THE TAMING

"Vintage Deveraux—a fast-moving, psychologically acute rendition of the battle of the sexes set in a richly textured historical landscape. . . . Deveraux's mastery of every trick of narrative art creates depth and resonance. . . ."

—*Publishers Weekly*

"Delightful . . . *The Taming* is a winning combination . . . a very funny, engaging, fast-paced read that's sure to please."

—*Rave Reviews*

THE AWAKENING

"A tender, hilarious, intense love story. . . . Everything Jude Deveraux readers expect from her passionate pen. . . . This is a keeper."

—*Romantic Times*

WISHES

"In *Wishes,* one of Jude Deveraux's most enchanting stories, she blends a pinch of magic, a dash of Cinderella fantasy, and spoonfuls of fun into a stunning romance."

—*Rave Reviews*

"Jude Deveraux always spins a gripping tale. . . . Plenty of passion—and the plot never slackens."

—*Booklist*

Books by Jude Deveraux

Published by POCKET BOOKS

Jude Deveraux

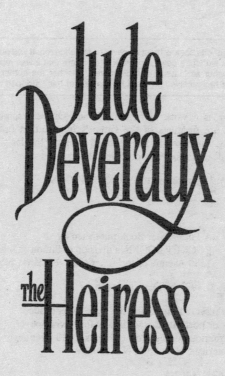

the Heiress

POCKET STAR BOOKS

New York   London   Toronto   Sydney   Tokyo   Singapore

This book is a work of fiction. Names, characters, places and
incidents are products of the author's imagination or are used
fictitiously. Any resemblance to actual events or locales or persons,
living or dead, is entirely coincidental.

An *Original* Publication of POCKET BOOKS

A Pocket Star Book published by
POCKET BOOKS, a division of Simon & Schuster Inc.
1230 Avenue of the Americas, New York, NY 10020

ISBN: 0-671-74462-3

First Pocket Books printing December 1995

10 9 8 7 6 5 4 3 2 1

POCKET STAR BOOKS and colophon are registered
trademarks of Simon & Schuster Inc.

Front cover illustration by Brian Bailey

Printed in the U.S.A.

the Heiress

Chapter 1

England
1572

*T*he Maidenhall heiress!"

Joby could hardly contain herself as she looked at her brother Jamie and her older sister, Berengaria, sitting so close to each other at the high table. She was no longer dazzled by the beauty of the two of them as she had been when she was small. Her father used to lift her high above his head and promise her that she was going to grow up to be as beautiful as her sister, Berengaria.

But he'd not told the truth. Not about that or, as it turned out, about a great many things. He'd not told the truth when he said they'd always have enough to eat and always have a warm, comfortable place to live. He'd not told the truth when he'd sworn that her mother would soon stop talking to her spirit people.

But most of all he'd lied about living forever.

1

Joby tossed her head of dark curls and looked up at her brother with stars in her eyes. Her hair had been shorn after she'd beaten some of the boys at sword play, and in retaliation, they had slathered her head with warm honey and pine pitch. Now her hair was growing back into glossy curls, and she found that she did indeed have one quite beautiful feature.

"The Maidenhall heiress," she repeated. "Oh, Jamie, just think of all that lovely money. Do you think she bathes in a gold tub? Does she wear emeralds to bed?"

"Nothing else is in her bed," Rhys, Jamie's man, said under his breath. "That father of hers keeps her as locked up as his gold."

Rhys gave a soft grunt as Thomas, Jamie's only other retainer, kicked him under the table.

Joby well knew the kick was to silence Rhys because they thought that at twelve years old she knew nothing about anything, and they wanted to keep it that way. Joby wasn't about to tell them what she knew or did not know, because in her opinion, there were already too many restrictions placed on her freedom. If any of the many adults in her life found out just exactly how much she did know, they'd start trying to find out where she had been to learn what she wasn't supposed to know.

Jamie's eyes were twinkling. "Perhaps not emeralds. But maybe she wears a silk nightgown."

"Silk," Joby said dreamily, her head propped on her hand. "Italian silk or French?"

At that everyone at the table laughed, and Joby knew she had an audience. She might not win attention for her looks, but she knew that she could make people laugh.

Maybe their branch of the Montgomery family couldn't afford jesters and other entertainers for dinner, or even much dinner for that matter, but Joby did what she could to enliven their otherwise dreary existence.

With one great leap she sprang to the top of the table, then bounded over it to the cold stone floor of the old castle.

With a bit of a frown, Jamie looked across the room at his mother, sitting so quietly, eating so little that no one could figure how she survived, but Joby's mannerless enthusiasm did not penetrate their mother's eternal dream world. She was vaguely looking in her youngest daughter's direction, but Jamie had no idea if she could see her or not. Or if she did, whether or not she remembered who she was. Their mother was as likely to call Joby Edward or Berengaria or, sometimes, Joby's real name of Margaret.

Jamie looked back at his young sister, as always dressed as a knight's page in tights and jerkin. For the thousandth time he told himself he had to force her to start dressing as a girl, but even as he thought it, he knew he hadn't the heart. Time enough for her to grow up and face the harshness of life. Let her be a child as long as possible.

"And how do you think she dresses each day?" Joby was saying as she stood before them. There were only five people at the table and a few servants—all that were left to them—beginning to straggle in from the kitchens, but Joby liked to imagine there were hundreds and she was on the stage before the queen.

Joby mimicked a woman awakening in the morning, stretching and yawning. "Bring me my gold chamber pot," she commanded imperiously and was rewarded with a laugh from her sister. If what she did made Berengaria laugh, then Jamie would allow her to continue.

Joby began making rather vulgar movements of a woman lifting her nightgown and settling herself onto a chamberpot. "Oh, my, but these emeralds do give me the most delicious pain," she said, wiggling about.

Jamie, who was whispering to Berengaria, raised one black eyebrow at Joby, letting her know she was not to go too far.

Joby straightened. "Here, bring me my dress. No! No! Not that one. Nor that one or that one or that one or that one. No, no, you fool. How many times have I told you that I have worn that gown before? I want *new* clothes. Always new clothes. What? This *is* a new gown? How do you expect the Maidenhall heiress to wear such as that? Why that silk is so thin it would . . . Why it would *bend* if I were to wear it."

At that Rhys began to laugh, and even Thomas, who rarely laughed, crooked one corner of his mouth up. They'd seen women at court who wore gowns so stiff they might as well have been carved of wood.

"Now," Joby said, standing back and looking at an imaginary gown, "this is more to my taste. Here, you men there, lift me into it."

At that even Thomas smiled broad enough to show his teeth, and a laugh escaped Jamie too.

Joby gave a great leap as though being lowered into the stiff dress, then waited while the hooks were latched.

"Now for my jewels." Joby pretended to be looking at several displays of jewels. "Yes, here are the emeralds and the rubies and diamonds, and here are pearls. Which shall I choose?" she asked as though in answer to a question. "Choose? How does one choose jewels? I shall, of course, wear them *all.*"

Spreading her legs apart as though bracing herself for a storm at sea, Joby extended her arms. "All right, men, put your hands behind my shoulders and brace me. Now, you there, put my jewels on me."

Everyone at the table was laughing as Joby extended first one foot, then the other, then an arm, then stretched her neck as though a hangman's rope had elongated it for her. Then, with her neck still stretched, she somehow managed to convey the impression to her audience that her head was now being weighed down with great, massive earrings. And when the jeweled headdress was placed on top of her head, she visually swayed under the weight.

By now everyone, servants, retainers, family, all except Joby's mother, were laughing helplessly.

"Release me now," Joby said to the imaginary men still bracing her shoulders. For a moment she swayed dangerously, about to go down, first one side, then the other, looking like a drunken sailor standing on the deck of a storm at sea. Just when she was about to go down, she righted herself and finally, at last, with great dignity, held herself erect.

With difficulty, the audience quieted and awaited what came next.

"Now," Joby said with gravity, "I shall see this man who is to escort me, the richest woman in all of England, across the country. I will see if he is worthy of taking me to the man my father has contracted for me to marry. But wait, tell me of him."

Everyone at the table was sneaking looks at Jamie as he ducked his head shyly, holding Berengaria's hand close to his heart. He'd only been home for a few days, and he found he could not bear to allow any of his family out of his sight or touch.

"James Montgomery," Joby said. "Ah yes, I have heard of that family. A bit of money there, but not much. But then no one has riches to compare to me, do they? What?! Speak up! I cannot hear you. Yes, yes, that is better. I know in my heart how rich I am, but I am still a woman and I like to hear it said aloud."

For a moment she was lost in thought as she admired her left arm. "Now, what was I speaking of? Oh yes. This man who has the privilege, the honor, of escorting me. He is a Montgomery. What is it you say? He is of the *poor* branch of the Montgomerys?"

Joby's pixie face with its sharp nose wrinkled in puzzlement. "Poor? I do not believe I know this word. Please explain it to me."

When the laughter had quieted again, she continued. "Ah, I see. People who have only a hundred silk dresses and only small jewels. What? No jewels? No silk? What's that? You say this man lives in a house with only part of a roof and sometimes no meat on the table?"

At this Jamie frowned, knowing that this was why he'd agreed to take on the degrading employment of escorting some spoiled heiress across England to join her almost-as-rich fiancé. But even so, he did not like to hear it said aloud.

Joby ignored her brother's frown. "If he has nothing to eat, he must be rather . . . small," she said in wonder, making Jamie laugh and forget his very real problems. Small he was not.

"Shall I carry him about in a box?" Joby asked, holding up her hands, not forgetting to act as though her arms were weighed down with hundreds of jewels.

She kept her fingers spread wide because her imaginary rings were so large they wouldn't allow her to close her fingers. "A jeweled box, of course," she said. "Ah yes, perhaps this is good. I see a way to carry more jewels. What! Is this box not made yet? You are dismissed! And you! And—Oh, I see, he is not small. He does not eat, but he is not small. I do not understand. But perhaps you had better send him in and let me see this . . . this . . . What was that word again? Ah, yes, poor. Let me see this moor, er, ah, poor person."

At this Joby did a pantomime of the Maidenhall heiress standing utterly still, weighed down with all her many hundreds of jewels, and awaiting the arrival of James Montgomery.

Out of the side of her mouth, Joby made a creaking noise as of rusty door hinges trying to open. "I have it on authority," she said as an aside to her audience, "that gold hinges creak abominably. That's why we refuse to have them here."

In the next moment Joby's face changed to astonishment: her mouth dropped open, her eyes widened, then she threw her arm across her eyes as though to keep a bright light from blinding her. "You are too beautiful," she said in a loud stage whisper.

At that, Jamie's face turned red, and his two men, who were sick of seeing women make fools of themselves over the extraordinary beauty of Jamie, fell about themselves laughing.

"No jewel in the world," Joby shouted above the loud laughter of the men, "could compare with your beauty. Oh, I must have you. Must, must, must have you. Here!" she said and began pantomiming the removal of all her jewels, sliding them off her arms,

7

her neck, her ears; running her hands along her head to remove great handfuls of them; tossing each precious piece at him.

"You must marry me," Joby cried. "I cannot live without you. You are what I have been looking for all my life. Next to you, emeralds are dark; they do not twinkle as brightly as your eyes. Pearls have no luster next to your skin. Diamonds cannot—"

She broke off because Jamie grabbed the worn cushion from under him and threw it at her, hitting her squarely on her flat chest.

Catching it, she clasped it tightly. "This is from my most beautiful beloved. He . . . Oh, heavens, but he *sat* on it. That most tender part of him has touched it. Would that my eyes and lips could share what this lowly cushion has—"

This time she stopped because Jamie had bounded over the table and clasped his hand over her mouth. She nipped his little finger with her sharp teeth, and taken in surprise, he released his grip on her.

"His arms about me," she said loudly. "I shall die from the pleasure of it."

"You shall die if you do not shut up," Jamie said. "Where have you learned such things as you have said? No, do not tell me. But if you have no care for my own delicate sensibilities, think how you shock your dear sister."

Joby peeped around the great bulk of her brother to see her sister's lovely face flushed with merriment. It suited her and her sister to pretend that Berengaria was as innocent and as angelic as she looked. The truth was that Joby was completely honest with her sister, often keeping her up half the night with tales of her latest escapade.

"Go!" Jamie commanded, motioning his arm to include everyone in the room. "Your ridicule of me is at an end. Tell me, little sister, what did you do for entertainment when I was not here to make merry of?"

Never at a loss for words, Joby said, "It was a solemn household. With only Father and Edward—" She broke off, the back of her hand going to her mouth.

For a moment there was silence in the worn, old hall as everyone seemed to have forgotten that just two days ago they had attended a double funeral. Technically, the household was in mourning, deep mourning, for the loss of the father and the eldest son of this branch of the Montgomery family. But the son, Edward, had never shared in the simple joys of family life, and their father had been absent, barricaded in his room at the top of the tower. It was difficult to weep for people who you rarely saw or, in Edward's case, did not miss.

"Yes," Jamie said calmly. "I think it is time we remembered what we are about." With his back rigid, he walked around the table to escort Berengaria from the room.

It was only minutes later that he was alone with his sister.

"Why did someone not tell me?" Jamie asked, standing before the tiny, crumbling window in Berengaria's room. Reaching out his hand, he broke a piece of stone away. Water damage. Years ago, while he'd been away, the lead gutters had been sold off the old stone keep, so the water seeped into the stone.

Turning, he looked at his sister as she sat serenely on her cushioned chair, a chair more suited for a peasant's hut than what had once been the keep of a proud and glorious estate. "Why did no one tell me?" he asked again.

Berengaria opened her mouth to give the explanation she'd planned to give, but instead, she told the truth. "Pride. That great Montgomery curse of pride." She hesitated, then smiled. "That pride that is now making your stomach churn and bringing out the sweat on your brow. Tell me, are you toying with the dagger Father gave you?"

For a moment Jamie didn't know what she was talking about but then realized that he was indeed holding the beautiful golden-handled dagger his father had given him long ago. The jewels in the hilt had been replaced with glass years ago, but if the dagger were held just so in the sunlight, one could see the gold that still coated the steel handle.

He gave a laugh. "I had forgotten how well you know me." With one easy movement, he sat on a cushion at her feet and leaned his head against her knee, closing his eyes in pleasure as she stroked his hair.

"I never saw any woman who could compare with you in beauty," he said softly.

"Is that not a vain thing for you to say as we are twins?"

He kissed her hand. "I am old and ugly and scarred, whereas you are untouched by time."

"Untouched is true," she said, trying to make a joke about her virginity.

But Jamie did not smile. Instead, he put his hand up before her face.

"It is no use," she said, smiling sweetly, catching his hand. "I cannot see lighted twigs before my face.

There is no sight for me, and no man wants a blind wife. For all the use I am to the world, it would have been better had I died at birth."

The violence with which Jamie arose startled her. "Oh, Jamie, I am sorry. I did not mean—It was thoughtless of me. Please, come sit down again. Let me touch you. Please."

He sat down again, but his heart was pounding. Pounding with guilt. He and his sister were twins, but Jamie had been quite a bit bigger than his sister and so had taken hours to be born. When Berengaria was finally allowed out, the umbilical cord was found to be wrapped around her neck, and it was soon discovered that she was blind. The midwife said it was Jamie's fault for taking so long to be born, so all his life Jamie had lived with the guilt of what he'd done to his beautiful sister.

And all their lives he had been close to her, never once losing patience with her or tiring of her company. He helped her in everything, encouraging her to climb trees, to walk miles into the hills, even to ride a horse alone.

Only their brother, Edward, thought Jamie less than a saint for helping his blind sister. Whenever anyone remarked on how good Jamie was to give up time with his rowdy boyhood companions to take his blind sister berry picking, their older brother would say, "He stole her sight, didn't he? Why shouldn't he do what he can to give it back to her?"

Jamie took a deep breath. "So no one told me what Edward was doing out of pride?" he said, coming back to the present. Guilt still weighed him down. Guilt over leaving his sister who needed him so much, guilt for what had happened after he left.

"You must cease this flagellation of yourself," Berengaria said, pulling Jamie's thick black hair with both her hands, making his head come back so he looked up at her. It was difficult to believe that those perfect, lushly lashed blue eyes of hers could not see.

"If you give me a look of pity, I shall snatch you bald," she said, pulling harder.

"Ow!" He laughed as she released his hair, then he pulled one of her hands to his chest and kissed it. "I cannot help the guilt I feel. I knew what Father and Edward were like."

"Yes," Berengaria said with a grimace. "Father never took his nose out of a book if he could help it, and Edward was a pig. There wasn't a village girl over the age of ten who was safe from him. He died young because the devil liked him so well he wanted him near him forever."

In spite of himself, Jamie laughed. "How very much I have missed you these months."

"Years, my dear brother. Years."

"Why do women always remember the most inconsequential of details?"

She tweaked his ear and made him yelp. "Now stop telling me of your women and tell me of this task you have taken on."

"How kind you are. How you make escorting a rich heiress across the country sound like a knight's holy quest."

"It is if *you* are involved. How Edward and you could be brothers bewilders me."

"As he was born five months after our parents' marriage, I sometimes wonder who his father was," Jamie said with great cynicism.

Had anyone else said this, Berengaria would have defended her dear mother, whose mind had long ago slipped away. "One time I asked Mother about that."

Jamie was surprised. "And what did she say?"

"She waved her hand and said, 'There were so many lovely young men that summer I'm afraid I cannot remember who was what.'"

The maleness in Jamie reacted first, making anger surge through him, but he knew his mother too well to take offense and so relaxed and smiled. "If her family found she was pregnant, who better to marry her to than Father? I can hear his mother, 'Come, dear, put down that book. It's time to get married.'"

"Do you think he read on his wedding night? Oh, Jamie, do you think *we* are . . . ?" Her eyes widened.

"Even scholars put down their books at times. Besides, look you at us and our cousins. We are alike. And Joby is the mirror image of Father."

"Yes," she said, "so you have thought of this, too?"

"A time or two."

"Perhaps every time Edward pushed you into a pile of horse dung? Or tied you to a tree branch and left you? Or destroyed your possessions?"

"Or when he called you names," Jamie said softly, then his eyes twinkled. "Or when he tried to marry you to Henry Oliver."

At that Berengaria groaned. "Henry still petitions Mother."

"Does he still have the intelligence of a carrot?"

"More of a radish," she said bleakly, not wanting anyone to see her despair that the only honest marriage proposal she'd ever had came from someone like Henry Oliver. "Please, no more talk of Edward and how he decimated what little we had. And definitely no more talk of—of that man! Tell me of your heiress."

Jamie started to protest but closed his mouth. "His" heiress had everything to do with the gambling and whoring and general depravity of his "brother" Edward. In Jamie's mind no one as degenerate as Edward deserved the title of brother. While Jamie had been away fighting for the queen, performing tasks for the queen, endangering his life for the queen, Edward had been selling off all that his family owned so he could afford horses (whose legs or necks he broke), fine clothes (which he lost or destroyed), and his never-ending gambling (where he invariably lost).

While Edward had been rapidly bankrupting the family, their father had imprisoned himself in a tower room to write a history of the world. He ate little, slept little, saw no one, spoke to no one. Just wrote day and night. When Berengaria and Joby confronted their father with proof of Edward's excesses, including deeds of land he'd signed over to pay his debts, their father had said, "What can I do? It will all be Edward's someday, so he may do what he likes. I *must* finish this book before I die."

But a fever had taken the lives of both Edward and their father. One day they were alive and two days later they were dead.

When Jamie returned for the funerals, he found what had once been a moderately profitable estate now unable to support itself. All the land except what the old keep was standing on had been sold. The manor house had been sold the year before, along with all the fields and all the cottages where the farmers lived.

For days Jamie had been inconsolable in his rage. "How did he expect you to live? If there are no rents or crops, how did he expect you to feed yourselves?"

"With his gambling wins, of course. He was always saying that he was going to win *next* time," Joby had said, looking both prematurely old and heart-breakingly young. She raised an eyebrow at her brother. "Perhaps you should spend less time ranting about what you cannot change and do what you can with what you have." She had given a meaningful glance toward Berengaria.

Joby meant that no man wanted a blind wife no matter how beautiful she was or even what her dowry was. Always it would be Jamie's responsibility to provide for her.

"Pride," he said now. "Yes, you and Joby had too much pride to call me home."

"No, *I* had too much pride. Joby said . . . Well, perhaps it is better left unrepeated what Joby said."

"Something about my cowardice at leaving you two at the hands of a monster like Edward?"

"You are kinder to yourself than she was," Berengaria said, smiling, remembering exactly what Joby had said. "Where *does* she learn all those dreadful words?"

Jamie winced. "No doubt about Joby being a Montgomery. Father was right when he said that Job had not been through so much as he had with his youngest child."

"Father hated anything that took him from his precious book." There was bitterness in her voice. "But Joby could read aloud to him and I could not."

Jamie squeezed her hand, and for a moment they were lost in unhappy memories.

"Enough!" Berengaria said sternly. "Heiress. Tell me of your heiress."

"Not mine by any means. She is to wed one of the Bolingbrookes."

"Imagine such wealth," Berengaria said dreamily. "Do you think they burn great logs each day so all the house is warm?"

Jamie laughed. "Joby dreams of jewels and silk, and you dream of warmth."

"I dream of more than that," she said softly. "I dream of you marrying your heiress."

Annoyed, Jamie pushed her hand away and got up to go to the window. Without realizing what he was doing, he pulled the worn dagger from its sheath by his side and began to toy with it. "Why do women put romance into everything?"

"Romance, ha!" she said with passion. "I want to put food onto the table. Do you know what it is like to eat nothing but moldy lentils for a month? Do you know what they do to your stomach, not to mention your bowels? Do you—"

Putting his hands on her shoulders, Jamie forced her back into the chair. "I am sorry. I—" What could he say? While his family had been starving, he had been dining at the queen's table.

"It is not your fault," she said calmly. "But weevils in the bread do take the romance out of one's life. We must look at the facts, look at what we have. First of all we could go to our rich Montgomery relatives and throw ourselves on their mercy. We could move into their houses and begin to eat three good meals a day."

Jamie looked at her for a moment, one eyebrow raised. "If that is an alternative, why did not you and our foul-mouthed little sister go to them years ago?

Edward would not have cared, and Father would not have noticed. Why did you choose to remain here and eat rotten food?"

Slowly, Berengaria smiled, then as they often did, together they said, "Pride."

"Too bad we cannot sell our pride," Jamie said. "If we could, we would be richer than the Maidenhall heiress."

At that they burst into laughter, for "richer than the Maidenhall heiress" was a saying throughout England. Jamie had even heard it in France.

"We cannot sell pride," Berengaria said slowly, "but we do have something else that is very valuable."

"And, pray tell me, what is that? Is there a market for crumbling stone? Perhaps we should say the well water has healed us so we could bring wealthy patrons here. Or we could—"

"Your beauty."

"Sell the dung from the stables," he continued. "Or we could—My what?"

"Your beauty. It was Joby who said as much. Jamie, think of it! What cannot money buy?"

"Very little, if anything."

"It cannot buy beauty."

"Oh, I am beginning to see. I am to sell my . . . beauty as you call it. If I am for sale, then money *can* buy beauty—if that is what I have." His eyes twinkled as they always did when he teased her. "How do you know that I am not as ugly as . . . as a pile of your mouldy lentils?"

"Jamie, I cannot see, but I am *not* blind," Berengaria said as though talking to a simpleton.

Jamie had to suppress a laugh.

"Do you think I do not hear and feel the sighs of the

women when you walk past? Do you think I have not heard filthy things said by women when they say what they would like to do to you?"

"This interests me," he said. "You must tell me more."

"Jamie! I am serious."

Taking her shoulders in his hand, he put his nose close to hers. "Sweet little sister," he said even though he was only minutes older than she, "you are not listening to what I said. I'm to escort this rich heiress to the man she is to marry. She does not need a husband; she has one."

"And who is this Bolingbrooke?"

"As you well know, rich is what he is. His father is almost as rich as hers is."

"So what does she need of *more* money?"

Jamie smiled indulgently at his beautiful sister. She had lived all her life in the country, and to her, wealth was warm clothes and plentiful food. But Jamie had traveled, and he knew that there was no such thing as "enough" money, "enough" power. For many people, the word *enough* did not exist.

"Do not patronize me," she snapped.

"I said not a word." He held up his hands in protest, the dagger in one of them.

"Yes, but I could hear your thoughts. You know that the queen has hinted that titles could be given to Perkin Maidenhall if he paid enough."

"And he has refused. The man's miserliness is known throughout England. And for once I am glad of it or else he would not have hired a man as poor as I to escort his precious daughter."

"Poor, yes, but you have now inherited all Father's titles."

For a moment Jamie was startled. "So I have," he said musingly. "So I have. So I am an earl, am I?"

"And a viscount, and you have at least three baronetcies."

"Hmm, do you think I can make Joby kneel before me and kiss my ring?"

"Jamie, think of the marriage market. You are titled; you are gorgeous."

At that he nearly choked. "You make me sound like a prize bird to be auctioned for the Christmas table. Lord Gander. Come, ladies, look at his fine plumage. Will he not look splendid on your table? Take this bird home, and your husband and children will love you forever."

Berengaria tightened her lips into a fine line. "What else do we have if not you? Me? Is a rich man going to marry *me*? Blind with no dowry? What about Joby? She has no dowry, she will never be a beauty, and her temper leaves a great deal to be desired."

"You are being kind," he teased.

"And you are being stupid."

"I beg your pardon," he said, anger in his voice. "When I look in a mirror, I see only myself, not this Apollo my two sisters seem to see." He took a breath and calmed himself. "Sweet sister, do you not think I too have thought of all this? Not quite in the way you have stated it, but I know that if I made a good marriage, it would solve many problems. And do you not think that my first thought of this heiress was that she would be a way to solve all our problems?"

Berengaria smiled in a way that Jamie knew too well.

He did not return her smile. "What are you and that hellion sister of ours up to? What are you planning?" For all that two people could not be more different, Joby and Berengaria were thick as clotted cream.

"Berengaria!" he said sternly. "I'll not participate in anything you two have devised. This is a job. Honest employment. If I deliver this girl safely into her fiancé's hands, I will be paid handsomely. There is nothing more to it than that, and I refuse to allow you or that brat sister to—"

He stopped and gave a groan. He could fight wars, lead men into battle, negotiate contracts between countries, but heaven help him when his two sisters got hold of him!

"I will *not* participate," he said. "I *will not!* Do you understand me? Berengaria, stop smiling in that way."

Chapter 2

*I*f she falls in love with you, Jamie, of course her
father will allow her to marry you. She's his only
child, she's to get everything, so of course he'd give
her anything she wanted."

Even to Jamie's ears, Joby sounded convincing. He
had a few comments to make, but he couldn't say
anything because his mouth was full of pins. He had
been standing in his undershirt, his legs bare, all
morning and half the afternoon as Joby directed the
village tailor and six seamstresses in the fashioning of
a wardrobe meant to win an heiress's heart.

Last night he'd drunk half a hog's head of horrible
wine while he listened to an outrageous plan that Joby
and Berengaria had concocted. Distasteful as the plan
was, that they had done so much work in so few days
impressed him.

As he listened, he heard more than he ever cared to

know about the perfidy of his brother (or, as he liked to think, his *half* brother). Edward had not only sold the Montgomery land but had sold it to men whose characters matched his own.

"Stinking, lying, murdering—" Joby started.

"Yes," Jamie interrupted, "but what have they actually *done?*"

Estate management was not a strong point of any of the new owners. Terrorizing peasants seemed to be their only real passion. They burned crops and houses, raped any nubile girl they could find, ran their horses over newly planted fields.

When Jamie heard that Joby had calmed the peasants by telling them that when Jamie returned he'd fix everything, Jamie nearly choked.

"It is no longer my land," he pointed out.

Berengaria shrugged. "Montgomerys have owned that land for hundreds of years, so how does your responsibility cease after a mere two years?"

"By the exchange of gold, that's how," Jamie nearly shouted, but they knew he felt the weight of all those hundreds of years on his shoulders.

"Speaking of gold," Joby said, then nodded to a servant standing in back of Jamie.

Later, Jamie thought that if he hadn't been drunk, he would have jumped out a window and kept on running. It had been only two weeks ago that he'd accepted this job of escorting this extremely wealthy young woman across England, but during that time his sisters had organized all three of the tiny villages that used to be on Montgomery land, land that Edward had sold.

Thinking of what must have been said, Jamie's face turned scarlet. His men had laughed so much they'd had to leave the room. It seemed that his two sisters had "sold" their brother.

"Just your beauty," Berengaria tried to reassure him—as though that would help.

"You know, like a stallion or a prize bull," Joby'd said, then laughed when Jamie tried to catch her as she darted out of his reach.

Last night, one by one, a representative of every village house had come to the old hall and shown what wealth he'd managed to save or—Jamie suspected—steal. There were parts of silver spoons, a handle from a gold ewer, coins with faces of long dead kings, bags of goose down that could be sold, piglets (one of which tried to join Jamie in getting drunk), leather pelts, a belt buckle, a few buttons from a rich lady's dress. The list seemed endless.

"And what, pray tell, is all this for?" Jamie asked, looking over the heaping table and the piles on the floor. The inquisitive piglet had overturned every wooden goblet on the table and drunk all the remains. What men found unpalatable, he found delicious.

"We are going to make you a fine wardrobe," Berengaria said. "We shall dress you as an earthly prince, and the Maidenhall heiress will fall in love with you at first sight."

At that absurdity, Jamie threw his head back and laughed, and the piglet, now by Jamie's wrist, looked up at him and began to laugh too.

When Jamie looked about him, he was surprised to see that no one else in the room, now probably a hundred people (some of whom had obviously never had a bath), was laughing.

"Jamie, you are our only hope," Berengaria said. "You could make any woman fall in love with you."

"No!" he said, setting his cup down with a splash and nearly hitting the piglet's tiny hoof. He was holding the stem of the cracked mug so hard he did not feel the piglet climb onto his hand and stick its face into the mug.

"I will not do this! The woman is to marry another. Her father would never give permission." He would have liked to have said that he meant to marry for love, but poor, landless earls could not afford such a luxury. But when he did marry, he wanted it to be in an honorable manner. He had no money, but he did have titles. Perhaps a rich merchant's daughter . . .

Which, of course, described the Maidenhall heiress perfectly. Not that many people had seen her to describe her in any way except as "rich." She was as elusive as a lady in a fairy story. Some said she was as beautiful as a goddess. Some said she was deformed and hideous. Whatever she was, she stood to inherit millions.

"I cannot. I will not. No. Absolutely not."

That's what he'd said last night, but today he was being measured and fitted. He was *not* going to ask where or how his sisters and the villagers had obtained such extraordinary fabrics. He suspected that Edward's coffers had been regularly emptied, and since he recognized some of the women as having worked in the manor house that had once been theirs, he figured the new owner was also missing some articles of clothing.

But he wasn't going to ask because he didn't want to know.

"Mmed eig!" he said through the pins, his arms outstretched.

Joby removed them. "Yes, dear brother?"

"Get this damned pig out from under my feet!"

"But it loves you," Joby said, everyone in the room trying to suppress their laughter. They all felt happy because they knew that Jamie would solve all their problems. How could any woman not love him? Six feet tall, two hundred pounds, with broad shoulders; a slim waist; huge, muscular thighs; and a face like a dark angel: beautiful dark green eyes, black hair, honey-colored skin, lips sculpted like those on a marble statue. It wasn't unusual for women to be struck dumb at the sight of him.

"The piglet is *female,*" Berengaria said, and everyone released their pent-up laughter in shouts.

"Enough!" Jamie roared above the people falling all over themselves in laughter, then gave a pull to the black velvet jacket that swathed him. With a cry of pain, he pulled back, two pins embedded in his palm, and waited impatiently as Joby removed the pins.

Grabbing his own old, worn clothing from atop a chest, he started for the door, not bothering to dress, when the piglet ran under his feet and nearly tripped him. Angry, Jamie grabbed the animal up and started to toss it out the third-story window. But as he did, he looked into its eyes.

"Hell and damnation," he muttered and slipped the fat creature under his arm. As he slammed the door behind him, he heard gales of laughter. "Women!" he muttered and practically ran down the ancient stone stairs.

Chapter 3

*A*xia neither saw nor heard the man before he threw one strong arm about her waist and a big hand across her mouth and dragged her to a secluded spot behind the hedges. With her heart racing, she told herself, *I must remain calm. At all costs, I must remain calm.* And in that flash of a moment she forgave her father everything. *This* was why she'd lived all her life behind high walls, why she'd spent her life in near imprisonment. In another flash she thought, *How did he get into the garden?* The wall was topped with sharp iron spikes; dogs ran freely to give alarm at any intruder; workers were everywhere.

It seemed to take an eternity as the man pulled her to the back of the hedge. One minute she'd been sketching a portrait of her beautiful cousin Frances—what surely must be the twentieth portrait this year—

and the next she was being kidnapped. *How did he know?* she wondered. *How did he know who I am?*

The man stopped, holding Axia close to his body, her back to his front, his muscular arm tight under her breasts. She'd never been this close to a man before. Her household was full of her father's spies, and if a man, a gardener, a steward, whoever, so much as smiled at her, she'd find him gone within days.

"If I remove my hand, will you promise not to give an alarm?"

His breath was in her ear.

"Perhaps you will not believe me, but I mean you no harm. I merely want some information."

At that Axia almost relaxed. Of course. *All* men wanted information from her. How much gold did her father have in the house? How many estates did he own? What was her marriage portion to be? People's desire for knowledge about her father's wealth was endless.

She nodded. Of course she'd tell him all she knew. She'd tell anyone all she knew—which was exactly nothing.

But the man didn't remove his hand from her mouth right away. Instead, for a few seconds Axia was aware that he was looking down at her. Her neck was bent backward, the top of her head nestled into his shoulder; his cheek was pressed against her forehead.

"You're a nice little handful," he said, and for the first time Axia was afraid. She struggled against him. "Stop that! I have no time for dalliance. I have to attend to business."

At that Axia turned to give him a look. Should she apologize for delaying him from kidnapping her?

But his head was turned away, peering through the shrubs toward Frances. "She is beautiful, is she not?"

At that Axia bit his hand, and he freed her mouth, though not her body.

"Ow! Why'd you do that?"

"I will do more than that if you—"

He clamped his hand over her mouth again. "I told you, I mean no harm. I have come to lead her, the Maidenhall heiress, across England."

At that Axia calmed and at once understood the situation. He wanted to see what this woman was like, and it was only natural that he should think Frances—who hadn't a bean to her name—was the heiress. After all, Frances dressed in finery that outshone the queen's, and she lived as she thought a rich woman should. In other words if she dropped a needle, she'd call a servant to pick it up for her.

Yes, Axia nodded.

"Will you be quiet if I remove my hand?"

Again Axia nodded vigorously.

He removed his hand from her mouth and loosened his hold on her waist at the same time.

Axia, being a sane and sensible person, made a great leap to get away from him.

He flattened her. Slammed her against the ground so hard the breath left her, then threw his great, heavy body on top of hers.

When she recovered enough to be able to see, she looked up at him. Heavens but he was stunning. Not pretty, but just divinely male. He looked like something off the pages of a fairy tale.

As for Jamie, he saw a very pretty young woman, not beautiful like the heiress, but the animation in her face made up for everything. She had a heart-shaped

face with dark brown hair, huge brown eyes surrounded by short, thick dark lashes, a little nose, and
the most perfect little mouth he'd ever seen. Her eyes
were gazing at him levelly, as though she expected
him to prove himself. No woman had ever looked at
him this way before, and he found it intriguing. As for
the rest of her, she had a full bosom, a tiny waist, and
full, curving hips. She made a man's hands itch—or
at least his anyway.

After she recovered from her shock of the beauty of
him, she wondered why her father had hired such a
beautiful man to lead her to her fiancé. Always her
father hired ugly men, men who would not tempt a
rich young woman. But above all, her father got value
for his money. As she'd learned from Frances, beautiful people were useless. They seemed to believe that
their mere presence was all that was needed from
them. So why had her father sent this beautiful,
useless man to be the heiress's escort? What was her
father up to now?

"Would you please listen to me?" he said.

As he spoke, he looked down at the small, curva-
ceous body under his, and she felt his hand on her
waist move upward. She had never seen that look
before, but instinctively, she knew what was in his
mind.

"Touch me and I'll scream," she said, her eyes cold.

"I'm not usually given to rape," he said as though
she'd wounded his pride.

"Then remove your hands and your body from
mine."

"Ah yes," he said, smiling in a way that she was
sure had devastated many women. But then handsome young men *always* smiled beatifically at the

Maidenhall heiress or, in this case, at a woman he thought was connected with her.

Yet he did not roll off of her. "You'll be quiet?"

"Only if you remove your person from atop me. I cannot breathe."

With seeming reluctance, he rolled off of her, but this time when Axia made a try for freedom, he was prepared, catching her skirt and pulling her slightly back under him. "You are not a person of honor, are you?" he asked seriously.

"I have a great sense of honor," she said, eyes flashing, "when I deal with honorable men. You, sir, are trespassing."

"I prefer to think that I am a day early, 'tis all."

Once again, his hand was creeping upward.

She narrowed her eyes at him. "If you will unhand me, I will tell you *anything*," she said, sounding as though his touch was more repulsive than all the sins of the world.

She could see by his expression that he was shocked by her words. No doubt he'd never heard any word except *yes* from a woman. Having spent most of her life with Frances's beauty, Axia knew the power it had. Axia could argue for an hour with a gardener over how to prune the apple trees, but Frances would stroll toward them, bat her lashes, and say *she* thought the trees should be cut such a way, and two minutes later three men were falling over themselves to cut just where she'd said. In the herb garden a lovesick boy had trimmed the rosemary into great F's for Frances. And there were swans—Frances's favorite bird—everywhere.

Perhaps it was going too far to say so, but Axia hated beautiful people. Oh, she liked to make sketches and paintings of them, but as for company, she much preferred men who looked like Tode and the head steward.

"Yes, of course," he said, rolling off her once again. "But please do not run or make any noise. Or I will have to—"

Axia raised herself to a sitting position. "Put your hands on me again? To prevent that I will tell you *anything* you want to know." His look of puzzlement at the disdain in her voice made her smile.

Once he was on his feet, he held out his hand to help her up, but she ignored it. Standing, she said, "What do you want to know? Pound per pound the amount of gold owned by Maidenhall? Or will you take an estimate in cartloads?"

"Cynical little thing, aren't you? No, I want to know about *her.*"

"Ah yes, the beautiful Frances." Axia was dusting herself off. He was dressed in black velvet, whereas she had on rough linen. But then velvet was so impractical for the muddy countryside.

"Is that her name? Frances?"

"Do you wish to compose love sonnets to her name? It has been done, and I warn you that it is difficult to rhyme."

Laughing at that, he glanced through the shrubs at Frances sitting on the bench in the sun, a book open before her. "Why does she sit so still? Is she such a scholar that the book engrosses her so?"

"Frances doesn't know how to read or write. She says reading would cause lines on her perfect brow and writing would wrinkle the white skin of her hands."

Again the man gave a bit of laughter. "Then why does she sit so still?"

"She is having her portrait painted," Axia said as though he were an idiot for not seeing the obvious.

"But *you* are the painter and you are here. Has she not noticed your absence?"

"The thought that she is being looked at is enough for her." Axia glanced down at his doublet. "Are you bleeding?"

"Hell and damnation," he said. "I forgot the cherries." He began pulling cherries from his pocket, some of them crushed.

"So you are a thief as well as a trespasser."

He had his back to the shrub. "What does she care? She is so rich she will not miss a few cherries. Want some?"

"No, thank you. Would you please tell me what it is you want to know so I can get back to my work?"

"Do you know her well?"

"Know who?" Axia pretended ignorance.

"The Maidenhall heiress, of course."

"As well as anyone. Is she who interests you? All that gold?"

"Yes, all that gold," he said, looking at her seriously as he spit a cherry seed onto the ground. "But I want to know about *her*. What could I do for her or give her that would please her?"

Axia looked at him a moment. "And why would you want to please her?"

The man's face changed, softened, and, if possible, became more handsome. Had he looked at another woman so, Axia was sure she would have melted as quickly as cheap candle wax. Leaning toward her, he whispered in his voice that was as splendid as his face and body. "Come, tell me," he said seductively, "what gift could I give her that would please her?"

Axia gave him a sweet smile. "A double-sided mirror?" Meaning, of course, that he could see himself as Frances looked at herself.

At that the man started to laugh, then caught himself from making noise that might call attention to them. Tossing the last of the cherries to the ground, he said, "I need a friend. Actually, I need a partner in some business."

"Me?" she asked with false innocence, and when he nodded, she said, "And what do *I* receive if I help you?"

"I am beginning to like you."

"As I do not feel the same about you, I wish you to get on with your request so we may part company."

"Go," he said, sweeping his arm out. "Go and leave me. I will be here on the morrow. Perhaps I will see you then. Perhaps not."

Axia cursed herself, but she was intrigued. "What do you offer me for helping you?" Heiresses were never offered money; they gave money.

"Riches beyond your wildest dreams."

Ah, she thought, *the Maidenhall gold—and silver and land and ships and warehouses and—*

"No," he said, "do not look at me like that. I mean no harm. I mean to . . ." He hesitated, looking at her as though judging her.

"You mean to have her for your own, do you not?" When, for just a flash of a second, she saw his eyes look startled, she knew she'd guessed right. But then he wasn't the first; he was one of thousands who wanted to marry the Maidenhall gold. But let him keep his illusions that he was the first to think of such a thing. *Why* did her father hire a man who looks like this one? she wondered again. A man who thought all women were dying to give him anything.

Axia smiled. "You are indeed ambitious. Is she not already engaged to marry?"

"Yes, well . . . ," he said and idly removed a little dagger from the sheath at his side. For a moment Axia's heart leaped to her throat in fear, but then she realized it was an unconscious gesture on his part and she doubted if he was aware he had the weapon in his hand.

"I see," she said. "On the journey you mean to make her change her mind and declare for you."

"Do you think I can?" he said, and it was the first honest thing he'd said to her.

She almost patted his arm in sympathy. "Frances will love you," she said while laughing inside at her lie. Frances hated anything as splendid as herself. She liked ugly things around her so she would glow more radiantly. "So, you've come to marry the Maidenhall heiress? Your family and lands fallen on hard times, have they?"

His eyes sparkled. "I knew I could trust you. From the moment I saw you standing there, brush in hand, I knew you were a trustworthy person. We shall be great friends, you and I. Do you travel with her?"

"Oh yes. Actually, we are cousins."

"Yes," he said, smiling, "I too have rich cousins."

"Tell me, er, ah . . . I do not know your name."

"James Montgomery, Earl of Dalkeith. A title, but, alas, no land and no gold to go with it. And you are Mistress . . . ?"

"Maidenhall, of course, but alas, I am only *Axia* Maidenhall."

"An unusual name for an unusual lady. Now tell me what I must do to impress her. A gift perhaps. Sonnets to her beauty? A rare fruit? Yellow roses perhaps? Come tell me, set me a quest. Nothing is too difficult to obtain."

"Daisies," Axia said without hesitation.

"Daisies? That most humble of flower?"

"Yes. Frances does not like anything to compete with her beauty. Roses are competition, whereas daisies are a plain setting for a sparkling gem."

"You're very clever, aren't you?"

"People in my station in life must be in order to survive."

He smiled at her. "Yes, we do understand each other."

"A cloak lined with daisies," Axia said. "To be wrapped about her shoulders while she stands with her eyes closed. Is that not romantic?"

"Yes, very." He was looking at her in speculation. "Do you tell me the truth?"

"I swear in God's Holy Name that the Maidenhall heiress loves daisies."

"And why are you willing to help me?"

She ducked her head shyly. "You will allow me to paint the portraits of all your impoverished family?"

"Yes," he said, smiling. "And I will pay you well. I have a twin sister."

Axia kept her eyes lowered so he would not see what she thought of his vanity, assuming she'd betray her own cousin just to paint some characterless beauty. "You honor me, my lord."

"You may call me Jamie." At that he leaned forward as though to kiss her mouth, but she turned her head so he kissed her cheek instead.

"That is *not* part of the bargain," she said in what she hoped was a good imitation of Frances warding off her twelfth suitor of that day. "Not yet," she added, then scurried away from him and back to her easel. Out of the corner of her eye she saw him running across the orchard, very fast for a man of his size.

Picking up a paintbrush, she held it toward her canvas but could not paint because she was laughing too hard. Wait until tomorrow, she thought, when he saw the truth, that she was the heiress and Frances was only a poor paid companion.

But in the middle of her laughing, her body changed to shaking. Fear was replacing her laughter. If this James Montgomery could so easily come onto the grounds, so could others, men who hated her father for one reason or another (and they were legion), men who wanted to hold her for ransom. Men who—

One minute she was standing behind her easel, and the next she had fallen to the ground in a swoon.

As promised, Jamie wrote to his sisters that night. *What to tell them?* he thought as he picked up a pen, then smiled. *They want a fairy tale so I shall give them one.* A man who has to struggle to reach the maiden, then the maiden being beautiful beyond all imagining, as Frances Maidenhall was.

My dearest sisters,

I have met her. My lessons learned in escaping Edward's tortures at last had some benefit as I used an overhanging tree branch to go over a high wall. The dogs were easy after I borrowed a cloth from a gardener's shed. It was an adventure worthy of Joby!

The Maidenhall heiress was in the garden sitting for her portrait, as still as a statue and as perfect as Venus. It does not surprise me that her father keeps her locked away, for her extraordinary beauty is worth more than jewels.

I did not speak to her, only gazed upon her, basking in the radiance of her and enjoying her loveliness.

Jamie paused. Yes, that should do it. Adventure and romance. What else to make them stop worrying? Ah yes, to reassure them that he had some help.

I questioned a girl painting the heiress's portrait. She was like a pretty sparrow caught in a cage, but she had a clever tongue on her and she is to help me win the heiress's hand. When this is all done I shall bring this sparrow to you to paint your portraits.

> With all my love,
> James

"That idiot!" Joby exploded upon reading the letter. "He thinks to use a plain woman to help him win the hand of a beautiful one? I know *I* would not help him." Several times young men had seen Berengaria from a distance and had asked Joby for an introduction. Without exception Joby had always been enraged at this.

"Our brother is in love," Berengaria said softly.

"Do you think so? Yes, yes, he does go on and on

about her beauty. I am glad. Jamie is plagued with scruples and a conscience. Were it me—"

"No, no, he is in love with that plain sparrow."

"You are insane," Joby said in a way that carried no animosity to it.

"We shall see," Berengaria said, smiling. "We shall see."

Chapter 4

"Well!" Rhys said, glaring at Jamie over a mug of ale. "You saw her. What was she like?"

The three of them, Thomas, Rhys, and Jamie, had been friends for years. They'd been through battles together, shared food when they had it, did without when they didn't. Jamie had a way about him that could make a person feel that he was soft and sweet and easy to manipulate, but Rhys and Thomas had learned all too well that when anyone overstepped the mark, Jamie's temper could make heads roll.

But over the years Rhys and Thomas had learned that Jamie had one major weakness: he thought women were angels come to earth. Of course, with Jamie's looks, women often were angelic. Everywhere they went, every country, whether women were fair Danes or the dark beauties of the Holy Lands, the most vile-tempered virago turned to honey when Jamie approached.

Rhys remembered in France being held off by a farm wife with a pitchfork, then Jamie walked up and smiled at her, and minutes later she was digging out bottles of wine from under the floorboards and offering them feather beds for the night. Or at least one feather bed. To Jamie. To Rhys and Thomas she pointed at the floor.

Had Jamie been a different sort of man, he could have taken advantage of this, but he did not. He was polite and courteous and turned down most offers made to him. "It would not be right to the woman's husband," he'd said more than once, a statement that made any man within hearing distance shout with laughter.

What time the men had spent at court could have kept Jamie very busy as there were few women, married or single, who did not try to get Jamie into bed with them, but for the most part, he declined. Not that he was a prude or celibate by any means; he was just cautious.

"I do not try to get myself killed on a battlefield, so why should I risk death for a night with a married woman?" Jamie asked. "Or have the father of a virgin come after me? And I cannot afford mistresses."

As close as he was to his men, as much as they'd been through together, they knew little about Jamie's life with women. Sometimes his bed was left empty for nights in a row and the next day he yawned often, but he would say nothing about where he'd been or with whom he'd been.

Now that Jamie would consider marriage showed how worried he was about his family's finances.

"What is she like?" Rhys demanded again. The Maidenhall heiress. A person of legend, like Midas or Croesus. From the day of her birth, the only child born to a man whose wealth was unimaginable, she had been the object of people's daydreams. "If I were as rich as the Maidenhall heiress" was something every person in England had said at one time or the other. Even the queen was said to have asked a foreign ambassador if he thought she was as wealthy as the Maidenhall heiress.

However, no one had ever said, "If I were as rich as Perkin Maidenhall" because that had no romance to it, especially since Perkin Maidenhall was known for his parsimony. Stories of his tightness with a coin were legendary. It was said that he wore the same suit of clothes until they hung in rags on his body, and he was emaciated because he would not spend money to feed himself. He had no pleasures, spent no time in games. It was said he'd married once (because the bride's father would not sell him some land that lay between two pieces he already had), gone to bed with her once, and his daughter was the result. His wife died just days later.

No, few envied Maidenhall himself, just his daughter, a motherless girl who was never seen in public but lived behind high walls in the south of England. Even the villagers near the estate where she lived had never seen her. And if anyone on the estate talked about her, he soon "disappeared," as Maidenhall had spies everywhere.

"Yes," Thomas said, "out with it." Usually he allowed Rhys to find out what he wanted to know, but this time Jamie's silence called for drastic measures.

"She is a pretty little sparrow," Jamie said, his eyes

far away. "Big brown eyes that can look through a man, plump bosomed, with the quick, sure movements of a sparrow." A slow smile spread over his face. "And she has a tongue as sharp as a sparrow's beak. She could make a man bleed with that tongue of hers."

Throughout this, Rhys and Thomas showed their shock, their jaws dropping open. Rhys recovered his powers of speech first. "You have fallen in *love* with the Maidenhall heiress?"

Jamie looked at the two men as though they were daft. "Axia?" The word had hardly left his mouth before he realized that he was saying too much. Some things deserved privacy. "Love? Love has nothing to do with this. I am to escort a woman to her—"

"Plump-bosomed sparrow, eh?" Rhys said with a laugh, poking Thomas in the ribs. "I think we will be eating fat this winter if he has set his sights on the Maidenhall heiress."

Thomas did not smile. "Who is Axia?"

"She is to help me win the heiress," Jamie said glumly.

"But I thought your plump sparrow *was* the heiress," Rhys said in confusion.

"No," Jamie said, looking into his mug. "The heiress is named Frances, and she is as beautiful as sunlight. I do not know that I have ever seen a more perfect woman: golden hair, lashes like fans, rosy cheeks, lovely mouth, a chin of perfection. She is a pink and white goddess."

Rhys was trying to understand. "Your words and your tone do not agree. You describe a wonder of nature, but you sound as though she is a virago.

Come, tell me, what could a woman who looks like that do to discourage a man?"

"She cannot read or write," Jamie said. "And she loves to have her portrait painted. She—"

Rhys laughed. "A true woman. Perhaps *I* shall try for her if you are too good for her."

At that Jamie gave Rhys a look that stopped him cold. "I must do what I must. I have to think of my sisters, and if this woman is winnable, I shall do it."

"I do not believe it will be such a hideous task."

"You have not seen how beautiful she is," Jamie said. "She will take much wooing. It is what she is used to."

"As opposed to your plump-bosomed sparrow?" Thomas asked as he studied Jamie. He was older than Rhys or Jamie, neither of whom had reached the age of thirty. But Thomas, at nearly forty, had seen enough of the world to know to attach himself to a man like Jamie. Once James Montgomery thought of a person as "his," he took care of that person, going without if need be, but he made sure that those who belonged to him had what they needed.

Jamie smiled. "Ah, to be free," he said. "To be a farmer's son and marry whom I wish." He raised his mug. "To freedom," he said, draining the contents.

Rhys and Thomas exchanged looks before drinking. No matter how long they were with Jamie they'd never understand him. He was one of the few men to ever see the Maidenhall heiress, and he was complaining because she was beautiful.

"To freedom," they said and drank.

Chapter 5

"Did you see him!" Axia said, her face flushed with anger.

"No, I did not," Tode answered, cleaning his nails with a penknife, not betraying how upset he was.

When a burly gardener had carried her into the house, Tode's heart had nearly stopped at the sight of her unconscious form. For a moment he thought she was dead. He had her taken to her room, and there he'd bolted the door against intruders, demanding that a doctor be sent for from the village. But when Tode realized Axia had merely fainted, he wouldn't allow the man inside. Instead, he'd given Axia a strong drink and had made her tell him everything that had happened. And as she spoke, he did his best to conceal his fear, for she could have been hurt by this intruder.

"He does not walk, he struts," Axia was saying.

Now fully recovered, she was pacing about the room in anger. "He swaggers. He throws back his shoulders and walks as though he owns the earth. Why? Because he is an earl? Ha! My father has two earls a day for breakfast."

"No wonder he is choleric," Tode said.

Axia did not smile at his jibe. "You should have seen him lusting after dear cousin Frances. It would make you sick."

Tode doubted it would but did not say so, especially since he tended to agree with her about Frances. "You were clever to tell him she was the heiress. He might have taken you else."

"No, no, not him. Not James Montgomery. *He* wants to *marry* me. Her. Marry her gold, that is." Axia landed hard on a chair. "Why does no one see *me*? My father locks me away as though I have done something wrong. Criminals have more freedom than I do."

"No heiress or young woman of your standing chooses her own husband," he said, trying to inject some reason into her anger.

"Yes, but she does not have men coming over the wall just to *see* her. See how she glitters, that is. Sometimes I am grateful to my father. What do *they*"—she waved her hand, vaguely indicating the people beyond the garden walls, people she'd never met—"think I do all day?"

Tode knew he had to, at times, live up to his title of jester. "Eat hummingbird tongues covered with a sauce made of pearls. Spend the afternoons counting your jewels. Choose silk for new dresses every day."

Axia did not laugh but glared at him. "You speak the truth."

"I am paid to make you laugh, and what is more humorous than the truth?" With difficulty, he moved away from the plastered wall. His damaged legs were bothering him a lot today.

"Here! Sit down," Axia said gruffly, knowing he hated her to be soft toward him. "You bother me when you creak about like that."

"Then pray forgive me for bothering you," he said as he sank onto a cushioned chair in the rather small and unnecessarily shabby room. Perkin Maidenhall had bought the estate because it was part of a larger tract of land he wanted. When his daughter was born, he'd sent her here to live, hidden away inside the high walls. In the nineteen years since her birth, she'd had only two companions: Tode and Frances. When Tode had arrived, he was twelve years old and had lived a life of endless pain and fear, and he had expected more of the same inside the high walls of the Maidenhall estate. But Axia, only eight years old but more like a small adult than a child, had taken him to her heart and had given him the best the estate had to offer. Under her loving care he had learned to laugh and had found out what warmth and kindness was. It was inadequate to say that he loved her.

"This Montgomery is to escort you—or is it Frances?—tomorrow?" His eyes, Tode's one truly beautiful feature, were sparkling as he teased her and tried to distract her from the realities of her life.

"Frances or me or you," she said angrily. "He wants only the Maidenhall gold. Were I to put a wig on you, he'd fall to one knee and declare his love for you."

"I should like to see that," Tode said, running his thumb across the scars that extended down his neck.

Not many people knew that from collarbone to midthigh, he was perfect, unscarred, unbroken.

Suddenly, Axia deflated and sank onto a chair, her head back, her face showing her misery. "Is this the way it is to be on the coming journey? Am I to be courted and lied to by every man from here to Lincolnshire? Shall handsome young men pull me into bushes and speak false words of love in hopes of getting my father's wealth?" She snorted. "If they only knew! My father *pays* for nothing. He is *paid* for everything. Only a rich man's son, like Gregory Bolingbrooke, could afford to pay enough to marry *my* father's gold."

Tode did not interrupt her, for he was fully on her side, but he'd never tell her so. It would only make her feel worse. In her whole life, she'd never been off these grounds. She'd grown up surrounded by people who were paid (as little as possible) by her father. And the people were given bonuses for spying on his daughter and telling her father everything she did. She was a rich piece of property to him, and he was not going to lose something as valuable as her virginity to some lowly retainer.

Therefore, the moment Axia seemed to grow fond of any male, he was removed. Because her friendships with females might cause her to be influenced by them, they too were removed when there was any sign of attachment. Besides Frances, only Tode had managed to stay near her. Perhaps looking at him, no one could imagine Tode inspiring love in another human. But, in truth, Tode was the only person Axia did love.

"Oh, Tode," she said, and there was despair in her voice. "Do you know what awaits me in this marriage?"

He was glad she was looking up at the ceiling (which needed replastering) or else she would have seen the despair in his eyes. He knew a thousand times better than she did what awaited her.

"There will be no love. No, I am not naive. Being a prisoner all my life has made me old. There is something wrong with this Gregory Bolingbrooke that his father must pay mine to marry me. I cannot look forward to a life of love with a healthy young man. I wonder if there will be children?"

When she abruptly lowered her head and glanced at Tode, he turned away so she could not see his eyes. "Do not tell me!" she cried. "I do not want to know."

Jumping up from her chair, she flung her arms out. "I would like to live for once in my life. I'd like to look into a man's eyes and see that he loved me or hated me for myself, not for my father's gold. I am not Frances who cannot wait one second before she tells that she is the cousin to the greatest heiress in the land. You know that I'd rather talk with the cook than with those old men my father sends to visit me."

Tode's eyes twinkled. "You, dear Axia, would talk to anyone from outside these walls, ask questions of anyone."

"Oh, to see the world," she said, twirling about, her skirt belling out about her. "That is what I'd like, to see the world. Oh, heavens, but I'd like to *paint* the world." She stopped spinning. "But to see it properly, I must be someone ordinary, like . . . like Frances. Yes, to be as ordinary as Frances, that is what I would like."

Tode had to bite his tongue to keep from making a comment. He disciplined himself to keep from again saying what he thought of Frances. When Axia was twelve years old, she'd received a letter from her father saying he was sending her a thirteen-year-old female cousin for a companion. Axia had been so excited that Tode was jealous, and for months Axia had turned the estate upside down as she prepared for the arrival of Frances. Axia had moved out of her own room, the best bedroom in the house, and completely refurbished it for her cousin. When Tode had protested this extravagance, Axia had said, "If she does not like it here, she will not stay," as though that ended the discussion. And even though Axia lived in fear of displeasing her father and made it a policy to ask for nothing for herself, she never hesitated to ask for something for someone under her care. So before Frances arrived, new curtains, new bed hangings, new cushions, were commissioned for her room. And as the day drew near, Axia was beside herself with anticipation.

But on the day Frances arrived Axia was nowhere to be found. After much searching, Tode found her hiding high up in an apple tree. "What if she doesn't like me?" Axia had whispered. "If she doesn't like me, she will tell my father and he will take her away." It had taken a great deal of talking to persuade her that no one could help but like her before Axia would come down and greet her cousin.

But Frances had not liked Axia. Tode, more worldly than Axia and hardened in the first horrible twelve years of his life, saw that Frances had learned to take what she could when she could and with anxious, eager-to-please Axia hovering about her, she managed to take a lot. It was no wonder this James Montgomery thought Frances was the heiress because she dressed as she thought someone who was related to the Maidenhall heiress should: dressed, ate, lived. And the more Axia gave, the more Queen Frances seemed to believe was her right. In the seven years since Frances's arrival, many times Tode had tried to get Axia to stop giving so much to Frances, asking her father for whatever Frances wanted, whether it was oranges in winter or a special shade of silk, but Axia just waved her hand and said, "If it makes her happy, why not give it to her? My father can afford it." But Tode knew that Axia, so lonely, imprisoned all her life, would always be that little girl, afraid of being left alone with strangers. And all these years, even though Frances had never reciprocated, Axia had never stopped taking care of Frances. Axia's only retaliation to Frances's ingratitude was barbed remarks and a pretense that she didn't care. And, Tode thought with a smile, an occasional practical joke, such as painting an ugly woman on one of Frances's mirrors or putting daisies under her pillow because daisies made Frances sneeze.

Tode was suddenly brought back to the present when Axia turned a face full of wonder toward Tode. "I shall *be* Frances."

"Ah yes, of course. We shall cover the walls of your bedchamber with mirrors as hers is and remove all those dreary books you love so much. And of course your paints must go. And—" He broke off. "Pray tell, who will Frances be?" But as he said it, he knew. "No! Your father—"

"Will not know, will not care. I will tell him I did it to protect his precious commodity. If the Maidenhall heiress is kidnapped, it will be worthless Frances, not I, who is taken captive. And I am sure she would soon enough tell her captors the truth. But this is of no concern as we will be under guard. There will be no danger."

"This is because of that Montgomery, isn't it? He put this idea into your head."

"He can go to blazes for all I care. He has no honor, no sense of decency. He has no soul that he would lie and deceive so."

Tode well knew how Axia felt about men or women who wanted to be near her because of her father's money. Once she'd said about Frances, "At least her friendship can't be bought. I've tried."

Going to his chair, she put her hands on the armrests, her face near his. She was the only person in the world who did not turn away in revulsion at the sight of him, and when she put herself this close to him, a wave of love ran through him.

"Do you not see?" she said. "It is my only chance. My *one* chance. I could travel as my rich cousin's poor companion."

"Poor indeed if you have less than Frances," he said, his eyes soft as a doe's.

Axia was not oblivious to Tode's love for her, and when needed, she used it to get round him, for ostensibly, he was her father's chief spy. She gave him a sweet smile. "It all depends on you."

"Away from me," he said, throwing up his arm, for he saw what she was up to. "You think you can persuade me to anything. This is dangerous. Your father's rage is—"

"What would be his rage if I were taken by brigands and held for ransom?" Looking at him, she lowered her voice and hoped he would not catch the hole in her logic, as just moments before she had been reassuring him that she would be safe. "What would you feel when my father refused to pay the ransom and they murdered me?"

When she saw his eyes flicker, she knew that she had won. Clapping her hands, she laughed aloud as she danced about the room. "No one will know who I am! No gawking boys staring at me as the new men my father hires do. No one staring at my clothes and food, asking whether I wear silk in bed or not. No one judging every word I say because England's richest heiress has said it. No marriage proposals at the rate of three a day."

At that Tode smiled. Axia exaggerated, of course, but declarations of love were tossed over the walls regularly. Young men sang love songs from outside the walls. They wrote sonnets to Axia's beauty and said they'd glimpsed her in a dream or "from afar" or had climbed a tree and watched her and fallen hopelessly in love with her. Whenever Frances heard that, she always said, "They must have seen *me.*"

"Will Frances agree?" Tode asked softly, buying time to allow him to think this out. "You know how she loves to thwart you."

"Agree?" Axia asked, aghast. "Agree! Are you asking me if she'll agree to have it *all?* To have the gold *and* the beauty? Do you ask me if this is what she wants?"

She laughed happily. "You leave Frances to me."

"And may God have mercy on her soul," Tode said under his breath so she could not hear him.

Quietly, Frances listened to what Axia was saying. Her room, half again the size of Axia's, had walls covered with drawings and paintings of herself, each of them expensively framed.

"You want me to be you?" Frances asked, her nose in the air. "I am to risk my life as every criminal in the country tries to take your father's gold?"

Axia gave a sigh. "You know my father would not send me across the country if it were not safe."

Frances gave her a little smile. "Safe for you perhaps, but if I am the heiress, what of *my* safety?"

"Safety? You act as though brigands with swords will attack this caravan. You know that tomorrow my father is sending new men to escort me. Escort *us*. No one will know us. And the few here who do will say nothing. No one *cares*," she said with bitterness. Besides, she knew full well that she would give Tode enough money to pay all employees well to say nothing.

Axia continued. "Frances, this is to be no passage of a queen. You know how cheap my father is; all of England knows of his stinginess. Our caravan will no doubt be so poor no one will know of the wealth that is my father's. They will think I—you—are an ordinary merchant's daughter, no more, no less. It is your one chance—"

"Cease!" Frances said, putting up her hand. Walking away from her cousin for a moment, she looked out the window, and when she turned back, her face was hard. "You always *do* get your way, don't you, Axia?"

"How can you say such a thing to me? I live as a prisoner."

"Prisoner! Ha! You don't know what prison is until you've been poor. As my family was and still is. But you, all your life you've had anything for the asking.

Whatever you want, all you have to do is ask your father for it, and he gives it instantly. And here on this estate your word is law."

Axia kept her fists clenched but said nothing. Everything Frances said was true: Axia knew nothing of poverty. While the world hungered, she lived in splendor, yet ungratefully, she wanted freedom. Frances always knew what to say to make Axia feel guilty.

"All right, I will let you see what it is like to have no power," Frances said when Axia did not respond.

Axia nearly choked at that. "Power? Do you think I have power here?"

Frances laughed. "You are queen here, yet you do not know it."

"It is you who flirts with the gardeners, teases the grooms, who—"

"It is all I have! Can you not see that? You do not even have to say, 'Open the door,' for it to be opened for you. You do not see that everyone is aware of who you are and jumps to find favor with you."

"I live as economically as possible, while I have heard of—"

"Heard of! Oh, Axia, you are so naive you think fairy tales are true. All right, we shall see how you will do as a commoner, but I warn you, once this is started, we will play it to its finish. *I* will be the Maidenhall heiress until we reach our destination. If you come to me a week from now or even a day from now and tell me you want to be yourself again, I will deny that I know what you speak of. And only under this agreement will I do this."

Axia raised one eyebrow at her. "You think it is

easy to be something out of a legend, to never know who is your friend and who your enemy? Three years ago I was nearly kidnapped. Do you think it is good to live in daily fear?"

"As I live in fear of you? All you have to do is write your father and tell him to send me away and I will be poor again. As it is now, all that your father pays me to live with you is sent to my father and younger sisters. Living with you I have given up all chance of making a good marriage; I never meet anyone suitable locked away here with you. But perhaps my sisters will make good marriages because of my sacrifice."

"I would not send you away," Axia said softly as she'd said many times before, but Frances never believed her. Every time they had a disagreement, Frances had said, "Now you will send me away, and my family and I will starve."

After a while, Frances gave a slow smile. "Perhaps we should work out a financial arrangement. I do not think you believe I am so stupid as to risk my life for nothing."

Axia smiled. "If you are asking if I thought you would do something for me out of friendship, no, I can honestly say that never crossed my mind. I took the liberty of making a list of possible payment," she said, unrolling a parchment.

Taking it, Frances glanced down the list, then smiled. "Not nearly enough. I do not risk my life for so paltry an amount."

As always, Axia was prepared for this. "Shall we sit?" she asked tiredly. Bargaining with Frances always took time.

Hours later, gold, jewels, cloth, and even revenues

from land that had belonged to Axia's mother had exchanged hands. Truthfully, it was less than Axia had expected to pay.

Standing, Axia rolled up the parchment. "You will not like being me," Axia said at last.

"Nor will you like being me," Frances answered.

Then, tentatively and very, very quickly, they shook hands.

The bargain was made.

Chapter 6

Jamie was in a foul mood.

At home, laughing, teasing with his sisters, it had seemed like a splendid idea to try to win the hand of a rich young woman. It was time he married; he was not averse to the idea. He was tired of sleeping on the ground or in flea-infested inns. He'd like to get back what his father and brother had sold, but to do that he needed money. And so it had seemed the answer to everything to make a young and protected girl believe she loved him, loved him so much that she'd beg her father to allow her to marry someone other than the one he'd chosen for her.

And of course, Jamie thought in his vanity, he'd felt that he was the better prospect than the one who she was to marry. He was a Montgomery, of an ancient family, and if he had no money, his titles and blood would surely make up for that.

But last night, as he paid halfpence to children to gather daisies to be sewn into a cloak, his conscience began to hurt him. Perkin Maidenhall had given him this job on trust. Trust. He was to guard a woman from enemies, not become her enemy.

How could he do this to either of them? he asked himself. Yet never once had he wondered if he'd succeed. Whatever his pretended modesty, he knew that women liked him. But every time he thought of courting the beautiful Frances, he remembered the feel of pretty little Axia under his body. He remembered her breasts against his arm; remembered her brown eyes looking at him with disdain. Maybe that's what he liked about her: she wasn't falling all over herself at the sight of him. She stood with her shoulders back as though to say, I'm worth something!

Just thinking of her made him smile, but the smile didn't last long. How was he going to travel for weeks with *her* while trying to get the Maidenhall heiress to love him, which of course was a dishonorable thing to do since he didn't love her and very much doubted that he ever would, and besides she was engaged to another, and besides that—

"Hell and damnation!" Jamie said. "What in the name of the devil is *that?*"

Sitting atop his horse, Jamie looked down at the sight before him and rubbed his eyes. Surely what he was seeing couldn't be real. It must be the early morning sunlight playing tricks on him. After all, he'd been up late last night supervising the sewing of daisies into a cloak (which he could ill afford), and now the cloak with its lining of hundreds of daisy heads was carefully packed into the wagon of goods he and his men needed for this trip. It had taken a great deal of work to be ready to meet the Maidenhall heiress.

Now, coming over the hill, he could not believe what he was seeing.

"How many are there?" Thomas asked from beside him.

"I count eight in all," Rhys, on the other side of Jamie, answered. After a moment, he said, "It looks like a circus."

All Jamie could say was, "How will I protect her?"

Standing in front of the stone walls that guarded the heiress were eight wagons, but not ordinary wagons. Six of them were made of massive oak timbers bound all the way around with thick iron bands. And in huge letters was the name Maidenhall. They were treasure chests on wheels. Had Maidenhall hired a trumpeter to announce that he was moving valuable goods across the country he could not have been more blatant.

As for the other two wagons, they were newly painted in red and gold, with cherubs on the side, painted draperies across the tops and sides. In the Holy Lands Jamie had seen wagons containing the sultan's wives that were less gaudily painted. Nothing could more obviously announce the transport of the Maidenhall heiress and her dowry as these wagons did.

"We will attract every thief in the kingdom," Thomas said.

"And every lovesick swain trying to win her hand," Rhys responded, then saw Jamie glance at him. He cleared his throat. "Except you, of course. I did not mean—"

"Someday, Rhys, you are going to trip on that tongue of yours," Jamie said as he kicked his horse forward.

For a moment Thomas held Rhys back. "He is in a venomous mood today. Best for both of us to keep our own counsel," Thomas said, then followed his master down the hill.

"Probably an attack of conscience," Rhys muttered. "Conscience is his weakest point." Then he too went down the hill.

Jamie was indeed having trouble controlling his temper. He knew Maidenhall was only a merchant, a great one perhaps, but a merchant only. He could not be expected to know about soldiering and strategy, but to send his only child across England accompanied by wagons that looked to be full of gold was too dangerous to contemplate.

The day was just coming dawn, and in the gray light, he could see men, obviously drivers, just waking. Where were the guards? Surely even Maidenhall did not expect a mere three men to guard so many wagons?

It did not take long before he saw them: three huge men coming out of the shadows of the wagons, yawning and stretching, and right away Jamie did not like them. It looked as though Maidenhall had made a common error: he thought size equaled strength. But Jamie knew you did not hire men the way you bought beef—by weight. These three men were as tall as he was but weighed half again as much, and Jamie could tell from the way they moved that they'd had no training.

I will not do this, he thought, but as he thought it, he knew he was lying to himself. Had not the Maidenhall letter—he had not met the man—said he'd hired Jamie because he was someone to be trusted? Was it not enough that Jamie was thinking of betraying the man's trust by trying to win his daughter in marriage? But now to leave her and her wagons of gold in the hands of another was more than his conscience could bear.

"James Montgomery," he said, introducing himself as he dismounted. As he assumed they would, the three men gave him insolent looks. Jamie could have groaned, for those looks confirmed his knowledge that he'd have to show these men that he was to be obeyed. "There are only three of you?"

"Never had any complaints before," one of the men said, puffing out his chest. "In fact, usually one's enough." He looked to the other men, and they smiled smugly in return.

Fat, Jamie thought. *Fat bodies, fat brains.*

"You forgot one," one of the men said, repressing a derisive laugh. "There's *four* of us." At that the men fell into great guffaws of laughter, nearly crying at their own witticisms. One managed to recover himself enough to point. "Him. He's the fourth."

Standing to one side was a tall, thin, plain-faced boy. At his side was a sword that looked as though it had been brought to England by the Romans. He gave Jamie a tentative smile.

At that Jamie threw up his hands and walked toward a tree where Rhys and Thomas were standing and observing.

Thomas raised his brows in question.

"We will camouflage the wagons as best we can," Jamie said. "To protect them as it is, I'll need a hundred soldiers, not just that fat lot. I will get rid of them as soon as I can. As for now, I'll have to put up with them."

"And the boy?" Thomas asked.

"Send him back to his mother. Now, go, talk to the drivers. And, Rhys, do *not* get into a fight with those braggarts. I do not need your temper today."

Rhys gave Jamie a hard look, but he nodded. Truthfully, he'd taken an instant dislike to those three, and he'd like to slice a bit off each of them.

"Merchants!" Jamie muttered as he strode back to the wagon.

The gate in the wall was still bolted, and Jamie now rang the bell for entry. But no one came. He rang again, but still nothing.

Much to his disgust, he found the three men standing behind him, doing their best to loom over him. He knew their posture, what their bodies were saying: they meant to establish their superiority from the beginning.

"We must warn you," one of the men said in a smug way, "of 'it.'"

Jamie did not have time for games. "Open the gate," he bellowed. How could he protect a lone female if she were surrounded by wagons full of gold? What if something happened to Axia—no, he corrected himself—to Frances, the heiress? He was so busy with his own thoughts he hardly heard the men behind him.

"Have you seen it?" a man said, too near Jamie's ear, as though they were confidants. "I cannot call it a man. It is stunted, with a raw face. A freak."

Jamie did not turn around. He daren't. Sometimes people called Berengaria a freak.

"If it comes out, I'll have a hard time keeping my breakfast down." The other men laughed at this.

"It can't travel with us. I'll be sick to look at it every day."

One man laughed aloud. "We should throw it to the dogs along with the rest of the beggars and blind men."

One minute Jamie was pounding on the door and the next he'd knocked one man to the ground, his foot on his throat, while his sword was at the second man's throat. Out of nowhere Rhys and Thomas appeared, Thomas with a dagger at the neck of the third man, Rhys taking charge of the one under Jamie's foot.

"Out of here," Jamie said through his teeth. "All of you leave before I drain your blood just for the pleasure of it." He could see that the men wanted to retaliate, and he knew he'd have to watch his back for a while, but they soon scurried away, mumbling curses under their breaths.

"And now how do we guard the wagons?" Thomas asked in disgust as he resheathed his sword. He'd heard what the men said, and when the word *blind* was mentioned, he'd known what was going to happen.

"And what about the boy?" Rhys asked, as annoyed with Jamie as Thomas was. "We don't need children along when we have women to protect."

Suddenly, Rhys was flat on his back. One minute standing, the next sprawling. Over him stood the boy, his corroded, pitted old sword at Rhys's throat, "Shall I slay him, my lord?" the boy asked.

Although Rhys could see no humor in the situation, both Jamie and Thomas did, as well as the wagon drivers who'd eagerly watched all of it. When Rhys moved in a way that let Jamie know he was going to teach the boy a lesson or two, Jamie prevented him with a wave of his hand. "What is your name?"

"Smith, sir."

"Have you done any fighting?" Jamie knew of course that he hadn't, but his test was of the boy's honesty.

For a moment the boy looked as though he were planning an elaborate story, but then he grinned, his face as plain and as wholesome as the daisies inside the cloak Jamie had in the wagon. "Never done anything except help my father farm, sir."

Thomas and Jamie smiled at that, and Rhys almost did. He was never one to hold a grudge, and the boy had courage. "You are hired," Jamie said. After directing the boy to fetch the cloak from the wagon, he turned to the gate bell again.

But before he touched the bell, the gate swung open, and standing there was the "it" he'd heard of. He was a young man, with a tall, strong upper body but made short by crippled legs. Down his face were long, deep scars, all on the left side, running down his neck and into his shirt. The scars had healed at odd angles, and so they pulled his face into a grotesque caricature of a human face. And, obviously, when the cuts were new, something had been put into them so they were forever red and raw looking. It was Jamie's guess that this man had not been born with these physical deformities.

Jamie did not flinch as the people behind him did. "What is your name?"

"Tode," he said, meeting Jamie's gaze levelly. He

knew everything about what had just happened, about what had been said and what Jamie had done.

"What is your real name?" Jamie demanded, frowning, remembering how many times he'd used his fists to inform people that Berengaria had a name besides Blind Girl.

No one had asked Tode this before. His one concession to vanity was to change the spelling from Toad, as his father had called him. "I do not know," he said honestly, "but Tode does well enough." At that he stepped back and allowed Jamie and his men to enter, and as Jamie passed him, he put a hand on Tode's shoulder and gave a squeeze of reassurance. And it was in that moment that he won Tode's allegiance forever. Only Axia ever touched him and she rarely. No man had ever touched him in friendship.

As well he could, Tode hurried to keep up with Jamie's long-legged stride. Even he could see that Jamie's mood was not something to be toyed with, and he didn't blame him. To travel the country with those iron-bound wagons with the name Maidenhall painted on the side of them was not what he wanted to do either. Axia would be in constant danger. No, he corrected himself, Frances would be as she was now the Maidenhall heiress. For a moment Tode suppressed a groan. Axia had had to pay every person on the estate to lie about who she was and who Frances was. Thank heaven the secret would only be entrusted to them for a few hours before they left the estate forever.

Frances was waiting for them in the withdrawing chamber, just off the entrance hall.

Now, standing outside the door, Jamie tried to get

his bad temper under control. Guilt and fear for the woman's safety raged inside him. Whatever happened, he would treat her well, he vowed.

She was standing in front of a wall that had been painted with a beautiful scene of Greek legends, and she was so lovely she made Jamie smile. But his smile was not so much for her as at her, for Frances looked exactly like Joby's parody of the Maidenhall heiress. Her dress of dark green brocaded silk must weigh as much as a small pony. Gold embroidery encrusted the bodice. Across her white-skinned bosom were emeralds, and if the enormous baroque pearls hanging from her ears were real, they could be sold to pay for a war. Even her hair was encased in a net of jewels.

"Lord Montgomery," she said, holding out her hand, and he warmly kissed the back of it, noting the rings on each finger. "So, you are to escort me to my fiancé."

"If I may be so permitted," he said, smiling as he withdrew a document from inside his cloak and handed it to her.

But as Frances touched the paper, Jamie's face turned pink, and he withdrew it. "May I be permitted to read this letter from your father to you? 'Montgomery,' he begins, 'I would like to employ you—'"

Frances held out her hand. "Perhaps it would be better if I read it on my own."

Jamie's eyes widened. "You can read?"

Around them, everyone stopped, stunned at the oddity of Jamie's remark.

"I mean . . . ," he said, even more red faced and clearing his throat. "I meant no insult. I was told—"

"He cannot believe anyone as beautiful as you can read. It is like covering a pearl's surface with diamonds. Is that not so, my lord?" Axia said from behind Frances. She was smaller than her cousin and dressed as plainly as Frances was splendid. In her clothing, she was a sparrow next to an exotic bird. But her soft brown dress with white embroidery on the sleeves seemed to make her big eyes more brilliant than any of Frances's jewels.

However, Jamie looked over Frances's shoulder and gave Axia a hard look that let her know what he thought of her lying to him. And immediately, he thought of the cloak. No doubt Frances hated daisies. Any woman who dressed as Frances did would not like something as humble as a daisy. But then what woman truly hated any flower? And he had no other gift for her. Better to give her something than nothing.

"Mistress Maidenhall," he said, smiling sweetly at Frances, doing his best to ignore Axia's smirking behind her, "I have a gift for you."

"Do you?" Frances said, seeming to be genuinely pleased, and Jamie wondered at this. Surely the Maidenhall heiress received gifts daily.

Suddenly, Jamie wanted to wipe that smirk off Axia's face. "It is nothing," he said in his sweetest tone. "The most unlovely to the most lovely; the lowest to the highest."

"Now I am intrigued," Frances said in delight, very aware of Axia hovering behind her. "Pray, may I see this gift?"

"Not yet," he said. "You must close your eyes."

"Oh yes," Frances said and happily closed her eyes.

Jamie motioned for the boy Smith to come into the room, the red velvet cloak across his arms. With a great show of tenderness, Jamie draped the cloak about Frances, hundreds of daisy heads soft against her body. He pulled the hood over her head so the daisies framed her face, swathing her in them, surrounding her with them, and fastened the intricate hook at her throat.

When Frances took a breath, there was a little catch in her throat.

"Now," Jamie said, stepping back to let all see her, for she looked like a mystical lady of legend, a maiden of spring.

Frances looked about her, but she was feeling so strange she could not at first comprehend what was going on. Then she saw them. "Daisies!" she gasped, and her reaction was so strong that Jamie was pleased he'd done this.

Putting her hands to her throat, Frances's fingers fumbled with the clasp, but she could not unfasten it. When the cloak remained around her, she closed her eyes, her face turning pale, then she fell to the floor in a swoon.

Bewildered, Jamie caught her before she hit the floor, then rapidly carried her to the window seat. "Wine!" he ordered. Was the woman unhealthy? Is that why she was kept hidden away? Did she have a disease that was gradually taking her life? He pushed the hood of the cloak back and unfastened it at the neck. She laid with her head on his lap, her long, thin body stretched out on the bed of daisies. She seemed to grow paler by the second. Was she dying? "Wine, damn you! Get a doctor."

At that moment, Tode appeared on his damaged legs, a pewter goblet full of wine held out, but when he saw Frances, he threw the goblet aside. "Get her out of that cloak."

"What?" Jamie was not sure what he meant.

"It is the flowers. They make her sneeze, make her dizzy. Get it off her!"

Within seconds, Jamie reacted, the cloak was torn off Frances and tossed aside onto Smith, who ran from the room with it. Sensing that she needed air, Jamie tried to open the window, and when it stuck, he used his foot to force it open, then half threw Frances across the sill, her head and upper body in the fresh air.

Within moments, she was breathing again. She still looked near death's door, but she was indeed breathing again.

When his heart stopped pounding and he could think once again, Jamie knew who had caused this: Axia. And it took no wizardry to figure out why she had done this: her petty jealousy of her richer, more beautiful cousin had caused her to do something that had almost killed Frances.

With a nod to Rhys to take over, Jamie stood and looked through the crowd of retainers and servants who had gathered around them, searching for Axia. She was standing stone still, her face unreadable, but as far as Jamie could tell, she was not shedding tears of remorse. What had she planned to gain by her cousin's death? Did she stand to inherit?

Had a man done such a thing he'd have drawn his sword on him, but she was not a man. And at the moment, in his eyes, she was not a woman either.

"What do you think you are—" Axia said as Jamie grabbed her wrist and began to pull her.

Quickly, the crowd's attention turned from Frances to Axia, for although they had been paid to keep the secret, they each knew that Axia was the Maidenhall heiress, the person who had to be obeyed at all times.

"You lying little sneak," Jamie said as he sat down on a stool and pulled Axia across his lap, bottom side up.

"Stop it," she screamed. "How dare you do this to me? I am—"

A hard smack to her back side cut off her words.

"Your prank could have *killed* her," Jamie said, administering another smack.

"I'll have your eyes for this," Axia screamed. "My father will—"

"Thank me!" Jamie shouted back. "Your father should have done this to you long ago. You are a liar and a self-centered little brat." With that he shoved her off his lap onto the floor where he proceeded to step over her.

Axia, her face red with humiliation, sat up and saw the looks on the faces of everyone in the room. They all knew the truth of who she was yet they'd raised not a hand to help her. And where was Tode?

Across the room Frances was leaning on the windowsill, still pale, but her happiness at Axia's humiliation was bringing color back to her cheeks. She knew full well that Axia never meant to actually harm her. Axia had put daisies under her pillow, in her wardrobe, in her clothes, everywhere, since Axia had found out how they made Frances sneeze. Neither of the girls would ever have dreamed Frances would react so violently when she was trapped with the daisies. So why wasn't Frances telling this odious man the truth, that it was a prank and nothing more?

"He means to get your money!" Axia bellowed across the room, making Jamie halt, his back to her. "He plans to court you, and when you believe you are in love with him, he plans to try to get you to persuade your father to marry him," Axia said. How dare he humiliate her! And it felt good to let Frances know what it felt like to be smiled at, not for her beauty but for her father's money.

Jamie did not turn around but stood frozen where he was. When he met this girl yesterday, he had liked her, liked her *very* much. How could he have misjudged anyone so completely?

"Then I hope he succeeds," Frances said as loudly as she could manage.

And at that the household burst into laughter. Smiling, Jamie left the room. And he did not stop smiling until he got to the nearest tavern, where he began the long process of getting drunk.

Chapter 7

Axia doubled up her fists and hit the bed again and again. She had not meant for this to happen! She had not meant to *kill* Frances as everyone seemed to think. She had just meant to give her a sneezing fit. How was she to know that spineless Frances would nearly stop breathing just from getting too close to a bunch of daisies? But even Tode had looked at her in accusation.

And that man Montgomery! Axia fell back against the bed, her arms flung out. He had *liked* her when he first met her. She was sure he did. Not her father's money, but *her*.

But now, of course, his eyes were on Frances and on the wagons full of whatever her father had filled them with, and he hadn't so much as looked at Axia. After this morning, Axia had retired to her room to pack her pigments and brushes, her sticks of charcoal and the wax crayons, and she'd stayed there the rest of the day. Maybe she should be saying good-bye to the people here in this beautiful prison, but her father had changed them often, so she'd never become attached to any of them except Tode. And to Frances, if unholy bonds counted.

For a moment tears came to her eyes, but by force of will she made them retreat. There wasn't a person on earth who understood how she felt. After all, who was going to have sympathy for the richest woman in England? No one, that's who. Even as a child when she cried, some undergardener would say, "Use gold to wipe away the tears." Never had there been anyone in her life who was there only because he wanted to be. Because she'd never been allowed off these grounds, every person she'd ever met had been paid by her father to be there.

For years she'd been introduced to people and watched their eyes change. So many times young men had come to the house and, not knowing who she was, looked at her in speculation, either their eyes roaming her body or they'd dismissed her according to their taste. But when they'd heard she was the legendary Maidenhall heiress—oh yes, she was not so isolated that she'd never heard that—their eyes changed. Interested eyes turned to fawning. Disinterested eyes became alert. Never once had Axia not seen the change in the eyes. Or in the manner and voice. Sometimes people were rude to her to show they didn't care. When she was a child, a few people that she'd just met told her they weren't going to allow her to treat them badly, as though it were a foregone conclusion that she would be a monster. She'd had a teacher whose favorite expression was, "Your father's money doesn't allow you to—"

"My father's money doesn't allow me freedom," she said aloud. *The freedom to walk through a village fair and watch a puppet show, the freedom to have someone like or dislike me according to who I am.*

"The right to have a normal marriage," she whispered and had to swallow tears. Any man who would imprison his only child so that the mystery of her would enhance her worth was not going to waste her on a strong, healthy husband. She wasn't sure what was wrong with Gregory Bolingbrooke, but she knew something was. Every time she asked one of her father's emissaries what her betrothed was like, the man's eyes skidded to one side. It was her guess that he was mad. Or evil. Or diseased. Or maybe all three. Whatever he was, his father was willing to pay Perkin Maidenhall a fortune to bring the Maidenhall heiress into the family, with the stipulation, of course, that upon Perkin's death his daughter was to inherit everything.

Of course, Axia knew her father better than other people did. It wouldn't surprise her to hear that her father had sold everything just before he died and buried all the proceeds where no one could find them. Maybe he wouldn't be able to take it with him, but he could prevent others from getting it. And Axia knew better than anyone that he loved to lock his possessions away.

So now, tomorrow, she was to start on the greatest adventure she was ever going to have in her life. She had no illusions that her life as the wife of Gregory Bolingbrooke would be any freer than her life had been so far. At least her father allowed her painting and drawing materials. What if her husband—or his father who seemed to control everything—believed that women should sew and pray and nothing else?

"Aaaargh!" Axia said, again beating her fists against the bed. So far she'd done well. She'd arranged to escape being the Maidenhall heiress for the entire journey. Oh, in the last day, the men and women on the estate had taken delight in not opening doors for her; the cook had chased her out of the kitchen, and one of the servants had snapped at her to get out of the way, but nothing really awful had happened. No, they were just pleased to be able to pretend that she was an "ordinary" person.

But in Axia's eyes she *was* ordinary. "Ordinary as a weed in a flower patch," Frances had said once when they were children. "And just as strong," Axia said before she pushed Frances backward into a newly manured flowerbed.

"Ordinary," she said aloud now. "Ordinary, but not free."

So, she thought, what would an ordinary person do now? She would apologize to James Montgomery and get on his good side is what she thought. Her immediate response to that thought was, *I'd rather eat dirt.*

Her nails bit into her hands at the memory of how he'd looked at the beautiful Frances. Yesterday he'd been looking at her, Axia, with interest, and the next day he was swooning over the rich Frances.

As for what he did afterward, Axia refused to remember. The many snickers she'd heard throughout the estate might have something to do with why she'd been hiding, er, resting in her room most of today.

"Damn him!" she said aloud. He never even asked,

just assumed she was jealous, spiteful, and . . . and was capable of *murder!*

The tears returned, but she made herself sit up and clear her eyes. Just in front of her was an embroidered plaque, *Carpe diem.* Seize the day. It was her motto. Take everything you could get from every day. Take the sunshine; take the raspberry tart off the window-sill; steal a kiss if you could; stay up all night and let the next day take care of itself. Tode said such a motto was going to get her into trouble someday, but Axia had laughed and said, "I hope so. Just so I am not bored."

Trouble is what I want, she thought now, then giggled at a thought. "I ought to show up on Gregory's doorstep pregnant. *That* would break the contract." She stopped smiling and grimaced. "Or at least prevent me from having a madman's mad baby."

Abruptly, she realized it had grown dark, and no one had come in to light her candles. She realized that this night people were showing the Maidenhall heiress that they were just as good as she was.

Frowning, feeling sorry for herself, Axia got off the bed, rearranged her clothing, combed her hair, and started to leave the room. On impulse, she turned back and snatched a pretty little embroidered cap off the wooden stand on the table under the window. It was the only thing she possessed that had belonged to her mother: several layers of dark blue silk embroidered all over with fantastic beasts such as dragons and unicorns and griffins. As a child Axia had spent hours contemplating the cap, and now it was her most precious possession. She rarely wore it and only when she needed comfort—which she did now.

Outside it was a cool spring evening, but the budding trees made the air fragrant. If she wouldn't miss any of the people from the estate, she'd miss her garden, she thought as she ran across the grounds, securely pinning her mother's cap onto her thick hair. Because most of the staff were inside having their supper, Axia had nearly all the garden to herself.

Walking along the north wall, farthest from the house, she noticed the top of one of the walls had been damaged and the guarding spikes were missing. As she made a mental note to tell someone to fix it, she saw fresh cuts on the overhanging branch of an oak tree. Puzzled for a moment, she wondered what the gardeners had been doing to create such marks.

"That's how he got in," she said in wonder, then looked to see if anyone had heard her. No one was about. She could see now that he'd thrown a rope over the branch and swung up and over. Simple when you knew how to do it.

Axia didn't hesitate but lifted her skirts and ran for the nearest garden shed to get a length of rope. Fifteen minutes later, after very little struggle, she was over the wall.

For a moment, Axia leaned back against the bricks, still warm from the day's sun and looked about her. In the growing dark, she could see across fields to houses, to pastures. She could see people—strangers, people who were not paid by her father—walking down lanes. Her heart was pounding, and she almost grabbed the rope to swing back inside the safety of the walls.

But her fear soon turned to curiosity when she heard voices around the corner of the wall to her left.

Slowly, tiptoeing so as not to make noise, she crept around the wall to see three tents there, one of them flying a flag of three gold leopards.

"Maybe if I shoved a barrel of sugar down his throat, that would sweeten his temper," she heard a man say, and Axia flattened herself but not before she saw that they were the two men who'd been with *him*. That man who'd—She was *not* going to remember that!

"With or without the barrel?" the other man said.

"With. Staves and all. Wide end first."

Who were they talking about, Axia wondered. Whose temper needed sweetening? Not *hers?* Please, not her. But no, the first man had said *he*.

"Something set him off," the second man said, and he had a nice, pleasant voice. He sounded older than the other man.

"Couldn't be the heiress. What a beauty. Sweet tempered, gentle, shy. No wonder her father kept her hidden away."

Axia's fingers were biting into the rough brick behind her.

"I think it's more the other one who's bothering him," the second man said.

The first man snorted. "The pretty little one. It's true she has a bosom to make a man weep, but a man would be insane to take on a temper like hers. Ah, there he is. Hide."

Axia's eyes were so wide they hurt. A bosom to make a man weep? Was this *her* bosom? Was she the "other one"? She looked down as though seeing her own chest for the first time. She *did* have a great deal of trouble sleeping on her stomach. But she wasn't sure how she compared to women in the world at large.

It was nearly full dark now, but Axia's eyes were adjusting. She saw the slim boy, one of the guards her father had hired, slip out of the tent with the leopard pennant and hurry away toward the road leading into the village. And a moment later she saw *him* leave the tent and disappear into the darkness.

Overwhelmed with curiosity, Axia ran toward the tent quickly and silently. What was this man like? she wondered as she quietly slipped inside. There was only one candle lit, and it made shadows inside the tent, which was disappointingly empty: a folding table, a folding camp chair, and in the back, a bed of sorts, more a pallet with coarse linen sheets and a wool blanket than a real bed. His clothes were lying across a big leather trunk, and she could not resist looking at them, touching the fine velvets and the satins. Without a doubt in her mind, she knew her father had not paid anyone enough to buy clothes like these. Unbidden, the thought came to her: courting clothes. Clothes made to entice an heiress.

In disgust, she dropped a velvet sleeve, then heard a noise, and he was *there*, entering through the open flap. Instantly, Axia blew out the candle.

"Who is it?" he asked, his voice menacing, and she could see the outline of the sword in his hand.

Would he murder her for trespassing? She gulped. "It's me," she said, her voice a high falsetto out of fear.

"Oh," he said flatly. "Get your clothes off and lie down. I will be there in a minute."

Axia's jaw dropped nearly to her knees. Who did he think she was?

Frowning into the darkness, he said, "You are the girl Smith sent, aren't you?" Between the darkness and all that he'd had to drink, he was having difficulty concentrating.

"Y-yes," she squeaked. Better that than the girl he had raged at this morning.

"Good! Then take off your clothes and light that candle. I like to see what I am paying for."

Ah, now Axia understood. *My goodness. Paying.* He thought she was a—

"Light the candle, I said," he barked out.

"No!" Axia snapped back, then caught herself. "Can't, my lord." She kept her voice slightly higher.

"And why can't you light the candle?" He sounded bored.

Axia's mind raced. "Ugly, sir. I am very, very ugly. Smallpox. Really hideous."

She could feel his revulsion. "But," she said suggestively (at least she hoped it was suggestive), "I have been told I have a bosom to make a man weep."

At that he gave a little laugh. "I guess I'll have to find out, won't I?" he said, then took a step toward her.

Now what? Axia thought. Reveal herself? If he hit her in public, what would he do to her in private? And heavens, what would he do if she did *not* reveal herself?

Carpe diem, she suddenly thought. Seize the day.

He was standing in front of her, but the tent was so dark she could only feel his presence but not see him. She could smell his breath, soft and masculine. And, she realized with a bit of shock, he was more than a little drunk.

"Well?" he said as though expecting her to do something.

But what? Axia wondered. *Throw all my clothes off and . . .* "I am a virgin, my lord," she said.

"You're a what?"

"Yes," she said more positively, "I am a virgin. Well, anyway, that's what I'm very good at pretending."

She could feel him frowning, so she put out a hand and touched the tip of her finger to his hard chest. "Surely, my lord," she whispered, "there's a virgin you'd like to touch. One with a bosom to make a man weep."

He hesitated, but then he said softly, "Yes, there is," and the way he said it made Axia's heart leap. Now she could return to her bedchamber and feel that a man had really and truly desired *her*.

But as she stepped forward, the man did the most extraordinary thing: he reached out and put his hand on her left breast. Axia was too shocked to speak. But then she wouldn't have been able to anyway because he bent down and kissed her half-open mouth.

His kiss was soft, gentle, and when he started to pull away, she leaned toward him.

"You are an excellent actress," he whispered, one hand still on her breast, the other on her neck and moving up to caress her cheek. "I would think you'd never been kissed before."

"I haven't, so will you teach me?"

Jamie didn't answer before he kissed her again.

To be touched, Axia thought. How utterly divine just to be touched. By her father's orders, no one, male or female, was allowed to touch her: must keep the heiress healthy. Only Tode touched her but only in private and then only her hand or his fingertips on her cheek.

She couldn't help herself as she kissed the palm of his hand, and he leaned forward to kiss her neck, her jaw, her ear lobe, as Axia began to lean toward him.

"My name is Jamie," he said. "And yours is?"

"Diana," she whispered, her breath catching in her throat. Just to feel his face on her skin, his big body hovering over her, not really touching her, was joyous.

"Yes, the virgin goddess," he said, and she could feel him smiling.

His thumb caressed her cheek. "You do not feel pockmarked. Your skin feels as smooth as marble."

"But warmer?"

"Oh yes, much warmer."

Expertly, his hands began unfastening the laces of her gown, and she knew that now she must stop him. But then his kisses turned to little nibbles.

"Do you like this?" he asked. "Tell me what you like."

"I do not know." Her head was back, giving him free access to her throat. "Everything is new to me, but so far I like everything."

She could feel his soft laughter, feel his hands moving over her body, and magically, her clothes fell away. His hands were everywhere, sliding over her smooth, warm skin, and when one hand moved lower, she felt weak with desire. At first she was shocked as his hand slid between her legs and she felt his fingers inside her. But when he removed his hand, she was disappointed. "No," she whispered.

He stepped back from her, his hands on her shoulders. "You *are* a virgin."

"Is that bad?" she whispered. It was so dark in the tent she could not even see the outline of his face.

"It is a responsibility to take a maidenhead," he said seriously, suddenly wishing he hadn't drunk so much. "I will not do it."

Please do not leave me, she wanted to say. "I—I need the money. My family is poor." It is what she had read or heard many times from young men.

"Then the coin is yours. Take it and go."

As he started to turn away, she flung her arms about his neck, pressing her naked body against his fully clothed one. "Do not leave me, Jamie, please," she said in a hoarse whisper. "My life is so lonely, and you do not know what awaits me in the future. It will be horrible, I am sure of it." There was absolute truth in her words.

For a moment he hesitated, and although he misinterpreted them, he could feel the truth in her words. If she was hideously scarred and from a poor family, perhaps prostitution was the only course open to her. And perhaps the man who did take her virginity would not be as gentle as he would be. And the truth of it was that he wanted her very, very much, wanted her in a way that had nothing to do with how much he'd had to drink.

His arms went around her, pulling her to him, his hands on her back, sliding over her firm round buttocks. He'd never had a virgin before, someone untouched by another man.

"I want to remember this night all my life," she whispered. "To remember it always. Maybe you could pretend that—that you love me?" she asked tentatively. "No man has ever loved me. Or ever will, I guess," she said sadly.

He assumed she meant because of her damaged face, but now Jamie couldn't imagine anything wrong with this woman in his arms. To him, she felt clean and pure and more beautiful than Diana, the goddess of the moon. "I think perhaps I do love you," he heard himself whisper, then some intelligence returned to him. "For tonight anyway."

"It is enough."

He was holding her, caressing her while she kissed his neck and chin. "Do you not remove *your* clothing?" she asked.

She could feel his smile. "No, you do."

"Do I?" she said with such interest and enthusiasm that he laughed. "And may I touch you?"

"Yes, Diana, my love, you may touch me," he said, laughing, then picked her up in his arms and whirled about with her. "It has been a horrible day, truly horrible, but you are my treat, my reward at the end of the day."

And you, tonight, are the reward for all my life, she thought. Clutching him, she knew she'd never felt so good in her life. "Oh, kiss me a thousand times. Kiss me and kiss me until my lips are numb and I can no longer speak."

"Yes," he said, laughing, "I shall kiss every inch of you."

"And I you, but how *do* I get your clothes off?"

He helped her, but not much, and her childish curiosity about his body was very exciting to him as she ran her hands over him, exploring.

"And may I touch this part of you?" she asked, her

hand between his legs, but all Jamie could do was groan his assent.

Lifting her, he carried her to the bed where he began kissing her beautiful body, enjoying her pleasure in his touch.

Axia lay still, enjoying to its fullest all that he was doing to her body, all the touching, his lips on her breasts, his hands on her thighs and between her legs, his fingers slipping inside her. When he moved on top of her, she had never felt anything as deliciously right as his weight on her.

"I love you, Jamie," she whispered. "I love you."

Jamie didn't answer, but when he started to enter her and she gasped in pain, he drew back.

Misunderstanding, thinking she'd displeased him and he was going to leave her, she awkwardly thrust her hips upward so that he entered her fully—and she nearly cried out in pain.

"Sweetheart," he said, using all his control to keep still as he kissed away the tears that had formed at the corners of her eyes, "slowly. We have all night."

When the pain eased, she found that she liked this sensation of his filling her body. "This is nice," she said as she flung her arms out to the side. "Take me, Jamie, I am yours."

He laughed again. She was unlike anyone he had ever met before. It was as though she knew none of the rules of behavior. "Yes," he murmured and began to move within her.

Axia's eyes widened in surprise. She'd thought his being inside of her was all there was, but now . . . Oh, now, this was even lovelier. Closing her eyes, she instinctively arched her hips upward and felt his silken strokes. And when he began to move faster and deeper, she flung both her legs and arms around him and pulled him as close to her body as she could.

Then he seemed to stop, shudder, and in the next moment he collapsed on top of her and she thought how sweet and tender he felt. He'd been so heavy and strong moments before, but now he was as light as a child.

Gently, she stroked his hair, glad she had been able to give him this pleasure.

"Did I hurt you much?" he asked softly.

"No, not at all," she said honestly, then had a horrible thought. "I must go." Tode would be looking for her, and if he didn't find her, there would be an alarm sounded.

"No!" he said sharply. He'd moved so he was only half on her, his arm tightly around her waist. Relaxing his grip, he turned his head away from her. "Yes, of course, you must go."

Let them look for me, she thought. In truth, what did she care if they *found* her? How were they going to punish her? Lock her up for the rest of her life?

Wiggling her body back under his, she stroked his face so he turned toward her. "What plagues you?" she whispered. "Tell me."

After days of worry, it felt good to Jamie to be so relaxed. "I do not know how to protect her," he said, knowing the woman would have no idea what he was talking about.

"Ah, yes," Axia said. "The heiress." Her arm was under his neck, his cheek on her shoulder, one of his heavy thighs across hers. How intimate, yet how right, she thought. "Is she so valuable to you?"

"I cannot fail. People depend on me. But the wagons . . ." He was feeling drowsy.

"Yes, the wagons," Axia said with a grimace. She had dreamed of a trip across England without people gawking at her—or now it was Frances—because of the Maidenhall name. But her father had sent those heavy wagons that were no doubt full of untold wealth, and all along the journey they would create curiosity. She gave a great sigh. "Were I the Maidenhall heiress I would want to be someone else."

He gave a sleepy smile. "And who would be greater than she? The Queen of England?"

"No, of course not. I would be . . . someone ordinary. A merchant's wife mayhaps. Staying at inns or in a tent like this one. I would want no one to know who I was."

"Yes, but people have seen her."

"Who?" she asked. "I have heard she's been a prisoner all her life. Never allowed out of the gates. It is my guess that she has never seen the world, never seen a puppet show, never seen a cathedral, never met anyone who was not properly introduced to her, never—"

Jamie chuckled. "You do have an imagination. Frances is so beautiful she would call attention to herself wherever she went. If I traveled alone with her, I'd have trouble protecting her."

"Shall I infect her with smallpox?" Axia asked helpfully.

Jamie laughed again. "I wish I could take you with me. You please me. You give me ease."

"Oh yes! I would like that," she said, sounding like a child.

"Alas," he said sadly, "I cannot."

"Why? Because I am so ugly? You would be ashamed of me?"

He didn't know how he'd feel to see her in daylight, but that was not his worry. "She might try to kill you."

"Who? Why would anyone try to kill *me?*"

"The heiress's cousin. Frances, the heiress, is a sweet-tempered, lovely woman, but she has a cousin who is eaten with jealousy."

"Oh?" Axia's voice cracked. "How do you know she does not have cause for her—her misdeeds? Sometimes women appear one way to a man and another way to a woman."

"Like you? Do you appear attractive to me yet hideous to others?"

"Sometimes. But what of the cousin? Does she have nothing to recommend her?"

"I thought she did, but no, she is not what I thought. I do not like liars."

"But perhaps there were reasons why she lied." Her voice was rising above a whisper.

Jamie raised himself on his elbow. "You sound as though you know her."

"No, of course not. How could someone like me know *her?* But I know what it is to have a beautiful older sister."

"And how do you know that the cousin is not beautiful?"

Axia's mouth was a tight line. "From the way you speak of her. There is a different tone in your voice when you speak of the beauteous Frances than when you speak of the cousin. I have heard that tone all my life when people speak of my sister. But never have I heard it addressed to *me.*"

"Sometimes a woman needs more than beauty," he said, thinking of Berengaria. Axia could feel a change in him. "You shall go to my sister," he said softly, as though this were a great honor.

"Go to your sister? Why? What—?"

"I will not leave you to your fate. I feel responsibility toward you after tonight. Yes," he said, and she could feel that he was smiling, pleased with his idea. "I will leave money and a letter with the Maidenhall steward, and tomorrow you shall leave. I will write my sisters and tell them you are to arrive."

For a moment Axia was overwhelmed by his generosity. No one gave gifts to one as rich as she. At Christmas she was expected to hand out gifts to everyone, but only Tode ever gave her anything in return. Frances had never once given her a gift. But this man, a stranger really, was asking to take on responsibility for her entire life. Were all poor people so kind and generous to one another? She had always fantasized about poor people's lives of loving each other, helping each other. Every year Frances went home to her family for one month, and Axia dreamed of what it would be like to have a family.

"Your sister is beautiful?" Axia asked. "As you are?"

"How do you know what I look like?" He had his hand on her stomach, touching her, feeling her thighs, moving up toward her breasts.

Axia was having trouble thinking. "I have seen you. You are—"

He kissed her. "Do not say it. I do not want to be judged by my looks any more than you do."

She smiled. Turning, she let her arms slide around him. "Make love to me again. Please."

"Yes," was all he said before his mouth covered hers.

This time he was slower, and Axia enjoyed their union very much, but what she loved most was the closeness, the feeling of not being alone.

When at last he collapsed on her, she knew that this time he was going to fall into a heavy sleep, but she also knew that she had to leave. After planting many kisses on his sleeping face, she struggled out of strong arms that held her to him as tightly as her father held onto his gold. Quietly, she found her clothes and dressed, but look as she could, she could not find her little embroidered cap. Her mother's cap, she thought in a panic. She'd rather lose anything than that. Including her virginity, she thought and couldn't suppress a giggle.

"What was that?"

Axia froze as she heard the man's voice outside the tent.

"All this gold makes me nervous. If a shadow moves, I may kill it before I see what it is."

That statement made Axia realize that she had to get out quickly. Now that she was no longer in Jamie's arms, she was beginning to wonder what her father would do if he found out she'd surrendered her virginity to someone he had not chosen. If Jamie did leave money for the woman he knew as Diana, maybe he'd leave the cap also.

"Farewell, my love," she said and silently left the tent.

Her eyes were adjusted to the dark, and the guards were carrying lanterns so she was able to slip past them without being seen. For a few moments she panicked when she couldn't find the rope hanging over the wall. After she found it, it took her three mighty swings before she could get enough height to get over. She knew she'd made noise and she heard the guards, but by that time she was on the other side of the wall, leaning against it, her heart pounding.

"Must have been a squirrel," a guard said.

"A squirrel the size of a man," the other guard said before they left.

When all was silent again, Axia ran through the dark, across the orchard, and back to her own bedchamber.

She did not see Tode rise from his huddled place in the deepest, darkest corner of the wall and, frowning, slowly and stiffly go to his own bed, his head bent in thought.

Chapter 8

He is here!" Frances said as she burst into Axia's room and threw back the bed curtains. Because the window curtains had not been drawn the night before, sunlight hit Axia square in the face. "Oh, he is divine, so kind, so considerate. Manners like a prince. And he is the most handsome man on earth."

There was no need whatever to say who "he" was. "And *my* lover," Axia muttered, only reluctantly waking up.

"What? What was it my poor cousin said?"

"Nothing, Frances. Why are you up so early? And what do you have on?"

"Yellow silk. Is it not divine? I have been saving it."

Axia grimaced. Her father often used the estate as a stopping point for his wagons of goods traveling across the country. Whenever a load of silks came from France or leather from Italy, Frances helped herself. Of course she told the steward to report that the fabric had been used for the heiress. As for Axia, she found that stiff silk impeded her climbing of ladders to pick apples. And paint did not wash out of satin. Truthfully, clothes had never been of much interest to Axia.

"Saving it?" Axia asked, yawning. "And how many other gowns have you 'saved' for this journey? A queen's wardrobe perhaps?" Both of them knew that Axia knew to a penny how much Frances spent or took.

Frances looked at herself in the mirror on the little stand on the table under the window. "You should hear his plan," she said, watching Axia in the mirror. "I am to be his wife." To Frances's *great* satisfaction, Axia sat bolt upright in bed.

"His what?"

Turning, Frances gave her cousin a sweetly catty smile. "Oh, my, it is getting late. I must run. I am so glad you slept late, cousin, as you have given James and me time to become such good friends this morning." With that, she slipped out the door.

Axia looked about her for something to throw at the door and found only her shoes, which made an unsatisfyingly weak sound when they hit the door. However, Frances must have been listening because her laugh rang out loud and clear before she ran down the hall.

Throwing back the covers, Axia thought, *His wife? Now what has Frances been up to? And how can anyone cause so much trouble in so little time?*

She dressed quickly, pulling her own laces together, gave a regretful glance toward the stand where her mother's cap usually sat, then ran from the room. How her life had changed! First last night and now today! Today she was to start the most wonderful journey of her life. As she ran down the stairs, tying her hair into a tidy knot, she thought, *What will I see on this journey? Who will I meet? What food have I not tasted? What smells will be new to me? What sounds are to be heard?*

When she opened the door of the withdrawing chamber, she stopped short. He was there, standing so the sunlight hit the back of his head, playing on the dark curls of his hair, then running down his warm neck that she'd kissed so many times last night and onto his shoulders, so broad and strong. He was standing by a table, a map in his hands.

At the sight—and memory—of his hands, Axia had to catch herself against the door jamb. Would he recognize her? Would his spirit know who she was?

Blinking, she looked away from Jamie, bent so intently over the map, to see that both Tode and Frances were staring at her, Frances with a smirk on her face. Axia forced herself to remove the expression from her face. She wasn't going to let anyone know what she was feeling.

"Good morning," she said lightly. Tode nodded at her silently, still looking at her in an odd way; Frances continued smirking, and Jamie looked up frowning.

"You sleep late, I see," Jamie said flatly, as though he now had further proof of her worthlessness.

From the way he glared at her, she knew that he did not recognize her from the night before. "Not usually," she began, because he made her sound as though she were lazy. "Usually I—"

"No matter." He cut her off, and looking back at

the map, he continued as though she were of no consequence. "We will meet the wagons here and here—"

"What are you doing?" Axia asked, leaning over the map as close to Jamie as possible. Tode had moved to stand on the other side of her.

"Lord James has the most marvelous plan," Frances purred. "Oh, please, do tell her," she pleaded prettily.

Involuntarily, Axia smiled. Frances would do *anything* to get a man's attention, pretend to be stupid, helpless, whatever. Axia had seen her ask men shorter than she was to reach for things for her. Frances could gag a person, but the men all seemed to love whatever she did.

Frances batted her lashes at Jamie. "Please," she repeated.

With obvious reluctance, Jamie turned to Axia. "I have sent a messenger to my relatives to send guards for the wagons. Anyone who sees them will think they carry the Maidenhall heiress and her dowry. But in truth I have hired someone else to take her role."

"And you will never guess who is to be *me,*" Frances said as she put her hand on Jamie's forearm.

"Me?" Axia asked tentatively. Was she to be the heiress playing someone playing the heiress?

"Of course not!" Jamie snapped as though she had offended him. "I do not risk women, and any woman traveling in those gaudy wagons is at risk."

Axia was glad he did not mean for her to be harmed, but the way he was looking at her made her think he hated her.

"Smith!" Frances burst out. "The tall boy who Father hired is to be me."

It took Axia a moment to remember that "Father" was actually *her* father. She gave a weak smile, but she didn't like the way Jamie was staring at her.

"Tell her the rest," Frances urged. "It is such a brilliant plan."

Jamie began rolling up the map, obviously very reluctant to tell Axia anything. "I and my two men will take another two wagons. We are to be cloth merchants, and Mistress Maidenhall will travel as my wife. That way, I will be able to protect her, free of the Maidenhall name."

Thrusting the map under his arm, he looked at Axia, almost sneering at her. "Is there anything else?"

Axia swallowed. Why was he looking at her with such anger? "How do *I* travel?"

He gave her a look up and down. "You do not. You remain here."

For a moment Axia could not speak. It was as though the bottom of her world had fallen out. Not to go? To remain here?

"You are not necessary," Jamie was saying. "I was hired to protect the Maidenhall heiress, and you are one of the dangers. You have shown your jealousy and the lengths to which you carry it."

Axia was in such a state of shock that it was as though her soul left her body and, hovering above the room, she could look down on everything and everyone. Not to go? She had been put inside these walls when she was three weeks old, and until last night she had never been outside of them. And after this journey she knew she would be locked up again. But now this man was saying that this one bit of freedom was to be denied her.

She could see Frances's face. Never had a countenance registered such joy as Frances was feeling at this news that Axia would not be allowed to go on this journey.

Maybe James Montgomery did not remember last night, but she knew that she had given him her most precious gift, had told him she loved him, and today he was saying there was no reason for her to be given these few weeks of freedom. He was denying her what she most wanted on earth.

Axia went into a rage such as she'd never felt before. Leaping on Jamie, her hands formed into claws, she raked the skin of his cheeks. Her attack was so unexpected, it stunned everyone in the room. No one could move. Jamie tripped over his own feet, staggering backward in his confusion as he tried to shield his face from her hands. Doubling her fist, Axia hit him in the face as she kicked him at the same time, all the while screaming, "I hate you, I hate you, I hate you."

Tode was the first to recover. He was the only person in the room who knew what Axia was feeling. Wrapping his arms around her, pinning her arms to her sides, he pulled her off Jamie. By this time, Jamie's men had recovered enough to step between him and the little wildcat.

"Ssssh, quiet," Tode was saying, holding Axia as tightly as possible. "Of course you can go. You will not be left behind."

Jamie, the back of his hand to his scraped face, looked up. One of his eyes looked as though it might turn black. Looking at the blood on his hand, he said, "She is insane."

At his words, Axia began to struggle again, but Tode bellowed across the room, "Frances! Tell him!"

Frances gave a great sigh because she knew exactly what Tode wanted her to say. "I will not go if my cousin Axia does not go with me," she said tiredly, obviously not wanting Axia to go but still saying what was demanded of her.

Jamie looked from Frances to that crazy girl being held by Tode. What was this? What hold did that murderous girl have on the heiress?

"You do not have to do this," Jamie said to Frances. The scratches in his face were beginning to sting. "She is a madwoman. She has tried to murder you, to murder me. Am I to carry her in a locked cage?"

Shaking all over, still trembling in the aftermath of her rage, Axia had not known she was capable of such anger. But not to go? *Not to go?!*

Tode relaxed his hold on Axia as he felt her subside. "Frances," he said in a voice that carried warning, "if you do not say what needs to be said, then I will tell him all."

Frances grimaced. She very well knew that Tode— that hideous little monster—would tell Lord James that she was not actually the heiress; then it would be Frances who would be left behind. She took a deep breath. "Axia did not try to murder me yesterday. She wanted only to make me sneeze. No one knew the daisies would . . ." She waved her hand. For all that her words were correct, her tone could not have been more flat.

"And?" Tode said, letting Frances know he would allow her to leave nothing out.

"Axia is angry because she wants to go."

At that Rhys gave a guffaw of laughter and even Thomas smiled. Anger? Is that what they had just seen was called? Anger? Men fighting in battle, trying to save their own lives, fought with less passion than they'd seen in this young woman.

Rhys looked at Axia now, her waist-length hair, thick and shining, twisted about her like a rich auburn cloak, her breast still heaving. All in all, she was quite a bit more attractive than even he'd originally thought.

When Jamie hesitated in giving his approval, Frances glanced at Tode and saw that he was about to tell the truth of who was the heiress. "Please," Frances said and her begging was genuine. "She can go as—as my maid."

"I would rather eat—" Axia started, but Tode cut her off.

"Not satisfactory," he said to Frances.

Frances gave a little moué of disgust. "All right, then, she can be my cousin or sister or whatever."

"I *am* your cousin," Axia yelped.

"So you are," Frances said, giving Axia a look up and down, Frances in her yellow silk embroidered with thousands of blue butterflies, Axia in drab, serviceable wool. Frances's look said she couldn't understand how the two of them could be related.

Seeing the look, Rhys guffawed again; Thomas put his hand over his mouth to hide his smile.

"Are you sure Maidenhall paid you enough?" Rhys said under his breath to Jamie.

Jamie put up his hand for the cat fight to stop. "If I must take you both, I wish I could send you on separate caravans, but I cannot." He glared at Axia. "You will travel as my sister." Moving close to Axia, he nearly put his nose to hers. "And if I have *any* trouble with you, I will send you back here with an escort. Do you understand me?"

Axia wasn't afraid of him, and she wasn't going to allow him to intimidate her. Standing on tiptoe, she looked him square in the eyes. "I swear here and now that I will do everything I can to make your life as miserable as possible, and if you attempt to retaliate in any way, you will regret it."

Jamie, never before having encountered hostility from a woman, merely stared at her. Frances broke him from his trance.

"Is *he* going?" she asked Jamie as she nodded toward Tode, her voice letting him know that she did not want Tode to go with them.

Jamie ran his hand over his eyes. He'd once been caught at sea in a storm that had destroyed the other four ships near them; he, Rhys, and Thomas had once fought twelve Turks at once; he'd spent seven months in a prison that was filled with rats and unspeakable filth. But, by God, right now he'd rather deal with any of those things than these two women.

Jamie took a deep breath. "Yes, Tode goes with us. Maidenhall has expressly requested that he remain with his daughter." He narrowed his eyes at Axia. "As for you—" He couldn't think of anything to say to her because if he opened his mouth, he feared what might come out of it. "You—paint the wagons as for a cloth merchant. Perhaps you can make yourself *useful.*" With that he stormed out of the room, his two men following him.

The single candle glittered in the barren little room, and Jamie thought how his youngest sister would not like to hear that the Maidenhall estate was comfortable but did not have the richness he'd expected. Truthfully, only Frances glittered as he'd expected.

But he must write them a letter and reassure them that all was well.

"The woman Axia is insane," Jamie wrote his sister. "But Frances the heiress—" He put down his pen. Frances what? *Loved* her insane cousin? Jamie ran his hand over the scratches on his face, then winced when his thumb touched his sore, swollen, and blackened eye. No, that girl Axia had some rule over Frances. What could it be? What secret could a nineteen-year-old heiress have that would cause her to do anything rather than have it found out?

And what was between Tode and Axia? Were they lovers?

At that Jamie smashed the end of his quill and had to use his dagger to cut a new point.

It was not his concern what went on between the cousin of the Maidenhall heiress and . . . whatever capacity Tode occupied in this strange household.

He turned back to his letter.

But Frances the heiress will not allow her cousin to be left behind. I do not believe Frances sees her cousin for the threat she is.

We will be traveling in disguise, with Frances as my wife, and I shall be pretending to be a cloth merchant. Shall I not make a fine one in my new clothes? Axia, the cousin, is very jealous of Frances, so I will need to watch her closely. She is to travel as my sister. No set of traveling players ever had such a farce as this one.

I am sending a girl to you. Her name is Diana, and she is badly marked. Be kind to her as she has been to me.

My love to both of you. May God watch over you.

> Your loving brother,
> James

"Well," Joby said. "Do you still believe he is in love with this Axia?"

"He is in love with someone or else he would not be so miserable," Berengaria answered. "Who is this Diana and how has she been so kind to our brother?"

"The same ways that *all* women are kind to men like our divinely handsome brother," Joby said sagely.

Reaching out her hand, Berengaria waited until Joby put the letter into it. Jamie always said Berengaria could feel what was not written in a letter. "Yes," she said, holding the letter, then turning it round and round. "Something is bothering him very much. He is . . ." Her face lit up. "He is looking for something."

"Probably lost that little dagger of his," Joby said, trying to sound flip when truthfully she wanted to ask Berengaria to say more.

Her elder sister was not fooled. "He is looking for someone, but she is hidden."

When Berengaria said no more, Joby said, "He should try the cellars. What do you think he means that this Diana is badly marked?"

"We shall have to wait and see, will we not?" Berengaria answered, knowing Joby would be her eyes. Still holding the letter, she was frowning. Something was troubling her brother very much.

Chapter 9

Dawn was breaking and the inhabitants of the Maidenhall estate were just waking when Axia, yawning, walked into the house. The steward was moving toward the front door.

"Did he give you something to give to a girl named Diana?" she asked, watching the man's eyes.

It was on the man's lips to protest that according to what he'd been told, she was no longer the heiress and therefore need not be obeyed. But when he looked into Axia's eyes, he could see that she was indeed the daughter of a man who was said to know more about business than anyone else on earth. Putting his hand inside his doublet, the steward withdrew the letter and handed it to her.

"There was no little blue cap with the letter?" When he shook his head no, she said, "Then give me the money he left for this Diana."

He dropped coins into her outstretched hand.

Axia looked at the coins, then looked at the steward. "While I am reading this letter, I suggest that you put the rest of the money in my hand."

To my dearest sisters Berengaria and Joby,

This is Diana. Take care of her and watch over her. Do not let anyone harm her in any way. She is my gift to you as her spirit is a happy one. I hope she gives you as much joy as she has given me.

                    With all my love,
                    James

As she was reading, Axia felt the clink of coins in her hand, and she closed her fist over them as the steward left the house. Clutching the letter and the coins, she climbed the stairs to her bedroom and smiling, she fell across the bed, still wearing her paint-smeared clothes. By her calculations, she could get at least one hour's sleep before what she'd done was discovered. Smiling, she was asleep instantly.

About ten minutes later, shouts woke her.

"Where is she?" she heard shouted from below and knew that sound could only be the unmistakable roar of James Montgomery.

With a one-sided grin, Axia shoved the letter and money into her pocket. Without the least concern for his rage, she fell back asleep.

The door being thrown open woke her. "Axia!" Tode said sternly, but there was also exasperation in his voice.

"Yes, yes," she murmured sleepily. "I am ready."

Dragging herself off the bed, yawning, she walked past him.

"Why have you done this?" Tode asked, following her down the stairs. "Why are you inciting him? He thinks you are dangerous, that you aim to hurt Frances. Why cannot you—?"

She had reached the bottom of the stairs, and standing there, his face red with anger, was Jamie. At least his face was partially red, red under the three bluish scratch marks along one cheek and a black and purple eye above the other cheek.

"Tried to shave yourself, did you?" she asked calmly as she walked past him and out the front door.

Of course she knew what he was angry about, but then she had merely obeyed him, hadn't she? Last night, all night long, by lantern light, she and a cook's helper, two undergardeners, and the steward's wife had painted one of the wagons that was to be used in their disguise as cloth merchants. She had painted the faces and the outlines, and the boys had filled in the large areas. The steward's wife had painted the letters according to Axia's direction.

Now, standing before the wagon, as was nearly all her household plus the wagon drivers her father had sent and the newly arrived guards from Jamie's relatives, Axia thought it looked good. Oh yes, very good. And from the awed faces of those around the wagon, each of them slowly circling it, she knew they liked it too.

Larger than life size, she had painted Jamie in armor as he slayed a glorious dragon, while looking on in fear, her eyes wide, her foot chained to a post, was Frances. If Jamie did not save her in a minute, she was going to be killed. The dragon's huge green, scaly tail circled around the wagon . . .

And became the tail of a monstrous lion on the other side. Here again was Jamie, but this time he was wearing very little clothing, only a sort of short leather skirt and a white shirt that hung in rags off his muscular body. Behind him, Frances, completely clothed, struggled against a post where she was tied by her hands.

All in all it was the most extraordinary, most exciting thing most of the people there had ever seen. And Axia's likenesses of Jamie and Frances were remarkable.

"I shall *kill* you, Axia," Frances screamed when she saw the wagon, then drew back her hand to strike her cousin.

But Jamie caught her arm, and Frances, never missing an opportunity, turned in his arms and "cried" against his chest. Of course Frances would never actually redden her eyes with real tears, but she liked the effect.

Rocking back on her heels, Axia smiled, knowing full well that Frances did not object to having her picture anywhere. What she objected to were the words painted on the wagon.

"See Frances, the most beautiful woman in the world." "Buy the cloth and see her." "No sale, no sighting."

There were words all over the wagon. "See her! Inside! Live!" "See Jamie, the only man on earth beautiful enough to match her." "Watch them eat. Watch them breathe."

The people who could read were telling those who

couldn't what the words said, and gradually, everyone was turning to look at Jamie and Frances with wonder on their faces.

"You have made me a freak!" Frances said, turning to glare at Axia. "Am I to be put in a cage and the cover lifted when anyone buys so much as an inch of cloth?"

Axia was solemn. "Frances, that face of yours is worth at least a foot of the best linen."

Again Jamie held Frances back from attacking Axia.

"Cover it!" Jamie ordered. "All of it. Paint over it."

There was a horrified silence around the wagon. To paint over something as beautiful as this?

"I will *not!*" Axia said indignantly, hands on hips, glaring at him over Frances's head. "This will sell much cloth."

Jamie spoke through his teeth. "The objective of this journey is not to sell cloth like some—some . . ." He could not think of a word bad enough. "Some tradesman, but to get her safely to her destination."

"Tradesman?" Axia said, making it sound as though he thought the word was dirty. "Might I remind you, *Lord* James, that my father—" Catching herself, she said, "Perkin Maidenhall is just that, a *tradesman.*"

It was at this point that Thomas stepped forward. "If I may, my lord," he said.

Jamie, glad for any excuse to get away, thrust Frances toward Tode. "Protect her," he said, then followed Thomas away from the gawking crowd, which was growing in size by the minute.

"Perhaps I could offer some advice."

"At this moment I would appreciate advice from the devil. That . . . girl, that hellion, makes me so I cannot think."

Thomas cleared his throat. That was obvious to everyone. He'd known Jamie a long time and had always admired his calm under even the most horrible of circumstances. But this young woman seemed able to do what war could not. "The wagon is quite beautiful."

"Beautiful?" Jamie was aghast. "Did you see what she has painted? It is *me.*" He winced as his anger hurt his face, then forced himself to calm. "Thomas, you would not feel the same if it was *your* face up there."

"*My* face would not sell a bag of ashes."

"And I do not plan to allow my face or Frances's to be used to"—his lip curled with distaste—"sell something. The world will come to an end when the face of a beautiful woman is used to sell merchandise."

"I leave the end of the world to God," Thomas said. "However, I know we will be traveling together for weeks, so I beg of you, do not make this girl your enemy more than she already is. Leave the pictures, have her paint out the words. She has been up all night painting, and after all, you did order her to paint the wagon. You did not stipulate how it was to be painted."

"Must you remind me of my every word?" Jamie started to run his hand over his face, but it hurt too much. "Yes, I can see your point. Tell them what is to be done," he said, waving his hand. "I still might kill her if I get too near her. Then load the wagons. We leave on the morrow." Turning, he looked back and saw that his Montgomery cousins' men were laughing and pointing, and he knew full well that his cousins would be told in detail about this wagon. "Thomas! Have her put clothes on the man with—with . . ."

"The lion?"

Jamie threw up his hands in disgust and walked away.

"Do you understand me?"

Axia, sitting primly on the chair, tightened her lips as she looked up at him. "Yes, my lord," she answered, putting as much sarcasm as she could in the statement.

Jamie turned to glare down at her. For thirty minutes he'd been trying to make her understand how serious the forthcoming journey was. He was beginning to fear that she would announce to the world that Frances was the Maidenhall heiress.

He'd had some time to calm down this morning, and while the wagons were being loaded, he'd talked to people on the estate. As far as he could tell, this little Axia was a master of control. No matter what he asked about, from accounts to cross-pollination, the answer was, "Axia does that." Frances was always Mistress Maidenhall, but Axia was Axia to everyone, old and young alike, from the housekeeper to the pig boys.

And Axia ran everything. It was as though she were steward and grand vizier all in one. And no wonder Frances was afraid of her. Axia had so much control that people were afraid to do anything without her permission. "I daren't without asking Axia," he heard more than once.

As the day wore on, Jamie wondered how he could

have misjudged her so completely. That first day he'd liked the way she looked at him, the way she seemed to say, I am worth something! But now he thought, *No wonder she thought so highly of herself when she had control of the finances of the Maidenhall heiress!*

Well, she wasn't going to control him, he vowed as he looked down at her. *"What* do you understand?" he asked.

"That I am not to cause any problems on this journey or you will—What is it you threaten me with? Tying me to a wagon wheel?"

"Not quite. Tying you inside the wagon."

"Ah yes, I knew it was some violence you planned for a woman half your size."

Jamie grimaced. Why would she understand nothing? "It is not *me* I fear for but Frances," he said with exaggerated patience. "You cannot understand how the world sees her." With some guilt he remembered Joby's pantomime. "Her father's money makes people blind to her as a human. Were anyone to know who she is I would fear for her very life."

"And of course her life is everything since you plan to marry her money yourself."

"Why did I ever think I could trust *you?"* he spat out. "If I had not told you—"

"Then Frances would think your liking of her is *real!*" Axia spat back. "At least now she is warned against you." Standing, she sneered at him. "You say you hate liars, but you are the worst sort. You lie to all women about love and honor. You attacked me that first day, looking at me as no man ever has before, yet all the while you were lusting after Frances's gold. Then you take an innocent girl's virginity and—"

Startled, she stopped. She had *not* meant to say that, but it was too late now. She buried her clenched fists in her skirt.

"What do you know of her?" Jamie snapped.

"She came to me as she knew you were with the Maidenhall estate. Poor ugly thing, her face all—" Axia took a breath. "Foolish girl, she thought you loved her. But you love only the Maidenhall gold, do you not?"

Jamie turned away so Axia could not see his face. That night with that girl haunted him. He seemed to remember the smell of her hair, the feel of her skin. "What has happened to her? I left money for her," he said softly.

"Do you think I was going to send her to *your* family? I sent her to—" *Where?* Axia thought, then remembered she was supposed to be Frances. "I sent her to my family, to my father and sisters." Now she watched Jamie's face carefully. Why couldn't he see that she was Diana? And what did he feel for her? Why was he so gentle to Diana and so harsh to Axia?

Taking a deep breath, Axia gave him her coldest look. "As for your sermon on my behavior, yes, I will stay away from you. But for Frances, she has been under my care for years, and as you can see, she has come to no harm. As for you, in truth, nothing will please me more than to forget that you are alive." As she stepped past him, she moved her skirts aside. "To me, sir, you are dead." With that she left the room.

Jamie collapsed onto the window seat. All his life he'd been blessed with having *no* problems with women. Really, none at all. His sister Joby, who plagued every other male she met, only amused Jamie, and when she did get too outrageous, he merely had to lift an eyebrow to bring her back into line. Berengaria was an angel. The queen, who gave so many problems to so many men, smiled at Jamie and danced with him.

It seemed that all over the world women smiled at him. But not this girl with the big brown eyes and hair that had to be the thickest, most luxurious, most—

"Hell and damnation!" he said, then purposefully touched his swollen eye so a shaft of pain shot through his face. She wasn't human! She'd tried to kill her more beautiful cousin, had made him and her cousin into a public freak show, had ridiculed him, taunted him, embarrassed him. The list never seemed to end.

And now she'd interfered with Diana, his sweet, funny Diana, who'd given him a wonderful gift.

"Damn her!" Jamie said aloud. All he'd wanted of her was her word of honor—if she knew what that meant—that she would behave on the journey. Why did she have to dramatize everything? And what did she mean that he was dead to her?

When the door opened and he saw Rhys, Jamie knew his time for reflection was over. Frances, he thought. He must think of Frances and what his family needed. It didn't help any that that brat Axia had said what Jamie felt, that he was courting the Maidenhall gold.

"The wagons are ready for your inspection."

"Yes, of course," Jamie said, rising. They would leave early in the morning, and there was much to see to. At the door, he paused. "Rhys, do you know anything about women?"

"Not a drop in the ocean," he said pleasantly. "And if any man says he does, he's a liar."

"Mmmm," was all Jamie could say in agreement as he left the room.

Chapter 10

Three days, Axia thought, stretching in the delicious sunshine. She was sitting on a little ridge, the wagons below and behind her. Before her was a field of wildflowers, a pretty little village in the distance. If she were a landscape painter, this is what she'd paint, but now she wanted to sit here alone and look at the world, or at least this tiny bit of it.

She'd had three days and two nights of freedom, of seeing something besides what was inside brick walls. There'd been villages with houses with the upper floor hanging over the street. There were shops full of goods she'd never seen before, such as religious relics and children's toys.

There was food: cream cakes, honey cakes, sugared currant buns. The Maidenhall cooks had been adequate, but none of them had ever been creative. When Axia saw a baker's shop with a loaf of bread in the front that had been shaped into a standing, roaring bear, a snarling dog before it, she nearly swooned with delight.

And Rhys had bought the loaf for her. *Dear Rhys,* she thought now. Both he and Thomas had been so kind and generous to her these last days.

After that horrible lecture by the traitor, James Montgomery, the day before they left, Axia had vowed never to speak to him again except when it could not be helped. And so far she'd not had to address a word to him. In the first wagon was Frances, her maid, Violet, and the driver, George. In the second wagon was Axia, Tode, and their driver, Roger. Jamie and his two men rode along on horseback.

From the first day the journey had been joyous to Axia. For the first half of that day she'd said not a word but had gasped at people and houses, at the rutted road, at dilapidated carts carrying goods. On the first afternoon they had stopped to water the horses, and there were three boys playing with a hoop. Another child held a wooden cup that had a ball attached to a string; the child was trying to bounce the ball into the cup. Curious, Axia went toward the children, and because she was small and not much older than they were, she was soon taking lessons from all four of them on hoops and ball bouncing. When Rhys came to fetch her, he informed all of them he was the champion ball bouncer and was soon trying to prove it. When Thomas came to fetch Rhys, Thomas said he could twirl a hoop the best of anyone in the world and started to show them. When Jamie came to get all of them, he found four children and three adults laughing hilariously and playing children's games. Smiling, Jamie went toward them, but Axia froze, handed the cup back to the child, and walked away, her back stiff. And that abruptly ended the laughter.

After that day, Axia and Rhys and Thomas had become great friends, the men riding their horses on either side of her and answering all of Axia's questions. Tode liked to drive the wagon when there were no people near, so Roger went inside and slept. And the four of them made a merry group, laughing, telling riddles, trying to dredge up every children's game they could remember. Because Axia had spent the first several years of her life exclusively with adults, she had missed most childish activities. The first child Axia remembered seeing was Tode when he was already twelve and the second one was Frances, who had certainly never been any fun.

In the evenings she drew portraits. Each night they had pulled their wagons into a field, and under Axia's direction, the drivers had built a camp fire and hung the cast iron pot full of a stew made from meat purchased in the nearest village.

During the day Rhys and Thomas fed Axia. When the road passed through a village, one of the men would stop at the local bakery or sweet shop, the butcher's, or even the grog shop to see what he could find that perhaps Axia had not eaten or drunk before. At first they'd bought two of everything and had offered one to Frances; after all, she was the heiress, the one who'd been locked away all her life. But Frances looked at the men as though they were daft. "How can I eat that now?" she asked, annoyed. "My hands would be sticky."

They never tried Frances again after the morning of the second day, but they delighted in feeding Axia anything they could find. And in the evening she rewarded them by sketching events of the day. It was as though her mind memorized everything she saw in perfect detail. There was Rhys reaching for a bun, the baker's wife's spoon just about to come down on his hand. There was Thomas puzzling over a wooden toy and a little girl looking up at him in impatience because he could not figure the toy out. There was Tode driving the wagon, showing only the unscarred side of his face, and smiling. There was Roger asleep and snoring, a fly hovering over his lips.

"And what of Jamie?" Thomas asked softly, marveling at her drawings.

After a quick look at Jamie, standing some feet away, Axia dipped her pen into ink and sketched quickly. In minutes she showed the drawing. There was Frances's beautiful face, but her body was only a pile of bags of gold. Jamie leaned over her, his face leering, kissing her fingers that peeped out of the bags, his other hand behind his back holding a certificate of marriage.

No one meant to laugh. It was a hateful drawing and they knew it, but Roger the driver thought it was hilarious, and when he howled with laughter, so did the others.

And, of course, that was when Jamie chose to walk over to see what everyone was enjoying.

With a smug little smile, Axia handed him the drawing, even though Tode nearly fell into the fire as he tried to catch it before it reached Jamie's hands.

"So that is what you think of me," he said before handing the drawing back to her, then walking away.

So now Axia was alone, enjoying her freedom, and it seemed that every part of her body was tingling. Leaning back on her arms, she put her head back and breathed deeply of the clear, cool air. How different this air felt than that inside the walls of her father's estate.

Carpe diem, she thought. Seize the day, and with each precious minute, her short time of freedom was ending. Three days were already gone, and it seemed that she had done very little except eat half of England. Throwing out her arms, she thought that she wanted to try more, to fly. "Yes," she said aloud, "I want to fly. I want to . . ." Yes, what did she want most in the world?

"I want to prove that I am more than money," she said to the wind. Ever since she was a child, she had been reminded constantly that she was the Maidenhall heiress. Frances never missed an opportunity. "If he likes you, then I am sure it is because of your money," Frances had said a hundred times. "She is being nice to you because of your money." Again and again, always her father's money!

"Am I not worth more than my father's gold?" she asked. "Why is it never questioned that no one wants anything except gold from me? Why—?"

She stopped because she heard Tode's whistle, his call that she was to come to him. Slowly, she went down the hill toward the wagons.

"What is she doing up there?" Jamie asked Tode, his voice showing his annoyance. "She is the strangest person I have ever met. One minute I hate her and the next I—"

"The next you are intrigued by her," Tode finished

for him, then saw Jamie give a reluctant nod of agreement. "Axia has been isolated all her life; she does not know the ways of the world. Everything is new to her."

"As she has made abundantly clear as she makes fools of my men," he said tightly.

Tode shook his head. "I think that you will find Axia quite a, ah, useful person."

"Ah yes, she does help about the camp."

Tode smiled, something he rarely did because it made him look more grotesque than usual. "I think you will find Axia is a bit more useful than flavoring the stew. Axia is quite knowledgeable about money."

Jamie gave a snort of disbelief. "Only a fool would allow that brainless harridan to touch his money."

"Blood will tell."

"What did you say?" Jamie asked quickly.

Tode cleared his throat. "I said that only time will tell."

Jamie grimaced and walked away, but Tode's words affected him. Unfortunately, yes, he *was* intrigued by Axia. And it was true, she was unlike anyone he'd ever met. First of all, she seemed to have no understanding of the class system. Her relationship with a man as rich as Maidenhall would naturally give her some rights, but Axia didn't seem to understand this. Whereas Frances seemed to thoroughly understand her place as the leading actress in a play, Axia just seemed to do what needed to be done, whether it was washing dishes in a stream or helping Frances find a ring she'd misplaced.

What Axia did, he thought, was make everyone's life easier. The first night they had camped he'd found the three servants going about their duties silently and efficiently. In his experience new servants stood about scratching themselves until someone told them exactly what their duties were. Upon questioning, he found that Axia had given them instructions before they'd halted for the night.

At first he'd resented her presumption. She wasn't going to control *him* as she did poor Frances, he'd vowed. But then he'd found the rabbit stew flavored with wild thyme Axia had gathered during the midday halt, and there was always fresh bread for supper, so he forgot about "control."

And the oddest thing was the way she took care of Frances. From what Jamie had seen and heard, he'd feared that Axia would creep into Frances's wagon at night to do her harm, but it was quite the opposite. Axia directed Frances's maid about what Frances liked to wear, to eat, even to how she liked her bedding arranged. Jamie would have thought Axia was an excellent lady-in-waiting except for the frequent barbs sent in Frances's direction.

All in all, after three days it was becoming more and more difficult to reconcile what he knew about Axia and what he saw. And what he heard. Already, the camp was beginning to echo with, "Ask Axia." She seemed to know where everything in the wagons was stored, knew that Rhys liked dark meat and Thomas, white. When bread was bought, she insisted on caraway buns for Frances. And Tode! Princes of the realm had not been treated with as much attention as Axia routinely and efficiently gave to him.

The only person she neglected was Jamie. Although Axia saw to the setting up of the tent Rhys and Thomas shared, Jamie had to direct—each night—that his tent be erected. Each morning Axia took a little brush to the clothes of the other men, but Jamie had the same dirt on him for days. She drew pictures of the others, even Frances, but Jamie might as well have stayed behind for all the notice she took of him.

And heaven help him, but her neglect of him made him unable to take his eyes off her. There was no rational thought behind his feeling, of course, but he noticed everything she did for the others and resented everything she did not do for him.

For the first time in his life, Jamie found himself trying to get the attention of a woman. And with Axia, he thought with half a smile, giving attention to Frances seemed to be the most certain way of getting Axia's attention.

An hour later, sitting around the campfire, Jamie turned to Frances, and smiling, he said lightly, meaning to tease her, "I wonder if the Maidenhall heiress looks like Perkin Maidenhall?"

Frances was so lost in thought that she did not think what she was saying, so her voice was sarcastic. "How would she know what he looks like? She's never met her father."

Immediately, a deep silence descended around the fire, and Frances frantically tried to cover her error. "I mean that I have never met my father."

"Never met your father?" Rhys asked. "Not once?"

Frances looked down at her plate to keep people from seeing her shining eyes. It had annoyed her that this man Rhys had ignored her since he had met her and given all his attention to Axia. There had been that one morning when he'd offered her some disgusting sweet as though she were a child, but since then he had not looked at her.

When Frances looked up, her eyes were sad. "It is

true, he writes letters and sends messengers, but he has never come to me in person."

Jamie could not help frowning as he looked in sympathy at Frances—as everyone was looking in sympathy at Frances.

"I have always envied others for having a family, as I have had no mother or father," Frances said as she looked across the fire. "The only family I have had is Axia. And Tode, of course."

At that Axia opened her mouth to speak, but Tode put his hand on her arm and gave her a look that said that she was the one who had wanted to play this game.

Axia did not like anyone disparaging her father. Whatever he did, she was sure he had reasons for his behavior. If she did not know what they were, that was her problem, not his. "The Maidenhall heiress has had other things in life to compensate her."

"Such as love?" Frances snapped, then she turned to Jamie, her eyes shining with unshed tears. "I do not ask for sympathy, but the cousin has never even given the heiress a Christmas gift, but the heiress always gives the cousin a gift. Is that not true, Axia? Tode? *You* can swear that what I say is true, can you not?" She looked directly at Tode.

"Yes, Frances, you are right," he said coldly. "The cousin has never given the heiress anything. Nor has she ever shown gratitude for all the heiress has given her."

Axia could now feel all eyes upon herself and realized she needed to defend herself. Or was it now Frances she was defending? She seemed to have lost track. "Perhaps the cousin could not afford a gift for the heiress. What could she give the daughter of the richest man in England?" It was what Frances had said to Axia a thousand times.

To Axia's disbelief, Frances began to laugh. "No money! Why Axia, you are the richest person on the estate."

Confused, Axia could not say a word. Was Frances now going to tell everyone the truth?

Frances turned to Jamie, still laughing. "You have never seen anything like her. What do you think she did with the apples in the orchard? The berries? She sent them into the village to be sold, that's what!" Pausing for effect, she looked hard at Jamie. "Axia cut every flower on the estate to try to make perfume out of them. I tell you, she has the heart and soul of a greedy little merchant. She is no lady!!"

Calmly, Axia put her plate to the ground, then stood. "Frances, I'd rather eat a mouthful of needles than spend another minute in your company," she said before walking off into the darkness.

When Frances looked back at the group in triumph, not one person was smiling at her and she couldn't understand why. James Montgomery was an *earl* and hadn't he said the word *tradesman* with disgust? She had seen how offended he'd been when he'd seen the way the wagon had been painted. He hated the lower classes, the merchants, didn't he?

It was Thomas who spoke first. Standing, he stretched and said he thought he would go to bed so they could get an early start in the morning, and minutes later, Rhys said the same thing.

When she was left alone with Jamie, Frances put her hands over her face and said softly, "They do not like me. I know they do not."

Jamie knelt before her; he hated to see anything

female cry. "Of course they do. I am sure they like you very much."

"No, they like Axia. Since I was thirteen years old, everyone has *liked* Axia better than they liked me. You cannot imagine what my life has been like. My father imprisoned me and kept me away from all the world, and people only care about my money, nothing else."

"Like me?" he asked softly. "You know that I have had every intention of marrying your father's gold."

Lightly, she clasped her hands behind his neck, her face very close to his. "Is it truly only my father's gold that you care about? Do you not find me even a bit attractive?"

"Yes, of course," he said and moved his lips close to hers to kiss her.

But his lips did not reach hers because Axia kicked at a burning branch so hard it went flying through the air and landed on the ground near Jamie's leg, where it promptly set the edge of his doublet on fire.

All hell broke out as Tode and one of the drivers helped put out Jamie's burning clothing, with Rhys and Thomas leaping out of the tents, swords drawn.

When at last he was safe, unharmed, Jamie, shaking with rage, looked down at Axia.

"So sorry," she said, smiling at him. "I must have kicked a bit too hard. I hope I did not disturb your courting of my rich cousin."

"Axia," Frances said under her breath, "I will get you for this."

Jamie was beginning to recover his power of speech. "Tonight you sleep in my tent with me. I will watch that you do nothing else to harm anyone."

She smiled at him. "I'd rather spend a week buried

up to my neck in horse manure than spend one night in the same tent with you."

Jamie took a step toward her, but Tode put his body between them. "I will watch over her and protect her."

"Protect her?" Jamie gasped. "And who will protect *us* from *her?*"

"I am not hurt," Rhys said. "Are you injured, Thomas?"

Thomas gave a tiny one-sided grin. His own father was a merchant, what Frances the heiress had referred to with so much disgust, so he wanted to take Axia's side. "I am not injured in any way. Perhaps only one man in this company has been injured by this daughter-of-a-merchant."

Blinking, Axia looked up at the two men with love in her eyes.

Jamie threw up his hands. "Go to bed all of you. I do not care where anyone sleeps."

And with that they dispersed for the night into two tents and two wagons.

Chapter 11

"Wake up," Axia whispered to Tode. He was sleeping under the painted wagon, next to the driver Roger, while Axia had the interior to herself. She had a bed on top of the bolts of cloth they'd stored there as part of their disguise.

Sleepily, Tode roused himself. "Axia, it is not daylight yet. Nor will it be for hours by the look of it. Go back to bed."

"Where are all these wagons going?"

With half-closed eyes Tode looked at the many wagons slowly making their way down the road but a few yards from their camp. "I do not know. I have never been here before. Go to bed."

"If you do not tell me, I will ask *them*." Meaning that she would cause a commotion and wake up the entire camp, then no one would get any sleep.

"I would assume it is market day in this village, and

they are going to sell their wares," he answered, then lay back down again.

Standing, Axia looked at the wagons. Market day! She'd always wanted to see market day in a village. What Frances had said so nastily was true: Axia did send produce to the village, and afterward she asked hundreds of questions of the vendor.

Bending, she shook Tode awake again. "Get up. We are going to the market."

"I . . ." Tode began, frowning.

She knew what his worry was. He did not like to be seen by people. "Oh, do not fret. You will stand inside the wagon, and no one will see you."

Slowly, painfully, he crawled out from under the wagon. "You cannot do this. He will be very angry."

"He already hates me, so what does it matter?"

"Axia . . ." Tode began in warning.

"Please," she whispered. "You know what awaits me. Do you think my new husband will allow me to attend the village market day? Or will he exhibit me like a freak? The Maidenhall heiress!" She said the last as though it were something vile and dirty.

The words *exhibit* and *freak* made Tode agree. "But he will hear and—"

"Not over the noise of the other wagons. Oh, Tode, please. I cannot allow this man to lock me away from all life. Maybe he will hear, but at least we can *try."*

Tode grinned, something he did only with Axia. "We can try to seize the day, can we not?"

On impulse, she threw her arms around his neck and gave him a quick, fierce hug. "Thank you so much."

Axia didn't spare the time to see the way her hug

had affected Tode but scrambled under the wagon to wake Roger and try to silently escape the ever-watchful eyes of James Montgomery.

"She has gone," Jamie said under his breath. His anger would not allow him to speak out loud, or he'd bellow so the stars would fall from the sky.

Rhys, just crawling out of his tent, looked at the place where the big painted wagon had been last night. Over the last days he'd grown to like the fire-breathing dragon and the lion that Jamie—a still nearly nude Jamie—was ready to slay. Under normal circumstances, he would have worried, would have suspected a kidnapping, but now he knew without a doubt that if there was a domestic problem, Axia would solve it. Yawning, he wondered what delicious thing she'd bring back for supper.

"Wonder where she has taken it?" Thomas asked as he looked about as though the big wagon might be hiding behind a rock.

Only Jamie was in a rage. "I see that neither of you think there has been foul play."

"She is with Tode," Thomas said. "He will see that she is safe. And I am sure she will return soon."

Jamie looked at the two men as though they had lost their minds. They did not seem overly concerned that he had been commissioned to get the heiress safely to her fiancé. But this—this Axia thwarted him at every opportunity. "She must be found." Turning to the maid who was laying out bread and cheese on the little table from Jamie's tent, he said, "You must wake your mistress as—"

He broke off because Frances came slowly out of the wagon, and insignificantly, he thought that she did not look so beautiful first thing in the morning. "She has stolen a wagon and gone," Jamie said, not explaining who "she" was. "And I must find her and bring her back."

Frances did not like the early morning and especially did not like being confronted with Axia's misdeeds the first thing of the day. "She has taken the wagon into the village," she said, reaching for a mug of cider from her maid. Her gown was wrinkled, and she was annoyed with Axia for not having seen that it was properly packed.

Jamie was too busy saddling his horse and too angry to hear her, but Rhys and Thomas, hands full of bread and cheese, turned to look at her. "Why did she want to go into the village?" Thomas asked.

"To make a penny, of course," Frances answered.

When all three men looked at her in consternation, her lips tightened. When did she become Axia's keeper? Nodding toward the people on the road a few yards away, all of them walking or riding toward the village in the near distance, she said, "There is a merchant's fair, is there not? And money is exchanging hands?" Her voice was sarcastic. "If there is money to be made, then *that* is where Axia is." She looked up at Jamie, her eyes narrowed. "I told you she had the heart and soul of a greedy little—"

She didn't finish the sentence because Jamie had mounted his horse and was lost in a cloud of dust as he thundered toward the village.

As Jamie rode, he thought that he wasn't sure he believed Frances. Why would a girl who lived with the Maidenhall heiress want to go into a country village on market day? And even though he remembered Tode's words about Axia being good with money, he didn't believe that termagant was good at anything except drawing pictures. How could she be when she'd been locked away all her life?

No, he corrected himself, it was Frances who had been locked away. Axia had a father and sisters and had lived with them half her life and now visited them regularly.

"Have you seen a wagon with—?" Jamie started to ask as soon as he reached the outskirts of the village, but he broke off when someone pointed and said, "It's him. The dragonslayer. The lion killer. It's *him!*"

Jamie, teeth gritted, reined his horse away from the man and into the crowd of people. Obviously, she was here and people had seen his picture on the side of that odious wagon.

Always, it seemed that Axia had the ability to humiliate him. For twenty-eight years he had conducted himself with dignity and pride, but since he had met her, his life had become a farce. "A Greek tragedy," he said under his breath as he wove his horse through what seemed to be a few hundred people who were buying, trading, bartering, or just visiting each other.

"Dragonslayer!" he heard called out more than once. Cynically, he wondered how they recognized him, what with the scratches still visible on his cheeks and one of his eyes still bruised.

Toward one end of the town was a large crowd of people, and just above their heads he could see the colors of Axia's painted wagon. And, believe it or not, he could hear Axia's voice. How could such a small female be so loud?

In order to get near the wagon, he had to go around the crowd and come in the back way, and then it was only because he was atop the horse that he could see what was going on.

He'd purchased the wagons as a pretense only, never thinking what they were meant for. Tode had told him that there was cloth in the cellars, so Jamie had decided to use some of it as part of their disguise. But now he could see that this wagon had been built for what Axia was using it for. One side of it, most of the dragon's belly, had been raised, making an overhead door, held aloft by two posts that were fitted into iron rings bolted to the side. There was a shelf, which had probably been attached to the inside of the wagon, fitted across the bottom of the opening, making a convenient counter.

Axia had draped a bolt of cloth across one end of the inside of the wagon, forming a curtain, and Jamie had no doubt that Tode was hiding behind that, out of sight of the crowd. Inside the wagon was Axia, Roger with her as he rushed to cut and measure, according to what Axia was telling him to do.

But what confused Jamie at first was why there was so large a crowd around the wagon. Had they never seen a cloth merchant before? Or was it the way the wagon was painted? He could imagine that they would gather in crowds to see it, but these people were buying as fast as Roger and Tode, hidden behind his curtain, could cut. Jamie knew that a few hours ago there had been tall stacks of cloth inside the wagon, but now there was very little. However, there did seem to be a huge wheel of cheese, some bags of flour, a haunch of beef, and, unless he missed his guess, a couple of chickens, and they were only what he could see. He had no doubt that there was a great deal more on the floor out of his view.

He had just urged his horse forward when Axia's voice rang out, making him halt.

"My ancestors were the greatest merchants ever put on this earth," she shouted, even though she seemed to be talking to a man only a foot in front of her. "I'd sooner give this cloth away than accept what you are offering. See that glimmer? Dragon scales, that's what makes that shine. Have you never wondered what happened to the slain dragons of old? The great knights killed them, true, but my ancestors skinned them and salted the skins, scales and all. They saved them for generations, not knowing what to do with them, but then my own grandmother, blessed be her name, discovered a way to spin the scales into threads and my sainted grandfather oversaw the massive looms it took to make the scales into cloth. Now, see the way it shimmers in the sun? Dragon cloth," she shouted. "Dragon cloth for sale. It never wears out."

It took Jamie some moments to clear his head of the lies he had just heard. Dragon cloth? It never wears out?!

Every knightly vow he'd ever taken rose up in him. How could she lie like that? How could she—?

He didn't bother wasting any more time thinking but kneed his horse forward into the crowd, scattering them as he rode to stand in front of the wagon.

"What—?" Axia began, then groaned when she saw who it was. "Close up, men. The devil has eaten the sun," she shouted, ostensibly toward Roger and Tode in back of her.

"Get out here," Jamie said to her, his jaw clamped shut.

A man standing by his foot, a fat goose tucked under his arm, stared up at Jamie and started to say,

"Dragonsl—" but the look Jamie gave him kept him from finishing his cry.

"Now!" Jamie commanded to Axia. "Leave the wagon and let the *men* take care of it." He turned to Roger and Tode, who he knew was listening, "And that wagon had better be back in camp immediately." Roger just nodded as Axia opened the door and stepped out.

"Could someone ask this man what he is angry about now?" she asked, squinting against the sun as she looked around the crowd but refusing to look up at Jamie. "Or perhaps it is just the fact that I live and breathe that offends him?"

Jamie wasn't about to make himself more of a laughingstock before this entire village and the neighboring population than her half-dressed painting of him had already done. "You there!" he said to a burly man with muscles bulging. "Lift her up to me." Nor was he going to dismount and get closer to these people who were comparing the painting to the actuality.

The man's face lit up as though he'd received the keys to the kingdom, and in an instant he had put his hands under Axia's arms and was lifting her into Jamie's saddle to sit before him. But as the man started to drop her, he felt the sharp point of Jamie's dagger just under the tip of his chin.

"If you would like to keep those thumbs of yours," Jamie said, "watch what they touch."

The man looked properly chastised, but the crowd, already excited by the wagon and Axia's promise of dragon cloth, found this whole scene appealing to their imaginations. One man in the back, far away from Jamie, yelled, "Dragonslayer!" and within minutes the whole of them had taken it up. "Dragon-slayer! Dragonslayer! Dragonslayer!"

Rolling his eyes skyward, Jamie, Axia before him, turned his horse and started to make his way out of the village. With some effort he was able to disentangle himself from the crowd and head toward the fields that lay in the direction of the camp. But he did not go quickly there, for he wanted some time to try, once again, to talk some sense into this disruptive young woman.

"You are drawing attention to us," he began, meaning to wait until they were someplace where he could dismount, but he couldn't seem to wait. "What is the use of a disguise if you parade us before the whole town, making us a spectacle and a laughingstock?"

She did not say a word.

"Do you have no answer?" he demanded. "Do you never have an explanation for your actions? Do you never think before you act?"

Axia was in the saddle before him, both her legs to one side, his arms were around her, albeit to hold the reins but still around her, and her entire left side was pressed against his body. In spite of the fact that she had decided that she hated him for all the things he had done to her and most of all for not recognizing that she was Diana, he did feel rather nice.

"Axia," Jamie said sternly, "what do you have to say for yourself?"

Axia bent her head forward. "Horse, do you hear anyone talking? No? Nor do I. It must be the breeze in the trees."

Jamie gave a heavy sigh of exasperation. "When I received a letter from Perkin Maidenhall asking if I would escort his daughter across England, I thought it would be an easy way to make money," he said as though talking to himself. "But now I know that I'd rather rout criminals in the Highlands of Scotland than deal with—with . . ." As usual, Axia seemed to defy his powers of description.

He took a deep, calming breath. "Axia," he said softly, for now, holding her like this, he could remember that she was a woman. Most of the time it was difficult to remember that she was anything but an imp put on earth to harass him. "You cannot take the wagon and disappear at will. You and your cousin are under my protection. I must know where you are and what you are doing at all times. Do you understand me?"

Again he awaited her answer, even if it were addressed to his horse, but when he looked down at her, he saw that she had fallen asleep. Her head was nestled into the hollow of his shoulder, her hands were primly in her lap, and she had fallen asleep against him.

And no wonder, he thought. She did twice as much work as anyone else in their troop. Not that she ever did any work for *him,* but he saw all that she did for the others. And now, from the look of the contents of the wagon, he wouldn't have to buy food stores for the coming week. Maybe, he thought reluctantly, Tode had been right and Axia was, well, competent with money.

However, he *must* speak to her about her outrageous lies about "dragon cloth."

A few hundred yards before him, he could see the camp, and he knew that the others awaited them. But Jamie was sure that soon Tode and the driver would bring the other wagon, what Rhys called the dragon wagon, and shortly they would be off on the day's journey.

Knowing that he should join them at once, instead, on impulse, Jamie turned his horse off the road and rode up a hill toward a huge oak tree that provided deep shade. It wasn't easy, but he managed to get off the horse while holding Axia and without waking her, then, carrying her as though she were a child, he sat down under the oak tree, Axia cuddled on his lap.

She slept for nearly an hour, curled on his lap, his hand holding hers. He hadn't realized before now how small she was. Maybe it was just her character that was large, he thought, because now, as he looked at her little hand and felt the way her head did not reach his chin, she made him feel very protective. Somehow, right now he felt as though he actually was the man she'd painted on the side of the wagon.

Fastening his arms about her tightly, he pulled her close to him, put his head back against the tree, and began to doze himself.

Minutes later, he awoke with a start.

"Get your big, horrible hands off of me!" Axia yelled at him, hitting him in the ribs with her elbow. "Do you think that I am a loose woman who you can be free with?"

Jamie blinked at her, for a moment not knowing where he was or what was happening to him. Confusion seemed to be a normal state with him lately. It had become a way of life ever since he had climbed over that wall and met this extraordinary young woman.

Although she was still sitting on his lap, she was angry at him—as she always seemed to be. "Do you think *I* am another Diana?" she asked him, her nose close to his.

Had she been any other woman in the world and he'd awakened with her on his lap, he would have kissed her, but Axia wasn't like anyone else.

Unceremoniously, without saying a word, he pushed her off his lap onto the hard ground and went to his horse.

Axia was confused herself. Did he fondle *every* woman he met? "Lecher!" she said but without the venom that such an accusation required. Then, standing, she dusted herself off.

"I will not—" she began when he approached her, but he grabbed her around the waist so tight he cut off her breath, then he lifted her onto the saddle. However, he lifted her a little too high, then dropped her so she landed hard on the leather and wood of his saddle. When she said, "Ow!" he gave a little smile as he threw his leg over the saddle and sat behind her.

And as soon as the horse took a step, Axia leaned back against Jamie in a familiar way that made him smile. And, although he didn't see, she smiled also. She didn't really believe he was a lecher. He'd wanted to *kiss* her.

After a while, she said softly, "I had a choice of cheeses so I got that hard white kind you like best."

"Did you?" he asked, trying to keep his voice calm, but inside he was leaping with joy. It was the first time she'd ever done anything for *him*. But best of all, she had noticed what he liked.

He searched for something else to say. "Maidenhall gave me a purse for expenses, and what you traded for today will save me."

Twisting in his arms, she looked up at him, "Oh, Jamie, I would like to help save expenses. I *liked* buying and selling today. Oh, but it was fun, and . . ." She looked down. "And maybe I was good at it."

He smiled at the top of her head. "You were magnificent."

"Really? Do you truly think so?"

"Yes, the best. You are as talented at selling as you are at drawing."

Her eyes wide, she looked up at him. "But I'm not so good at drawing. I'm sure you've seen much better."

"Never. Not anywhere in the world."

Opening and closing her mouth for a few moments, Axia seemed at a loss for words, and that pleased Jamie very much. "I noticed you like almonds, so I shall stuff a duck with almonds and here . . ." Reaching inside her bodice, she pulled out several sprigs of wild sage. "I found this and thought it would help the dressing."

Jamie smiled at her. "I shall relish every bite," he said in a low voice.

For a moment Axia had no idea what he meant, then she blushed because she realized he was referring to where the sage had been. Her face still red, she turned around and settled back against him.

When the camp came into view, she said, "May I try to help with expenses? I so like to be useful."

"If you like," Jamie said. "But no lying. No more promises of cloth that will never wear out. And no more disappearing so I don't know where you are. You can't imagine how worried I was this morning when I awoke and you weren't there."

"I would think you'd be glad," she said, tight-lipped. "Your life would be much easier if I fell into a hole and stayed there."

He laughed as he put his arms tighter around her. "Axia, I think I would miss you if you were gone. I know you cause me nothing but trouble, but I would miss you."

She knew he couldn't see her face, so she indulged herself in a wide grin. "I have turnips and carrots and a huge slab of butter. And, oh, yes, tiny onions. And I could pull the feathers from the geese to start making you a pillow."

"That would be very nice," he said softly as they entered the camp, and Rhys put up his arms to help her down. "Very nice indeed."

Chapter 12

As soon as Frances saw Axia sitting on the horse in front of Jamie, she knew that things had changed between the two of them. And of course it would, as it seemed that Axia had a way with men. Frances wasn't sure, but she thought perhaps it was the way Axia was always feeding them.

"They are men, not hogs to be fattened for market," Frances had said more than once. "If I were them, I'd worry you were after my liver."

Now, looking at Axia getting down from Jamie's horse, Frances gave a great sigh. This trip was not going as she'd hoped. When she agreed to be the Maidenhall heiress in Axia's place, she had envisioned traveling the country with everyone knowing who she was. That way she would have had much interest from men, and she had planned to choose one for a husband. Perhaps it would be trickery to make a man believe she was an heiress before they were married and later tell him that she was poorer than he was, but then Frances hoped that her beauty would inspire a man to love her. Frances knew that if she was to make a good match, she had to do it now, on this trip.

Axia knew what awaited her at the end of this journey, but Frances did not. In usual Axia-fashion, she refused to brood about her approaching marriage, but Frances knew that somewhere inside her, Axia knew. As for Frances, she had no idea what Perkin Maidenhall had planned for her. Would a letter be awaiting her, telling her she was no longer needed as a "companion" to Axia? Would she be sent back to her "family"? Sent to that group of people who she always described to Axia as a set of angels but who, in truth, never stopped badgering Frances to get more goods, more money, more anything from the Maidenhall estate?

Frances knew that Axia thought her life in her "beautiful prison" was the most horrible existence on earth, but then Axia had never experienced much of life. She was protected from it, sheltered, had never really seen it.

But Frances knew what happened to women without money. Her mother had been beautiful, from all accounts more beautiful than Frances ever thought of being. But her mother had married for love. She had run away from a marriage with a prosperous, but old and boring, banker and married a handsome ne'er-do-well who refused to stay at one occupation for more than a few months. Within five years, her mother was no longer beautiful but worn out from bearing children and taking in sewing.

While her mother was still alive, Frances, dressed in patched and worn clothing, used to walk past the banker's rich house and wondered how her mother could have married her father. She used to look at the banker's children in their clean and pressed clothing, looked at their toys, and she vowed that she would never do what her mother did. If she, Frances, was fortunate enough to inherit her mother's beauty, she would *use* it.

It was her idea to write to Perkin Maidenhall and point out that her family was distantly related to his through his father's brother and ask him for employment. Sometimes Frances thought of that letter, remembered how she had laboriously written it again and again, then thought how she'd stolen the good-quality writing paper from a printer's desk. She wrote that his daughter must be very lonely as no one ever saw her and could she, Frances, go and be her friend?

When the answer came, along with a pouch of money, no one had ever been more joyous than Frances and her family. They had celebrated for a week, until nearly all the money was spent. And when the Maidenhall wagon came to take Frances away, she never looked back.

So now Frances had seen a way to get away from Axia, from her parsimonious father, from horrid Tode, and from dependence on the Maidenhall money. If she could get a man to fall in love with her, she'd marry him. She did not ask for someone fabulously wealthy nor a man who was a blushing maiden's dream of handsomeness. All she wanted was someone like that banker her mother had turned down.

But who? How? Frances wanted to scream. How was she going to meet an eligible man if she was traveling as James Montgomery's wife? Which, of course, was a joke. Other than the mention of this before they'd left the estate, nothing had come of it. And for all that Axia seemed able to sneak away from the man's eagle eyes, Frances was not so daring.

So Frances tried to look at her prospects. There were the earl's two men, but Frances knew poverty when she saw it. They weren't a great deal better off than she was. Which left only the earl himself.

And of course he had eyes only for Axia.

Damn her! Frances thought. Axia had no idea how men looked at her. She was so ignorant she thought men looked at her because she was the legendary Maidenhall heiress, but the truth was that what Axia missed in classic beauty she made up for in vivacity. Having been shut up all her life, Axia had no idea what was suitable behavior and what was unacceptable. She was as likely to serve her father's ancient ambassadors dinner in a barn as she was to have them sit at a table.

Axia had no idea about titles and treating a man of rank with reverence. Two years ago a decrepit old duke had demanded entrance to the estate. He said he was tired of hearing of this heiress and wanted to see her for himself. Axia put him to work pulling feathers out of the chests of squawking geese, then later gave him a drawing of himself and the geese. The old man went away swearing he'd never had such an enjoyable afternoon in his life. And the next year when they heard he'd died, Axia wept with grief.

So now it didn't surprise Frances that James Montgomery was watching Axia in fascination. But what did surprise her was the way Axia watched him in return. And the way Tode watched both of them.

Something was indeed going on, and Frances would love to know what it was.

Love, Frances thought with disgust. That was the key word in all this. She had no doubt that what was happening was the beginnings of love, that stupid, useless thing that everyone spoke of but no one needed. Love was what had caused all her mother's unhappiness. Love was—

Love was what was going to be Axia's undoing if she were not careful, Frances thought. What would happen if Axia went against her father's wishes and demanded to marry some impoverished earl? Her father would disinherit her, no doubt, and of course her earl would leave her. Then where would Axia be? Her cousin was pretty, but it took great beauty to make a good marriage without a dowry. If Axia were poor, Frances was sure her cousin would be quite unmarriageable.

Perhaps I should save her, Frances thought. *Save her from herself. If I took James Montgomery from her, then Axia would no longer be in danger of angering her father. No longer in danger of being disinherited.*

And if I married an earl, I would be Lady *Frances,* she thought, smiling. *Wouldn't my sisters eat their hearts out at that?*

Of course, there was the fact that Lord James *said* he was poor. That's why he had undertaken this employment. But how could someone with a title be poor? Besides, he had many rich relatives who were very willing to help him. She'd seen that when he'd sent messages to those relatives and they'd quickly sent men with armor and weapons to protect the Maidenhall wagons.

Compared to her other prospects, James Montgomery was wealthy all right. He was rich, and it looked as though he were the only man she was going to meet. Too bad he was so handsome. Frances had found that the uglier the man, the easier he was to enthrall.

Frances looked up at Axia, then her eyes narrowed and she set herself a goal. By the time this journey ended, she was going to be the wife of James Montgomery. Whatever she had to do; however it could be accomplished, she was going to do it. And someday Axia would thank her.

Axia was rearranging the contents of one of those horrible, uncomfortable wagons. If the Queen of England could travel around England freely, why couldn't the Maidenhall heiress? The answer of course was that Perkin Maidenhall was too tight to pay for sufficient guards so his only child was forced to travel like some anonymous merchant's daughter. But then Axia seemed to be having the time of her life with all her low-class bartering. Just like her father, she loved to make money.

Standing, Frances dusted off her gown. She, on the other hand, hated traveling in these wagons. When she was Lady Frances Montgomery, she'd have a coach with velvet-covered seats and a dozen footmen. She'd have—

"What are you planning?"

Frances jumped at that whisper in her ear. She didn't have to turn around to know it was Tode, that odious little man.

"I think I may save Axia from herself," she replied, then put her nose in the air and walked away from him. *Let him think on* that, she thought. *Let him sit*

*with his beloved Axia and try to figure out what I have
in mind.*

Smiling, she walked over to Jamie.

"Would you like to walk with me?" Jamie asked
Frances, holding out his arm for her to take. "It is
such a beautiful night."

Wrapping her fingers about his arm, Frances walked
with Jamie down the little road where they had made
their camp.

Trying his best to make conversation, he said, "In a
few days we shall stay in a house," he said. "With
beds."

Frances smiled. "I should like that. I should like
something besides just what can be cooked over a
campfire," she said with a grimace.

"Axia does well, does she not? I have never known
almonds to taste so good," Jamie said, smiling in
memory.

Frances looked up at him through her lashes, the
fading daylight making her look especially beautiful.
"Will you walk with me and talk of another woman?"

"Why, no, I guess not," Jamie said, then had no
idea what else to say.

They walked in silence for a few moments, then
abruptly, Frances burst out laughing.

Puzzled, Jamie turned to her, a smile ready.

"We are alike, are we not?" she said companionably.

"I am sure we are, but how are we alike?"

"Tell me, James Montgomery, have you ever had to
court a woman? I mean, have you ever had to work to
get a woman to pay attention to you? Flowers?
Poems?"

Jamie ducked his head. "Actually . . ." He hesitated.

"Nor have I," Frances said. "All I have ever had to do was sit still and they came to me. I have had men fight each other over the privilege of sitting next to me. Boys fall over themselves to be allowed to hand me a cup of sweet cider." She looked up at him. "And no doubt it has been the same with you."

With a chuckle, he looked down at her. "I admit that I have had an easy time until . . . lately."

Frowning, Frances looked up at him. "I think it is time you and I discussed business."

But Jamie's mind was on the "lately." Had there ever been a time when he had not known Axia? There was the first day with her body under his, the time he'd turned her over his knee, when she'd attacked him and blackened his eye, the painted wagon, Axia asleep in front of him in the saddle, later with her head on his lap and—

". . . and make plans for the marriage. Perhaps it should be secret and later we will tell my father and—"

"Marriage?" Jamie said blankly, not having heard the first of what she was saying.

Frances batted her long lashes at him. "I thought you wanted the Maidenhall gold. My inheritance."

"I . . ." He didn't like to hear the case stated so bluntly.

"It is all right," she said, pressing her breasts against his arm, then seeing his mind was elsewhere, she suddenly released him, and putting her hands over her face, she began to cry. "Oh, James, you do not know what awaits me. My father has chosen a horrible man for me. I will never have love and children, I know it. I have been a prisoner since I was three weeks old and I will continue to be a prisoner after I am married. Oh, how can I bear it?"

Jamie did what he always did with crying women: he pulled her into his arms and held her, stroking her back to calm her.

"I know Axia meant to be mean and hateful when she told me that *you* hoped to marry me, but it was the answer to my prayers. I have dreamed that my father would send someone handsome and charming to me and that we might—No, I daren't say it out loud."

"Tell me," he whispered, fearing he already knew the answer.

"That this man would save me from this horrible marriage that I know will be worse than the prison that I have already lived my life in."

"Your father has placed great trust in me. He—" Jamie began.

"What of your family?" Frances argued. "Are they as poor as Axia's? Are they warm in the winter? What is their food like?"

Jamie swallowed, remembering Berengaria's description of moldy lentils, her dream of warmth. Lately, his time with Axia had made him begin to forget his duties and responsibilities, but now Frances was bringing him back to reality.

Frances, her hands gripping Jamie's arms, looked up at him pleadingly. "We could be married secretly. If we are already married, there is nothing my father can do about it. He cannot dissolve our marriage."

"But . . ." Jamie didn't want to say anything, but what if Maidenhall was so angry, he disinherited her?

Smiling as though she could read his mind, Frances said, "People are so enchanted with my father's wealth that they forget that my mother was the only daughter of a very wealthy man. If my father gives me nothing, I have my grandfather's estate of land, houses, a castle or two. I have considerable income of my own." She smiled at him. "And I do not believe my merchant father will be disappointed that I have married an earl bearing the ancient name of Montgomery."

"Probably not," Jamie said distractedly.

She looked up at him, tears just about to spill over her bottom lashes. "You will rescue me, will you not? For me? For your family?"

Firmly, Jamie gripped her shoulders and held her at arms' length. "I will do my best to—to rescue you, but my honor forces me to ask your father's permission. I cannot do this in secret. He *must* give his approval."

Frances looked away to prevent him from seeing her face. Above all, she could not allow knowledge of their marriage to reach Axia's father. "What do I care for his approval? He has imprisoned me all my life. He will sell me to any man who has the gold. Do I not deserve happiness like everyone else?"

"Do not speak of your father so. Do not—" Jamie knew that what was wrong with him was that he could not seem to think. Marriage was a major decision, and it could not be taken lightly. If he enraged someone as rich as Maidenhall, what would happen to his family? He must think of them. "I will—"

"You do not like me," Frances said, her lower lip stuck out in a pretty pout. "You do not like me at all."

"But of course I like you," Jamie said, but even he knew there was no conviction in his voice. Truthfully, he hadn't thought much about Frances one way or the other.

"I believe I understand," Frances said coldly. "It has often been this way. I am, after all, the Maidenhall heiress, and that tends to frighten men. No man can love me for who I am. It is only the money they want. It is Axia who inspires men to love her. Look at Tode, horrid thing that he is. He loves her. Your man Rhys cannot take his eyes off her. He is courting her. Even your Thomas has thoughts of her. It is only me men cannot see for my gold. Axia is right: I am not human, I am my father's gold."

With that she turned back toward the camp, but Jamie caught her arm. Joby had always said that a woman had only to tell Jamie a sad story and he turned softer than rainwater.

"Frances," he said softly, "it is not so. You are a very sweet woman. Any man would be happy to have you for his wife."

"Oh, Jamie," she said and threw her arms around his neck. "I knew you loved me. I knew it. I will make you the best of wives. And your family will have warmth and food and all the best that the Maidenhall money can buy. You shall see. You will be the happiest man on earth."

Pulling away from him, she took his hand. "Come, let us tell the others." Her eyes lit as an idea came to her. "Yes, and you must write my father. I will write him too. We will put our letters together and send them by the same messenger. I am sure my father will agree, as he will love having a daughter called by the title of lady. Come, come, do not hesitate." Pausing, she looked at him. "Is something amiss? Is not this what you wanted? You are going to be married to the Maidenhall heiress. Please tell me now if this is not what you wanted."

"Yes," he murmured. "This is what I must do. It is what my family needs."

Stretching out her arms, Frances twirled about. "I am the happiest woman on earth. And you? Are you not also happy?"

"Oh yes," he said, "very, very happy. Truly happy." But there was only the sound of sad resignation in his voice. "Come," he said slowly, "we must return to the others."

"Yes, we must tell them," Frances said happily, then paused. "But, Jamie, dear, let us not tell about the letters to my father. Axia will . . . Well, you know what she is like. We will just say that we are to be married secretly. Is that all right with you?"

"Yes, of course," he said, then with a great sigh, Jamie followed her down the path back to the camp.

My dearest sisters,

All your dreams may come true. It seems that I may be married to the Maidenhall heiress. No, do not think it is a love match, it is not. Frances is in need of rescuing. She needs protection and we need a new roof. Is that not how all the best marriages are arranged?

However, I do not believe this marriage will take place as I am insisting on begging her father's permission. As he has already contracted for his daughter's marriage, I cannot see how he will agree. But Frances thinks he will give his permission; then we must be married immediately.

I will let you know what comes of this.

Do you remember Axia who I told you about? She is proving herself to be quite useful, as she buys and sells wherever we go. Although she told outrageous, but highly amusing, lies to make the sale, she sold an entire wagonload of cloth for coins and animals. Then she traded some of the animals to a country merchant for a hundred pairs of shoes, and she used the coins to buy a thousand buttons from a widow walking back from her husband's funeral. Afterward, she put all of us, except the heiress of course, to sewing the buttons on the shoes and the next day sold them for twice what she'd paid for them.

Rhys says that in one week she has tripled the value of the original cloth, and he laughs that in a month she will be able to buy a house. But I fear that Rhys may be in love with her. And Thomas too.

However, due to Axia's bargaining, I have not spent any from the Maidenhall purse for days now.

We will be staying at Lachlan Teversham's house for a few days while we await the arrival of the Maidenhall wagons and the letter from Frances's father, so you may write me there.

I send you both my love and my prayers.

> Your loving brother,
> James

PS. I am sorry, but that purple silk doublet was ruined when Axia set fire to it and to me, but do not worry, for the burns healed quickly.

* * *

"Well?" Joby asked her sister. "What do you think now? He is going to marry the Maidenhall heiress, I am sure of it. I am sure Perkin Maidenhall will be delighted for his daughter to marry Jamie. After all, he *is* an earl."

"I am not so sure," Berengaria said as she breathed deeply of the aroma of the flowers that grew in the tiny garden behind the old castle. "Do you think if this rich man had offered his daughter to Jamie, our brother would have refused the Maidenhall heiress? Would any man? So there must be hidden reasons that he offers her to a rich merchant's son, as there are many impoverished titled men who would have taken her."

"True," Joby said thoughtfully but not wanting to think about that. "What do you think of this Axia?"

Berengaria hesitated before answering. "I think she is the most interesting person I have ever heard of."

"Interesting? I would imagine that woman walking back from her husband's funeral did not find her 'interesting'. It is a wonder someone did not put this Axia in a dunking stool."

"On the other hand, what was the woman going to do with a thousand buttons? Perhaps she was grateful for someone stupid enough to want to buy them."

Joby stopped walking and looked at Berengaria. For some reason, their roles seemed to have reversed. Usually, it was Joby who was cynical and disbelieving, but now Berengaria was the one putting grief on a monetary level. For some reason, there was something about this Axia that Joby did not like.

"Oh, Joby," Berengaria said with a sigh, "are you never romantic? You are afraid that our dear brother, who is *very* romantic, will fall in love with this impoverished Axia and we will never have enough to eat."

"According to you, he already is in love with her," Joby muttered. "But what do you mean that our dear brother is romantic? Was it romance that has made him such a good soldier?"

"Of course."

"You are crazy! What is romantic about killing and maiming?"

"You know very well that Jamie hates all that. What he loves is the feeling of honor and justice and fighting for good over evil."

"True," Joby said slowly, "but what does that have to do with this Axia? I think she is making our brother demented. He says she has set fire to him." She narrowed her eyes. "I would like to set fire to *her.*"

Berengaria looked sightlessly into the distance. "Will you gather me some of those cherry blossoms? By the smell of them we will have a good crop this year."

Taking her dagger from her side, Joby cut some branches off the nearest cherry tree. "What shall we write to our brother?"

"You mean, what can we write to him to make him truly fall in love with this rich woman who he says he might marry but admits that all he wants from her is a new roof?"

"Exactly. You do not think Jamie's sense of honor would extend to love in a marriage, do you? We are too *poor* to think of love."

"And he has too many burdens," Berengaria said with bitterness. "Mother and I are—"

"And me," Joby said. "I want to be like the queen and never marry!"

"Well, I want to be like a queen bee and have a thousand children, all of them pulling on my skirts and wrapping their arms about me."

Joby gave a little smile. "There's always Henry Oliver. He'll give you—"

"I'll get you for that," Berengaria said and reached for her little sister.

Chapter 13

*I*t had been raining heavily for several days. The streams were swollen, and the roads, already bad, were quagmires, sucking at the horses' feet, amassing on the wagon wheels so that they would hardly turn.

Jamie knew that he was feeling sorry for himself as he tried to direct the moving of the wagons through the mud. When had he become responsible for merchant wagons and quarreling civilians? He had always been a soldier, a younger brother who was not to inherit the title and the estate so he had to make his own way in the world in his chosen profession of the military.

But there was no estate, was there? he thought as pulled his horse to stop once again. The rain was coming down so hard that he could barely see, could hear nothing over the pelting of the heavy stream onto the ground.

Dismounting, he stalked through the mud to the wagon where it was once again stuck. The mud was up to his ankles, and it seemed as though he was covered with the cold, wet slime. Of course, even as he made his way through the muck, he knew that his real problem was not the rain, but Axia. Sometimes it seemed that before he met her he'd never had a problem in his life. What was the struggle between life and death compared to what he had been through since he'd met her?

Just when he'd thought they were becoming friends, everything had changed in an instant. Before he could stop her, Frances had run back to the campfire and loudly announced that she and Jamie were to be married. Jamie didn't think he'd ever forget the look on Axia's face. Betrayal, hurt, disbelief, all registered in her eyes for just an instant before she turned away and stopped speaking to him altogether. Since then, twice he had tried to talk to her, tried to explain that he was not a free man, that, for him, marriage was business and he could not follow his heart. For if he did follow his heart . . . But Axia would not listen to him. Each time, she'd jerked away from his grasp and refused to speak to him. And later, when he thought about his heart and his duty to his impoverished family, he thought that perhaps it was better that Axia wasn't speaking to him. But two days later when she informed the others that there had been an accident and the rest of that wheel of cheese had somehow rolled from the wagon, he felt like weeping.

But his mood had reversed when this morning Axia had presented Rhys with a little pillow stuffed with the goose down that she had been saving for Jamie.

So now, in a few hours, God willing, they would be at the house of his friend and former comrade-in-arms, Lachlan Teversham, and there would be dry beds and hot food and perhaps they would all feel better.

Through the rain, Jamie could just see the dragon wagon, as everyone insisted on calling it, as it made its way down the road ahead of them. On Jamie's orders, the two women were in that wagon, as it was lighter and had a better chance of getting through the mud. This wagon, fully loaded down with tents and what furniture they had, tended to get stuck often.

It didn't take Jamie but a second to see that he was going to have to push. Rhys and Thomas both—damn them!—were riding by the other wagon, so that left only the driver and him and Tode, who was inside, to try to get the thing out.

At first Jamie was studying the wheel so intently that he didn't hear Tode's voice as he shouted from beside him. "Rocks! Put rocks under the wheels. Tree branches. Anything."

Jamie nodded. Of course. His mind was so distracted by his personal problems that he couldn't think of the simplest things. George sat in front, trying to control the nervous horses from the lightning that flashed all about them, while Jamie and Tode tried to find anything they could to put under the right rear wheel to give it some solid ground to move onto.

"Can you push?" Jamie shouted to Tode and saw him nod. Water was cascading down his face, dripping off his nose, and making runnels in the deep scars that distorted his face.

After Jamie alerted the driver, he put his shoulder

to one side, and Tode followed him, his short legs deep into the mud.

"Ready?" Jamie shouted, then as they heard George crack the whip, they pushed. It was not easy to find traction in the ooze, and they kept slipping, but Jamie could see that the wagon was about to be freed. "Again!" he yelled. "Harder! More muscle!"

Just when the wagon was nearly free, when it looked as though another two minutes would have them on their way, Jamie landed flat on his back in the mud with a hundred pounds of enraged female on his chest.

"He cannot! He cannot!" Axia screamed at Jamie, hitting him about the face and chest.

Putting up his arms, Jamie tried to protect himself from her blows; beneath him, the mud sucked at him like a great sea monster meant to devour him. It was Rhys who grabbed her about the waist as though she were a sack of grain and lifted her off Jamie.

Jamie was so deeply stuck in the mud that he had to pull himself up by holding onto the wagon wheel. "What is wrong with her?" he yelled, swiping at the mud covering his face with his hands.

Still holding Axia's struggling body as best he could, Rhys gave a shrug.

"Let me go! Let me go!" Axia screamed with all her might, struggling as hard as she could against Rhys.

After bracing himself in preparation for her attack, Jamie nodded to Rhys to release her.

But once free, Axia did not go to Jamie, but ran as best she could through the mud, her skirts thrown over arm, toward Tode, who was slumped against the back of the wagon. Putting her hands over his destroyed face and trying to wipe the water away, Axia looked at him hard, but Tode didn't seem to have any life in him as he leaned back against the wagon, his eyes closed.

"Look what you have done!" she screamed at Jamie. "May the devil roast you!" She looked at Rhys. "Help me. He must get inside the wagon."

Both Rhys and Jamie stepped forward, but Axia blocked Jamie and the look she gave him made him back away.

They are lovers, Jamie abruptly thought. *That is why she is so protective of him. That is why she does not want other men near her. Those two are lovers!*

Now, anger gave him new energy, and when Rhys stepped back out of the wagon, Jamie shouted to the driver and the two men pushed. Suddenly, Jamie seemed to have the strength of Hercules, and when the wagon rolled out of the mud, he kept on pushing.

When Rhys put a hand on his shoulder, Jamie ignored it and kept pushing. Under the rain and mud, sweat was pouring off of him. It took all Rhys's strength to pull Jamie away from the wagon. And when Jamie turned to his friend, the look on Jamie's face made Rhys step back. Without a word exchanged between them, Rhys mounted his horse and rode toward the other wagon.

Jamie, too angry to speak, too angry to give thought to exactly why he was angry, mounted his horse and rode beside the wagon until it reached the gates of Lachlan's house. And once inside, he was enveloped in the big, warm embrace of his friend.

"Jamie, lad," Lachlan Teversham said, his big arm around his younger friend's broad shoulders. Lachlan was a bear of a man, huge, with a mass of reddish-brown hair and great bushy eyebrows. As Jamie well knew, the man could be a terror on the battlefield, could strike fear in the hearts of men just by his presence.

But in spite of his size and sometimes fierce demeanor, Lachlan never seemed to frighten the women. As a woman once told Jamie, "Who could be afraid of a man with a mouth like that?"

"Is it you in there?" Lachlan asked, then used his big hand to try to clean a place on Jamie's face.

But Jamie was not in the mood to laugh. Angrily, he twisted away from Lachlan and went back to the wagons. "Secure them!" he shouted at the drivers. "And you, boy, take care of those horses. You'll regret it if I find they have been misused."

Standing in the rain, looking like some Norse god of old, Lachlan stared at Jamie in wonder. He had known him since he was a boy and he'd never met a more charming person. Never had Lachlan seen young Jamie be rude.

Dismounting, Thomas wiped rain from his face, then nodded toward the painted wagon where Frances was being helped out. A huge waxed cloth was being spread above her in an attempt to keep her dry, but not before Lachlan saw her beautiful face. Looking at Thomas, he raised his eyes in question, as though to ask, Is *she* what's wrong with Jamie?

Thomas, who had known Lachlan for years, leaned over and said, *"Two* women."

At that Lachlan put his head back and roared with laughter, for he understood that there was nothing wrong with his young friend except women. Lachlan would never have thought that Jamie, with a face like his, would ever have the least bit of trouble with women.

"Hell and damnation!" Jamie shouted as he looked inside the wagon and saw that Axia and her . . . her lover—he nearly spat at the thought—were gone.

"Where are they?" he shouted at a stable lad who was trying to get the horses out of the rain. Of course the boy did not know who Jamie was talking about and hastily got away from this enraged mud monster.

Jamie turned back to Lachlan. "Did you see them? A girl and a man, very short and—" How could he describe Tode?

He could see that Lachlan had no idea what his friend was talking about.

He would not want to be seen, Jamie suddenly thought and had an idea where Tode was, for Jamie knew Lachlan's place well.

"Take care of these," he yelled to Rhys, motioning toward the wagons, then he grabbed a lantern out of a boy's hands and began racing toward the stables. If a person wanted to be hidden, that's where he'd go. He couldn't imagine Tode walking into Lachlan's well-lit Great Hall.

Running, lantern aloft, Jamie went from one stall to the other, looking inside each of them. He wasn't sure what he was going to do once he found the two of them, but he knew that she was his responsibility and he had every right to—

At the end of the stables was an old tack room, long used for only storage, and just as Jamie was about to leave, he saw a faint glow of light from under the door.

Angry, he flung open the door, and to his horror and disbelief, he saw Axia *undressing* Tode!

His first impulse was to fling her across the room and possibly to use his sword on Tode. But then Axia turned a ravaged face toward him, a face not of a lover, but of one who is deeply afraid, afraid to the point of terror.

"Help me, help me," she whispered, her voice trembling.

Instantly, all Jamie's anger left him. Setting down his lantern, he stepped forward. "What can I do? I am yours."

"His legs," she managed to whisper as though the words were so disturbing she could not speak.

Lying on piles of straw and dirty horse blankets was Tode, his face turned to one side so that only his good side showed, and Jamie could see that he was pale to the point of death. "I will get someone to help so—"

"No!" Axia said as she grabbed his forearm with both of her hands. "Please," she said, tears in her eyes. She was dripping wet, her dark hair plastered to her head, her dress sodden, and he knew she was cold, tired, and hungry, but she did not seem to be aware of it. "He is proud, and he does not like to be seen. Can you understand that?"

Jamie was sure that no one could understand pride better than he. "What do you want of me?"

Wasting no more time, Axia turned back to her friend. "He is in pain. Great pain. Help me get him warm and dry. Get his clothes off."

"Yes," Jamie said, then went to Tode and began to remove his trousers, but they were wet and stuck to his skin so he took his dagger and sliced them off, exposing Tode's bare legs to the air and the light. Jamie had seen maimed men on the battlefield, and he thought he was hardened, but he had never seen anything like Tode's legs. They were like raw flesh, scars big and small, great ridges in the skin. And under the skin the bones seemed to have been broken and set at odd angles. How did he manage to walk at all? And if he did walk, how did he bear the pain of every step?

When Jamie looked up at Axia, he saw that she was holding a bottle of some dark liquid.

"Put some of this on your hands and rub it on his legs. Quickly!"

Even as she poured it into his hands, Jamie could feel the warmth of the oil. When he touched Tode's bare legs, they were as cold as death. Looking across at Axia, Jamie could see the terror on her face. "Give me that," he commanded, taking the bottle from her. He knew a bit about being cold as he'd spent some time in the Highlands with his relatives there. A Scottish summer could be colder than an English winter.

His hands were larger and stronger than hers, and he used her warming liquid lavishly as he rubbed it into Tode's cold skin. "Go into the stables, find my horse and look in the carrying cases on the saddle. There are clothes in there; they should be dry. Get them. Do not hesitate! If anyone sees you, tell them they are for me. And bring the flask in the pouch on the side."

With scarcely a nod, she ran out of the little stone room and into the stables where she quickly found Jamie's horse, his saddle thrown across a wooden trestle against the wall. It took her only minutes to get the clothes, good English wool, from the bag, then the silver flask. Holding them a bit away from her so they would not get wet from her dress, she started to run back to the tack room, but the words of a groom, hidden from her by a stall wall, stopped her.

"I hear she is the Maidenhall heiress," a man said quietly. "It is to be a secret, but everyone knows."

"I'd like to get my hands on that. Imagine all that gold! Anything you ever wanted for the asking."

"Shall you propose marriage?"

"Ha! I shall throw her over my saddle and charge her father to get her back."

At that, Axia kept running, her feet silent across the straw-strewn floor. In the tack room again, she saw that Jamie had Tode's clothes off except for the linen loin cloth, and he was rubbing her liniment on his chest and arms.

"Did anyone see you?" he asked, and when she shook her head, he said, "Good. I do not want them being curious. We should have thought of this before." He was thinking of the many times he'd tried to ride with Berengaria with him, but she always caused confusion, with children dancing about them and shouting, "Blind Girl! Blind Girl!" Jamie could not imagine what would happen if Tode walked down the middle of a village street.

"I am going to dress him," Jamie said, "and I want you to get that into him." He nodded toward the flask. "As much as he can hold." When she looked in doubt at him, he said, "It's good single malt Scotch. McTarvit. The best. Now do as I say!"

Axia gave the tiniest nod of obedience as she rolled up a horse blanket and put it under Tode's head, then slowly started forcing the whiskey between his lips. She knew from experience that he was conscious, but the pain in his legs made him wish he were not.

It was more difficult than Jamie had thought it would be to dress Tode's inert body. For all that his legs were frail, his upper body was that of a large and healthy young man, and he was heavy with muscle that he'd developed in compensation for his weak lower half. It seemed forever before Tode began to cough at the whiskey that Axia was judiciously forcing down him.

"No," Tode managed to say, turning his head away. "Let me sleep."

"Yes," Axia said, sitting by his head, smoothing his hair back from his face. There seemed to be a tiny bit of color in his cheeks now. "Please sleep. I will be here with you. I will not leave you." Reaching under the blanket that Jamie had spread over him, she took Tode's big hand in hers and held it to her wet bosom.

She had no idea how long she sat there, but when Jamie started to pull her away, she fought him.

Clutching her chin in his hand, he turned her face to look at him. "I am heartily sick of being regarded as your enemy. You are wet and cold and—"

"I will not leave him," she said fiercely, jerking away from him. "It is because of you that he is like this."

For a moment Jamie stood back, running his hands over his eyes, and with every movement he made, half-dried mud flaked away. How well he had learned not to argue with her. He could force her into the house, into dry clothes, but he had no doubt that unless he tied her inside his friend's house, she would find a way out.

Without saying a word, he removed a thick horse blanket from a hook on the wall, then wrapped it around her body. When she was encased, he picked her up, wrapping his arms tightly about her. "Quiet or you'll wake him," he said into her ear when she began to struggle.

"Unhand me," she said, but Jamie held on.

Sitting on the straw-covered floor, leaning back against the cold stone wall, he pulled her onto his lap, her back against his front. When she continued struggling, he said low into her ear, "Please do not hurt me more. My body is a mass of bruises and cuts from my days with you. I begin to bleed at the sight of you."

If he'd said anything else, she could have retained her anger, could have fought him, but humor took all the rage out of her. To her great embarrassment, she dropped her head against his strong body and began to cry.

Jamie cuddled her on his lap as though she were an infant, wrapped in the thick blanket, her head against his neck, and her tears further wetted him.

She did not cry for long. "I am sorry," she whispered. "I never cry. No one can make me cry."

"Except me. Yes, I always have that effect on women."

"You are a liar," she said, sniffing. "I doubt if you have ever made a woman cry."

He had no intention of replying to that remark, but he was sure that he'd never enjoyed holding a woman as much as he was enjoying holding her, for all that she was a shapeless lump in a smelly blanket. "Tell me about Tode," he said softly. "Why is he like this?"

Axia felt that she was warm for the first time in days as the rain had not stopped long enough for them to have a fire. Frances had begged to stop at an inn, but Jamie had said it was too "dangerous." Since people did not know who they were, how was it dangerous? However, the idea of danger made Axia think she should remember something important, but at the moment she couldn't think what it was.

Curled in his arms, she felt so warm and safe. Her forehead was snuggled into his neck, and when something scratched her, she drew back and pulled a big chunk of half-dried mud from his face. Unfortunately it took away a bit of his hair with it.

"Ow!" he said, and when he looked at her in accusation, as though to say, You are hurting me again, she smiled and put her head back down.

"Did you know that mud is very good for the skin?" she said. "I have been experimenting with mud mixed with the green from the pond and—"

"Mud and slime?"

"Mmmm. Very fine mud, very fine slime. When the mixture is allowed to dry on the skin, there is much improvement."

She was sounding so scientific that he replied in the same tone. "Yes, Frances has nearly perfect skin."

"Ha! Frances is a coward. She never allows me to try anything on her. But Tode—" She looked anxiously toward him, sleeping on the makeshift bed.

"Tell me of him," he whispered, sensing that she didn't want to.

She started to move off his lap. "You must be cold. Let me fetch you another blanket from the stables. Or, better yet, you can return to the house. You must be hungry, and your soldier friend will be looking for you." It was difficult to move since her arms were cocooned inside the blanket, but when she moved, he pulled her back, his arms tight about her.

"For once you are not going to have your way. I know you plan to stay here with him, but I mean to stay with you. Do you understand me? For once I am going to win."

"Do you not *always* win? You have had your way about everything."

"Oh? I did not think it was necessary for you to come on this trip. I wanted that horrid wagon to be painted over. I—"

"You wanted to marry the Maidenhall heiress."

"I do not think *want* is the correct word. I have a family to support, and I cannot marry whom I please. Perhaps you do not know that men of my—of my rank, we are not free. Were we free to marry whom we wish, we might marry the chambermaid."

"Or pockmarked girls?"

"Yes," Jamie said in a way that let her know that this was a subject he was not going to talk about. "Now, tell me about Tode. We have all night, and you *are* going to tell me."

Axia took a deep breath. "His father did this to him."

Jamie had already formed a suspicion that what had been done to Tode was no accident. "To make him into a beggar?" he asked as he had heard of this practice before and he'd seen cripples who he thought were not that way by nature. But he had never seen anything like Tode's legs.

"To exhibit him," Axia said softly. "To take him around England in a wagon and charge people to look at him."

"But he was sent to the heiress instead."

Axia wanted to say, To me, he was sent to *me*, but she did not. If James Montgomery knew that she, Axia, was the heiress, would he then propose marriage to her? "Yes," she said softly. "Perkin Maidenhall saw him in the making, so to speak, and he bought the boy and sent him to—to the heiress."

"Along with you?"

"Oh yes," she said, as though making a joke. "He seems to like misfits and oddities."

"You are not a misfit. You are—"

"Yes? What am I?" Feeling herself stiffen, she awaited his answer.

"You are unique. You are different from anyone else."

"Ah, yes, I am as unusual as Frances is ordinary."

"Frances," he said heavily, "is beautiful."

Abruptly, Axia moved so she could glare at him. "Frances is *not* beautiful."

"Oh?" he asked, one eyebrow arched. "Then what is she?"

"You laugh at me, but I say to you that you do not know what beauty is."

"It is what you paint, and since you seem to draw Frances often enough, you must think she is beautiful."

"No, beauty is what inspires love. It is . . ." She lay back in his arms, her head tucked into his neck. "To be beautiful is to make someone love you. It is when a woman is old and fat, and her husband still sees her as slim and radiant, her eyes bright, her hair dark. To be truly beautiful you have to think more of other people than you do of yourself."

"So are you beautiful?"

"You are laughing at me! No, I am not beautiful. I never think of anyone but myself. But Tode is very beautiful. You could not know, but he runs all the

Maidenhall estate. He knows every person on it, knows all their problems. When a person is ill, Tode sees that he is taken care of; if he is melancholy, Tode sees to him—or her, he makes no distinction. Small children are the special concern of Tode, for they do not see him as different but . . ." She smiled. "Children see the kindness within him. Tode is a very good person."

"But he does not like Frances."

"No one who sees past her face likes Frances," Axia said in disgust. "Except you. You see past her face to her money. As does everyone else in the outside world."

"Frances did not take care of the people on the estate?" He was thinking of his sisters telling him that he was responsible for the surrounding villagers: "Montgomerys have owned that land for hundreds of years so how does your responsibility cease after a mere two years?" was his sisters' philosophy.

"Frances does not know their names. Frances wants—"

"Yes, what does Frances want?"

"Do you ask me again how to court her? Shall I tell you to give her more daisies? Perhaps you should seal her in a room full of them."

"No, I was not asking you how to court her. I was . . ." Yes, what was he asking? "What do *you* want in life?"

"Freedom," she said quickly. "To not live locked away, secret. To be able to go where I want when I want." Quickly, she turned to look up at him. "Have you been to France?"

"Many times." Smiling, he looked down at her. He was still damp, parts of his body were cold, he was caked with thick patches of dried mud, and he held a girl wrapped in a smelly horse blanket. None of these things in themselves were conducive to romance, but he felt as though he wanted to—

Axia drew back from him in disgust, tried to get away from his grasp. "Do you mean to try to seduce *me?*" she asked in horror. "Is that the way you are looking at me? First poor scarred Diana, then witless Frances, and now *me?*"

"No, of course not," Jamie said tiredly. "What could I have been thinking of? When I am around you, I should not take my clothes off—I should put my armor on." With more strength than he meant to use, he pulled her back down on his lap.

"I can remain here alone," she said stiffly. "There is no need for you to stay with me. I am sure that Tode is all right. He has had many attacks with his legs, and I have been there with him. Tode and I need no one else."

Abruptly, Jamie tightened his arms around her, pinning them immobile to her sides so she would not be able to fight her way out of the blanket. "Are you two lovers?"

For just a second, Axia tried to loosen herself, but his hold was too strong, so she gave a great sigh and quit fighting. "No, we are but friends. Why do you put everything in such terms? Is it the great love for Frances that runs through your veins night and day that causes you to think of nothing else?"

"I do not love Frances, and you know I do not."

"But you plan to marry her."

"As you said, I plan to marry her money. It will be a good match for us."

"For her perhaps, but you will be very unhappy. Frances is quite stupid, you know."

"So is my horse, but I still like him."

Axia gave a sigh. "It is not my concern who you marry."

Jamie was thinking that her father would never give his permission. Or was he just hoping that Maidenhall would refuse? He took a deep breath. "I have heard that Gregory Bolingbrooke's father paid a lot to have her inheritance."

"Where did you hear that?" Axia snapped.

"What the Maidenhall heiress does is the interest of all England. But then, perhaps her father will not accept me as his son-in-law."

"I'm sure he will love having his daughter at court," Axia said.

"If Maidenhall charges a man to marry his daughter rather than giving her a dowry, why would he welcome the marriage of his only child to a penniless earl like me?"

"Perhaps he loves her and will allow her anything," Axia said softly.

"A man who has never bothered to see his daughter in all of her life cannot bear her much love."

"That is not true!" Axia said fiercely. "Perhaps he loves her very much. You do not know."

"Perhaps," Jamie said, puzzled by the vehemence of her outburst.

"Perhaps he locked his rich daughter away to protect her," Axia insisted.

"The queen was not so protected in her childhood as the Maidenhall heiress is. Prisoners have more freedom than she does. Criminals—What is wrong with you?" he asked when she began to try to get off his lap.

"There is naught wrong with me. I do not think it is amusing to make light of parents who do not love their children."

"Oh," Jamie said in understanding. "Because of what Tode's father did to him?"

"Yes," she whispered, refusing to think about what he had said. It was not something she wanted to think of. When she was with Tode or Frances, Axia mentioned her father often. Even though they'd had a regular correspondence since Axia was a child, it was true that she had never seen him, never once held his hand . . . No, she did not like to think of that.

Settling back against Jamie, Axia took deep breaths to calm herself.

"What do *you* think Perkin Maidenhall would say if I were to marry his daughter in secret?" Jamie asked honestly. Twice now since that first night, Frances had said they must marry in secret.

Axia liked this kind of question as it implied that she knew her father well. Tode often asked her what she thought her father would say about this or that. Pulling back, she looked at him. "I think Maidenhall would like to have his daughter marry into the aristocracy if he can get the man without paying him anything."

Immediately, Jamie thought of his leaking roof and the villagers who wanted the Montgomerys to again be their landlords. "Nothing?"

Axia smiled. "No major capital outlay. The husband of the heiress would, of course, receive what is her due from her mother, but the bulk of the wealth, the fabulous hoard as it were, will not come to her husband until after the death of Perkin Maidenhall. That is, if he so wills it."

"Ah, well, if there is enough to put food on the table and buy a few acres of land, I am content."

"If that is all you want, then why bother with the riches of the Maidenhall heiress? Surely, with your looks you could entrap any wealthy young woman."

Jamie shrugged. "Frances is here and there is some—some urgency."

"I see. It does not matter who you sell yourself to."

"Stop it!" he commanded. "You do not know what you speak of. I am not free to marry. I have responsibilities that you know nothing about. What of you? Who do you marry? How will you be supported?" As he said the words, he felt himself stiffen. What did it matter to him who she married? But even as he thought that, he was very aware of her body in the circle of his arms.

"I do understand responsibility and lack of freedom," she said softly. "I understand as well as anyone." For a long while she was silent as she lay back against him, for she well knew that her father would not allow his daughter to marry a penniless knight or to remain married if she dared such. If he were to hear of this, Perkin Maidenhall would react in a rage that such a thing had been done. Her father had not become wealthy by giving anything away for free. Even his daughter. He sold everything.

But he would not care that Frances had married this penniless knight. Perhaps it was cruel of Axia to continue this charade, but if Jamie secretly married Frances for her money, then found she had none, he deserved what he got. But then Axia well knew that she would stop this charade before he went to the altar. It did not matter what happened now, just as long as her father was not involved.

With a crooked smile, Axia imagined halting the wedding ceremony with an announcement that Frances wasn't worth the clothes on her back. Oh, how she was going to enjoy the look on James Montgomery's face then.

Just so her father did not know of this, she could play out the game to within seconds of its conclusion.

As for answering him about her own marriage, she did not want to think about that. As soon as they reached their destination, the charade would end and she would have to marry the man her father had chosen for her.

Jamie put his hand on her forehead. "I think something plagues you. You have secrets," he said softly. "Tell me what is in your thoughts."

No! she screamed in her mind as she began to remember that night he had made love to her. Sometimes it seemed far away and sometimes only yesterday that he had held her and kissed her and said that he loved her.

"You!" she said. "You make me sick. You try to seduce me as you do Frances. Or do you leave her chaste for your wedding night? Or is it only poor girls like Diana and me who you use for your lechery? What if you have impregnated poor Diana? Who will take care of her?"

Abruptly, Jamie dropped his arms from around her. "You are free to go," he said coldly, then when she struggled to free herself, he helped with the blanket and she got away from him.

Feeling angry and not knowing the cause of her anger, Axia went to Tode and felt his hands to see that they were warm. When Jamie came to stand near her, her lips tightened. "You may go. Had you better not spend time courting your heiress? I can attest to the fact that Frances will have all the men in the hall swarming about her. And since everyone knows that she is the Maidenhall heiress—"

"What?!"

Axia could not resist a smile at his reaction; obviously he thought his secret safe. "I heard it in the stables when I went to get the blanket."

"And you did not tell me?" he demanded.

"I beg your pardon, but the life of my friend was more important to me than the protection of gold."

"The gold you refer to is in the person of your own cousin."

That sobered Axia. "Yes, do go." Her head came up. "Yes, please do go. I do not need you."

"Axia, you . . ." Words seemed to fail him.

"Yes? I what?" she asked, shoulders back.

For a moment, Jamie could only stare at her. *Are beautiful,* is what he wanted to say. If beauty was thinking of others, then Axia, standing in this cold room in her wet clothes while nursing an injured friend, was more than beautiful. But self-preservation kept him from saying such. *She is not for you, Montgomery. Not under any circumstances can you have her.* He had to marry for money. *Think of Berengaria,* he reminded himself. *Think of the villagers who pawned everything they had to make you clothing meant to entice an heiress. Think of . . . Oh, think of anything except this muddy, damp, bad-tempered, big-hearted witch who has occupied your every thought since you met her,* he told himself.

"You are every man's nightmare," he said softly,

meaning that no man wanted to meet a woman who overtook him as completely as she had.

"Of course," Axia said, misunderstanding. "Go to your heiress and leave me alone," she said as she turned away.

"Yes," Jamie said and left the tack room.

A few hours later, after a bath and a hot meal, Jamie lifted the quill and began to write to his sisters.

I am sending a letter to Perkin Maidenhall to ask for his daughter's hand in marriage. I do not know if he will give permission or not. Axia thinks he would like to have an earl for a son-in-law, but I am not so sure.

I have not talked to Lachlan yet, as everyone has now gone to bed. Since it has rained for days here, the roads are like the bottom of a pond, and the wagons were stuck repeatedly. It has caused us some problems, mainly that Axia's friend was injured.

I have not told you of Tode and I will not now, but suffice it to say that I might bring him home with me. We will need an estate manager, and he comes highly recommended. Berengaria, you will like him very much. You will see him as he really is, as only Axia sees him now.

I must go now as it is late. I would like to sleep, but I must watch for Axia as she is nursing her beloved Tode, and I must see that she is safe.

My love to you both. You are in my prayers always.

With great affection,
James

"One, two, three, four," Berengaria said. "Yes, I counted that he wrote this Axia's name four times. Is that right?"

"Mmmmm," Joby said in disgust. "You are right. And he mentions the heiress only once. Oh, but I would like to go to him and put some sense into his head! One of those odious Blunts burned a field today."

"Their own field," Berengaria reminded her sister.

"My point exactly. No longer a Montgomery field. I am tempted to write our Montgomery cousins and tell them what is going on."

"Jamie would skin you."

"Better to die that way than of hunger."

"And how does the burning of a field that is not yours affect your belly?" Berengaria asked her sister, but they both knew the answer. Under no circumstances could they look like failures to their rich, successful cousins. Berengaria took a deep breath. "We should write him. Ask him to tell us more of the heiress. What does she say? What is her favorite music? Flowers? We will think of many things to ask her, so he will have to talk to her to find the answers."

"If this Axia allows him near her," Joby said spitefully.

"Do not tell me you have grown to dislike this Axia?" Berengaria said hesitantly.

Joby eyed her sister thoughtfully. "As I think you have also. I am sure she has set her eye on an earl and means to have him. It is her only opportunity to meet a man of his rank. What do you think she does to entice him away from the beautiful heiress? Does she wear gowns that reveal an excessive amount?"

Berengaria was thoughtful. "No, Jamie would like

intelligence, someone who can talk to him. Do you think she entices him with discussions of Aristotle's theories? Does she read books in Greek to impress him?"

"Come, we must set our minds on this. What can we do to make him love the heiress?"

"I wish we could get them alone, away from this Axia. You know that Jamie cannot resist a weak creature in need."

"A damsel in distress," Joby said. "Yes, let us see what we can arrange."

Chapter 14

The sun was well into the sky by the time Axia left Tode. Only after he had assured her that he could take care of himself did she leave him. Truthfully, all she wanted to do was take a bath and sleep. She'd had all the trauma she could take for one day.

Axia didn't know her way around this walled estate, and it was drizzling rain so she couldn't see very well, but she knew she didn't want to enter through the front. No doubt the tables for breakfast would be set up, and everyone would be eating. Looking as she did, the last thing she wanted was to encounter Frances and Jamie, both of them, no doubt, dressed in clothes made of sunbeams and starlight.

Making her way to the back of the castle, to what had to be the oldest part, she went in through the kitchens—and as soon as she saw them the sleepiness left her.

Chaos was the general air of the place. No one could walk for the number of people in the kitchen: a couple of enormously fat cooks; boys running around with pans and kettles; children chasing each other; men shouting over the heads of others; women screaming at children to behave; dogs rooting in the garbage shoot.

Waste! she thought, looking about her. *Incredible waste!*

On the floor were great bags of flour, fresh from the mill but open to rats and pilferage; herbs and vegetables had fallen off the center table and were being trampled underfoot. And all the people in the kitchen seemed to be eating anything that came out of the ovens as fast as they could be opened. Axia was nearly knocked down by a man carrying half a cow carcass on his way into the larder, the cold room for meat.

No one noticed her as she slipped past them, where she saw unlocked spice cabinets that could be ransacked by anyone and meat that could be used for soup and stew bases thrown to the dogs. In the buttery, she saw open kegs of beer and imported wines that were free for the taking. The pantry contained great crocks of pickles and salted meats that had been opened and were now being left to ruin.

"Disgusting," she muttered. "Truly disgusting." Whoever owned this place was paying twice as much for food as he needed to. There was no order, no organization, and as far as she could tell, no one in charge.

In spite of her exhaustion, Axia had an urge to take a broom, or perhaps a sword, and clear out these superfluous people and stop all this waste. With management, she thought, more people could be fed and less money spent.

"Look out!" she heard just in time to step aside as a piece of meat landed at her feet. To her disbelief, she saw that the meat was an entire cow's liver, and in the blink of an eye, two dogs had eaten it.

"Aren't you a tasty bit," said a man with two hog's heads in his arms, eyeing Axia up and down, but when she turned on him with a look of fury in her eyes, he backed off. "Sorry," he mumbled and went into the larder.

Axia didn't know what made her angrier than waste and the misuse of funds, and this was worse than she'd ever seen before. However, she did not stop to think that this was the *only* estate she'd ever seen besides her own and that maybe all of them were run this way. Such horror was unimaginable to her.

As she made her way down the corridor from the kitchens to the Great Hall, she saw that the rushes on the floor had not been changed in many months and that, all in all, the place needed a thorough cleaning. If this man, this Lachlan Teversham was feeding all these people, why wasn't he putting them to work?

As she stepped into the Great Hall, she saw as much chaos as she'd seen in the kitchen. More dogs (how many did this man have?) nosing about under the tables for scraps, dusty pennants hanging from the ceiling, tables with too much food on them. The tables were set in a semicircle, and in the middle of them, wrestling on the floor, were four or five little boys, a bit tattered, but dressed well enough that Axia assumed they were the sons of the owner. If he had children, where was his wife that she could allow such disorder in her house?

Standing in the doorway, Axia saw that Frances was the center of attention, sitting in the middle of the high table, a big good-looking man who was no doubt Lachlan Teversham leaning over her, attentive to everything she had to say. On the other side of her was Jamie, also leaning toward her. He was wearing a dark green velvet doublet, and he was as clean as Axia was dirty, as fresh as she was tired.

Sure that no one would notice her, Axia walked into the middle of the room and into the melee of boys and began grabbing shirt collars as she attempted to pull them apart.

However, she miscalculated the size of the boys, or perhaps her own lack of size was her underestimation. The boys, not used to any form of discipline imposed on them, thought she wanted to play with them. One grabbed her ankle, and with a scream, Axia went down into the middle of them. In seconds, she was nearly smothered by a tumbling, laughing heap of arms and legs and sweaty torsos.

She had no idea what would have happened if someone had not lifted the largest boy off of her. On her back, her arms over her face in protection, Axia looked up to see the smiling face of a big, handsome man, gray at his temples, the man who had seconds before been giving all his attention to Frances. She couldn't help herself, but she smiled back up at him.

The next second, she was grabbed about the waist and lifted, then slung across Jamie Montgomery's hip like a lumpy bag of beans. Her hair had come unbraided during the tussle and now surrounded her so she was like a fish caught in a net. If she moved her arms, she pulled her own hair.

"Jamie, my lad, what do you have there?" Lachlan asked.

"Put me down, you great buffoon!" Axia shouted at him or tried to shout as her lungs were nearly cut in half by his hip and his strong right arm.

"An imp. Satan's very own imp," Jamie said casually but then yelped when Axia bit him on the leg, and he almost dropped her.

It took Axia a moment to right herself, get her hair out of her eyes, spit it out of her mouth, and look up at the big, red-haired man. He was very nice looking, not at all gorgeous like Jamie, but then who was? However, she did like the way he was looking at *her*.

"Axia Mai—" she began, but Jamie grabbed her upper arm tightly. "Ow!"

"Matthews," Jamie said plainly. "A cousin to Frances. Isn't that right?"

Behind this big man were standing four handsome little boys, their eyes bright with interest at what was happening.

"Children," Axia said calmly, "if I give you swords, will you kill this man for me?"

At that the children's eyes widened as they looked up at Jamie. Their father roared with laughter.

"What's this, Jamie? Do I hear aright? This is a woman who does not love you at first sight?"

Jamie grimaced. "Shall I show you my scars?"

Lachlan was looking her up and down and Axia found that she was warming to the way he was looking at her. "I do not think she could give *me* scars," he said softly.

Dropping Axia's arm, Jamie smiled knowingly. "You, my innocent friend, do not know her. I saw you," he said to Axia, "come through the kitchens and I saw your anger. Tell my poor, naive friend what is on your mind."

With a smug expression, Jamie looked at Lachlan as he waited for Axia to speak.

Axia well knew what Jamie was doing. Taking a deep breath, she tightened her lips. She was *not* going to hide what she was! "Waste is what I saw," she said, looking Lachlan Teversham in the eyes. "Food thrown to the dogs, trampled in the floor, too many people, filth everywhere." She took a step toward him. "You ought to be ashamed of yourself for the way this place is run. Look at it! Dirt everywhere, your children with the discipline of puppies. You should be ashamed of yourself."

She was advancing on him now, warming to her subject. She had no idea what a scene she presented; though she was rumpled and dirty, her body was small and trim within her pretty, big-eyed face and her hair like a lush curtain. With her hands on her hips, she faced Lachlan, as big as a bear but looking at her with an expression as though he were a schoolboy being chastised by his teacher.

"And your wife should be doubly ashamed of herself. How can she show her face with such mismanagement? You should be running this place with half the expense. Have you no care for your future? Are you so rich that you can waste what other people need? Are you—?"

She stopped because Jamie had taken her by the upper arms and was pulling her back from his friend. There was a look on Jamie's face that said, See what I mean?

But Lachlan was staring at Axia in wonder, as were his sons behind him.

Then, suddenly, Lachlan grabbed Axia's face in his hands and gave her a hard kiss on the mouth.

Everyone in the hall, all of whom (except Frances) had stopped eating and were watching the scene in the middle of the room as though it were the most fascinating play they'd ever seen, blinked in wonder at Lachlan's reaction. But no one was more surprised than Jamie.

"I have no wife," Lachlan said when he released Axia. "Will *you* marry me?"

"Yes," Axia said at once. "I'd like that."

"You will *not!*" Jamie roared, startling everyone out of their motionlessness.

"I most certainly will," Axia said, turning on him. "I can marry whom I wish. It is no concern of yours."

"Your father——"

She well knew that he thought her father was Frances's father. "Died last year," she said quickly.

"I thought he was alive," Jamie said, confused, trying to think.

"You never asked. Plague. Body buried in a pit. Dissolved in lime. I never even said good-bye."

"Wait!" Rhys said, coming around the tables to join the group in the middle of the room. "I have some land from my father. I am not rich, but I too would like to marry you. If you will consider me."

"Like hell you will," Lachlan said as he reached for Axia.

But Jamie was faster than either man as he shoved Axia behind him. "This girl is under my protection and I must——"

"I am *not* under his protection. He didn't even want me to come on this journey. His only duty is to get the Mai—er, ah, Frances to her beloved fiancé. Besides, he's trying to marry Frances himself."

At that everyone turned to Frances, who was eating and doing her best to ignore all of them. Wherever Axia was, she managed to pull the attention onto herself. Frances would very much like to get rid of Axia. If Axia married this man Lachlan, who Frances had already discovered had no title and whose sons had the manners of wolf cubs, then Frances would be alone with Jamie.

"You forget, dear cousin," Frances said sweetly, "that your father left you in my care. And I give permission for you to marry either of these men. Now. Today, if you'd like." She gave her most beautiful smile to her cousin.

Wonder what's wrong with him? Axia thought, looking up at Lachlan. Frances was as anxious to marry and find herself a home as she, Axia, was, so what was wrong with this Lachlan? It never occurred to Axia that Lachlan had not first asked Frances to marry him and been turned down.

But the truth was that Lachlan had been widowed for two years now, and he'd had several opportunities to marry, but he wanted more in a woman than just a pretty face. He needed a woman who could control his unruly, headstrong boys, and he wanted wine without sand in it. He'd been raised with a strong mother and had thought he wanted a dainty wife so he'd married a fragile flower of a woman. But ten years of nursing an invalid had made him want a second wife with a whip in one hand and a crossbow in the other. He was sure it was the only thing that could control those boys of his.

Lachlan went to one knee, making his head level with Axia's. "Marry me. What is mine is yours. Come, boys!" he commanded. "Beg this sweet lady to be your new mother."

The boys had no idea what was going on, but they knew better than to disobey a direct order from their father. Usually, he didn't pay much attention to what they were doing, but when he did give an order, they obeyed. Flinging themselves on Axia, they wrapped their strong young arms about her waist, her thighs, her hips. "Please," they cried. "Please be our mother."

Axia was delighted. Touching other humans was something so wonderful, so delicious, and these beautiful boys—

Jamie put a stop to that though.

With his hands firmly on her shoulders, he extricated her from the clutching children, then turned her toward the stairs and pushed her up the first steps, all the while hissing in her ear. "Do you forget that this is supposed to be a secret enterprise? I do not want the world to discover who your cousin is."

"And how has *my* marriage anything to do with the secrecy of *your* marriage? You could leave me here with your dear, handsome friend, and it would not matter one way or the other." Oh, but she liked the anger in his voice. Could it be jealousy? But then, how could it be when he was engaged to marry someone else? "Or do you think I should marry Rhys? They are both handsome men, are they not? But if I were like you, I would go with the one with the most money and forget feelings." She paused on the stairs. "Which man do you think I should marry?"

"Neither!" he said emphatically. "I'm to take you to your—"

"My what? To *my* intended?" She smiled at him smugly. "As you said, there is no reason for me to go with you."

"You are Frances's companion."

At that, Axia laughed with such good nature at the ridiculousness of his statement that Jamie also smiled, but only for a second. "You are under my care and that is that. Until I have received instructions from Maidenhall, you will be allowed to do nothing except what *I* say. Certainly, you are to marry no man." Turning her around, he made her continue up the stairs.

"Yet Frances *can* marry someone other than the one chosen for her by her father. Is that true? She is engaged, but she is still free to choose. I am engaged to no one, but I am not free to choose. Do I have my facts right?"

"You ask too many questions. Perhaps Maidenhall will not agree to your marriage. If you are related to him and your father is dead, then you must be his ward and he has the right to decide your future. And I might remind you that I am not yet married to Frances."

"Is there hope in your voice that you may yet be saved? Or do you crave the beauteous Frances in your bed?"

"What do *you* know of beds?" he asked, sounding like a prim old lady as he opened the door to the room that had been assigned to her. Inside were three men with heavy buckets of hot water, and they were filling a big wooden tub for her.

"More than you think," she said, trying to sound mysterious, then she saw the tub of hot water and knew without a doubt that he was responsible for this great luxury. "Oh, Jamie," she whispered, feeling every bit of her cold, clammy skin and her dirty dress and hair.

When she turned to look up at him, he was smiling in a way that made him so handsome she had to take hold of the bedpost to keep from falling. It wasn't the smile she'd seen him give to women when he was flirting with them, but it was a little-boy smile of happiness filled with delight that he had pleased her. He looked like the young son who presented his mother with the broken and crushed head of a flower and his mother had told him she loved him best in the world.

"I thought you might like to take a bath," he said hesitantly. "But if you'd rather not . . ."

Knowing that what he wanted was more praise, she said, "Pearls could not have pleased me more." The sincerity of her words made him almost blush with pleasure. "I shall soak until my skin peels off. Oh, please tell them to make the water very hot." She had seen Frances do this, ask a man to give an order that she could very well do herself, and it never failed to please the men. To her utter amazement, she watched as Jamie told the servants how to adjust her bath water. "I shall wash my hair," she said in a voice that told how much she looked forward to that treat.

Jamie nodded toward the side of the bath. "Camomile soap and a rosemary rinse water. I hope it is all right."

"Yes," she said, looking up at him. She didn't know what would have happened if the men had not at that moment announced that the bath was ready. But they did, and the moment was gone.

"I will leave you then," Jamie said, giving her a weak smile before he left the room, pulling the door closed behind him.

For a moment, Axia whirled about the room. *Oh, how lovely freedom is,* she thought. Two men had asked her to marry them and now Jamie was—was . . . Well, she didn't know what he was up to, but she was certainly enjoying it.

In the next instant, she peeled off her clothes, her undergarments still wet, and gingerly stepped into the very hot bath water. As the warmth soaked into her skin, she leaned her head back and closed her eyes.

"He sent the letter!" Frances nearly shouted at Axia as she lay back in the big wooden tub full of hot water. "Did you hear me? He *sent* the letter."

Because Axia had not slept all night, the hot water had soothed her into a delicious and much-needed sleep. "Who sent what letter?" she asked tiredly. She did, of course, know who the "he" was, but not what letter. Now that Frances had ruined her bath, Axia began to soap her hair.

Frances plopped down on a stool at the foot of the bed. "The letter to your father. Lord James sent a letter to him asking to marry his daughter, Frances. Not you. Frances. Me."

Axia was so tired that it took her a moment to comprehend. Then her eyes opened in horror. "Jamie sent a letter to my father?" she whispered. Putting her hand to her forehead, she tried to think. After Frances had so proudly announced that she and Jamie were to be secretly married, Axia had been too angry to think. She had not looked too deeply into her reasons for her anger, but whatever the reason, it blocked out all rational thought. Why hadn't she asked Frances questions at the time? "Tell me everything," she said softly.

"I wanted a secret marriage, with no one else involved, but Lord James said that his honor forced him to ask your father for permission—"

"Now he is *my* father," Axia muttered.

Frances ignored her. "I agreed, of course. What else could I do?"

"Oh yes, your trickery of the man must make you very thorough in your lies."

Frances's eyes flashed anger. "Axia, I have done all this for you."

"You have what?" Axia's eyes were wide.

"I can see that you are attracted to him, and if you married him in secret, your father would disinherit you."

For a moment Axia could not speak. "So you thought to make yourself into *Lady* Frances in order to save me? I do apologize for ever having had an ungenerous thought about you. Frances, you are the very personification of kindness."

Frances looked at Axia to see if she was telling the truth or not. With Axia, one could never really tell.

Axia leaned forward, her eyes narrowed. "Please spare me your fairy tales of all you have done for me. I want to know about this letter to my father!"

Frances should have known better than to think

Axia would believe anything she said. "As I said, Lord James wanted to send a letter to your father asking permission to marry his daughter, only it would be me, Frances, who was the daughter. I couldn't very well say no, so I said that I would write a letter too and we'd send them together. And then, of course, I would never send the letters."

Axia was staring at her cousin in disbelief. "Did you think he would not notice when there was no reply? Or were you planning to write the reply in my father's hand?"

Truthfully, Frances hadn't thought that far ahead, but she'd die before she told Axia that. "None of that matters now. His letter has been sent to your father, and it asks for permission to marry his daughter." Frances's mouth tightened, something she did not do often as she knew facial movement would give her early wrinkles. Her voice lowered. "What do you think your father is going to do when he reads that *I* am his daughter and not you?"

Axia did not like to think about any of this. It was difficult to control her anger at Frances. "I do not know. Perhaps he will yawn and say, 'My goodness, there must have been some mistake.' Or do you think he will send an army to fetch me? To escort me under military rule to my beloved fiancé's house?" She took a deep breath. "And you, dear cousin, what do you think he will do with *you?* My guess is that he will dump you naked in the mud at the side of the road. Let us see what your beauty will attract *then.*"

For a second Axia closed her eyes; she needed time to think. "Dump that bucket of hot water over my head so I can rinse."

Frances stiffened. "For all that you might think it, I am *not* your maid."

"All right then," Axia said sweetly, "you can use *your* brain to come up with a solution to this problem."

Frances only hesitated for a second before lifting the heavy bucket and sending water cascading over Axia's soapy hair.

When she'd finished, Frances used the one dry towel to wipe imaginary droplets off her blue satin dress. "Perhaps we can intercept the reply to the letter."

Axia's head was now beginning to clear enough so she could understand what had happened. Because of this letter, her freedom could end much sooner than was originally planned. "It is not the reply that worries me, but the hundred or so armed men that my father will send *with* his reply." Again she tried to calm herself, as she'd never be able to think if she were this angry.

Standing in the tub, Axia took the towel from Frances, and while she dried herself, she tried to think. "You must disappear."

"Excuse my vanity, but do you not think someone will notice that I have gone? And really, Axia, I do not understand why *I* am the one to disappear. Your father will be angry at *you,* not at me. I am only the cousin."

"A cousin with no funds," Axia reminded her. "And besides, you are the one who caused all this with your talk of a secret marriage."

Frances gave her a stubborn look, and Axia knew that it would do no good to remind Frances that all of this was her fault. From experience she knew that Frances never seemed to remember that anything had ever been caused by her own errors.

Axia took a deep breath. "When did he send the letter?"

"I think this morning, I am not sure. Yes, yes, it had to be this morning, as he was out all night." Frances looked from Axia's uncrumpled bed to her. "Where were you last night?"

"With Tode," she answered, waving her hand in dismissal. "His legs. You cannot be here when my father sends his reply. He will—"

"Yes," Frances whispered in fear, "what will he do?"

"Throw you out and clap me in chains. Frances, why can't you think of these things first, before you get into these messes?"

"I wanted him to marry me. Is that so bad? He is an earl. An *earl!* Oh, Axia, you cannot imagine what it is like to never be safe. Every day I live with an ax hanging over my head. I do not know what will happen to me, what will—"

"And I do?!" Axia exploded, then forced herself to calm. A clean white linen nightgown was hanging over the back of a chair, and she put it on. With this news of Frances's, it didn't look as though she were going to get any sleep, but for a while she could be comfortable. "Let me think. I am tired."

Why hadn't she thought to warn Frances about this "engagement" of hers? Why hadn't she thought of what her father would do if he heard that his daughter was to marry someone not of his choosing? In reality, Jamie and Frances's marriage would be a union between a poor middle-class woman and a poor aristocrat. It was their own business and no one else's. But the lie of the switched places and the involvement of Perkin Maidenhall made it all very serious.

Now, thinking of all this, Axia realized how stupid she had been. Why had she not thought of all the possible consequences of this switch with Frances? Why had she not thought of what would happen if her father became involved? For a moment fear ran through Axia. It was true that she'd never met her father, but she'd corresponded with him since she could write. But no matter what she did or how well she did it, there was never any hint of a visit from him.

As Axia well knew, Perkin Maidenhall was the overruling force in all their lives. Even if he wasn't a physical presence in their lives, the force of his personality always ruled them. And all her life, Axia had wanted to please her father. Maybe if she pleased him, he would visit her. Maybe he would say, "Well done."

The truth of the matter was that, for all that she liked flirting, liked these men asking her to marry them, she well knew that she'd only marry the man her father had chosen for her. No matter how horrible the man was, she would marry him. If she did not, what would her father do to her?

For all that she'd lived a life of great isolation, Axia was not naive in the ways of the world. Her father had not made his great wealth by being a kind and loving person. He was ruthless, and when someone did not give him what he wanted easily, he found other ways to get it. He had married her mother because he wanted a piece of land her father owned. No matter what he had to do to get what he wanted, in the end, he got it.

If her father received the letter from James Montgomery asking if he could marry his daughter *Frances*, what would be his reaction? Rage? For surely he'd figure out about the switch, and Perkin Maidenhall was not known for being kind to people who played him false. Would he decide it was his mission in life to bankrupt James Montgomery? Would he really throw Frances out without so much as a copper penny? Or would he marry her off to someone who made the devil look sweet tempered?

And, heaven help her, how would he punish his disobedient daughter?

"It is bad, is it not?" Frances whispered, watching Axia's face anxiously.

"I think we have gone too far," Axia answered, and Frances was so relieved at that "we" that she could have burst into tears.

"What do we do?"

"You must not be here when my father's men arrive. And we must get *him* out of here. Jamie must not receive the reply from my father. If we could make him think there was some danger and he had to move quickly—"

"He will not leave without you," Frances said grimly. "He will want to get *you* away from those men. All of them fawning all over you. As always, you made a spectacle of yourself."

At the thought of this morning, Axia smiled. "Two men proposing marriage in one day. Was it not divine?"

"Am I to say yes? From where I was sitting, it was

disgusting. You are not considering marrying either of them, are you? That Rhys has nothing, and the other one breeds animals for children."

"You know that I am not to be given a choice for a husband," Axia snapped. "That is what this is all about! I am not free as you are. You can have any man who wants you, but I cannot. You are free to marry your earl if you can continue tricking him all the way to the altar."

Frances brightened at that thought. She would not tell Axia, but she was beginning to like this James Montgomery, not just because he was an earl, but because he was always so polite to her. It was a change from men clutching at her, wanting to touch her, for Frances did not much like being touched.

"Kidnapped!" Axia said brightly. "You shall be kidnapped."

Instantly, Frances said, "I do not like that idea."

"You should have thought of that before my father was informed of your marriage plans." Sitting on the edge of the bed, drying her hair with the damp towel, she looked at Frances. "I will get Tode to arrange a kidnapping. Yes, yes, this is right. I have told Jamie that I heard in the stables that they know you are the Maidenhall heiress, so it will seem natural that you are abducted."

"Is this true? Am I in danger?"

"Only from your own imagination," Axia snapped. "Yes, you will be kidnapped, in secret, of course, and Jamie will go after you."

"And you?" Frances asked archly. "While I am being bruised in a wagon, what will *you* be doing? Sitting in hot baths? Eating stuffed peacock?"

"What does it matter to you if you are alone with

your beloved James? I will . . ." She couldn't think what she would do, for surely the letter identifying Frances as the heiress would make her father send someone who could identify Axia as his daughter. Or would he send Jamie a written description? "My daughter is the ugly one," her father would write. "How could you have confused Frances with my plain, insignificant daughter?"

Now, Axia looked at Frances, and the early morning sunlight creeping in between the shutters in the room touched Frances's perfect cheek so it looked as though her skin were made from peaches. Her dress was bright blue satin trimmed in black, and Axia knew to the farthing how much it had cost. For herself, she never wore such gorgeous clothes, as it seemed that to adorn herself so was to put diamonds on a donkey. No matter how you dressed it up, it was still just a plain little donkey.

"I hate it when you look at me like that," Frances said. "You aren't planning something horrible for me, are you? You and that dreadful Tode?"

"Frances," she said patiently, "you got us into this. I had nothing to do with it, but as always, I will be the one who has to repair the damage." *And bear the consequences,* she thought, but she wasn't going to let Frances see her growing misery. "I will get Tode to take you away, then Jamie will follow you. He will tell everyone here that you were called away to home, but he will know the truth, and he will go flying out of here, his men behind him in pursuit of you. Therefore, when my father's men come they will—"

Frances looked at her cousin. "They will take you," she said softly.

Axia turned away so that Frances could not see her

face. "It does not matter. It was only a few weeks of freedom that I was to have. And I have seen much and eaten much and met people who were not paid by my father. It is enough. It is more than I had expected." She would not allow herself to think about what was happening. "Here," she said as she fished inside a leather case and withdrew a little bag from inside the lining. "This is gold. Take it and go ready yourself. You must put what clothes you have back into the wagon, the unpainted one. Make some excuse, then stay in sight so Tode can find you."

"Will he be wearing that awful hood again? I hate it when he wears that."

"You hate his face; you hate his face to be covered. Whatever Tode does you hate. But yes, he will be in disguise, his face hidden. Go to him, and he will have arranged everything. It will be soon. Do you understand me, Frances, soon!"

"Axia, why do you always have to be so bad tempered?"

What had Axia expected? Gratitude? From Frances? Suddenly, she couldn't bear the sight of her cousin. "Go!" she said, and when Frances did not move, she nearly yelled, "Go!"

With that, Frances scurried from the room, closing the door loudly behind her.

Axia started to get up, as she had much to do. But then it all hit her. Her tiny bit of freedom was over. Why had she not thought of what would happen if her father found out about the charade?

But she knew why. Freedom had gone to her head and forced out all rational thought. And then, too, there had been Jamie. Her fights with him, the—Oh, heavens, but her lovemaking with him.

Flopping back on the bed, she closed her eyes for a moment and remembered. That lovely night when she'd been in his arms. She'd told him she loved him, and he'd kissed her and held her. Had made love to her.

But now that was all over. When he heard that his precious Maidenhall heiress was missing, he'd be out of here in seconds, and he'd never look back at Axia. After all, he thought that Axia had no money, and money was what he most wanted in the world.

Axia wanted to cry, to indulge in feeling sorry for herself. But she had no time, as she needed to get up and tell Tode what must be done. But first she needed to see if his legs had recovered. She knew that he'd never stay in bed for more than one day, no matter how bad the pain. And the driver, she thought, she'd have to hire a driver. She'd have to do everything for her cousin because Frances was so dumb she'd wait inside the wagon until doomsday for someone to come fetch her.

I must get up, was her last thought before she fell asleep.

Chapter 15

"What have you done with Frances?"

Axia was so hard asleep she couldn't at first understand what was being said or who was saying it. She was draped across the bed sideways, her feet hanging over the edge. When she opened her eyes in the dark room, she smiled. "Mmmm, Jamie," she murmured and closed her eyes again.

At a groan from him, she opened her eyes again. He was lying on the bed beside her, not touching her, his eyes closed and an arm thrown across his face.

"What is wrong?" she murmured and felt a surge of—of . . . Oh, dear, maybe it was just memory of that night they had been together. She so much wanted to kiss the skin of his neck, just above the soft velvet of his doublet.

"Why are you trying to kill me?" he asked, his voice

deep within his throat, his eyes still hidden, not looking at her.

There had never been any sex play in Axia's short life, but she knew when a man was angry with her and when he wasn't. And right now Jamie Montgomery was *not* angry at her.

Smiling, she rolled toward him and slipped the little dagger from its sheath at his side, then playfully held it to his throat. "Shall I do the job now? Take your life from you?"

Slowly, he moved his arm from across his eyes and looked at her with such a hot stare that her breath caught in her throat. "You do not know what you play at."

"I think I know more than you believe I do," she whispered, and for a moment she thought he was going to kiss her.

Abruptly, he sat up and glared at her. "I am not one of your pastries!"

"My what?" she said, smiling, leaning a bit toward him.

"Axia, I warn you, stop that. You do not know what you do. You may think you want to taste everything, see everything, that you want to touch all that is in the world, but you cannot—" He broke off and looked at her, covered only by her undergarment, the long linen shift that went next to her skin. He knew that she had on nothing beneath that thin piece of linen. Nothing. Absolutely nothing.

"Axia," he said, and his voice was a moan.

"Yes, Jamie," she whispered, leaning toward him.

One minute he was sitting away from her, his mind firmly made up in resolve that he was not going to touch her, then the next second he had her on her back on the bed, his mouth on hers.

Even as he touched her, he wondered at the ferocity of his desire for her. This was Axia, the girl-woman who'd made his life hell ever since he'd first seen her, yet he'd never felt such desire in his life.

His body was half on hers, his thigh pushing hers apart as his mouth devoured hers. Perhaps he could have controlled himself if she had offered even the least resistance, but she opened to him like a flower to a bee. Her mouth opened under his, her legs opened, her arms clasped him to her.

His mouth, hot and searching, was on her neck, her cheeks, his hands clutched her breast, his thumb on her nipple, then his mouth descended lower, seeking her breast.

"Axia?" came a whisper from the doorway. "Axia, are you in here?"

"Just—" her voice broke as she tried to clear her brain and throat. "Just a minute." Looking up at Jamie hovering above her, he looked as dazed as she felt.

But only for a second. With a soldier's sense of urgency, Jamie sprang off the bed, threw back the covers, tossed Axia under them, then he slipped behind the screen that was in one corner of the room.

"Axia?" Tode said, silently stealing into the room, making sure no one in the brightly lit hall saw him. His face and body were covered by a coarse robe, the hood of it cleverly made deeper on one side so it covered the mutilated half of his face.

"Mmmm?" she said, trying to pretend that she had been asleep.

"I apologize for waking you." His remorse for disturbing her sleep was in his voice, because he knew that she had been awake all night tending to him. "I think something is amiss. Your father—"

Axia started coughing so violently that his words were cut off. Whatever happened, she could not let Jamie, hiding behind the screen, hear the secrets that she and Tode shared. Nor could she give Tode a hint that there was someone else in her bedroom.

"Axia, are you all right?"

She flung back the covers. "I think we should discuss this privately."

"And where is more private than your bedchamber?" he asked archly. "Axia, what are you up to?"

"Nothing. Really nothing. Leave me that I may dress, and I'll come to you later."

Tode stood still and looked at her. "Something is wrong. You are upset about something."

"No, no, of course not." Nervously, she glanced at the screen to see if any of Jamie's long form could be seen.

Following her eyes, Tode walked toward the screen, but Axia leaped from the bed and ran behind it. "Let me dress, then we shall . . ." Now that she was behind the screen, she looked at Jamie sitting calmly on a little stool and grinning at her. His long legs were stretched from one side of the screen to the other, and the only place to stand was between them.

"All right, dress then," Tode said with annoyance in his voice, unable to figure out what was wrong with her. It wasn't as though he'd never seen her in her nightclothes before.

Jamie was looking at Axia as though to say, Yes, do. Please get dressed.

Reaching out, Axia put her hand over Jamie's eyes to let him know he was to close them, but he just pulled her hand away, kissed the palm of it, and grinned.

Narrowing her eyes, pursing her mouth, she gave him a look that would have been translated into a vulgar expletive—if she knew any. Then, with a nasty little grin on her face, she reached across Jamie and up to the corset that was hanging on the wall above his head. Unfortunately, or fortunately, depending on the viewer, her breasts were momentarily pressed firmly and fully into his face.

When she had the corset in her hand, the smug expression was gone from his face. Now he looked like a man in pain.

"Where is Frances?" Tode asked from the other side of the screen, having no idea what was happening behind it.

"How in the world should I know where Frances is? Did you look inside the largest cluster of men you could find?"

Axia slipped the corset about her middle, then turned and motioned to Jamie that he was to fasten it for her. To her great delight, his hands were shaking.

"Axia," Tode said, "do not toy with me. What have you done with her?"

"Me? Why do you suspect me?"

"I heard what happened this morning. What made you agree to marry that man? Do you know that he is telling everyone that you are to be married?"

"Ow!" Axia yelped as Jamie pinched the back of her with a corset latch. "No, I did not know that, but I rather like it," she said over her shoulder to Jamie. Turning, she started to reach for her dress, a long, seamless gown, perfectly fitted to her body, a dark gold color, trimmed in narrow black velvet ribbon. There was nearly a yard of lacing down the back to secure the dress.

But this time Jamie didn't allow her to press herself against him as she reached for the dress. Instead, he lifted it from the hook himself and sat with his arms folded across his chest as she struggled to get it on over her head.

"Axia, you are telling too many lies," Tode said.

Quickly, Axia glanced at Jamie to see if he'd heard this, and of course, he had. He lifted one eyebrow at her in question.

"I think we should talk of this later," Axia said loudly. "I will explain everything to you when we are in private."

"And we are not now private?" Tode asked quietly. "Axia, what is wrong with you? You have done something with Frances, have you not?"

"No, of course not," she said honestly, her head buried inside the dress. Usually, she didn't have trouble dressing herself, but then she didn't usually perform for some man, so now her arms and fingers seemed to catch in every seam and fold.

Then, as her head poked through the dress, she suddenly remembered everything she and Frances had talked about before she went to sleep. With the way Jamie had wakened her, no wonder she had forgotten the stupid thing Frances had done. She had told Frances to wait for her in the unpainted wagon and she would arrange for Tode to meet her there. But there had been no time to arrange anything. And from the look of the sun peeping down low in the shutters, she must have slept for hours.

In spite of everything, Axia smiled. "I know where Frances is," she said and almost laughed. For all Frances's insolence, she could be quite obedient. Once when they were children, Axia had told Frances to hide, saying she'd search for her. Something had happened on the estate that made Axia forget all about games, and so it was many hours before Tode noticed that Frances was gone. One of the gardeners had found her asleep inside a shed at the bottom of the garden.

So now Axia knew that Frances was waiting for her inside the wagon in the stables, waiting for Axia to tell Tode and for Tode to take her away—and get her out of the mess she was now in. Thinking of Frances waiting for hours inside a hot wagon, nervous and not knowing what was going on, made a little giggle escape Axia.

"Axia! What have you done?" Tode demanded.

Axia had to think quickly. She couldn't tell Tode the truth, not with Jamie listening to every word. What would he do if she told him that she feared that her father was going to send an army of men after them?

Instantly, Axia's mood went from laughter to fear. How many hours had she slept? "Did you look inside the wagons?" she asked as innocently as her nervousness would allow.

"Of course I did. The painted wagon is gone, and she's not in the other one. Did Montgomery take the wagon?"

After a glance at Jamie to see him shake his head, she said, "No. I mean, I doubt that he did. Maybe it needed repair. Maybe someone liked my painting." What in the world had Frances done now? Fallen asleep in a wagon that was to be taken to the blacksmith's?

Turning her back on Jamie, Axia stood still while he drew the laces together and fastened her dress. She could tell that he was extremely interested in what was being said.

The second the laces were tied at the bottom, she fairly leaped around the screen to see Tode standing by the window, his hood pushed back, and when he saw her, he opened the shutters, filling the room with the dying light of the day.

"I have slept most of the day," she gasped, and a faint feeling of alarm crept into her body.

"Axia," Tode said softly. "I think Frances has been abducted."

"No, of course she hasn't. How could she have been? I have not told you—" With a glance at the screen she stopped.

"Not told me what?"

"No one here knows that she is the Maidenhall heiress," Axia said loudly. "So why would she be taken? I am sure she is around somewhere. Did you look in both wagons?"

Tode narrowed his eyes at her. He was not going to answer the same questions twice, and he was growing more suspicious by the minute of Axia's behavior. "Why would Frances want to be in the wagons when there is a house? You know she hates the wagons."

"Frances hates so many things I cannot keep up with them. Let us go outside and—and look for her. Yes, I will help you search." Axia's mind was racing. Frances couldn't have arranged her own abduction, could she? She did not like Tode, so maybe she had decided to get away without him. But the idea was to make Jamie leave as soon as possible in pursuit of her so he would not be here when Axia's father sent an angry army. So a silent departure was defeating the purpose. Even Frances would understand that, wouldn't she?

Axia was saved from answering by a loud, urgent knock on her bedchamber door. When the door was flung open, she saw Thomas standing there, his face showing that something was wrong.

"Is he here?" Thomas asked.

Axia did not like the assumption that she would know who "he" was. "To whom do you refer?"

Thomas didn't waste time telling her. "The Maidenhall wagons have come, and they bring with them the body of Rhys."

Jamie did not waste time as he knocked the screen to the floor and strode across it. Without one look at Axia or Tode, he followed his man from the room.

Axia started to run after them, but Tode caught her arm. "What is going on?" he demanded. "And I want no lies from you."

Axia took a breath. She didn't know why, but she was beginning to be sure that everything had gone wrong. "Jamie sent a letter to my father asking for permission to marry his daughter. Frances."

It took Tode a moment to comprehend what this meant. They had never before been so stupid as to incur the displeasure of Perkin Maidenhall, but they had heard of it. If Maidenhall knew of the switch, what would he do to Frances and Tode? Would he lock Axia away for the rest of her life?

Axia clasped Tode's arm with both her hands. "I was going to get you to fake a kidnapping and take Frances away. Jamie would follow you and so none of you would be here when my father and his—Oh, heavens, but I do not know what he will do to us when he finds out."

Tode pulled himself up to his full height. Had his legs not been as they were, he would have been a tall man. "This is all my fault. I take full responsibility. I should never have allowed you to do this, but—"

"But you loved me," she said with resignation. "That is the problem. You wanted me to have some happiness, some freedom for however long I could." Her head came up. "Rhys! I must go to him. Oh, Tode, what have we done?"

Chapter 16

"All right," Jamie said as he glared down at Tode and Axia, "I want to know what is going on."

It was two hours after he'd hidden behind the screen in Axia's room, and during that time he'd been through hell. Rhys had been shot through the leg with an arrow while attempting to follow the painted wagon out of Lachlan's land. It was only by chance that he'd seen the wagon when he was returning from a day's hawking with Lachlan. His first thought was that the wagon was being sent for repairs, but he decided to make sure.

He was still a hundred yards from the wagon when he was brought down by an arrow, an arrow with a crudely written message attached to it.

"You took my woman so I will take yours," the message read.

Jamie quickly ascertained that his man was not in

life-threatening danger, but he still didn't know who had taken Frances. How could a man walk into the gates and in the midst of a few hundred people take her without anyone noticing? Surely the man had to make a threat or cause some commotion to get Frances to go with him? Surely Frances would have raised an alarm. Her sense of self-preservation would undoubtedly cause her to do something to let people know she was in danger.

Jamie reread the message and knew it made no sense to him. Who had done this thing? Was it something personal to him, or did it have to do with the Maidenhall heiress?

All Jamie knew for sure was that Tode and Axia knew a great deal more than they were telling. Now, standing while they sat, he paced in front of them. "You have two seconds to tell me everything."

"Or you will do what?" Axia taunted, her arms folded. "I would rather eat live frogs than tell you anything at all. Not that I know anything, but I am sick of being blamed for everything. I had nothing to do with Rhys being shot. If you'll remember, Rhys asked me to marry him, and I think I might. I think I will nurse him back to health and marry him. Then—"

"Axia and Frances planned to fake a kidnapping," Tode said tiredly.

"Tode!!" Axia gasped, looking at him with hurt eyes for his betrayal.

He didn't turn to her, but she could see that his eyes were furious. "Do you not yet realize that Frances has actually been kidnapped? We do not know where she is, and if the villain knows that she is the Maidenhall heiress, he could ransom her piece by piece."

As though a mountain had dropped on her head, Axia suddenly realized that Frances could very well be in danger. And if anything did happen to Frances, it would be her fault. Frances had said that if she posed as the heiress, she would be the one in danger.

"Why?" Jamie said, looking at Tode, trying to keep his anger under control.

"The letter," Tode answered, not looking at Axia. "You said you were going to write and ask permission of Perkin Maidenhall to marry his daughter. Frances thought she could prevent you from sending such a letter because she knew that her father would *never* agree to her marrying anyone other than the man he's chosen for her. She desperately wants to get out of her marriage to Gregory Bolingbrooke any way she can, and she thought that if she could trick you into a secret marriage . . ."

Trailing off, he looked at Jamie, his eyes dark as he stared at Tode. Until now Jamie had been gentle and kind, but now Tode could see how he'd become a renowned soldier. Tode ran his hand about his neck as the room seemed to have become suddenly very hot. "When Frances found out that you'd sent the letter, she was afraid her father would send men. So we decided that I was to take Frances away, and we thought that you would follow so neither of you would be here when Maidenhall's men arrived."

"So you planned a fake kidnapping," Jamie said flatly.

"No," Axia said heavily, "*I* planned everything. Tode had nothing to do with it. I was going to put the plan into execution, but I fell asleep."

For the first time since he'd entered the room, Tode

looked at Axia. If nothing else, she was brave. But now all he seemed to remember was James Montgomery pushing down that screen in her room and walking across it. Axia had been behind that screen dressing. What had they been doing in the room before he entered?

"What other secrets do you have?" Jamie asked calmly.

"None that have any bearing on the matter at hand," she said honestly for Frances's safety was all that mattered now.

"It is not her fault," Tode said quickly before Jamie could ask another question of Axia. "She was trying to save Frances. Can you not think what Maidenhall will do to Axia? He thinks that the cousins should look out for each other." Tode swallowed as he thought of Maidenhall's wrath when he found out about the switch. "It was Frances who was trying to trick you into a marriage that her father would no doubt have annulled even if he had to buy half of London to achieve it."

"I see," Jamie said after a moment. "Every one has secrets, but now Frances really is kidnapped and we don't know by whom."

"And it is all my fault," Axia said, her heart in her eyes. "If Frances is killed, it will be my fault."

As Tode watched, Jamie went to her and knelt before her. "Come on now, imp, don't lose courage on me now. Whoever has her will probably fall in love with her at first sight." He put his fingertips under her chin. "And, besides, if this is anyone's fault, it is mine. The note said, 'You took my woman so I will take yours.' But the truth is, he should have given his name and his full address so I could distinguish him from all the other cuckolded men from my past."

When anger at those words replaced the misery in Axia's eyes, Jamie smiled at her, then stood, and he was serious once again. "You may sit, Tode," he said graciously. "I am sure your legs could use the rest. It looks to me as though I must find a solution to this," he said, but in the next moment the door burst open, and Thomas shoved two people into the room. One was a pretty little maid, the other, a stable lad by the smell of him, and from the color of their faces, it was easy to guess what they had been doing when Thomas found them.

"Tell him," Thomas said quietly but in a voice of command.

The girl sat on the floor, threw her apron over her face, and began to cry loudly. The boy looked as though he wanted to go to her, but he was shaking too badly.

After a confirming glance at Thomas, Jamie went to the girl and held out his hand to her. That was all that was needed to calm her. Between Jamie's looks, his beautiful clothes, and the very elegance of him, her tears dried instantly.

And when he spoke, his voice was as soft as honey, and Axia had heard that tone only once before: on the night she had been Diana. "No one is going to hurt you, and there will be no punishments. I just want you to tell me what you know."

The boy, still sitting on the floor, looked up at Jamie with jealousy. Standing, he moved toward Axia. "You mean about the lady? The beautiful lady? The most beautiful lady in the world? *That* lady?"

Turning his back to the girl, Jamie gave the boy a look that quelled him, then he returned to the girl. "Tell me what you know."

After a smug look at the boy, she looked up into Jamie's eyes. "She came to the stables by the wagons, the wagons you brung."

"Frances?" Jamie asked.

"Yes, that one. I was there to escape the heat of the kitchens if you know what I mean."

"Ha!" the boy said. *"That's* not why she was there."

The girl didn't even look at him but concentrated on Jamie's eyes. "The lady looked very upset and asked me which wagon it was to be, but then she said I wouldn't know. Which I didn't."

Axia gave Tode a look. Frances couldn't even remember which wagon she was to be kidnapped in.

The girl continued. "I, ah, I stepped behind the stable wall for a moment and—"

The boy gave a derisive snort at that.

"But I could hear everything, and since I wasn't very busy . . ." She paused to give a triumphant look at the boy who had been trying to keep her *very* busy. "I happened to see this big man, quite huge he was. I like a big man," she said, looking up dreamily at Jamie, "not little men or boys."

"Get on with it, girl!" Thomas snapped.

The girl lost her dreamy expression. "This man asked her, this Frances, if she was looking for someone, and she said yes, had he come to kidnap her? I think this surprised the man, but he said that yes he had. 'If you are the Maidenhall heiress, then I've come to kidnap you.' That's exactly what he said." She looked up at Jamie in awe. "Was she really the Maidenhall heiress?" Her eyes were wide.

Jamie smiled at her but didn't answer. "Then what happened?"

"He walked with her to the painted wagon and said it was the prettiest wagon he'd ever seen. Then he said, 'That's you painted on that wagon,' and he said she was the most beautiful person he'd ever seen in his life, 'cept maybe for one, so he wanted her to sit by him on the wagon so he could look at her and decide which was the prettiest."

"And they drove away," Jamie said softly, then turned to Thomas. "Start searching. Ask anyone anything. We must find her. Someone must know something." After Thomas had taken the young people with him, Jamie turned back to Axia and Tode. "Go now," he said distractedly, and they could see the worry in his face.

Outside the room, Tode said he was going to help search. "Are you all right?" he asked Axia.

"Yes, of course. I feel fine," she reassured him. "Go and help look. Look in places other people can't."

With an encouraging smile, he left her.

But the moment she was alone, she found that her knees were shaking. What had started as a joke, switching places with Frances, was turning into a nightmare. And what if she had not switched places, would she now be the one held hostage? Perhaps Frances was wise in not struggling. If someone had taken Axia, she would have yelled and screamed and bitten and no doubt ended up dead.

After a word with a servant asking for directions, Axia found the Tevershams' private chapel and went there to pray. She prayed that Frances would not find out that the kidnapping was for real, for if Frances were afraid, she might cause the kidnapper to do something that he might not do otherwise. She prayed for Frances's safety and asked her forgiveness for getting her into this mess.

And even though she told herself she had no right to ask God for this, she asked that He might make her father a tiny bit less furious than she knew he was going to be when he received Jamie's letter.

Chapter 17

Tode wasn't a drinking man, but he felt that now he would like to drown himself in something that would make him forget. Everything horrible that had happened in the last weeks was his fault. Like Axia, he had no doubt that Perkin Maidenhall was now on his way to the Teversham estate with an army of men. And now, because of Tode, Axia's bit of freedom was to be over.

A vision of Axia chained inside one of the Maidenhall wagons danced in front of his eyes, and it was a moment before he could clear them.

And not only Axia was in danger, but what would happen to Frances at the hands of the kidnappers? At this moment Jamie was tearing the estate apart to find anyone who had seen or heard anything that would give him a clue as to who had taken Frances. So far, there had been nothing.

Axia was in her room, where Jamie had set her to drawing pictures of Frances that he could send with messengers around the near countryside to ask if anyone had seen her.

Axia drew one picture after another, each of them an excellent likeness of Frances. But Tode, while concerned for Frances, found his thoughts returning again and again to the end of Axia's freedom. In what had to be only hours now, Maidenhall would come and take her to Gregory Bolingbrooke.

And at that thought, Tode shuddered. Bolingbrooke might be wealthy, but Tode knew that, due to an accident when he was a child, Gregory wasn't a complete man. As Axia had guessed, there would be no children, no hope of a normal life.

Gregory's father worked hard and paid much over the years to keep this information from the outside world, but sometimes Tode's scarred face could be used to advantage. No one paid much attention to what a jester knew or didn't know, and traveling players and singers, going from one estate to another, gossiped a great deal. It had not been a difficult task to find people who had been to the Bolingbrooke estate and knew the truth of that household.

So Tode knew exactly what awaited Axia. Her father would come and take her to that horrible boy and force her to marry him. And Axia would do it without complaint, because above all else in the world, she wanted to please her father.

Knowing what was in store for her, Tode had been unable to deny her these few weeks of freedom from being the Maidenhall heiress. To the very depths of his soul he knew what it was like to be stared at and considered a freak; it was one of the things that he and

Axia had in common. In order to give her a brief time as a normal pretty girl, he had allowed her to switch places with Frances and now everything had gone awry. Frances's life was in danger and Axia was going to be taken by her father.

"I must *do* something," he said aloud. "I should have taken care of both of them. Both of them were under my care." Guilt nearly overwhelmed him at the way he had always favored Axia over Frances. Maidenhall had put him in charge of both females, yet he had neglected Frances to the point where she was so lonely that she'd marry the first man she saw, namely, James Montgomery.

But all anyone could do was wait. Jamie was combing the countryside, asking questions of everyone, but so far, nothing had come of his questions. In the morning, Jamie planned to go with Thomas, leaving the injured Rhys behind, and ride north, as that was where they were heading when Frances was taken.

Tode knew without a doubt that he too would be left behind. Jamie and his man would want to travel fast, and Tode would only be in the way. He wondered if Jamie planned to leave Axia behind or to take her with him. It was Tode's guess that he'd leave her behind, especially since he didn't believe she was in any danger from Maidenhall's men. Perkin Maidenhall would be interested in the whereabouts of his daughter, who Jamie thought was Frances, so he'd think Axia was safe.

But Tode knew, and Axia knew, the truth.

Since they had arrived, Tode had stayed in the old tack room off the stables. In his years with Axia he had grown used to comforts, but he well knew the worth of someone like himself in the outside world. For the most part Tode had stayed away from strangers, hiding inside his coarse robe, keeping his face hidden.

But now he picked up his gnarled staff and walked into the stables, looking into each stall until he found the boy who had seen the man who had taken Frances. He was angrily rubbing down a big horse.

"Go away," the boy said without looking up. "I have no more answers."

Tode had had years of sitting on the sidelines and watching; he was good at assessing what people were thinking. Jealousy was what was wrong with this boy. "I just wanted to tell you that you do a better job of taking care of a woman than *he* does. You didn't lose yours." With that, Tode slowly turned away.

"Wait!" the boy said, then watched as Tode turned back. Turning his head like an inquisitive bird, he was peering into Tode's hood. "You one of his men?"

"Hardly," Tode said with a laugh. There was a torch on the wall just outside the stall, and a small stream of light flowed over the wall. Moving into the weak light, for just a second, Tode lowered his hood so the boy could see his lacerated face. It was more than enough time, and Tode turned away from the look of revulsion on the boy's face, then his superior laugh.

"I don't think *you'll* be taking anybody's girl," the boy said, unconcerned with Tode's involuntary wince.

"No," Tode said jovially. Long ago, he'd learned to hide his hurt. "I wanted to ask you about what you saw, but then you must be sick of speaking of it. But, still, it all must have been very exciting."

Tode watched the boy as he seemed to consider this. Truthfully, he had been so busy trying to get his hands under his girl's skirts that he hadn't paid any attention to what other people were doing. That she had was another sore point with him. Since this afternoon, the girl had talked of nothing but this earl— "An *earl*," she'd gasped for the thousandth time. An earl talking to her and looking at her as though she were the most important person on earth.

"Nobody wants to listen to *me*," he said bitterly. "No one wants to know what *I* saw."

"You did see something," Tode said eagerly. "I knew when I saw you that you were a clever boy. I thought then that Lord James should have paid more attention to you." Leaning toward the boy, he was careful to keep his face in shadow. "I travel from house to house, and I look for stories to tell. Your exploits could be told from one great house to another, but I would need to know more than I do now."

For a moment the boy stared in wonder. "He had half an ear."

"I beg your pardon?"

"The man had half an ear. Cut off right here," he said, motioning to just above the hole of his ear. "The top half was missing."

Tode could have kissed the boy, he was so pleased with this information, but instead, he forced himself to sit still for thirty minutes and listen to the boy tell everything that he imagined had happened since he'd seen the man with half an ear.

When, wearily, Tode was finally able to leave the stables, his first impulse was to take his new-found information to Jamie, but as he walked across the courtyard, he changed his plans. If he told Jamie, no doubt he would go charging off with men and weapons, and perhaps Frances would be hurt in the fracas.

No, Tode thought, he would do better to do this himself, and as he well knew, he would be able to get into places that other men couldn't. And besides, this was all his fault, wasn't it?

Tode knew that from the way the message on the arrow sent into Rhys's leg was worded that it was expected that Jamie would know who had taken Frances, so perhaps someone close to Jamie would also know. Tode had no hope of duping Jamie into giving him information that he did not mean to give, but perhaps Rhys would like to have some company.

"I have come to make you laugh," Tode said as he poked his head around the door to Rhys's room, a skin full of very strong wine under his arm.

"And welcome you are," Rhys said, sitting up, then wincing with the pain. "Tell me what has been found. Any news on Frances?"

"Nothing yet, but that is not why I am here. Come, come, you must forget that, or your leg will never stop aching. Let me tell you an amusing story I heard."

Two hours later, Tode left Rhys's room, and he was smiling beneath his hood. It had not been difficult to get Rhys to talk about extraordinary people he had known in his life.

"But no one is dumber than Henry Oliver," Rhys had said after the first hour of gossip and stories. "He thought he was deaf because he had only half an ear." When questioned, he told how Jamie's older brother, when they were children, had hit Oliver on the side of the head with a sword, and when the top half of his ear had fallen off, Oliver had cried that now he would be deaf.

"To this day, I think he still believes he can't hear well out of that side of his head."

"And what sort of man is this Henry Oliver?" Tode asked, trying not to sound frantic. "Dangerous?"

"Oliver? No, not at all, unless blind stupidity makes a man dangerous. He loves Jamie's sister, and he's been trying for years to force Jamie's family into allowing them to marry."

"Force them?" Tode was glad Rhys was getting drunk so that he couldn't hear the rising panic in Tode's voice.

"For years he tried to buy her from Jamie's older brother, and Edward would have sold her, but Jamie's father looked up from his books long enough to say no, that he didn't think that was a suitable match." Rhys chuckled. "I think this decision was influenced by Berengaria saying she'd throw herself off the roof before she married Henry Oliver. And since the death of the brother and father, Oliver has offered Jamie some lands that flood every spring, a few run-down cottages, and some ancient horses in return for Berengaria's hand." Rhys took a deep swig of the wine. "And once he tried to kidnap Berengaria."

"Kidnap her?" Tode asked, unable to breathe.

"Well, at least he threw a sack over her and carried her off."

"What happened?" Tode asked.

Rhys could hardly contain his laughter. "Some-how—Oliver has very poor eyesight—he got the other sister in the bag. Joby. You don't know her, but believe me, no man wants to rile that girl. I'd rather open a bag full of Scottish wildcats than one that contained an angry Joby."

"Like Axia," Tode said softly.

Rhys smiled in a dreamy way. "No, they are not at all alike. Axia is a terror to one man only. Joby makes everyone's life difficult. Except for Jamie's and Berengaria's. Let me tell you what she used to do to her brother Edward."

And with those words, he launched into a completely different story, but Tode had his information, so now it was going to be an easy matter to find out where this Henry Oliver lived and easier still to guess where he was going. No doubt he was taking Frances to his home. No wonder Jamie had not understood his message: "You took my woman so now I'll take yours." In Jamie's eyes his sister never had and never would belong to Henry Oliver, but obviously Oliver thought differently.

So now, leaving Rhys's room, Tode was smiling. He'd found out a great deal, but what could he do with this information? Take it to Jamie? But he knew what Jamie would do, he'd run after Frances and leave Axia behind, as was right. But Tode knew that it was Axia who needed protection, and Tode knew that if Jamie knew that, he would protect her with his life.

How could he get Axia and Jamie away from the Teversham estate before Jamie found out what Tode knew? How could he get Jamie to protect Axia and leave Frances to Tode?

Chapter 18

Jamie angrily crumpled the message into a tiny ball. He was going to show this to no one. With every passing minute he felt more stupid, more helpless, as he couldn't figure out what he should know. Who had taken Frances? From the way the first message was worded, it seemed that he was supposed to know, but he didn't.

He hadn't slept in two days now, and his chin was black with whiskers, but he wasn't going to rest until he found out something. There had to be a clue somewhere. He'd just told Thomas to bring him the stable lad again when this second message had arrived. It said that Jamie was to go west to his uncle's house and wait there for another message.

But what bothered Jamie was that at the bottom of the message was written, "Better take care of your women."

Not "woman," but "women." Maybe it was a mistake. Maybe the writer's pen slipped. Maybe he meant that only Frances was in danger and no other woman.

And too, Jamie was bothered that he'd found the message on his bed, which meant that it had come from inside the Teversham household. It had been put there by someone who was inside the castle, someone so familiar his presence would interest no one.

Jamie could not lose much time in contemplation. He would go to his uncle's house and await further instruction. In the meantime, to make sure she was safe, he'd send Axia away with Tode and Thomas; they were the only people he could trust.

Thirty minutes later, Jamie was cursing, for both Thomas and Tode were down with a debilitating flux. Clutching his stomach as he ran to the garderobe in agony, Thomas was ashen, his guts gripping.

As for Tode, he was so weak he could hardly look up as he clung to Jamie's arm. "Do not let the kidnapper take Axia. You must protect her. I fear that she is not safe here. That man took Frances with everyone looking on. He could do it again."

Tode echoed Jamie's worst thoughts. As Axia had told him, people knew that Frances was the Maidenhall heiress, and perhaps because Axia was traveling with them, they would think that she had something to do with all that gold as well.

Because Jamie had not slept in days, he was not aware of time, was unaware that it was the middle of the night when he burst into Axia's room. Frowning, he was instantly aware that there was no maid sleeping in her room. She was unprotected.

When he touched her shoulder, she snuggled deeper

under the covers, so deep in fact that he had to reach down under them and pull her up.

"Axia," he said softly, "I want you to get up. I want you to go with me."

"Sleep," she murmured, keeping her eyes closed.

"No, not sleep. You have to get up. Where is the maid to help you dress?"

"Jamie helps me dress."

Tired as he was, he smiled at that, then gave her a little shake. "We are going to my uncle's. He has a very nice wife named Mary, and she will take care of you."

Yawning, Axia was beginning to wake up. "What are you doing in my room again?" she asked. "Why are you always in my room?"

"I'm a soldier, remember? I go where the danger is."

Axia tried not to smile but couldn't prevent it. "Have you found Frances?"

"No, but I've received a second note, and I'm to leave here at once and go west to my uncle's. It is about a day's ride from here, and you are to come with me."

"Why?" she asked, one eyebrow raised.

"Both Thomas and Tode are ill, so they can't take care of you, and since there is no one else, you must go with me."

He was not prepared for the suddenness of her leap from bed. As she flung the covers back on him, one corner caught him on the eye. Pushing the covers off his body, his hand to his eye, he wasn't surprised to see a spot of blood on his finger.

With a hand to his eye, he pivoted on one foot and,

stretching, caught Axia by the arm before she ran out the door in her nightclothes.

"Tode!" she gasped, pulling against him with all her strength. "I must go to him if he is ill."

Jamie held her easily. "Axia, I am tired; I am worried; do not make my life more difficult. Now come here and see if you have blinded me."

Turning, she saw a tiny spot of blood at the edge of his eye. That didn't bother her, but when he sat down on a chair by the bed, she saw his shoulders sag, and that posture made her see the burden he felt. "Your beloved Tode is all right," he murmured, "merely a flux."

She was fully awake now as she went to a basin and wet a cloth, then standing between his knees, she touched the cloth to his eye. "What is the news?" she asked softly.

"None. I am to wait."

When he looked up at her, she saw the strain of him. There were black circles under his eyes from lack of sleep. If she were missing, poor that he thought she was, would he be looking for her this hard?

She knew the answer to that. Yes, he would.

Fighting an impulse to put her arms around him, she stepped away to stand by the bed, her back to him. "You want me to go with you?" She hated how much hope built up inside her as she waited for his answer.

"I cannot leave you here. I wanted to send you away with Thomas and Tode, but they are both ill. Thomas will join us as soon as he is able."

"And Tode?"

"He is to remain here. Lachlan will look after him."

Whirling about to face him, she said, "Could not Lachlan look after *me* as well?"

"No," Jamie said. "The note hinted that more than one woman was in danger. That could mean you as well as Frances."

"But Lachlan could take me away somewhere," she said, her eyes pleading. "Oh, Jamie, please. Do you forget that he has asked me to marry him?"

"He meant it in jest!" Jamie snapped. "You had made a fool of yourself in front of all the company so he tried to save you embarrassment."

"Oh? Is that what he did? Then he is indeed a good man. He would be a good match for me, so perhaps if you could persuade him to take me away somewhere, he would propose again. This time not in jest."

He was frowning at her, but he did not answer.

Moving toward him, she again stood between his knees. "Please, Jamie, please. You know that I have no money. Like you I must make a good match, and this Lachlan with his adorable sons would be a very, very good match for me." She was standing very close to him. "Please," she whispered.

Jamie was too tired to think what he was doing, but he pulled her into his arms and kissed her hard on the mouth. At least the kiss started out hard, then it turned into such soft sweetness that he was all too aware that they were alone in her bedchamber and she was naked under her nightclothes.

Abruptly, he thrust her from him. "Are you so eager to get a husband that you will take *anyone?*"

"Oh yes," she said happily. "Anyone except you, that is. You would make me remember that I was poor all the days of my life and that I had cheated you out of the Maidenhall heiress."

With that, Jamie jumped up from the chair, raising his hands skyward. "You know that Frances's father will not allow the match. Most of the trouble now—" Halting, he glared at her. "What is the use trying to talk to you? You are not going to remain here with Lachlan and make a fool of yourself. You are under my protection, and until I am released from that duty, I will see to your care. Is that understood?"

"Quite well. And I am sure that half the household heard you too."

Jamie grimaced. "Get dressed. We ride at dawn." With that he left her room, not bothering to close the door behind him.

But Axia closed the door. Closed it, leaned against it, then smiled. Then she moved away from the door and danced about the room, humming a very happy little tune to herself.

Chapter 19

Jamie was tired, and his temper was blacker than the circles under his eyes. What in the world had made him decide to take Axia with him? He knew very well that Lachlan would guard her with his life, as would Rhys, and when Thomas got out of bed, so would he. She would have been safe. They would protect her from kidnappers and from Frances's father.

But even knowing that, he could not leave her. It made no sense to him, but he knew that he had to have her with him, where he could see her. Perhaps later he could leave her with his uncle, but truthfully, he wasn't sure if he'd be able to then either.

So now dawn was breaking and sleepy servants were milling about, he was ready to go, but there was no sign of Axia. She was not in her room, and no one had seen her. For a few seconds, his heart leaped to his throat in fear, then he calmed. Without a doubt, he thought, she was with her beloved Tode.

As a surge of jealousy flooded him, he didn't bother to tell himself that it was only right that she'd want to say good-bye to her childhood friend. All he knew was that he didn't want her alone with another man.

"I will be alone," Axia was saying to Tode as he lay on the hard bed of horse blankets.

"Your Jamie will be with you."

"He is not mine. If he belongs to anyone, it is to Frances."

Tode gave a snort of laughter. "You do not believe that. Frances wants him because he is available, and he wants her to help support his family. You cannot fault him for that. Axia," he said softly, "Jamie is a good man, and I think he loves you."

"Me? Loves me? You must be very sick indeed. James Montgomery cannot wait to get rid of me."

"Oh? Then why is he taking you with him to his uncle's?"

Axia gave a little one-sided grin. "To keep me away from Lachlan."

"Exactly. And why does he want to keep you away from Lachlan if he does not care for you? Since he thinks you have no dowry, he must know that a match between you and Teversham would be a good one."

"The best." Axia was grinning. "I begged Jamie to let me stay with Lachlan and his dear sons."

"Those demons from hell, you mean. They think it is a great joke to put burrs into people's beds."

"And tadpoles and other crawly things," Axia said with a grimace. "You cannot believe what they offered the chief steward to drink!"

"Mmmm. Unfortunately, I can imagine. I have done the best I could to hide myself from them as I do not want to be on the receiving end of their merriment."

At that thought, Axia's eyes widened. "You must go with us," she said. "You do not seem so ill that you cannot go with us. I will tell—"

Tode caught her arm as she started to rise from the side of his makeshift bed. "I am not ill," he said softly. "I am going to ride ahead and see if I can stop your father."

"My—? Oh, Tode, he will murder all of us. Why is Frances *always* stupid? Could she not once offer some variety? If she'd just come to me and told me that Jamie wanted permission from my father, I could have arranged something."

"What would you have done? Written the letter yourself? Given permission for the marriage to take place? By now Frances would have connived to marry your dear Jamie."

"My *what!*" she gasped. "You know very well that I hate people who think more of their looks than they do of anything else."

"Jamie is not like that, and you know it. You delight in tormenting him."

She looked down at her hands. "But he has no use for me."

"The man is nearly insane with wanting you. I thought he might cry when you gave that pillow to Rhys."

"This is true? Do you think he likes me? No! Do not answer. He thinks I am a great nuisance and no more."

"Oh yes. That is why he is taking you with him." At

a sound outside, Tode said, "Listen. He will be here soon, and you must leave." His voice lowered. "Axia, do you know that I—that I . . ."

She well knew what he was trying to say, words that they had never before exchanged. But then there had been no need for an exchange of words. Since she was a child and her father had sent her a thin boy who was in constant pain from what had been done to him, Axia had loved him. It had taken years to make him trust her, years for him to get over his fear of other people, years for him to stop hating, but they had done it. They had learned to give and receive trust, and together the two misfits had made a life for themselves inside the beautiful prison.

Axia threw her arms about his neck. "I love you, I love you, I love you. I will love you all my life, and what will I do without you for even a day?"

For just a moment Tode held her close, but then he pushed her away. "Go on before I make a fool of myself. Please do not hurt Jamie; I do not want him to wind up looking like me." He was smiling, but his eyes were serious.

Axia was working too hard at not shedding tears at leaving her friend to be able to think of a clever retort. And she was trying not to let him see that she was afraid to be without him.

Tode put his hand under her chin and tipped her head up. "And do not worry too much about Frances." Guilt ate at him as he could not tell her that he was sure her cousin was in no danger.

"Oh, Tode, Frances does not even know how to dress herself. What if she tells the man she is not the Maidenhall heiress and he tosses her out? Who will take care of her? Frances wouldn't know what to do to save herself even if she is given the opportunity."

"There you are wrong. Frances has the cunning of a cat. Didn't she manage to take an obscure relationship with the Maidenhall heiress and get herself out of her father's poor household? If not for Frances's shrewdness, she would no doubt be a washerwoman with two children by now."

The image of beautiful Frances doing any work was so ridiculous it made Axia smile.

"There, that is better. Now go. He is waiting."

"You will not allow my father to harm you?" she said. "And remember that no matter what he says he will do to you, I will take care of you. If I have a penny, you will have half of it."

Tode lifted her hand and kissed it. "Axia, if *you* have a penny, you will somehow manage to turn it into a hundred pennies."

"Then you shall have half of that," she said smiling, then quickly, she rose and ran from the room and ran smack into Jamie's hard chest as he stood outside the door. "You were spying on me!" she accused, looking up at him with defiant eyes.

"I have much more interesting things to do with my life than spy on you. Now come, we will lose the whole day if we continue to dawdle." Taking her by the arm, Jamie led her back to the middle of the courtyard, where two horses were waiting.

"What is this?" Axia asked, staring at a pretty little mare that was fitted with a saddle and loaded with leather bags full of goods.

"That is a horse," Jamie said without looking up. "Have you not seen one before?"

Axia was nearly as tired as Jamie and not about to put up with his bad temper. "I know *what* it is, but who is to ride it?" Her face brightened. "Tode will come with us after all!"

"Axia, I do not have time for this. We must ride. Now get on that horse and let us go. There might be news of Frances awaiting me at my uncle's."

When Axia didn't move, he stopped tying things onto his horse and looked at her. "What is wrong now?"

She gave him a weak smile. "I have never been on a horse before. Not alone anyway."

"Never . . . ?" he began, then shook his head. "Pretend you want to sell it and the buyer wants to see that it is docile, so it is up to you to demonstrate it."

Axia didn't smile at that but nodded, turned toward the horse, then turned back again to Jamie.

"And what is it now?"

"Tode," she said softly. "I have never been without Tode before. He—he takes care of me. Could he not come with us?"

Jamie felt an emotion run through him that he'd never felt before. Of course, he told himself, he was tired and under strain, so he was bound to feel things that under normal circumstances he would not—He didn't want to think anymore, so he picked Axia up and dropped her into the saddle, then handed her the reins.

"Chairs are not as safe as this horse. Now throw your leg over and follow me." He had not given her a woman's saddle, as he'd realized that she might not know much about riding. With a man's saddle, she would be able to balance easier.

When she was atop the horse, she looked down at

him with big eyes that seemed to say, Don't leave me! In spite of himself, Jamie liked that look. And he liked the fact that on this journey she would be dependent on him and him alone. He put his hand on her calf, hidden under layers of skirts. "I will take care of you, Axia. I swear it." When she still looked doubtful, he grinned. "Seize the day," he said, "and today you get to ride a horse."

For just a bit of a second, she looked frightened, then she put her chin in the air. "If you can do it, so can I. And did you pack my paints?"

"No," he said, smiling as he mounted his horse. "No pens or ink or paints or paper and no Tode. It is just you and me and the stars." With that he nudged his horse forward and she followed him.

Chapter 20

I hate this animal. I hate it. I hate it," Axia was saying through teeth clenched so tightly her jaws hurt. But her jaws weren't the only thing that hurt. Every muscle, bone, and nerve in her body cried out in pain.

"Stop complaining and get down," Jamie said, looking up at her. He had led her to an inn, pulling their horses to a halt before the Golden Goose, and was now waiting for her to dismount.

All day they had been riding. A day that was to Axia the longest in her life. The insides of her thighs were raw, and the muscles of her legs screamed in pain. And the rest of her felt shattered from hours of constant jarring.

"These animals were not created by God," she told Jamie. "The devil made them. They are meant to destroy mankind." As though the pretty little mare heard her, she turned baleful eyes up at Axia. Axia, however, was completely hard hearted and would have sneered, but her face hurt too much to move it.

"Axia, I am tired," Jamie said. "I haven't slept in days; I haven't eaten in many hours. Have some mercy on me and get down."

Axia looked at him in disgust. "I cannot. I cannot move any muscle on my body. They are all frozen into place."

Jamie ran his hand over his eyes. For the life of him he could not now remember why he had insisted that she come with him. He held up his arms to her. "Then fall onto me, and I will catch you."

"I cannot," she whispered, and Jamie saw that she was serious.

Maybe his heart should have gone out to her, but he was too worried and too tired. Reaching up as far as he could, he caught her about the waist and pulled. When she didn't budge, he released her, then went to the other side of the horse and removed her foot from the stirrup. But when he moved her, as far as he could tell, her body was entirely rigid; she didn't bend at all.

Since he had spent most of his life on a horse, Jamie hadn't thought much about riding, but now that he thought on it, he had been gradually introduced to the saddle. Maybe it was too much to spend twelve straight hours in the saddle on the first time out.

When Jamie pried Axia's hands loose from the reins and saw that they were indeed frozen into place, he did feel a bit of sympathy for her. He had to hand it to her though: she'd not complained once all day. Except maybe to tell him in detail how much she hated horses. But he hadn't paid much attention to that, as his only goal had been to get to his uncle's house and find out what he could about Frances.

After Jamie had freed both of Axia's feet and her hands, he again put his hands about her waist and pulled. But since her legs didn't bend, she still didn't come off the horse.

"Could I give you a hand?" asked a fat, red-faced man who was probably the owner of the inn.

"Please," Jamie said, glancing up at Axia, but she was staring at the sign hanging over the inn with absolute fascination. If her face hadn't been crimson with embarrassment, Jamie would have thought she wanted to start painting public house signs.

On the opposite side of the horse, the tavern keeper put his hands under Axia's foot and pushed as Jamie pulled her from the other side. As though her legs were a dowsing wand, Axia's legs stayed rigid and as far apart as the width of the horse.

Holding her about the waist, her legs immobile, Jamie found that he couldn't pull her completely off the horse. "Er, ah," he said to the man on the other side. His battle training had not prepared him for this situation. "Perhaps if you gave the horse a bit of a nudge," he suggested.

"Ah, yes, of course," the man said, trying to keep his face serious, but his eyes were filled with merriment. Going to the front of the horse, he took the reins and led it out from between Axia's unbending legs.

But when he saw Jamie's look as he held Axia aloft, her legs wide apart under her skirts, looking like the fork of a tree, he could no longer retain his laughter. With his hand over his mouth, the man disappeared into the tavern.

Jamie wasn't sure what to do with her. He couldn't

very well stand her upright, as there had to be nearly three feet of space between her feet.

"Perhaps you'd like to sit down?" he suggested.

"I'm too sore," Axia said. "The backside of me is sore, the inside of me is sore. *All* of me is sore."

"Yes, but—" he began, then realized that they couldn't stand there like that the rest of the day. With a quick toss, he threw her across his shoulder, ran his hands down her legs, and began to push them together.

It was a harder task than he would have imagined, and by the time he reached her ankles, he was glad she was short and his arms were long or he would never have reached them. With a hand on each ankle, he pushed, and it was rather like trying to get the blades of a large, strong, and very rusty pair of scissors to meet. And the fact that Axia was whimpering in pain did not help the matter.

But through strength and perseverance, Jamie was at last able to succeed, and finally, Axia's feet came together.

Still holding her over his shoulder, he let her rest a moment before he slid her down his body and stood her in front of him. But the moment he released her, her legs started to collapse under her.

Holding her gently by the shoulders, he pulled her upright. "Come on, imp. Seize the day, remember?"

She gave him a hard look. "I would like to seize that horse and slit its throat. I would like to seize—"

Companionably, Jamie put his arm around her and led her into the inn, supporting a great deal of her weight with his own body as her legs were by no means fully functioning.

Inside the inn, there were four tables, three of them

full of other customers, but in the corner was one unoccupied table, and the owner had placed three cushions on top of a hard wooden bench.

When Axia saw the cushions, tears came to her eyes, and she whispered, "I love you," to the man, who beamed in pleasure.

At that Jamie gave her a rather hard push to sit down and stop flirting.

Once seated, Axia put her head down on the table and promptly went to sleep. She didn't awake until the smell of food surrounded her, at which time she had to wake Jamie and tell him to eat, for he had dropped his head back against the bench and was as sound asleep as she had been.

"Eat this," she said, shoving a pewter trencher full of food toward him.

But he just reached for the mug of ale and downed it.

"Travelers, are you?" the owner asked, his eyes twinkling every time he looked at Axia. He looked at Jamie, whose eyes were half closed in fatigue. "You and the lady be wantin' a room for the night?"

"Yes, oh yes," Axia said eagerly. "Something soft with sheets, and oh yes, flat. Very, very flat. I want a very flat bed."

The man chuckled. "The flattest beds in all of England. And they don't move unless you make 'em move," he said, winking at Axia and was pleased when she blushed prettily.

"Then we shall take your finest room," she said happily.

Jamie wanted to go on traveling until they reached his uncle's, but he knew he couldn't. The way he felt now, he would be no help to Frances or to anyone else.

He'd thought to get to his uncle's house by tonight, but all day he'd been aware that Axia was having trouble holding onto the horse, so he'd slowed for her. As a result, they still had half a day's ride ahead of them. After what had happened when he'd tried to pull her off the horse, he could not be so cruel as to make her get back onto the creature again so soon.

"Two rooms," he said to the innkeeper. "We will need two rooms."

"He snores," Axia said quickly, for some reason not wanting anyone to know that she and Jamie were not married. "No one can be in the same room with him." There was a man at one of the other tables who had turned to look at her when Jamie said they were to have two rooms, and he was still staring at her.

"Only have one room," the owner said to Jamie, "unless you want to sleep in the stables. You won't disturb the horses."

Jamie, who had woken up enough to turn to the food before him, had also seen the man staring at Axia, but he gave no indication of it. "It looks as though tonight, dear, you are going to have to endure my snores."

"Oh?" Axia said with interest, then caught herself as she looked up at the innkeeper. "I guess it cannot be helped. Endure I must."

Shaking his head, the innkeeper went back to the kitchen. He thought Axia was a nice handful, and he would keep her in his room no matter how much she complained about his snoring.

Axia was beginning to feel better now that she was no longer on that cursed animal, and she found that she was ravenous. Tearing off a hunk of tender beef, she chewed, all the while looking at Jamie.

"And what is on that devious little mind of yours?" he asked, not even turning to look at her.

"Nothing at all. *Do* you snore?"

Turning, he looked at her in a way that made her feel quite warm. "No one has complained yet."

"Jamie," she said, leaning toward him, but he looked back at his dinner.

"Do not say it," he whispered, making Axia sigh and give her attention to the food.

It was two hours later, alone in their room that Axia found out that Jamie meant to sleep on the floor while she took the rather narrow bed.

Jamie had given her time for privacy so she could undress and get into bed, but now he stood in the middle of the room, peeling off his clothes and carefully draping them across a chair. "Axia, you are in a marriageable state, and I plan to leave you as I found you. I plan to deliver you to your guardian as you were delivered to me. I do not seduce girls who have been put under my care."

"Except Frances. Her you cannot keep your hands off of."

"I never so much as touched her as I am sure you well know."

"But you want to, don't you?"

Jamie sat down on the chair to remove his leggings. "Are you jealous?"

"No, of course not. I have never been jealous of Frances."

Turning away from him, she put her hands behind her head. "I was merely curious, 'tis all. Someday I shall have a husband, and I would like to know what to expect." She looked back at him. "Is it wonderful?" As she asked the question, her mind filled with memories of her night with Jamie, his arms about her, his lips on her body.

Please remember me, she wanted to say. *Remember that I am the woman you made love to. Or was that night no different from a thousand others, and so it meant nothing to you?*

"Do not look at me like that, Axia," Jamie whispered.

"Like what?" she said, and all her thoughts were in her voice.

For a moment, Jamie closed his eyes as though he were trying to gather his strength. "Axia, I am only human and you are . . ."

"What am I, Jamie?"

"Beautiful," he said, then snatched a blanket from the bed, tossed it to the floor, and, like the soldier he was, rolled himself in it and turned away from her.

For several minutes, Axia lay staring up at the ceiling and smiling. "Beautiful," she whispered. She wanted to stay that way forever, dreamy, enjoying what had just been said to her, feeling how nice it was to hear Jamie's soft breathing so near her. He did not snore, she thought, smiling to herself. But then she wasn't sure she'd mind if he did.

Moments later she was asleep.

"Please, Jamie," she said, looking up at him with big eyes. "Please." They were sitting in the dining room of the tavern, an enormous breakfast spread before them.

"Do not look at me like that and do not call me Jamie like that."

"Do not call you Jamie? Oh, so now I am to call you *Lord* Jamie? After we spent the night together?"

That made him laugh as she'd meant it to. "You know very well that I never touched you, in spite of you, daughter of Eve, trying to entice me into your bed."

"I did no such thing!" she sputtered. "I merely asked you some questions."

"Mmmm. Now eat, so we can go."

"I'm not going to get on that creature-from-hell again," she said stubbornly.

"You are going to ride. You'll find that you're not nearly as sore as you—" He couldn't finish that sentence with a straight face because he'd had to help her down the stairs this morning, and she'd groaned with every step. "Well, it's not far now, and you will love my aunt. She will take very good care of you."

"I want to go with *you.*"

"We have been through this six times this morning. You cannot travel with me as I do not know where I am going. All I know is that a message is to be sent to me at my uncle's house, and I will then be told who has Frances and how much money is wanted for her. At that time I will go wherever I must."

"Without me," Axia said sulkily.

"Yes. Without you." He put his hand on hers. "You will be happy there. My aunt is lovely. She will—will entertain you. You can draw pictures for her."

"Strangers. They are strangers to me. *Why* can't I go with you? Frances is *my* cousin, remember."

"Axia, listen, I will have to move fast. You can't stay on a horse, and most of all, this may be dangerous. Whoever has Frances may—" Looking away, he didn't want to think on that. "This will be no place for you. You will be a hindrance."

Axia toyed with the food on her plate. She hated the

idea of being left behind, surrounded by strangers. Alone among strangers—it was her worst nightmare. And, truthfully, she hated the idea of being separated from Jamie. First losing Tode and now Jamie. She had not known Jamie for long, but now, sneaking a look at him while he ate, he seemed to have always been with her.

"Eat!" he commanded.

Axia started to say something, but a man's voice interrupted her. "It *is* you," the man said, looking at Jamie. "I thought it was last night, but I wasn't sure."

"And who may I ask do you think I am?" Jamie asked as he took a drink of his ale.

"The man on the wagon. The dragonslayer."

Jamie nearly choked. "You've seen the wagon?" he gasped out. "When? Where?"

"Heading due south."

"But that can't be," he said. "I was told—" With a quick glance at Axia, he saw that she was thinking what he was. Lies. The message had said Jamie was to go west to his uncle's and wait there, but if the wagon was going south, they were getting farther away from it, not closer.

"Did you see who was driving it?" Jamie asked.

"Sure. A big man. And the woman was with him, you know, the lovely woman on the wagon. We were laughing because the man was no looker, but in the painting he'd been made handsome. That was the best painting I ever saw, and do you know that the lady herself painted it? She told us all about how she painted it."

"*I* painted that wagon," Axia said. "Frances couldn't—"

Jamie put a strong hand on her shoulder, and painfully, Axia sat back down.

"We have been searching for those people," Jamie said quietly, "and we'd appreciate whatever you could tell us."

"You really did paint that wagon?" the man asked, looking at Axia.

Jamie took a deep breath. "She will draw a portrait of you and your friend if you will tell me all you know." When the man kept looking at Axia, Jamie added, "As a knight. She'll draw you as a knight in full armor."

"Saw it two days ago," the man said quickly. "It must be long gone by now."

"What of the woman? Was she well? Unhurt in any way?"

"Well enough to lie," Axia muttered.

"Looked good to me. She seemed right pleasant. They was stopped by the road for the night, and the man was waitin' on her like she was the queen of England."

"Now I am *sure* it is Frances," Axia said.

Under the table, Jamie gave her a little kick to tell her to be quiet. "What was the man like? Other than big, what did he *look* like?"

The man shrugged. "Nothing remarkable. Brown hair. Brown eyes. Not much to look at, but not ugly either. I don't think I'd remember him if I saw him again."

Frustrated, Jamie slumped against the bench. He still didn't know much more now than he had before.

"Except his ear," said another man who'd just walked up.

"Oh yes," the first man said, "he had half an ear. The top half was missing."

For a moment, Jamie just sat there, then he grinned, then he put his head back and laughed. Laughed wildly while everyone in the inn stared at him.

When Jamie could at last control himself, he managed to say, "Henry Oliver," as though that should mean something.

Jamie managed to collect himself long enough to thank the two men who had given him this very welcome information, then when they were gone, he turned back to his breakfast.

It took Axia a while to realize that he had no intention of explaining anything to her. "You are going to tell me nothing?" she gasped.

When he looked at her and smiled slowly, she knew he was well aware of her impatience.

"Tell me!" she hissed.

"Henry Oliver is harmless. Frances could not be in better hands. He will see that she is unhurt."

"But he has kidnapped her. Surely there is some harm in that. He must want a ransom from the—" She looked about to make sure no one was listening. "From the Maidenhall heiress."

"Henry cares nothing about money. He did this out of love."

"He *loves* Frances?" Axia sounded as though this were the most unbelievable thing she'd ever heard in her life.

"No, he loves my sister Berengaria. Since we were all children, he has been trying to get permission to marry her."

"But you would not allow them to marry?"

"Oliver is stupid."

"Ah, well, then he should love Frances. Kindred souls."

"No, no, you do not understand. Oliver is genuinely, truly stupid. He believes anything anyone tells him, such as that money is found in caves in Africa. When we were children and playing hide-and-seek, he would hide by closing his eyes. He believed that if he could see no one, no one could see him."

Axia had had too much of being the object of speculation. "But surely he has grown out of that. Perhaps now that he is an adult . . ."

Jamie looked at her with one eyebrow raised. "Last year he had a stone grain crib with a big hole in a wall, and rats kept getting in and taking the grain. So Oliver tore down the crib and burned the grain to keep the rats from getting it."

"But why didn't he just patch the hole?" she asked, then paused. "Oh, I see." Axia sipped her ale. "Would he like to buy some dragon cloth?"

Jamie laughed. "Oddly enough, he's not a bad businessman. When he makes up his mind, nothing on earth can sway him. There's no way a person can reason with him; there is no 'appealing to his finer sensibilities,' so to speak. He makes up his mind about what he wants and what he will pay, and nothing in the world makes him change."

"And now he wants your sister."

"Always has, and knowing Oliver, he'll probably die wanting her."

"But he'll die without her, I guess."

"As long as *I* live he'll never have her," Jamie said fiercely.

"And she is *very* beautiful, is she not? The maid said that Oliver said Frances was the second most beautiful woman he'd ever seen."

"Yes, Berengaria is beautiful." Jamie smiled. "Henry Oliver will take care of her and give Frances the best of everything. He hasn't a mean bone in his body. My brother, Edward, used to play endless tricks on him, but Oliver never resented him or got angry. Oliver thought Edward liked him because he paid him so much attention."

Axia grimaced. "I know too well that someone paying attention to you doesn't mean that he *likes* you." As she said this, she gave Jamie her best sigh, trying to make him tell her that he liked her very much.

But Jamie only winked at her.

Two hours later, after she had drawn pictures of every man in the inn, Jamie said, "We should go."

"Go where?" she demanded, stowing away her pens, which he had indeed packed.

"Henry will have taken Frances to his home, which is very near my home, so I am going there to get Frances. But first I am going to take you to my aunt, and please, Axia, do not argue more with me. I have decided."

"True, and I am sure there is no appealing to *your* finer sensibilities."

"None at all."

"But *why* cannot I go with you? Especially now that you know that it is only your Henry Oliver. You said there is no danger. Oh, please, Jamie, I will cause you no trouble at all."

"You would cause me trouble even if you slept the whole trip. Axia, do not look at me like that. You must know that it is not seemly for us to travel together alone. Your guardian, Maidenhall, has given you to me in trust. How will it seem if we have been traveling all over England together, just the two of us? Last night was bad enough, both of us sharing the same room."

"Maidenhall need not worry about *you* touching *me*," she said in disgust. "You are only interested in Frances."

At that Jamie took her hand and kissed the back of it. "There, my dear, you are mistaken," he said softly. "If I were free and had no need of making an advantageous marriage, I would court you so hard you would think a mountain had fallen on you. Landlord! Our bill please."

Axia was staring at Jamie with wide eyes. "Would you?" she whispered, but he was too busy handing out coins to the landlord to notice her. So Axia turned her mind to figuring out what to say to persuade him to take her with him.

"If I go with you, it will save you much time," had no effect on him. Eyes full of tears and telling him that she did not want to stay with strangers did not move him. Telling him that she was afraid that Perkin Maidenhall would show up and take out his wrath on her didn't make him so much as blink. Threatening to escape and return to the waiting arms of Lachlan Teversham only made him laugh. Telling him she'd tie the bedsheets together and escape out the window of his uncle's house made him laugh harder.

It wasn't until the horses were standing waiting and he was about to toss her into the hated saddle that she realized she was indeed going to be stuck with an old man and woman who she was sure would prove horribly boring. There was no adventure in spending her days behind a sewing frame.

Standing at the side of the horse, she gave a great sigh, the force of which almost turned her lungs inside out. "I guess there is no hope that this aunt of yours has children that I can play with."

Jamie snorted. "All of them grown."

"Grandchildren?"

He had his hands cupped to help her onto the waiting horse. "No," he said impatiently. "Aunt Mary has six grown sons, none of them married."

"Oh?" Axia said, and for the first time, she thought that perhaps visiting his aunt Mary might not be so boring after all. She put her foot into Jamie's waiting hands, but he didn't lift her onto the horse. When she looked at him to see why, he had the oddest expression on his face.

"Jamie?" she asked. "Are you all right?" When he didn't answer, she said louder, "Jamie!?"

"You are going with me," he said quickly, then tossed her into the saddle so fast and with so much force that she nearly went over the other side.

It didn't take Axia half a second to add up the facts. "No," she said with resolution, "I think you are right. I *should* go to your aunt's house."

Jamie didn't answer but grabbed the reins of her horse and led it out of the courtyard toward the road.

"But this is south," Axia said at the crossroads. "Jamie, I think we should talk about this. You are always taking me away from marriageable men. First that dear Lachlan and lovely Rhys and now your very own relatives. I really think you should take me to your aunt's house and leave me there in safety. It is not right that an unmarried couple such as you and me should travel alone. And, besides, to meet six full-grown Montgomery young men would be a magnificent opportunity for me! You can go and save Frances, and maybe Maidenhall will be so grateful that he'll reward you with her hand in marriage, and meanwhile, maybe I could find myself a handsome husband. And a Montgomery at that! Such a fine old name. And to think of it, Jamie, we will be relatives."

Halting his horse, Jamie turned to look at her. "Axia, if you don't close that pretty little mouth of yours, I am going to sell you to the gypsies. And I'll sell you to whichever one offers me the *lowest* price."

When he'd turned his back, Axia wiggled her shoulders and gave a silent laugh of triumph, then smiled at the sunshine.

Chapter 21

*F*our hours later, Axia was wishing that Jamie had kept to his original plan and left her somewhere soft and safe. As it was, it seemed that she'd never been off the horse, for her legs were stiff and sore. She very much wanted to beg Jamie to stop, but she knew she'd die before she did. With a crooked smile, she thought that Jamie really did have a soft heart. If she worked at it long enough, she was sure that she could talk him into anything.

She was riding beside Jamie, they were moving too fast to talk, and besides, it took all her concentration to stay on the horse. It was a beautiful day, and they were surrounded on either side by dense forest. Axia had asked if they could stop and eat the bread and cheese they had purchased in one of the villages, but Jamie had said they couldn't. She'd argued with him about that, but he'd warned her there were bandits in the forest, and he didn't want to encounter them.

Frowning, Axia had glanced into the dark forest, looming on both sides of them, wondering what was lurking inside there. From the way Jamie spoke he was very afraid of the bandits and didn't want to risk an encounter. Since she'd known Jamie, for all that he'd had enormous difficulty with her and Frances, he had been the soul of sweetness. For all that he had turned her over his knee—and she'd never forgiven him for that—he seemed to be a nonviolent man. He seemed to fight with words rather than a weapon. She could imagine Rhys and Thomas fighting, but she couldn't imagine Jamie in a fight.

This was one reason she was adamant about getting him away before he met her father. If a sweet man like Jamie met Perkin Maidenhall, Jamie would never live through it. Thinking of this, she smiled, because if she told Tode what she was thinking, he'd say she was a snob. He'd say that Axia believed that only people who were not born with money could actually *do* anything on the earth. The sons and daughters of earls would starve if their pretty clothes and houses were taken from them.

So now, glancing at the dark forest, she urged the horrible creature between her legs forward.

But only minutes later, she was startled by two men jumping out of hedges growing alongside the road, one of them grabbing the reins of her horse. "Your money or you won't see the sunrise," the man said, looking up at her with an ugly grin on his face.

Another man, a huge, bearded ruffian, his little eyes glittering, held the reins to Jamie's horse. "Ain't you a fine gentleman?" the man said, eyeing Jamie in his spotless black velvet doublet. "Get down."

"Please don't hurt us," Jamie said softly. "We will give you what you want if you'll just let us go free."

Axia saw that the man holding the reins of her horse had a pistol. Feeling real fear for her life was not something Axia had bargained for when she said she wanted to experience the adventure of life. In fact, fear was not an emotion she was very familiar with, so now she couldn't seem to move.

As Axia sat, staring, Jamie dismounted slowly and came to her, holding up his arms to her to help her down.

"I like this horse," said a third man behind them, a man Axia had not known was there. "Think I'll take it."

"Say *nothing*," Jamie whispered to her with warning in his eyes.

Axia did not have to be told that, for she was too afraid to say anything. What would she and Jamie do if the bandits took everything they had and left them alone on the road? Or what if they decided to kill her and Jamie? She had to think of something to do, some clever way to get them out of this mess.

"Over here," said the man with the pistol, motioning toward the shadow of the trees. "Come over here, rich man, and empty out your pockets."

"We have nothing," Jamie said in a voice full of fear. "We are merely traveling from one place to another. Please do not hurt us."

Axia, standing to one side, heard the fear in Jamie's voice and was disgusted. Even if he was afraid of them, he should not show it. He should stand firm and show them who was in charge.

"How dare you assault us!" she said loudly, her shoulders back, her chin high. "We are on the business of the queen and if you touch us, you will be drawn and quartered."

At that she had the satisfaction of seeing the three bandits and Jamie pause and stare at her. *Now they will leave us,* she thought in triumph.

But unfortunately, her words seemed to have the opposite effect. Whereas before they had paid no attention to her, now the biggest of them grabbed her from behind, one huge hairy arm about her waist, the other about her neck.

"On the queen's business, are you? Then a ransom for you should be high," said the man holding her.

Axia's eyes were full of terror as she looked at Jamie, and for just an instant, she saw his anger at her disobedience.

"We don't really know the queen," she whispered, but no one listened to her.

"Empty your pockets," the man with the pistol said, waving it at Jamie. "And do it quick before she dies." Turning, he grinned at Axia. "I'll make use of her before she goes, though."

To her shame, Axia could feel her knees weakening. She'd always hoped that in a situation like this she would be brave, but these horrible men were so awful and so frightening. Were they going to kill her and Jamie?

"There's nothing in my pockets," Jamie said, and his voice was nearly trembling now. "Please do not hurt her. She is an innocent, and she has no value."

"I'd say that parts of her have a great deal of value," laughed the man holding Axia so very tightly. She could smell his foul breath, and to her horror, he began to move one hand upward toward her breast.

"My money's in my boot," Jamie said loudly. "I keep all our gold in my boot, and I will give you everything if you will but leave us with our lives."

At that the man with the pistol laughed as he looked toward Axia. "I love these fancy gentlemen. Such fine clothes, such fat purses, and such weak stomachs."

Axia could feel her heart sinking as she watched Jamie bend down toward his boot. He was right to give in to the men, of course, but part of her wished that he'd show a bit of spine.

Everything happened at once, and it happened so quickly that Axia almost saw nothing.

Jamie did not draw a purse from his boot, but a thin dagger that she had never seen before, and with a flip of his wrist, he threw it. At Axia! She saw it coming, but it was so unexpected and so fast that she had no time to get out of its way. But, thankfully, it missed her, sailing right past her head.

In the next second, Jamie whirled in a blur of moving arm and flashing steel. He always carried a long sword at his side, but all gentlemen did. It had never occurred to Axia that the sword was for anything but show. Now Jamie seemed to extract it from its sheath in one blinding, fluid motion, and in the same movement, he stuck it straight through the man holding the pistol.

With her eyes wide in disbelief, Axia saw the man look down at the sword, where it was up to its hilt in his belly. What he could not see and Axia could was the long pointed tip of the blade protruding from his back.

The third man, standing on the other side of Jamie, could also see the tip, and with a glance at Axia and the man holding her, he disappeared into the forest.

But Axia did not move, for the man who had grabbed her still held her as tightly as ever, both his arms clutching at her in a deathlike grip. Now that Jamie had killed his companion, what would this bandit do to her?

Axia was too scared to speak as she watched Jamie withdraw his sword from the dead man, then saw the man crumple to the ground. She still did not try to speak while she watched Jamie clean the blood off his sword and resheath it at his side.

Axia didn't speak nor did the man holding her. Was he as afraid after what he'd just seen as Axia was?

When Jamie had his sword resheathed at his side, he walked toward her, unconcerned with the man holding her. To her disbelief, he put his hand on the man's arm and pulled it from under Axia's breast.

It was only then that Axia turned her head and saw the man, still in exactly the same position, but he had a knife sticking out of his throat. And he was very dead.

"Don't faint on me now," Jamie said as he pried the man's other hand from around her waist. "I think we should get out of here in case these fellows have friends."

Axia could only stare at Jamie.

He gave her a little smile as he pulled her away from the man, for her body was rigid with fear. "Do not look at me like that. There were only three of them."

She did not know what to say. Never in her wildest dreams had she imagined such action as Jamie's. He was like a prince out of a fairy tale come to save her.

"Hold on to me," he said, smiling in amusement at her expression. "I think your legs have gone again." He was chuckling at the way she was staring at him.

As Jamie bent slightly, Axia slipped one arm around his neck, then the other, then on an impulse she could not control, she put her mouth on his and kissed him. She kissed him long and hard, kissed him to say thank you, and kissed him to let him know what she was feeling about him.

After a long time, Jamie pulled her arms from around him, and his eyes locked with hers. "Axia," was all that he could say, and he kissed her chin and nose. Then with great reluctance, he pulled away from her. "We must go."

But Axia's legs didn't move, so Jamie swept her into his arms and carried her to the waiting horse, as usual, dropping her into the saddle. Within seconds he had mounted his own horse, and after urging her mount forward, they rode faster than Axia ever had before, and it was all she could do to stay in the saddle.

It was nearly sundown before they reached the end of the forest, and there was an inn where they could spend the night. During the hours of the ride, Axia had given her concentration to the horse and not to what had happened. In fact, she did her best not to think of it. But images kept flashing through her head: Of the man holding her, of his threats, of his malignant little eyes. She remembered Jamie tossing the knife and how close it had come to her head. But instead, it had sunk deep into the man's throat, just inches from her own head.

It seemed that the farther they got from the scene, the more frightened Axia became with her thoughts of what could have happened. Maybe she was better off locked away in the Maidenhall estate. At least there she'd never had to contend with bandits with pistols.

As the hours wore on and she grew ever more tired and more hungry, the forest seemed more threatening and more horrible.

When at last Jamie pulled the horses to a stop and helped her dismount, he frowned at her. "You are pale. Come and I'll get you something strong to drink." Putting his arm about her shoulders, he supported her as they walked into the inn. "Axia, it is over. Do not think of it more. I will keep you safe."

With that he pushed open the heavy oak door and went inside the warm, well-lit dining room, where a fat, cheerful-looking woman came bustling forward.

"Good evening," she said cheerfully, then looked at Axia. "Oh, my, the young lady has been hurt. Come, dear, sit down, and I will see to you."

Axia didn't know what the woman meant, but then she turned her head to the side and saw the blood on her shoulder and neck. She was drenched in the man's blood, blood that must have come from the knife that Jamie threw into the man's neck. And in that moment everything that had happened became completely real to her. All the danger, all the risk and threat, came before her eyes, and it all seemed to block out the light.

As she crumpled in a faint, Jamie caught her in his arms.

Chapter 22

$\mathcal{W}$hen Axia awoke, it was to Jamie sitting beside her on a bed in an unfamiliar room. It was dark, a single candle on the far side of the room, but she could tell that dawn was close at hand. She must have slept all night, and given how exhausted Jamie looked, he'd never left her side.

Opening her eyes more fully, she smiled at him, then startled, she tried to sit up, but Jamie pushed her back onto the bed. "Is it gone?" she whispered.

"Yes," he said softly. "All the blood is gone. I cleaned it off myself. Even washed it from your hair." As he said it, he looked at her lying there with great masses of soft brown hair spread around her. During the day she kept her hair pulled back and covered so he didn't see much of it, but now it lay about her like a soft, shining cloud.

"Why are you looking at me like that? You're

ashamed of me, aren't you? I *have* been a nuisance to you, haven't I? Ever since I met you I have been horrible."

"Yes," he said, reaching out to touch her hair. "Truly horrible. Before I met you my life was so calm and sensible, but now nothing is sane or logical."

"Are you teasing me?"

He gave her a little smile. "Of course not," he said as he leaned toward a table and picked up a bowl and spoon. "The landlady made you some soup, and I want you to eat it." Carefully, he brought a spoonful to her lips.

Whereupon Axia burst into laughter. "Oh, Jamie, I'm not an invalid." She was not going to allow him to see her embarrassment, for truthfully, no one had ever found it necessary to wait on Axia. She prided herself on never having been sick a day in her life, and it was she who nursed others, not the other way around.

"All right," Jamie said, setting the bowl down. "You are healthy and well, so I will go to my own breakfast. I bid you good morning."

She could tell by his voice that she had hurt his feelings, but she'd not meant to. Throwing back the covers, she leaped from the bed, then put her hand to her forehead and began to sway on her feet. "Oh, I think . . ."

When Jamie did not run to her rescue, she opened her eyes and saw he was smirking at her.

"Go on," he said. "You may finish your faint. The bed is behind you."

She laughed. "Oh, Jamie, I am starved. I do not want thin soup. I want beef and a couple of chickens and a great huge pudding. And——" She broke off as the images of that afternoon suddenly came back to her, and she sat down hard on the bed. "You killed them," she whispered.

Sitting beside her, Jamie put his arm companionably about her shoulders. "It was the only way. I had to do it. I never like killing anyone."

Turning her head, she looked at him. "I did not think you were capable of such a thing. You are so very nice."

"I am what?"

"You are very kind to everyone, such as Tode and Frances and your men. Everyone likes you."

Jamie was smiling at her as he stood up. "But you knew I was a soldier, did you not?"

"Yes, but I thought you sat on a horse in pretty clothes and——" Jamie was laughing too loudly for her to continue.

"Get dressed and I'll go see what the kitchen has to offer in the way of breaking our fast," he said, still laughing as he turned to leave.

Rising, Axia caught his arm. "I have never had anyone take care of me before," she said softly. "But you do. You see that I have hot water for a bath; you make sure I have paper for my drawings; you take care of Tode; you save me from bandits." In a very natural gesture, she stood on tiptoe and put her arms around him. "Oh, Jamie, I——"

"Axia, please do not say it," he said, and there was pain in his voice. "Please, I could not bear it. You do not know what is in my heart, the fight I have between duty and——and love. I must remember my obligations to others. Please," he said again, then firmly took her by the shoulders and held her away from him. "Get dressed and come downstairs. I will be waiting for you there."

With that he was gone. For a moment Axia felt bereft, but then she smiled as she leaned back against the door. It seemed that in the last weeks her mind had come to be filled with nothing but thoughts of Jamie.

Her dreaminess lasted only moments before she looked about the room and saw that Jamie had put clothes for her across the back of a chair. A dress of deep red wool with black embroidery all along the hem and up the front.

Dressing as quickly as she could, she flew down the steps and out the back toward the privy and nearly ran into Jamie where he was ransacking the great packs on his saddle.

"Couldn't bear to be parted from me, eh?" he teased.

"Actually, you are on the path to the . . ."

Chuckling, he stepped aside. "There is partridge for supper."

"Save me a dozen," she called and closed the door. Moments later, when she emerged, she saw Jamie still taking things out, putting things back, so she went to stand by him.

When something dropped to the ground, without thinking, she stooped to pick it up. "My cap!" she exclaimed. "My mother's cap! Wherever did you find it? I lost it in—" Suddenly, she remembered where she had left it: in Jamie's tent the night they made love. Cutting herself off, she looked at him, hoping that he would not remember where the cap had come from.

But it was obvious from his face that he did remember, and she did not like what she saw, for Jamie's face was a mixture of rage and—and, well, maybe murder. "Do not look at me so," she whispered as she held the cap behind her and began to back up.

"So, Axia," he said, and she did not like the tone of his voice. It was as though he were trying to control himself from doing something awful to her. "What were you playing at? Did you want to taste what it was like to go to bed with a man just as you taste one cake after another?"

"I did not mean it to happen," she said. "Truly I did not. I saw where you came over the wall, and I thought I'd—"

"You did not think. You tricked me and lied to me, just as you lied about your dragon cloth."

"I did not lie to you. I told you I was a virgin." He was still advancing on her, and she was still backing up.

"You said your name was Diana and that you had smallpox scars."

"I was afraid you would beat me if you found me in your tent; it was the only thing I knew to do." She tried to put as much reason as she could in her voice.

"You do not believe that lie. I gave you time and opportunity to tell me who you were."

Axia was now up against the stable and could go no further. "I did not mean to trick you. I—I . . ."

"Yes? I am waiting for your answer."

Axia put her chin up. "Seize the day," she said defiantly. "I was there, you were there, and there was opportunity for a new experience, so I took the chance. Perhaps I will die tomorrow or my father will lock me away and I'll never have such an opportunity again, so I took it."

"Your father is dead, remember? Dissolved in lime, according to you, but then you lie so often I cannot tell what is the truth."

Abruptly, he turned away and put his hand over his eyes, as though he were thinking about what to do.

Axia had seen how he worried about people under his charge, and she knew that his honor was everything to him. "I am sorry, really I am," she said softly, then put her hand on his arm. "We shall forget about it. I already have. If it hadn't been for the cap, you would never have known. You can go ahead and marry your heiress and—"

When Jamie looked up, his eyes were different. Without a word to her, he started toward the stables, Axia close on his heels. "Jamie?" she said, for she could tell by his expression that they were nowhere near the end of the matter. "Jamie, please say something. Tell me you don't hate me. Or maybe you do, but I swear to you that it was all just a mistake."

"Saddle that horse," he said to a boy walking about the yard, rubbing sleep from his eyes. "And be quick about it."

Axia saw that the horse he was having saddled was hers. "You are sending me away? Alone?" she gasped. "Oh, Jamie . . ." She sat down heavily on a wooden box covered with dirty bridles.

For a moment, Jamie glared at her. "What have I ever done to make you think that I am the kind of man to leave you alone and unprotected?" He didn't wait for her answer but went to his own horse, threw a saddle over it, and led the animal from the stall.

"Are you ready?" he asked, holding his cupped hands for her to mount her horse.

"I—I guess so," she said with resignation. She wanted to know where they were going, but she was much too frightened to ask. Better just to follow and leave her destiny unknown for as long as possible.

Thirty minutes later, Jamie reined into the pretty front garden of a lovely white cottage and told her to wait for him. Minutes later he returned and said, "Follow me."

She could only nod as she saw a clergyman leave the house and start up a hill toward a big stone church that stood at the top. *Oh,* she thought, *he's going to make me pray for forgiveness for all my many sins.* Her next thought was, *If I do that, we'll be here all night, and I'll never get anything to eat.*

At the church door, Jamie paused and looked at her, then removed a twig from her collar, smoothed her hair into place, straightened her little hood. "Are you ready?"

"Ready for *what?*" she burst out, very close to tears.

"Why to marry me, of course. What else can we do?" With that he turned on his heel and started into the church.

But Axia did not follow him. Instead, she collapsed onto one of the benches that ran on either side of the little porch over the church door. Moments later, Jamie came to sit beside her and took her cold hand in his.

"Horrified at the idea of marrying me, are you? I can understand that."

"Jamie, do not joke," she said in barely more than a whisper. "You must know that I cannot marry you."

"Axia, the only thing that would prevent our marriage is if you truly did hate me, and I don't think you do. Do you?"

She looked up at him, thinking of all the time she had spent with him, how he had changed her life. Maybe she'd fallen in love with him that first day. Maybe she had lied about being the Maidenhall heiress because she wanted him but desperately needed to know that he wanted *her* and not her father's money. And just maybe love for him had been the motive behind everything she'd said and done since she met him.

"No, I do not hate you," she said, looking into his eyes, and he smiled at her in such a way that she thought she might possibly melt into the bench and puddle on the stone floor.

"Nor do I hate you, so let us go. The vicar wants his breakfast and so do we. Let us not hesitate," he urged as he stood up.

Still holding her hand, he pulled, but Axia did not move, so Jamie sat back down. "Do you not *want* to marry me? You have said yes to half the men of England, but perhaps I am the only one you do not want to marry."

"It is not that, it is—Oh, Jamie, it is money."

"I see," he said stiffly. "I am not rich enough for you. Ah, then of course we will not marry. How presumptuous of me to assume."

When he started to get up, she flung herself on him, her arms about his shoulders, her cheek against his chest. "It is not that you don't have any money, it is that *I* do not. When my—my guardian knows that I have married without his permission, he will disinherit me. I will be penniless."

"You do not know that for sure," he said, putting his arm around her shoulders, holding her tightly. "If you were his daughter, I could understand your fears, but you are just his ward. I do not think his judgment will be so harsh as all that."

She pulled away to look at him. "If I were his daughter, would you still want to marry me?" she whispered.

"I would want his permission, but yes, with or without his permission, I would be forced to marry you—under the circumstances."

"You mean . . . ?"

"Yes, dear almost-wife, that night in the tent."

That did not make her feel better, for Jamie was admitting that he was marrying her because she had tricked him into making love to her. And he'd marry any woman who tricked him, and love or feeling made no difference. Obviously, his honor meant more to him than money.

"What else?" Jamie asked. "Tell me what else is on your mind."

"You do not know Perkin Maidenhall as I do. Money gives power, and if he wants it, he has all the power on earth. He will have the marriage annulled, then he will bankrupt you for having dared touch what is his."

"For all that Maidenhall is rich, there are laws in the land. Axia, you have been locked away most of your life, and your major contact has been with him and people who work for him. He is a rich man but not as powerful as you think. He cannot annul the marriage without a reason. And perhaps by the time he learns of us, you will be pregnant and that will hinder him."

"A baby?"

At her look of disbelief, he laughed. "It has been known to happen. Now, what else?"

"He will hurt you and your family when he takes away all that you own."

"There's not enough to hurt. If he takes away everything, it will be nothing."

"Oh, Jamie," she said, putting her head in her hands. "How will you live?"

"We," he said, emphasizing the word, "will live with my relatives. The Montgomerys are a nice lot, sometimes rather noisy, but they have much money and more houses and castles than they know what to do with, so I'll ask them to give me one or two."

"For me. You are forced to do this for me. Because I sneaked into your tent one night, you must give up your own lands and estates and go begging on your knees to your relatives for charity."

Jamie smiled at her. "It is not as bad as that," he said, although it was exactly the way he saw it too. "It is not as though my relatives earned the land they have. They conquered no countries and so were not given estates as rewards, but they married rich women. It is a talent my family has for marrying into money."

"Except you," she said. "You planned to marry some pockmarked girl you tumbled with in a tent."

"Yes," he said, looking at her face, touching her cheek. "I have been haunted by that girl since that night. Do you know that I carried that cap over my heart for days? I had it the morning you attacked me, remember?"

"Which time?" she asked seriously.

He chuckled. "The morning after I spent the night with Diana. When I awoke and she wasn't there, I was furious. I turned the place upside down. I thought she was but a girl destined to be a prostitute, but there was something unique about her. I found the cap, wrote a message to my family, and left money for her. And later, I had the cap next to my heart, looking at maps, and for some reason you attacked me."

"You said I couldn't go with you."

"Ah, yes, that was it. I remember now." He caressed her cheek and down her neck. "How different my life would have been if I had left you behind."

"Oh yes! Yes! Yes! Yes! If you had not taken me, you wouldn't be forced into marriage with me now."

"Axia, I am not being *forced* into marriage with you. No one is making me do this. See? No one holds a sword on me. Axia, please listen to me. I *want* to marry you. I want to. Do you understand that?"

Truthfully, it was difficult for Axia to believe that anyone wanted her. All her life she'd been surrounded by people who were paid to be near her. Not one person had been her friend because he wanted to be. And now Jamie was marrying her because she'd given him her virginity and he felt that he had to. His honor was so important to him that he'd give up all hopes of an heiress wife—which of course Axia would be no longer after her father heard of how she'd disobeyed him. Would Jamie hate her when he found out that she used to be the Maidenhall heiress?

Putting his fingertips under her chin, Jamie made her look up at him. "Where is your 'Seize the day'?"

"That motto is what got me into this mess in the first place," she said in disgust.

He laughed. "True, but I am glad of it. So, let us continue to live our lives day by day. We marry now, and if your guardian finds some way to annul it later, so be it." Inside, Jamie thought, *My death will be the only way this marriage will be annulled,* but he didn't say so, for he could see that Axia was very frightened of something. "In the meantime, we will enjoy each other as much as we can." His voice lowered. "Or perhaps I am mistaken, and you did not like making love with me."

"Oh, Jamie," she said, wide-eyed, "but I did. Oh I liked it ever so much. I like kissing and touching, and your body is very nice when you are naked, and I like—"

He gave her a soft kiss to shut her up. "It will be difficult enough to wait until the service is done, but do not make it more difficult. Listen, if we marry now, we can spend the night in the same bed together. If we do not marry, *you* will have to sleep on the floor tonight."

As she looked up at him, her reason warred with her emotions. She should *not* marry him. She knew that. Without any doubt in the world, she knew that her father would annul the marriage even if Jamie's baby was kicking inside her. Perkin Maidenhall was a law unto himself. But, truthfully, she didn't think he would hurt Jamie and his family, not if she went docilely and did what he wanted her to, which was to marry a man who had paid for her. But in the meantime, before her father found out what she'd done, she would have these days, maybe even weeks, when she would be Jamie's wife.

His wife! she thought, and a thrill went through her. She took a deep breath. "I hate sleeping on the floor."

At that Jamie gave a one-sided grin. "Come on then, the vicar is waiting." Standing, he held out his hand to her, and she put her small one into his. He clasped it tightly, and together they walked into the church.

Chapter 23

Smiling, Jamie watched Axia scurry about the chamber, straightening his clothes, making order out of chaos. Wherever she went, he thought, she seemed to think she had to buy her way into people's hearts. Not with money, but with deeds, kindnesses, and help. She never seemed to believe that anyone was going to like her for herself. It was almost as though she felt she had to compensate for something that was wrong with her.

But now, watching her, he knew that nothing in the world was wrong with her. With every movement she made, her hips moved, and he could see the outline of her breasts.

"Come here," he said huskily.

"But, Jamie, I need to get this mud off your clothes, and I need—"

"Here. Now."

After their hasty marriage, they had returned to the inn only long enough to pick up their belongings and a cooked chicken, which Jamie had torn in half, and they'd eaten as they rode. Now, hours later, as the sun was setting, they stopped at another inn, where Axia had gone into the kitchen to see to their dinner. Jamie had not been surprised when, moments later, the landlord had firmly escorted her out of his kitchen, for Axia had told him ways of better management, none of which he appreciated. "Keep her with you," the landlord had said with a jaw firmly set.

"Gladly," Jamie had replied as he pulled Axia onto the bench beside him.

"He is losing money through mismanagement," she muttered, but Jamie only laughed and kissed her forehead. He truly loved that she was taking care of him in the way he had seen her do for others.

So now, alone in their bedchamber, he pulled back the covers of the bed and held out his hand to her. Under the concealing covers, he wore not a stitch of clothing, and while he was undressing, Axia had turned her face away, blushing prettily at the sudden intimacy between them.

Hesitating, Axia looked at his outstretched hand.

"Come on, imp," he coaxed. "Afraid of me? You've scarred me, burned me, cursed me. I am the same now as I was then."

As always, Axia never did anything halfway, so she ran to him, flinging herself on him. "Oh, Jamie, I am so very frightened. I do not know how to be a wife. Even a temporary one. You have known so many women, and every one of them has been in love with you. Heavens, but how can I compete with French women and ladies of the court? I am only a merchant's daughter, nothing more. I think this will be an impossible task."

All the time she had been speaking, Jamie had been expertly removing her clothing, which wasn't easy since she was cuddled into a ball in his arms. But he managed. And with each bit of skin he exposed, he kissed it.

Axia stopped talking. "Oh, but that is nice, Jamie. You kiss so very well. Have you had a lot of practice?"

He smiled, for all women asked about his other women, always wanting to know that they were special or at least different. "None," he answered. "I am new at this, so if I make errors, you will have to tell me."

"You are a liar," she said happily, her eyes closed as his mouth moved down her arm.

"I learned how to lie from my wife."

When Axia giggled, Jamie smiled as he pushed her to her back and pulled more clothing off of her, flinging it about the room.

Then Axia didn't think anymore as Jamie's lips were on her body, his hands seeming to be everywhere as he caressed her and touched her.

"Show me how to please you," she whispered.

"You please me all the time, but you do not know it," he answered, his lips on her neck.

He knew that she thought he knew everything about being in bed with a woman, but the truth was, he'd never spent more than one night with any woman. He'd never wanted the complications or entanglements that frequent lovemaking invariably caused. And never had extremely experienced women appealed to him. So perhaps what he'd told Axia about being new at this was true. Other men would have laughed at him, but as his sister Berengaria often said of him, he was a true romantic, and maybe he had been saving himself for the woman he loved.

For sure, he knew that he'd never had the time to enjoy a woman as he was now enjoying his lovely Axia. He wanted to touch all of her body, to get to know it as he knew his own, and as he ran his hands over her from her scalp to her toes, he liked to think that no one else had ever touched her but him. He even liked that she had grown up isolated, few men having seen her, and his possessiveness surprised him, as it was a new emotion to him.

Now, on their wedding night, the first time he made love to her, he was too fast, but then he'd wanted her too much to allow any hesitation. So the second time, he took his leisure, toying with her breasts until she was arching under his body in a most provocative way. But he continued feeling her passion build, enjoying giving her pleasure, and when she began to give little biting kisses on his neck, he turned onto his back and pulled her on top of him.

"Oh, Jamie, aren't you clever," she murmured, her eyes closed as she instinctively moved up and down on him, and he thought he might perish from pleasure when her hips met his. Helping her with his arms, she moved fast and hard against him, until he threw her to her back and came inside her with a violent explosion that felt as though part of him died.

Collapsing against her, his sweaty body limp, she hugged him with glee. "I like this very much. Jamie, you haven't fallen asleep, have you?"

Laughing, he turned his head to kiss her. "We shall see who begs for sleep," he said as he put his hand on her stomach.

Yawning, Axia tried to mount her horse, but her eyes were so blurred from lack of sleep that she couldn't quite focus on the stirrup. After she'd missed it three times, Jamie shoved her foot into it, then put his hands under her seat and pushed her up into the saddle. She was still yawning when he handed her the reins.

Turning away, he couldn't help smiling. As a soldier he was used to fighting for days with no sleep, but Axia was accustomed to regular hours and sleep every night. But for two nights now he'd made sure she had no sleep at all.

And he had enjoyed every minute of their nights. For all that she was tired all day, even falling asleep during supper once, when they closed the door to their chamber, she was as wide awake as he was. Their clothes were off within seconds, and they ran at each other with arms open.

Jamie was delighted to find that Axia was anxious to try anything that he could devise, and as her body was as flexible as a willow wand, he rejoiced in figuring out new ways to make love. They twined their bodies about each other as though they were two snakes, twisting and turning, but above all, never letting go one of the other.

Somewhere about dawn, they'd fall asleep in each other's arms, but the sun and the noise of the inn would wake them. With great reluctance, they would pull out of each other's arms, dress, and go down to breakfast.

On the morning after their first night together, he had awakened to find an empty place beside him, and after his first moments of panic, he saw Axia curled up asleep on the only chair in the room. Beside her a candle sputtered, burned down to a nub, and all around her were pieces of paper covered with drawings. Curious, Jamie quietly got out of bed and held the sketches up, one by one, to the early morning light just coming through the window. All of the drawings were of him, but Axia had portrayed him as a man greater than life. He was atop his horse, controlling it as it reared dangerously. There were many pictures of him fighting the bandits, leaning over to draw the dagger in his boot, then she'd caught the knife flying through the air toward a leering criminal. There was Jamie thrusting his sword through the man; Jamie lifting Axia as she swooned in his arms; Jamie as he put his body between Axia and danger.

At first incredulous, then smiling and feeling bigger and stronger, braver and wiser than he ever had before, Jamie carefully stacked the drawings, then gently picked up Axia and carried her back to bed. And as he fell back asleep, he thought that she was right about one thing: he would give up his life to protect her.

But now Jamie knew that their "honeymoon" was nearly over. Today they would reach his home, and they would no longer be alone. As much as he loved his family, Jamie did not want to give up having Axia to himself. Even knowing it was the sin of jealousy, he still didn't want to share her.

Now, riding slowly, he glanced back at her, and when he saw that she was half asleep in the saddle, he smiled. In the last days she had called a truce with the horse she rode. As with everyone and everything she considered under her care, she asked Jamie after its welfare, making sure the animal was fed and watered, but she was not going to give the animal any love. And, he had to admit, she was never going to make a great horsewoman. At the slightest bump, she let go of the reins and grabbed the saddle, and if he increased the pace above a walk, she flung her arms about the horse's neck and held on with her eyes closed.

Bending, he caught the reins of her horse, and Axia was so hard asleep that she didn't awaken when they slipped from her hands. To his left was a field covered in daisies, and he knew that this land and all that they had passed for hours belonged to his Montgomery cousins. A narrow dirt path, barely wide enough for a horse, led through the field and up a hill to a beautiful glade where some Montgomery ancestor had built a tiny stone house. The roof was gone now, and one of the walls had fallen down, but when they were children, Berengaria had said it was the most romantic spot in all the world. Right now Jamie could not think of a better place to take his bride.

Axia did not awaken as he led her horse down the little path and up the hill. And she remained asleep when he halted the animals and pulled her down into his arms, carrying her into the shade of the ruins, where he sat with her cradled in his arms.

Jamie had slept in rain and with cannons going off near his head, so a small wife in his arms and a stone wall to his back did not hinder him from sleeping now. Snuggling Axia to him, he was asleep in an instant.

When he awoke, it was nearly sundown and growing cooler by the minute, so he held Axia closer to him, allowing her to continue sleeping as he looked out over the daisies.

"Still think I was trying to kill Frances by smothering her with daisies?" she murmured.

"I thought you were asleep."

"Yes and no. Jamie, these last days have been the happiest of my life. You are so good to me. Do you think your family will like me?"

"They will love you," he said with confidence.

"They won't be disappointed about the money? That I'm not an heiress?" *Or no longer an heiress,* she thought but refused to allow herself to think of that.

Jamie smiled. "They will love you as you are."

She kept her head against his shoulder, wanting to stay there with him forever. But Jamie had to ruin it.

"What is it that you hide from me?" he asked softly.

"N—nothing," she said, unprepared for the question. When she felt a change in Jamie's body, she could have cried for it.

"There is something that you and Frances and Tode know that I do not. I can feel it. I have seen the three of you exchange looks; I have seen the way Frances has threatened you."

"Threatened me? Whatever could you mean?"

At that Jamie nearly dumped her from his lap, but she clung to him. "Please do not be angry with me. Please, I beg you, Jamie. I love you. I love you very much. I told you so even when you thought I was Diana."

He was sitting beside her, but his body was half turned from hers. "Always, even from the beginning, you have lied to me. I did not know who you were that night in the tent, but I knew that you were unique, unlike anyone I had ever met before. Perhaps I should have figured out who you were because both Diana and you are—"

"Are what?" she whispered, suddenly acutely aware that he had never told her that he loved her.

"Close to me," he said. "I do not know how to describe it. I have felt close to you since I met you, as though you were mine. To answer your question, no, I do not think you tried to kill Frances. I did not think so then. Yes, yes, I know that I said so, but truthfully, I felt betrayed by you."

Turning, he put his hands on her arms, looked into her eyes, and continued. "You have no idea how I have felt about you from the moment I saw you. I sneaked over the wall and ran through the garden to the hedges, and for a long while, I stood there watching you paint. You were so very good at it, I was amazed. I must have watched you for an hour as you took a person's face and made it appear on canvas. Every movement you made was so quick and sure and so very perfect."

She was astonished, as she'd had no idea he'd watched her that day.

Moving one hand, he caressed her cheek. "I do not know how to describe how I felt about you, but I sensed that I had met a woman I could live with. Not just marry or even love, but a woman I could share my life with. I thought, This woman would understand if I told her about my father and brother, about my mother, about Berengaria, even about Joby. I felt I could talk to you about anything, and I had never felt that way about any other woman before. Nor about any man. I have never felt that I could . . ."

He looked deep into her eyes. "I have never felt that I could fully trust someone before, not Rhys nor Thomas, nor any of my family. I tell them only half-truths, only what I want them to know. But as I stood there watching you, I knew that there was something so sensible about you that I could trust you."

"You can trust me, Jamie," she whispered. "I would die before I betrayed you."

"Betrayed. That is what I felt that day when you lied to me about the daisies."

"I did not know—" she started in protest, but he cut her off.

"I know you did not. I knew then that you had not tried to kill anyone, but I felt so betrayed by you. I had cared about you so much, but you—"

Dropping his hands from her, he turned his face away. "And that is how I feel now." He looked back at her. "Axia, you are betraying me."

"I have never touched another man! You are the only one."

"Do not try to misunderstand me!" he said with anger, glaring at her. "What is the secret you are hiding from me?"

"I . . ." She wanted to tell him the truth, but if she did, she knew that the few days they had together would be shortened. He would be very angry with her, for it was not a small secret that she had, but a huge one, a great, enormous secret that the moment it was out of her mouth would change their lives. If she were to tell him that she was (or used to be) the Maidenhall heiress, no doubt he would toss her onto that hated horse, and they'd run galloping away to try to find her father. Would Jamie apologize to her father for being so presumptuous as to marry his daughter without permission?

"I can see that you have no intention of telling me what it is that you withhold from me."

"It is nothing, Jamie. Just childish secrets that mean nothing to—"

She stopped because Jamie had risen and gone to his horse. Following him, she clutched his arm. "Can you not accept me for what I am?"

"Do you mean accept you for the liar that you are?"

"No, of course not. I mean—" She halted when she saw his face, then drew herself up. "I am no more or less than what I am, and I have never meant you nor anyone else any harm. I ask you to accept me as who I am, nothing more."

"And I ask you to trust me." Turning, his eyes were pleading. "Axia, please tell me what it is that is between us. I feel it in you all the time. You live each day as though it is your last. Why? What fate awaits you? Are you ill? Is death imminent? I cannot believe that, as I have come to know your body well and I can find no symptoms. You always refer to our marriage as temporary, but I cannot see that your guardian will object to the daughter of a poor merchant marrying a peer of the realm."

Again, he clutched her upper arms. "Axia, please tell me what haunts you so. What makes you so afraid?"

"I cannot tell you," she said. "Please, I cannot. All I want is now, today. Nothing more. It will end soon enough, so do not make it end sooner. Please."

Releasing her arms, Jamie ran his hands over his

eyes. "All right, have it your way. Do not tell me; do not trust me."

"I *do* trust you," she said, trying to take his arm, but he moved away from her.

"Mount your horse. We will be at my home soon."

Axia could have cried at the coolness in his voice. Turning, she mounted her horse for the first time without Jamie's help.

Chapter 24

As she rode, knowing that her time alone with Jamie was nearing an end, she debated whether she should tell him the truth or not. Perhaps he would forgive her, perhaps . . .

In the early evening they stopped by the side of the road to rest, and she could see that Jamie was still angry at her, for he would hardly look at her as he handed her bread and cheese and a pouch of wine. She searched for something to talk about.

"You did not tell me of the Maidenhall wagons," she said, then could have bitten off her tongue for mentioning the name. But to her pleasure, Jamie smiled.

"You should have seen Smith; he made the ugliest female you could imagine."

"I am sorry I missed that." She looked at him

through her lashes. "Especially since, in truth, the heiress is so very beautiful."

Jamie didn't seem to hear her. "Smith's hands hung below his gown, you could take shelter from the rain under his nose, yet he showed me a box full of marriage proposals and letters declaring love. And he told unbelievable stories of what had happened to him."

The cheese and bread stuck in Axia's throat. If Jamie had not insisted on secrecy, these things would have happened to her. She didn't want to know, but like a child at the circus, she had to peek. "W–what happened?"

"Marriage proposals by the hundreds, letters begging money, pleas for favors. A woman was convinced the heiress could heal by the laying on of hands, so she followed the caravan for three days while holding her sick child in her arms."

"What did Smith do?" Axia whispered when she saw Jamie frown.

"Smith gave in and held the child for half an hour, but later . . ." He trailed off and looked at her, then quickly away. "Later the child died and the woman cursed Smith and spit on him. She said it was his lack of generosity that had killed her child, that the Maidenhall heiress had so much but would part with nothing, not even to save a child's life."

"That makes no sense. Because she has money does not mean she has any special powers." Axia knew that all too well.

"Exactly." Turning, he gave her a small smile. "Which is why I am glad I did not marry the Maidenhall heiress."

"You are?"

"I know you worry that I wanted the heiress, but it was all the idea of my family. I do not want to spend the rest of my life known as the man who married the Maidenhall heiress. Too much responsibility and too much speculation goes with such a marriage." He smiled broader. "So see, I would much rather marry you than the heiress."

Axia gulped. "But you might change your mind if the letter from Maidenhall gives his permission for you to marry his daughter. Then you will regret that you married *me.*"

To Axia's consternation, Jamie threw back his head and laughed at that. Opening the leather bag on his horse, he pulled out a folded piece of paper. "I never sent the letter."

Axia nearly choked. "The letter to Perkin Maidenhall? You never sent it? But Frances said—"

Bending, he kissed her cheek. "Frances is not too clever, is she? When she insisted that I send the letter to her father through her, I was suspicious, so I told her that I had sent it so I could see her reaction. As I feared, she was horrified. I do not think she ever had any intention of marrying me. It is my guess that she said she wanted to in an attempt to make you jealous. What do you think?"

Axia threw her arms around Jamie's neck. "I do not care a fig what Frances wanted to do. Oh, Jamie, do you know what this means? It means we have more time. More time!! What money cannot buy. Oh, Jamie, I love you so much."

Jamie was not sure why a letter not sent should cause her such happiness, but if it caused this reaction, he was glad for it. He was still hurt by her refusal to tell him what great secret plagued her, but he knew that only time could make her trust him.

But one minute he was thinking logical thoughts and kissing her, and the next he was thinking nothing at all and kissing her harder. There were tall hedges by the road so he dragged her into them as though he were a thief after her jewels—which maybe he was.

It amazed him that his passion for her seemed to grow, and now he felt as though he must have her or he would die. And she seemed to feel the same about him. They came together in a flurry of hurriedly thrown aside clothes and searching hands and mouths, rolling about under a hedge of blackthorn trees, clasping at each other, desperate in their attempts to get closer.

Within minutes their passion was spent, and he collapsed on top of her, sweaty and limp. But Axia was wide awake as she caressed his hair, touched his neck, and thought how much she loved him—and how happy she was. If her father had not been sent a letter, then he was not now leading an army to find her and take her away from Jamie.

"Whatever happens, Jamie, remember that I love you," she whispered. "I love you with all my heart. Even if—"

"If what?" he asked, turning to face her.

Smiling, she tried to sound as though she were making a joke. "Even if I am married to another."

But Jamie did not smile. "You belong to me and no one else. I have worked hard for you and you are *mine.*"

"Yes, I am yours no matter what happens."

He waited, hoping she would say more, but she did not. Again frustrated by her silence, by her lack of trust in him, he moved away and told her they must go, that soon they would reach his house.

Axia wanted to make him forget about her secrets. He would find out what they were soon enough. As he helped her onto her horse, she said, "Tell me of your family. I know your sister is your twin, so is she as ugly as you are?"

Jamie smiled. "I do not know how it happened but Berengaria is beautiful, and even though she is bl—" Breaking off, he had his hand on his saddle, about to mount, when he looked at her. Thinking of her love for Tode, he knew that he need have no fear that she would think Berengaria or Joby or his mother with her drifting mind would be anything out of the ordinary. Axia judged people by what was inside them, not what was on the surface.

Thinking this, when he smiled at her, there was love in his eyes.

"Do you think they will like me?" she asked again. "They will not be disappointed that you have wasted yourself on a poor merchant's daughter?"

"No, of course not," Jamie said with utter confidence. "I have sent a messenger on ahead, and they are planning a wonderful welcome for you. You will see. In days they will love you." With that, he reined his horse ahead of her to lead the way.

Behind him, Axia was not so sure. She'd already figured out that Jamie was as romantic as she was practical. If she were in his family's place, she was not so sure she'd be thrilled that her brother had passed up an opportunity to marry a great heiress and instead returned home with the penniless daughter of a merchant. But then maybe they were romantic like Jamie and loved love.

Axia was not prepared for the poverty of Jamie's estate. It was a run-down old castle, probably reeking with history, but it would have been better off with less history and a new roof. With her merchant's eye, she appraised that it would take a great deal of money to restore it, so much in fact that it would be better to build a new building, something modern and sanitary, and leave this monster to the history books. She couldn't imagine how cold the place must be in the winter.

Moving her horse near his, she asked about what land he had, then was appalled to hear that there were no more than about five acres, not even enough for a good crop. Perhaps a productive orchard could be laid out, she thought. If they had a good year, she might be able to make cider and sell it and—She sighed. No use planning, for she wouldn't be here, she reminded herself. By the end of the summer she would be somewhere else, probably someone else's wife; she'd be whatever and wherever her father wanted her to be.

"Is it so bad?" Jamie asked, watching her face, and she could see that he very much wanted her to like his home.

"No," she said, forcing a smile. "It is not bad at all."

"Are you getting worse at lying or am I getting better at detecting them?"

She laughed. "I think I can do something with it," she said, appraising the crumbling stone work.

At that Jamie let out a laugh, then leaned over and kissed her cheek. "I have no doubt that you will, my little wife. I fully expect that this time next year you will have found some way to make the place worth three times what it is now."

"Ah, then, that should earn me at least a copper," she muttered, making Jamie laugh again.

"My sisters will love you," he said.

"And what of your mother?"

"She, ah, I meant to tell you about her. She is, ah, well . . ." But Jamie didn't have to find the words to tell Axia that his mother had the mentality of a child and that with each day her mind was slipping further away because just then an arrow came zinging through the air. Landing a yard from Jamie's feet, it made his horse rear. Even as his horse's feet were high off the ground, he saw that Axia's was frightened, so in one motion, he leaned over and grabbed her bridle, bringing both horses under control at the same time. Then, as he looked at her face, he grinned. "Will that earn more drawings of me?"

"Oh yes, Jamie, yes," she said breathlessly.

Laughing, he dismounted and pulled the arrow out of the ground, unwrapping the message that was tied to it. As he suspected, it was from Oliver and what was written made him frown, but he would not tell Axia what the note said.

"He has not hurt Frances, has he?" she said in fear as he helped her dismount.

"No, but—" He cut off, still frowning, refusing to say more. "I must go. Now. I am sorry, but you must go to my sisters without me. I will come later."

"Yes, of course," she said, wanting to feel brave and adult, but the thought of meeting his sisters alone terrified her.

"Come, do not look so frightened. They will love you. I will return in a few hours."

"I will go with you and—"

"No!" he said sharply.

"There *is* danger! Something is wrong and you are not telling me."

"No, there has been no harm done," he reassured her, "but I must go now."

"All right," she said at last, then went to her saddle bag, removed a leather pouch, and handed it to him. "Inside are some herbal mixtures for Frances, and you must see that she has them. She has never been able to take care of herself, you know. One mixture is for colds, and one is to be soaked in hot water for a chest plaster if she coughs. The third is a drink she likes if she cannot sleep, and the fourth—"

Smiling, Jamie kissed her, then took the pouch. "I will see to her health, and I will bring her back safely to you. Now go inside and keep safe for my return." With a glance up at the windows and another at the people who were on the road around them, Jamie did not want to show a public display of affection, but when he weighed kissing Axia against the public, there was no contest.

Quickly, fiercely, he pulled Axia into his arms and kissed her hard and long, and when he pulled away, he had to support her for a moment until her legs steadied. "Wait for me," he said, and all she could do was nod. Then he mounted his horse, turned, and went at a gallop down the road, a cloud of dust behind him.

Standing in the road, Axia watched him until there was a sharp bend, then the trees closed around him and she could no longer see him. As soon as she was alone, she knew that for him to leave her alone in a strange place, the message on the arrow must have been very serious. Much more serious than he would allow her to see.

Turning, she looked back at the castle. When she'd been with Jamie, it had seemed a friendly enough place, but now the clouds had blocked the sun and a cold wind had risen. Goose bumps formed on her arms, and looking up at the sky, she thought a storm might be brewing. And as she looked back at the ramshackle old castle, she thought she could feel that another storm might be brewing inside. Maybe she was just being superstitious, but she thought she could feel animosity coming from the inside. Jamie's family wouldn't hate her, would they? No, of course not, she told herself. They couldn't. They had no reason to hate her. No reason at all.

Chapter 25

*J*oby," Berengaria whispered, "we have done a great wrong."

"Do not start on me again," Joby said with barely controlled anger. "I do not like her; I do not trust her."

"You have made that abundantly clear to everyone."

Joby wasn't going to allow Berengaria's soft heart to sway her. She had known what this Axia was like before she ever met her, and in the ten days she had been here, nothing Joby had seen since was going to change her mind. "How can you see the way she has tried to take over this place and still have sympathy for her?"

"Oh, Joby, what has made you so hard? Do you not think this falling down heap of stones could use some

301

management? All she did was roll up her sleeves and try to clean the kitchens."

"It is a matter of rule and power. Surely you must be able to see that."

"As opposed to not being able to see anything else, is that what you mean?"

"Now she has *us* fighting."

"No, *she* has not made us fight, *you* have. Oh, Joby, all of this started with that stupid Henry Oliver. Why ever did I allow you to bring him into this?"

"Someone had to do something. I couldn't very well allow our idiot of a brother to . . ." She trailed off because just what she hoped would not happen had. They had thought to get Oliver to "kidnap" the Maidenhall heiress, and Jamie would follow her, rescue her, and fall in love with her. But Oliver had, as always, done everything wrong. Instead of sending the note Joby had written for him, he came up with his own and had, by accident, sent it flying into poor Rhys's leg. With Oliver's poor eyesight, he had meant to hit the ground in front of Rhys. "Only Henry Oliver is such a bad marksman that he'd miss the *ground,*" Joby had said in disgust when she'd heard about Rhys.

But everything had backfired because for some inexplicable reason, their brother had taken this Axia with him when he went to chase the heiress, and along the way, he had married her. And now stupid Oliver was saying that he would not release the heiress unless Berengaria married him. So Jamie had been there for days trying to talk some sense into Oliver, and Jamie's new wife was here with Joby and Berengaria, doing her best to change everything in their lives.

But yesterday Joby had stopped her, for she had told this Axia how her entrapment of their brother had destroyed their family. Joby told her about the villagers giving up their last pennies, their tiny treasures, to make a wardrobe that would gain the love and admiration of the heiress.

"And he would have married her if it weren't for your interference," Joby had said nastily. "So now we have lost all our chances for any wealth. Do you think being called *Lady* Axia will keep you warm and fed this winter?"

In the face of such venom, Axia had backed away from her, whispering, "I am sorry. Please forgive me." Then she'd turned and fled up the stairs to Jamie's room and closed the door.

Since then she had not shown her face, not even for meals. As far as anyone knew, she had not left her room.

Now Berengaria and Joby were alone in the solar on the second floor, and Berengaria was full of remorse about everything she had allowed Joby to do. They had been in agreement about Axia, that from what they had read in Jamie's letters, this woman was a conniving schemer, but since Axia had arrived, Berengaria had begun to feel differently.

"If I could just see them together," Berengaria said, and they both knew that she meant that if she could be in the presence of Jamie with his new wife, she would know if Jamie really loved her or not. But Joby was convinced that her gorgeous brother could not be head over heels in love with a plain little thing like Axia. Truthfully, Axia was more like a housekeeper than an earl's wife, what with her sorting out the kitchens and going through the flour bins. She was certainly not of the same class as their beautiful brother.

"It is done," Berengaria said, "and we cannot change the fact that Jamie has married her."

"But I want her to see what her conniving and scheming have cost us. She may think she can earn her place here by sorting the beans, but because of her, there will soon be no beans to sort."

"What was that?" Berengaria said, her head tilted to one side, listening to the sounds coming from outside.

"I hear nothing."

"No, listen, there it is again."

Going to the window, Joby looked down into the garden below, and her temper soared as she saw the woman who had wrecked all their plans sitting on a stone bench beside their mother. Their poor, crazy mother.

"There!" Berengaria said. "What was that?"

It took Joby a moment to believe what she was seeing. "That Axia is writing something and showing it to Mother and she is . . . Mother is laughing," she said in disbelief.

"I am going down!" Berengaria said, standing and heading for the door. She was quite familiar with her home and knew the way perfectly.

"Do not let her sway you. Just because she—"

"Close your mouth!" Berengaria snapped as she went out the door, Joby close on her heels.

In the garden they stopped behind a rose trellis where Berengaria knew they wouldn't be seen. "What is she writing? Why did Mother laugh?"

"Wait a minute," Joby said as she ran back into the

castle. A moment later a child from the kitchens came out and asked Axia to return with him. As soon as Axia was out of sight, Joby picked up the pages that Axia had tossed onto the bench. As usual, their mother ignored them. She lived in a world all her own, and no one could pierce it. Not violence, not emotional drama, nothing ever took her from her own world. At least not usually. Not until today.

"What are they?" Berengaria said anxiously.

It took Joby a moment as she looked at the drawings one by one. "They are all pictures of Jamie," she said in a voice of wonder, for she had never seen anything like the drawings. They were so lifelike that she could almost feel the warmth of her brother's skin.

"Yes," Berengaria said impatiently, "but what about them made Mother laugh?"

As Joby looked from one drawing to the other, she could not repress a smile, then she began to describe them to her sister. "They are Jamie as we know him," she said. "In this one he is drawing his sword on some villagers as he "rescues" Axia from greedy-looking merchants. And in this one . . ." She trailed off, smiling.

"Yes! What is it?"

"Jamie is furious as he is looking up at a wagon, and on the side of the wagon is a picture of himself. And he seems to be fighting a lion. In this one Jamie is looking perplexed as two women quarrel with each other. One of the women is Axia, but the other is quite beautiful."

"That must be the heiress," Berengaria said. "What else?"

"Here is Jamie rubbing oil on the deformed legs of

a man, but only his legs are deformed, as the rest of him is large and well shaped. His face is turned to one side so I can only see half of it, but he looks to be quite handsome. And this one is—"

"Is what?" Berengaria encouraged.

Joby lowered her voice. "It is Jamie lying in a field of flowers, daydreaming, and there is a look of . . . I have never seen him look like this."

"Describe it to me!" Berengaria commanded.

"He looks silly, ridiculous actually," she said, but she did not really mean it, for she well knew that it was the look of a man in love.

"Have you spied enough?" Axia asked from behind Joby. "Have you finished laughing at me?"

"I wasn't spying, I was merely . . ."

"Yes?" Axia asked, hands on her hips. When Joby said nothing, she started to gather up her drawings. "You have made it quite clear that you do not want me here, and I will go soon enough. You do not have to worry about that. Now, if you will excuse me, I'll leave you and—"

She broke off because Jamie's mother had put her hands over her face and begun to cry. Immediately, Axia sat down on the bench and put her arm about her mother-in-law's shoulders. "Now look what you have done," she said to Joby, then turned and began to soothe the woman. "Here, I will draw more. Would you like to see Jamie as a dragonslayer?"

Joby and Berengaria were speechless as their mother quieted and grew calm again. They had not seen her cry or show any emotion for years.

As Axia began to draw, she described every stroke she was making as she drew Jamie with his clothes torn and ragged from the exertion of his fight, then she made the dragon with its long tail and fiery breath. It took a moment for Joby to realize that Axia's drawing was for their mother, but the explanation was for Berengaria. And when Joby looked at her sister, she could see Berengaria's face was alive with interest. Joby didn't recognize the emotion for what it was, but jealousy surged through her. Berengaria was hers and hers alone!

"Berengaria can smell the dragon," their mother said, and it was rare to hear her voice, at least in a coherent sentence.

Berengaria laughed. "Yes, I can smell it. It has iridescent green scales that change color in the sunlight. I can smell the char of its breath. And I can smell the sweat of Jamie. He is worried and afraid, but his honor will force him to do what he thinks is right. I can smell his bravery."

Axia stopped drawing and looked at Berengaria. "Can you really smell things? Better than other people?"

Joby spoke before her sister could. "Berengaria is only blind, but she has her other senses intact, better than most people. She is not a freak."

"Neither am I!" Axia shot back in a tone just as nasty.

At this exchange, Berengaria stood stone still in fascination. No one ever told Joby off! For all that Joby was kind and thoughtful to her family, to outsiders she was a terror, and people were afraid of her. But obviously this Axia was not. It was Berengaria's guess that Axia had done a bit of terrorizing herself.

Joby was not put off by this unusual retaliation. "Did you trick my brother into marriage?"

"Yes!" Axia answered immediately. "I put on an

alluring gown and used my fatal beauty to ensnare him. After all, he was such a marvelous catch. Not a penny to his name and three women to support. Of course, there is that beauty of his, and that certainly puts bread on the table. Tell me, how do you people make it through a winter here? I have never seen such mismanagement in a kitchen as in yours. And just look at these fruit trees! They haven't been pruned in ten years, so you'll get half the crop you should have. And look at those flowers. They're a waste of space. Since you have so little land, you should use all of it for what you need. Put beans in there or onions."

It took Joby a moment to catch her breath. "The flowers are for Berengaria. She happens to like them. She has little enough in life, so she can at least have flowers to smell."

"Heavens above, but your sister is merely blind, there is nothing *wrong* with her. She'll like the smell of a good bean porridge this winter more than all the roses in the world this summer."

"How dare you—"

Berengaria's laugh cut her off. "Joby, I think you have met your match. I think—" She cocked her ear, as she could hear someone coming.

With a smug look directed toward Axia to let her know that she understood Berengaria even if she didn't finish her sentences, Joby turned and ran through the gates. Berengaria knew the steps of every person on the estate and when there was a stranger, she was the first to know.

"What a truly horrid child," Axia said the minute Joby was out of sight.

Feeling a bit of a traitor, Berengaria could not help giving a small smile. "I am sorry—"

Axia cut her off as she did not want to hear what she had to say. There was part of her that wanted to tell them the truth of who she was, but she did not want to be hated because she did not have money, then loved because she did—if she hadn't already been disinherited, for surely her father had heard of her defection by now.

Joby was not going to leave her sister alone with the usurper, so she was back in seconds with a message. "It is from Jamie, and he says that he needs to stay longer. Oliver will not release the heiress."

"There was nothing else?" Axia asked, hating herself for lack of pride, but she so wanted to hear from Jamie, and now she wished that he had sent something personal to her. It seemed years ago that they had made love and he had held her in his arms.

"Nothing," Joby said in triumph as she handed the letter to her blind sister.

Watching, Axia saw Berengaria run her hands over the letter. "He is lying," Berengaria said. "Jamie is in danger. He wants us to get help."

"I will send a messenger to the Montgomerys, and they will come to us," Joby began. "And we will—"

Axia was silent as she thought about what had just happened, that Berengaria could feel a piece of paper and know what the writer was feeling when he wrote it. She was nearly faint with the implications of such a talent. "You can tell if someone is lying or not?" she whispered in awe. "Do you know how much *money* you could make with such a knowledge?"

Joby turned on her. "Berengaria is not to exploited! It is disgusting to think of Berengaria sitting in a booth and telling fortunes by holding someone's hand."

"You can do that *too?*" Axia asked, wide-eyed.

For several moments, Berengaria sat silently blinking as Joby, with great disdain, explained that she and Berengaria were not of the merchant class, to earn their living by pedaling themselves.

When she could stand it no more, Berengaria said, "But, Joby, we need money. And we tried to peddle our brother's beauty, so what is the difference?"

Joby turned on her sister in horror, feeling greatly betrayed. "It is not the same at all."

With a deep sigh, Berengaria dropped the issue. She was not going to be caught between Joby and her new sister-in-law, but she had to admit that Axia's words appealed to her. How very much she would like to be useful, to not be the Family Burden.

Chapter 26

Axia was looking from one of her sisters-in-law to the other. In the time she had been there, the youngest, a twelve-year-old daughter of Satan, had done all she could to make Axia's life hell. No matter what Axia did, according to the appropriately named Joby, she did it wrong. Even cleaning up that pigsty they called a kitchen was an act of aggression, according to Joby.

All Axia had been able to think of was Jamie's return. He could straighten his sisters out. But now it looked as though she would be here longer, for they were discussing sending for their illustrious relatives to help Jamie out of whatever problem he had. Meanwhile, Axia thought, Jamie might be in danger. This time he might have been attacked by twenty men, and even he couldn't fight off that many. They could lock him in a dungeon, starve him, beat him.

She had to shake her head to clear it of these horrible thoughts.

And immediately, she thought, *What about Frances?! Who is taking care of Frances? What if she is held captive near daisies?*

Suddenly, Axia's head lifted at the same time as Berengaria's. Someone else was coming, only this time Axia knew that step well. Without a glance to her new family, she picked up her skirts and began to run.

Tode barely reached the gate of the old castle before Axia saw him, and without a care for what the people around them thought, she ran to him, arms open wide. Catching her to him, he hugged her so hard, her feet came off the ground, and she buried her face inside his hood, tears of joy pouring down her face.

"I have missed you. I thought of you every minute," she said.

He was laughing. "Even when you were with your handsome Jamie?"

"Yes, of course," she said, laughing. "For what is a *husband* compared to a friend?"

For just a moment, Tode leaned back and looked at her with a raised eyebrow, and in that moment, she knew that something was different about him. Had her marriage affected him so that he would change toward her? Why was he not laughing at her joke?

"You must be tired," she said. "Come inside, and let me take care of you."

"All right," he answered, taking her arm and leading her, and again she thought that something was different about him. The minute they were inside, she meant to find out everything.

Stopping only long enough to order food and drink for her friend, Axia led him up the steep spiral stairs to the best room of the house, the solar. She could tell by the way he walked that his legs were hurting him very much, and when asked, he told her that today he had walked or been jostled in the back of a wagon for many miles.

When Axia entered the solar, her happiness faded as she saw her two sisters-in-law waiting for her, for now she'd have to share Tode with them. But then she thought how much Tode would like Berengaria, because she could not see what he looked like.

"I want you to meet my sister-in-law. She is blind!" Axia said, and there was much pride in her voice.

Both the beautiful Berengaria and the boy-dressed Joby were staring at Tode with blank stares. Because he was wary of beautiful women, Tode assumed it was Joby who was blind. Throwing back his hood, he smiled at her, then when he saw the look of revulsion cross her face, he instantly pulled the hood back up and looked away.

Axia gave Joby a look of anger, then pulled him toward Berengaria. "No, that is Joby. I want you to meet this one. This is Berengaria," she said, then introduced him.

"Ah," Tode said smoothly, again pushing his hood back, seeming to disregard Joby's stares as he gazed at Berengaria's perfection. "I could not guess that eyes so beautiful could be without sight. But then those of us who can see are allowed to endlessly bathe in your beauty without appearing rude." Reaching forward, he picked up her hand, and for a moment he caressed it. "May I?" he asked softly, then when Berengaria nodded, he kissed the back of her hand almost lovingly.

It would have been difficult to guess who was more

astonished: Axia or Joby. Never in her life had Axia seen Tode act so with another human being. She'd seen him with women, with blind women even, but he had always stayed in the background, never pushing himself forward as he was now. And he knew how to position his body and to turn his head just so, so the scarred side of his face would not show. But now he was standing with his hood back, the mutilated side of his face fully exposed to Joby and herself.

As for Joby, she was more interested in Berengaria's reaction to this deformed man than to his reaction. Berengaria was very shy with strangers; she never liked to be alone with anyone she had not known for years. But here she was, allowing this awful man to kiss her hand! In fact, he was still holding her hand.

It was Joby who recovered from her shock first, going to Tode and Berengaria and physically separating their hands. And Axia was right beside her. In one instant the two of them had gone from being enemies to allies, united in astonishment.

Turning, Tode gave Axia a fond look, an almost fatherly look, as he bent and kissed her cheek, then said, "Ah, the food has arrived. Come, ladies, and sit with me. I will enjoy your company."

Saying that, he easily and naturally slipped his arm around Berengaria's and led her to the table, where the meal was being spread out.

Behind them, in stunned silence, stood Joby and Axia. Axia was in shock because Tode's behavior was so out of character, and Joby could not believe that a man who looked as though he were part of a traveling show was taking over *their* household. Who was this man anyway?

Tode had seated himself at the small table with

Berengaria next to him, leaving the bench on the other side of the table for Joby and Axia. "Come, girls, do you not want to hear my news?"

Girls? Axia thought as she went toward the bench, Joby right beside her.

As soon as they were seated, Tode began to tell his story, but it took Axia a while to hear what he was saying. There was no mistaking that he still looked like her Tode, but his body now seemed to be occupied by the spirit of another. For one thing, he seemed to have taken possession of Berengaria. Only one plate had been set on the table, but Tode, in a natural gesture, had moved it to halfway between himself and Berengaria. As he ate, he placed small bits of food into her hand: succulent pieces of fruit, buttered bread, a morsel of beef on the end of a little silver knife.

It took Joby's explosion to make Axia hear what Tode was saying.

"Jamie!" Joby shouted. "Henry Oliver has put our brother in a dungeon?" At that she drew a dagger from its sheath at her side and stood. But Tode caught her arm.

"Sit!" he commanded, and she did so.

"There is nothing we can do now, at least not in full daylight," Tode said. "I would like a few hours rest, then I will return."

Joby, not liking the way this scarred man had come into their lives as though he owned them, said, "What can *you* do?" with a sneer.

"Joby!" Berengaria said sharply.

From the moment Tode had said that Jamie was in danger, Axia had not been able to breathe, but now she was recovering herself enough that she could whisper. "Tell me everything. I must know it all," she said softly.

"This Henry Oliver is not as stupid as people think. He has a bit of cunning, and he has set his heart on—" Stopping, he looked into Berengaria's lovely face. "On you," he said softly, making Berengaria turn pink with a blush. "I can understand that now."

"What of my brother?" Joby shouted at him.

Unperturbed, Tode started eating again. "Oliver is determined to have her, and he says he will hold Jamie until he agrees to allow him to marry his sister. And he will hold Frances until her father pays a ransom."

At this Tode looked hard at Axia, letting her know that her father had now been notified of the exchange. Joby looked at the dagger still in her hands, because she knew that she was the cause of two people being held prisoner.

Tode continued. "There are underground tunnels leading from Oliver's house to the sea. They are dark and damp, and cells have been carved out of them. Jamie has been held in one of these for days. I tried to get to him, but the guards saw my torch, and I was"— he smiled—"detained."

At this Joby and Axia nodded, but Berengaria drew in her breath. "How did you escape them?"

"I played the fool," he said simply. "I merely had to act idiotically, and they were laughing."

For the other two women this was easy to understand, but Berengaria was puzzled. "How could *you* play the fool?"

As Joby and Axia watched in stunned disbelief, Tode picked up her hands and put them on his face, guiding her fingers to feel the scars of his face, then downward onto his neck.

"My legs are also scarred," he said, looking into her eyes, their noses but inches apart.

"And if you think my sister is going to be allowed to feel *those,* you'd better think again," Joby half snarled.

Blushing again, Berengaria took her hands from Tode's face.

With a smile that Axia had never seen before, Tode turned back to the table and the food.

"We will get the Montgomery cousins here," Joby said. "They will raze that place of Oliver's and hang his fat body from the nearest gibbet. They will—"

"There is no time. I must return tonight and see what I can do."

"Yes, I'm sure *you'll* be a great deal of help," Joby said contemptuously.

Tode did not bother to speak, but the look he gave Joby made her shut up. He let her know that she was a child, and as such, if she wanted to stay with the grown-ups, she had better mind her manners. Neither Axia nor Tode knew it, but it was the same look that Jamie often sent his little sister's way.

"I can come and go freely. No one notices someone who looks like me. I came for just these few hours to explain to you what was wrong."

"What of Frances?" Axia asked. "Is she cared for?"

To Axia's disbelief, she thought that for a moment Tode blushed, but surely, she must have been wrong.

"Frances is all right. She is being held in a stone room at the top of the old tower. She is comfortable but frightened. Oliver tends to her himself and rarely allows anyone in to see her." He gave a bit of a smile. "Except for someone to cheer her up."

Axia reached across the table to take Tode's hand. "Tell me what I can do. I will give my life if it will get Jamie out. Please let me do something."

For a moment, his eyes locked with hers, and Tode saw there what had only been a shadow before. Axia loved Jamie. Loved him as she'd never loved anyone else. For a moment Tode felt jealousy, but then he controlled himself and squeezed her hand in return. "There is nothing you can do. I can get into the tunnels well enough, as the guard lets me pass. It is just getting Jamie out that is difficult. I cannot very well lead him through the Great Hall and out. For all that your Jamie is a great soldier," he said, smiling warmly at Axia, "I do not think he can fight all of Oliver's men."

"What other way is there to get him out?" Axia asked.

"I cannot tell what the tunnels were, but they seem to go on for miles. Whether they are old mines or crypts, I do not know. Nor do I think Oliver knows, or if he did know, he has forgotten. I think they are mayhaps Roman, and some of them have collapsed. Whatever they were, only a mole could find his way through them."

"Or a blind person," Berengaria said softly.

"Not on your life!" Joby shouted. "Jamie would—"

"Quiet!" Tode commanded, then turned to Berengaria, his eyes searching her face. "Yes," he said thoughtfully. "A blind person would have a great advantage in the darkness of those tunnels. The first day I was allowed to see Jamie, so I took a torch and tried to see where the tunnels led, but the guards saw my torch and stopped me. Another day I spent combing the forest near Oliver's, trying to find the exit to the tunnels, but I could find nothing. For all anyone knows, they have no exit."

"But if we could hide Jamie in the tunnels until a rescue comes, it will get him out from under this Oliver's rule," Axia said, her eyes showing her rising fear. When Tode would not meet her eyes, she said, "You are not telling all. I know it! You are holding something back."

"Yes," Berengaria said as she reached for Tode's hand and ran her thumb over the palm. "There is more danger than you are telling us."

"Yesterday morning, Oliver's brother arrived."

When Axia heard the sharp intake of breath from both Joby and Berengaria, she knew there was danger, true danger.

Tode lowered his eyes and his voice. "The brother, Ronald, told Oliver that he was stupid for wanting a poor Montgomery for a wife when he had the Maidenhall heiress locked away in a tower. Since the brother is already married, he is trying to force Frances to marry Oliver. But Jamie has told them that Maidenhall has made him Frances's guardian, and she cannot marry without his permission. But, of course, Jamie will not sign any papers giving Frances to Oliver, so he is being held without food and only enough water to sustain life." Lifting his head, Tode looked at Axia. "He will need a doctor when he gets out."

At that Axia rose from the bench and went to look out the window, not wanting anyone to see into her eyes.

"What has been done to him?" Berengaria whispered.

"Repeated whippings," was Tode's reply. "I was the only one allowed to see him and then only because they did not know that I had ever met him before. For all that has been done to Jamie, he is still making Oliver's brother believe that he has some hold over Perkin Maidenhall, and it is up to Jamie to agree to the marriage."

"So this protects Frances," Axia said softly, turning back to the group at the table. "Whether she marries or not is out of her hands and in Jamie's."

"Yes."

Chapter 27

Drawing the horses to a halt, Tode sat atop the wagon seat with his breath held as he watched the approach of armed men. Because he knew some of them by sight, he knew they were Oliver's men. One disadvantage of looking as he did was that people recognized him and remembered him.

But when the men saw him and started punching each other and grinning, he knew they would not be suspicious. Which was good, because he had three females hidden in the back of the wagon, lying under great mounds of flowers.

"And what do you have here?" one of the men asked, already laughing at the very sight of Tode.

"Flowers for the Maidenhall heiress," Tode said jovially. "What better way to court a woman than with flowers? She will be his by tonight. In marriage or out."

Under the coarse linen that covered the three of them, Axia listened in wonder, as she had never heard this tone in Tode's voice before. By nature, he was a somber man, taking his duties rather too seriously at times. But the man speaking now had a tone in his voice that seemed to expect people to laugh at whatever he said.

And Oliver's men did laugh. "You'd better replant those," one of the men called. "The heiress won't be needing them."

"At least not for marrying poor ol' Henry," another man called.

"Ah, then," Tode said, "I shall use them for my own wedding."

At that the men laughed as though that were the funniest thing they had ever heard. Inside the wagon, Axia felt Berengaria, lying beside her, tense, her hands made into fists at her side.

"Maybe you can marry the heiress," one of the men said. "If you can find her."

"Oh?" Tode asked as though it meant nothing to him. "Has she managed to hide herself, or has her father come to fetch her?"

Only Axia heard the fear in Tode's voice at the mention of Perkin Maidenhall.

"Escaped," one of the men said. "Painted her way out," he said, then shouted with laughter. "If you see her, tell her to find a door and come back inside."

After that the men were laughing too hard to speak anymore, and without a word, they left Tode and his wagon full of flowers alone in the road.

Ten minutes later, Tode had moved the wagon under the dense shade of an oak tree and stepped down to get a drink of water from a little barrel strapped to the side of the wagon.

"Did you hear?" he asked, looking through the great crack in the sideboards at the three pairs of eyes staring at him.

Joby did not wait to give an answer but threw back the covering. When she had agreed to being secreted inside a wagon, she had not thought how horrible it would be. "I will find her," she announced as she leaped over the side.

"You know nothing," Tode said, feeling that this girl was his responsibility until Jamie was freed.

"I know every rabbit hole of this country, and maybe I can find the exit to your tunnels. If this city-bred Frances of yours is lost, she will not know where to go."

"I cannot allow—" Tode began.

Pushing aside great armfuls of flowers, Berengaria sat up and said, "She knows all the shepherds and cowherds in the county. No woman will be able to escape their notice. She must go."

Beside Berengaria, Axia sat up. "And you said we do not need her. Oh, Tode, please do not allow Frances to wander about alone. You know that she is helpless. She can do nothing on her own."

"You are not right about that," Tode said, frowning, but then he knew there was sense in what the women were saying.

"Please," Berengaria said softly, and that decided Tode.

Joby didn't wait for the answer but ran across the fields toward Henry Oliver's house.

As Tode handed each woman a dipper full of water

in turn, he looked at them. With Axia's talent at painting, she had managed to transform herself and Berengaria into old, haggard-looking women. Although to Tode's eyes, nothing could make Berengaria less than exquisitely beautiful, and he'd told her so.

As for Joby, Tode had refused to allow anything to be done with her as a disguise. With her boyish haircut and clothes, what else could be done with her? "Shall we try to make her into a girl?" Tode had said, indulging himself in a rare moment of spite because of all the nasty things Joby had said about him. "But no, not even you, Axia, are *that* talented."

So now he was glad to get rid of Joby, for her constant disobedience was a trial, and now he needed cooperation for what he had planned.

It was full dark by the time they reached Oliver's house, and Tode was glad for the state of confusion that reigned, even though he was worried about Frances. How had she escaped from a stone tower?

It took just minutes to ascertain that Frances had not yet been found, that Jamie was still locked below, still refusing to sign anything. Once again Tode vowed that he was going to murder Joby when this was all through, for Oliver had told him that it was "the odd little Montgomery girl's idea" that he kidnap the Maidenhall heiress and thereby force Jamie to give him his beloved Berengaria. After meeting Berengaria, Tode refused to believe that she had any knowledge of what her young sister had done.

Tode knew that Oliver's brother Ronald had stationed men at the front gate, watching for anyone who remotely looked like one of their Montgomery neighbors. Ronald had said that he wouldn't put it past those Amazonian Montgomery women to try to rescue their brother themselves, so he wanted all women entering to be scrutinized.

But no one had looked at Tode with his wagonfull of flowers. Or if they did look, they burst into laughter.

"He has played the fool for many days if they have all seen him," Berengaria whispered to Axia beside her, and there was bitterness in her voice.

Her words echoed Axia's thoughts exactly.

Once they were inside the grounds, the women listened as Tode pulled Henry Oliver to the side of the wagon and offered his help in bringing Frances back. He knew how women loved flowers, didn't he? Yes. Well if he were to scatter them about, Frances would be attracted to them and come back. They would be a kind of bait, didn't Henry see?

"Like putting out cheese for a mouse," Henry said in wonder.

"Exactly," Tode answered. "But do not tell that brother of yours or he will find the heiress before you do and he will take all the credit."

"Yes," Henry said. "Ronald thinks he is the only smart person in the village."

Tode thought Ronald believed he was the only smart person in the world, but that was beside the point. "So where shall we put them?" Tode asked, and Axia could feel the blankness of Oliver's mind.

"In the dungeon with the prisoner?" Tode suggested. "She will try to go to him first, will she not?"

"Oh yes, of course." Leaning over, he whispered to Tode. "Do not let my brother see you, as he will let no one down there, not even me."

"Then why do you not go and tell him that this is *your* house and not his and that she is your heiress, and he is not to interfere in your life ever again? After all, it was *you* who was smart enough to kidnap the Maidenhall heiress, not him."

"But that will make Ronald very angry."

"Yes, and while he is raging, I will put the trap out for the heiress. You are not afraid of your brother, are you?"

"Well, maybe . . . No! I am not. You go and put your flowers out. What harm can flowers do?"

"Right." Tode waited a few moments for Henry to walk far enough away before he flipped back the edge of the canvas and said, "It is safe now. You can come out."

"You are the most brilliant man I have ever met," Berengaria said as Tode helped her down. "All my life I will owe you, and my sister will—Ow!"

"Sorry," Axia said, "my foot must have slipped. I think we shouldn't waste more time talking and should get on with it."

"By all means," Tode said, and there was a bit of a chuckle in his voice.

Twenty minutes later, Tode, Axia, and Berengaria, with Henry's permission, were on their way down the stairs to the dungeon. There was so much confusion since Frances's escape that no one noticed that Axia was holding Berengaria's hand, leading her across broken flagstones, and whispering when she was to step over a pile of offal on the floor.

"Disgusting!" she hissed, but a look from Tode silenced her. Once they had to stop while Tode made some foolish faces at the kitchen help, and both of the women held each other's hands so tightly they hurt. Neither of them liked that Tode had to humiliate himself this way.

Once out of the kitchens, Tode led them through a labyrinth of old stone corridors filled with barrels, boxes, and rusting farm equipment. It seemed that everything Henry Oliver's family had ever owned was stored in the cellars below, and at times Axia had difficulty keeping Berengaria from stumbling as they made their way through the confusion. Now and then there was a torch stuck in an iron holder on the wall, but for the most part they were in darkness.

After what seemed to be an eternity, they came to a small room, seeming to be brightly lit after the gloom of the cellars. The heavy oak door to the room was open and the three of them were able to walk through without making a sound. On three sides of the room were huge damp stones and on the fourth wall there was nothing, just the black emptiness of a tunnel that seemed to stretch into infinity.

Before the tunnel was a table, a chair, and a guard sitting alone, his chin resting on his chest and sleeping soundly.

Part of Axia breathed a sigh of relief when she saw that the guard was asleep and part of her was terrified. Tode had said that he would think of something when the time came to put the guard off, but he did not yet know what it was. He had said that at worst he would have to stay and entertain the man while Axia and Berengaria went to Jamie. When Axia had asked what would happen to him when they found Jamie was gone, he had not answered.

But now she could see that the guard was asleep, his head hanging down on his chest—and the keys were hanging on the wall near his head. If Tode could just get them down soundlessly, without waking the guard, she knew they would have passed the first step.

"What is it?" Berengaria whispered anxiously.

Axia shushed her, fearing that her voice would wake the guard, then she gripped Berengaria's hand hard while she watched Tode creep forward and remove the keys from the wall. When they jangled, Axia drew in her breath sharply.

"What is it?" Berengaria asked again, making Tode turn and frown.

Annoyed, Axia jerked on Berengaria's hand to let her know she should say nothing, but when she saw her open her mouth to speak again, Axia whispered, "The guard is asleep."

In a normal voice that in the entrance to the black tunnels was as loud as cannon fire, Berengaria said, "There is no one here but ourselves."

Axia thought the fear that ran through her might cause her to die on the spot. Anxiously, she looked at the guard, but he remained asleep.

With some annoyance, Berengaria said again, "There is no one here, I tell you."

At that, Tode stopped, keys in his hand, and looked at the guard. As far as he could see the man was not moving, not even his chest was lifting as he breathed. Slowly, tentatively, he reached out his hand and touched the man's shoulder. His body was warm, but when the man did not flinch at Tode's touch, he put his fingertips to the man's neck.

But when Tode touched him again, the guard fell face forward, the sound of his forehead hitting the table making Axia jump.

Only when Tode pushed the man's body back against the wall could he see the small knife wound in his chest. It wasn't very large, but it was exactly in the correct place; the man must have died instantly.

"Jamie!" Axia said, dropping her flowers, then running into the darkness of the tunnels without giving heed to where she was going.

Taking the torch off the walls, Tode grabbed Berengaria's hand and followed Axia as fast as he dared, for the floor was so slippery it was dangerous.

The horrid little cell where Jamie had been kept was empty, only a pile of bloody clothes to show that he had been there.

"Where is he?" Axia demanded, as though Tode and Berengaria would have the answer. But even if they had, she did not wait for their reply because she plunged into the darkness of the tunnels outside the cell. She was sure that Jamie could not have gone upstairs; there were too many people who would see and recognize him. The only way he could have escaped was into the tunnels.

As fast as he could, Berengaria's hand firmly in his, Tode held the torch aloft and ran after Axia, catching her as she was about to run down a black corridor. "We must not separate," he said, looking into Axia's frightened face. "We must stay together. Do you—?" He broke off at a sound coming from the entrance to the tunnels.

"He's dead! Get torches. I want him found!" they heard a voice shouting. "Look! There's a light."

Without thought, Tode threw the torch into a puddle of heaven only knew what liquid that ran the length of the floor, and they were plunged into darkness. Absolute, total blackness.

When Tode and Axia hesitated, Berengaria took the lead. "Follow me," she said, and never in her life had she ever loved saying words more. She was the leader now, and *they* were helpless.

The tunnels were dirty and long unused—and as she soon found, they were full of hazards. In places the floor had caved in or the ceiling had collapsed.

"Be careful here," she whispered. "There is a hole here. Do not step amiss."

"How can you tell?" Tode asked, holding her hand, Axia behind him.

"This place is less hazardous than my home, what with the fallen daggers and swords of my brothers. And Joby finds that moving a piece of furniture is easier than walking around it." For all that there was danger, she could not help feeling a sense of purpose and strength at this new responsibility. For these minutes she was no longer the Family Burden, but someone who was needed.

Now she concentrated on getting them out of there. Pausing, she sniffed the air.

"What are you doing?" Axia asked, impatient. Where was Jamie?

"I am trying to smell the sun," she replied cryptically. "This way."

Tode had to pull Axia along behind him, for he was afraid she'd start asking Berengaria questions about how and why, her curiosity overriding her fear.

Now and then Axia would look behind her to see if she could see the torches of Oliver's men, but she could see nothing. In the thirty minutes or so that they had been walking, she was aware that they had passed large obstructions and tiptoed around holes in the floor. She thought that if she could see, she would believe the tunnel to be impassable.

"Wait!" Berengaria said when they came to a wider place in the tunnel, a place so wide that Axia could open her arms and hit nothing. "Someone has been here."

"Jamie?" Axia asked, breathless.

"I cannot tell, but I feel that someone has been here."

"Can you *smell* them?" Axia asked in wonder, and the way she said it made the others laugh.

And it was while they were laughing that the man jumped from the shadows and held a knife to Tode's throat. "One word and you are dead," came a harsh voice in Tode's ear.

"Jamie!" Berengaria and Axia said in unison, then Axia made a leap in his direction, her hands outstretched, reaching for any part of him that she could find.

"Hell and damnation!" Jamie gasped in shock and some annoyance, but the next second he was pulling Axia to him and kissing her, holding her to him as closely as possible.

"Jamie, my love," Axia whispered, "I thought I would die without you. Are you well? Did they hurt you?"

"Not at all. They—Ow! Well, perhaps a bit." He nuzzled her neck. "Will you nurse me back to health?"

"I will do things that will make you want to live," she said throatily, then there was silence as they continued kissing, their privacy ensured by the blackness of the tunnels.

Standing just a few feet away, two people listened to them with mixed emotions. For many years, Tode and Axia had been everything to each other, but now he could tell that their friendship had changed forever.

And Berengaria could feel how much her brother loved this woman who had come so suddenly into their lives and turned it upside down. Now she knew that Axia had done nothing to entice her brother, nothing except love him, love him completely and totally, without thought for herself. Berengaria had not paid much attention when Axia had said she would give up her own life to save Jamie's, but now she could feel Axia's fear for Jamie's safety as well as her need of him.

Berengaria was glad that someone loved her dear brother the way she thought he should be loved, but at the same time, a great wave of loneliness washed over her. Jamie was her best friend, and he was the only male she had ever known who did not care that she was blind.

As Berengaria was feeling the loss of her brother, Tode slipped his hand in hers, then leaning toward her, he kissed her on the side of the mouth. "You will not be alone," he said, seeming to read her mind. "Not while I have breath in me."

"Come, imp, release me and tell me what you are doing here. As if I did not know. Tode! How could you bring her into this mess? Oliver's men are serious in their pursuit of the Maidenhall money. But you allowed Axia—"

"And me," Berengaria said softly.

While Jamie was speaking, Axia was running her hands all over him to find out what damage had been done to him. She felt him jump at his sister's voice; then she felt the anger rise in him.

"We needed her," Axia said, trying to head Jamie off. "She can see where we cannot."

"It is bad enough that you endanger my wife, but to take my bl—my sister," he corrected himself. "Tode, I hold you accountable for this. You should not have brought women into this. Especially not—"

"Go ahead and say it!" Berengaria spat out. "He should not have brought your useless blind sister into this. That's what you want to say, isn't it?"

"I did not say that nor did I mean that. *None* of you should be here."

"We came to save you, you ingrate!" Axia said. "And for your information, Berengaria is *not* blind down here. *She* can smell the sun."

For a moment, Jamie hesitated, then he laughed. "All right, I cannot fight that. Come, let us go." But to his consternation, neither of the three followed him. Turning back, he said, "They will be searching for us soon. We must find the exit and quickly."

Axia put her hands on her hips, knowing that he could not see her gesture. "Berengaria can see better than you, so we will follow her."

It was in that moment that Berengaria decided that she truly loved her new sister-in-law. No one had ever said that Berengaria could do anything better than anyone else. For all that she was blind, she was still a Montgomery, and her pride swelled. "Come. This way!" she commanded and began walking in the opposite direction that Jamie had started to lead.

Jamie was wise enough to concede leadership when he was not the best man for the job, so now he turned and followed the others.

Berengaria led them through what seemed to be acres of tunnel, and after a while Axia thought that she too could "smell" the sun. Once they came upon a ceiling that had fallen, blocking the path. Tode and Jamie cleared the rubble, neither of them allowing the women to help.

"Jamie is hurt more than he lets us know," Berengaria whispered, taking a sip from the water bottle they each carried. "He is bleeding. I can smell it."

Axia took a breath. "Yes. I could feel it when I touched him. Are you sure we are going toward the exit?"

"Oh yes. I can—"

"Berengaria!" Axia suddenly said. "Could you smell the sun if it were nighttime?"

She chuckled. "I cannot actually smell the sun but what the sun does to the land. It makes things grow, and I can smell the plants and the fresh air. It seems so obvious to me which way to go. Can you not tell?"

"Not in the least. Could you find our way back, the way we came?"

"Yes, of course." With one ear turned toward Jamie as he struggled with the rocks, she said softly, "My brother Edward used to take me into the forest miles from our house and leave me to find my way back. He said that dogs could do it, so I should be able to also. The first time he did it I thought I would stay there and wait for someone to find me, and if they did not, I would die, but then I remembered we had strawberries for supper."

"Do not tell me that you *smelled* them and followed your nose?"

Berengaria let out a laugh that made the men turn toward them, but neither woman would tell what had made her laugh.

"No," Berengaria said. "I walked back, stumbling, but I trusted my instinct and found my way."

Before Axia could ask another question, Jamie told them the obstruction was cleared and they could continue.

An hour later they came to a tangle of roots that blocked the tunnel. "Here," Berengaria said. "Cut this away, and we will be there soon."

And she was right when, a moment later, Jamie turned back to them. "I can see daylight."

The other three were jubilant, but Berengaria almost wished they could stay in the tunnels, for with light she knew she had to give up her leadership, her usefulness. Once in the light, she would again become the Family Burden.

Using his knife, which the guards had not found in his boot, and a great deal of muscle, Jamie reopened the long-covered opening and emerged into the forest not far from Henry Oliver's house. And the moment he stuck his head up, he saw movement. "Quiet!" he commanded the others still in the tunnel.

Crouching, he ran quickly across the forest floor, the thick layer of pine needles making his footsteps silent. The brilliance of the early morning sun nearly blinded him after so many hours in the complete darkness of the tunnels, and at times he had to shut them against the glare. But he knew he had seen someone move, and he was trying to pursue him.

With one leap, he pounced on him, realizing that the small body under his was that of a child. He was glad, for at the moment he did not feel up to wrestling a full-grown person.

"Hello, big brother," Joby said cheerfully, looking

up at him with laughter in her eyes. "Been playing in the pig pen again?"

With great relief, Jamie rolled off of her, then sat up and rubbed his eyes. He had not eaten in a few days, had had very little water, and there was, of course, his back and now this night spent in the tunnels. He was not at his best.

"Come," he said. "We must get the others." Painfully, he rolled to his feet, then looked at the bag Joby had slung across her shoulder. "That wouldn't be food, would it?"

"Two chickens, four cherry tarts, and a few early carrots." Smiling, Joby gave the sack a pat, which made it squawk and flop about.

"Raw is it?" Jamie asked, eyebrow raised.

"Fresh," she corrected him, not allowing him to see how bad she felt at the sight of him. He was filthy, but under the filth was dried blood.

"And who taught you how to poach chickens and steal pies?" he asked with disgust, but he was too glad to see her to actually be angry. He glanced at the bag at her side. "I do hope you have not put the chickens and the pies together."

"What's a pie without a little chicken . . ." One look at Jamie made her think again at finishing that sentence. "What have you done with Berengaria and the other two?"

Jamie didn't answer but turned, and Joby saw him wince with pain as he started back toward the exit to the tunnel where the others awaited. "Come," was all he said to his little sister, and she followed him.

Chapter 28

*T*he sun was low in the sky, and it was cool and quiet in the forest as five people dozed and waited for the concealment of night to make their escape. Twice they had heard the sound of hooves in the distance that told them Oliver's men were still searching for them. Jamie had wanted to press on as he knew his Montgomery cousins would arrive soon, because he had managed to get a message to them when he had first arrived at Henry Oliver's.

But he had been voted down by all of them when they saw him in the light of day. Axia, having known about the whippings, had brought a cooling salve for his back, and she had forced him to lie still on his stomach as she spread the ointment on the open cuts.

Now, hours after emerging from the tunnels, after an afternoon's sleep, all of them were beginning to wake up and become restless. They couldn't move until nightfall, and that was still an hour or two away. Axia's growing worry was that Jamie would try to be a hero and go after Oliver himself, alone with no help. She knew that only exhaustion had persuaded him to sleep this afternoon, and now he looked about restlessly.

"Can you really smell anything?" she asked Berengaria, desperately wanting to think about something other than what they had all been through and why they were waiting. "Did you know that that is a very valuable talent? I have often tried to make perfume like the French do. You can't just dry a bunch of violets and make violet-smelling perfume. I've tried it. You have to mix several herbs together to get something that smells like something else."

"Like verbena smells more like lemons than lemons do?" Berengaria asked.

"Yes, exactly. I've done some experiments, but after four or five plants I couldn't tell the difference between dirty socks and roses. But if I had someone with a nose . . ."

"My sister can tell the difference between a hundred plants at once," Joby said, still smarting from Berengaria's betrayal of her. What had happened in those tunnels to make her sister sit so close to Axia, laughing at everything she said?

At that Axia began pulling plants and holding them under Berengaria's nose and soon discovered that it was true: Berengaria could identify even types of tree bark one from the other.

"Amazing. Truly amazing. What I could do with you in business!!"

"We are not going to put our sister in some shop so people can stare at her," Joby snapped.

"Stare at her? Oh, you mean because she's so beautiful."

"No, because she is blind!"

"With a nose like hers, who cares if she can't see?"

"What?" Joby gasped.

Immediately, Axia was contrite. "I am sorry, I did not mean any disrespect. It is just that for a moment I forgot that she was blind. It slipped my mind."

At that Joby began to sputter, but Berengaria said calmly, "I wish everyone would forget that I am blind. I would like to be something other than the Family Burden."

"Burden?" Axia said, smiling. "With your talent, you and I could make a fortune." Standing, she saw that all eyes were on her, and she thought that maybe for a moment she could take their minds off their worries.

"With your talent, we could make a wonderful perfume. We'll call it Elizabeth, and Jamie can present it to the queen." When Axia saw her husband frown at this suggestion, she knew she'd never be able to stop. "With his looks he'll be the perfect one to woo her into liking it. No one else in the world will be allowed to wear that scent. We'll make it only for Queen Elizabeth, and she'll direct all her courtiers to buy her huge bottles of it for gifts."

Axia saw that Tode was smiling a bit, and the worry lines were smoothing from Jamie's brow. "Then we will make other scents for other ladies. Having your own scent will become all the rage at court."

Berengaria smiled. "We will get Jamie to smell the necks of all the ladies at court and tell them whether they are violets or jasmine."

Until now Joby had been silent, but as Axia continued, Joby lost her resentment. Putting on a face that was remarkably like Jamie's when he was thinking hard about something, Joby extended her hand, acting as though she were holding a woman's hand and sniffing it. "Yes, yes," she said thoughtfully. "You are a full, ripe beauty like . . . ah, yes, like the musk rose. And you," she said, pretending to take another hand, "are as sweet as violets."

Dropping the imaginary hands, Joby was suddenly quite serious. "We must give him a list of all the scents, so he sells them all."

"Yes, of course," Berengaria said. "And I think we should decide which lady gets which scent before he goes to court so he makes no mistakes. Men are so bad at this sort of thing. He might have a tiny countess smelling of lilies and a great horse of a woman smelling of morning dew."

"Unless, of course, that is how she sees herself," Axia said. "Mmmm. What do you think, Jamie?"

"I am honored that the three of you have remembered that I am here. My actions, my very character, are assessed without my input, but now you have decided to ask me a question. At last, my honor is restored." He smiled at them. "And I have no intention of participating in any of this. I am not going to spend my life kissing hands and telling women how they . . . how they smell."

Axia grimaced, then smiled as an idea occurred to her. "Yes! I think perhaps a blind perfume lady would be better."

"Me?" Berengaria said. She was sure Axia was teasing about all this, but was she? "At court?"

Axia's voice was excited. "You could sit on a velvet chair and allow the women to come to you, hold their hands, talk to them, then decide what scent most suits them."

"Berengaria cannot—" Jamie began, but Joby cut him off.

"But what of the men?" Joby said. "Do not forget the men who will want their own scent. What do you think the Richard will smell of? Earthy and rich?"

Berengaria giggled. "What would a perfume named Henry Oliver smell of?"

"Horse sweat!" Joby said, and the women and Tode laughed. Even Jamie gave a little smile, but Joby saw it and it was enough to encourage her. Standing, she puffed her chest out, her shoulders back, her thumbs in her waistband as she began to strut like a vain man. "I'm a *man!*" she boasted. "And I want something truly manly. For a *real* man."

Axia stepped toward her sister-in-law, acting as though she were holding out a bottle. "Oh, great heroic man, I have here the most manly smell ever made."

"I want no flowers!" Joby said in a deep, gruff voice. "I must protect my—my finer parts, if you know what I mean, little girl."

"Oh yes, sir," Axia said, fluttering her lashes coquettishly, "and I can see that your finer parts are very fine indeed. But I think you will find that we have used the most manly of ingredients."

"Flowers?" Joby growled.

"Oh, no, none at all. Well, maybe just one."

"No flowers! You understand me, little lady? I'm a man and *no flowers!* I'm leaving here!"

"But, sir," Axia called out toward Joby's back. "It is the flower from the skunk cabbage."

At that the others laughed out loud, even Jamie, so

Joby came back. "What else is in it?" she asked suspiciously.

"Saw blades."

At that even Joby nearly forgot her role and almost smiled. Joby was used to having center stage and making people laugh, but Axia was a match for her.

"Old, rusty saw blades. And broken swords and mud from places where men have died—in battle, of course."

Joby did smile at that. "Of course."

"And, as always, horse manure as a binder."

"I would want nothing else."

"But . . ." Axia looked around as though to see if any one was looking. "For you we have included a very special ingredient."

"What is it?" Joby loudly whispered back.

"Toe jam. From under the toenail of a huge Turkish man. Never had a bath in his life."

"I'll take it!" Joby shouted above the laughter of everyone, including Jamie. "I will pay you six castles and two hundred acres of land. Is it enough?"

"Make it three hundred acres."

"It is yours."

"Then I am—"

"Quiet!" Jamie suddenly commanded as, standing, he moved to the other side of the little camp, motioning with his hand that all of them were to crouch down and be quiet while his eyes searched the forest. Tode put his arm protectively over Berengaria, hiding her from whatever it was that Jamie saw.

After a moment, Jamie gave a little smile, then turned to Axia, who had flattened herself on the ground. "It is your cousin," he said, wonder in his voice. "I would recognize the brilliance of that dress anywhere."

With disbelief in her eyes, Axia lifted her head and looked over the fallen log Tode and Berengaria were crouching behind, and there, sauntering toward them, as though she had all the time in the world, was Frances.

As soon as Axia could believe what she saw, she jumped up and ran toward her cousin, then stood in hesitation when she was in front of her. For all that Frances must have been through, she looked the same, but at the same time there was something different about her. *Just like Tode,* Axia thought.

"Well?" Frances demanded. "Are you not glad to see me?"

With that she opened her arms, and the two women ran toward each other, hugging, and Axia was surprised to find that she *was* glad to see her cousin.

In the next minute Jamie was on the other side of Frances, ready to ask her many questions, but Frances said she had nothing to say until she'd had something to eat. Then she shocked Jamie by telling him where she had hidden a bag full of food.

"Do not look so shocked, Axia," she said, laughing, after Jamie was gone. "How do you think my family fed itself before they had access to the Maidenhall money?"

"I—I do not know."

"Thievery, that's how. When I was a mere four years old, I was an expert chicken thief, and I could steal eggs as fast as they were laid." With that, she turned away and went toward the others in the camp.

Axia stood staring after her cousin, because in all

the time she'd known Frances, all she'd heard was that Frances's family was the kindest, most wonderful she'd ever imagined. Recovering herself somewhat, Axia followed her cousin back to the camp.

An hour later, a meal had been cooked—Frances had helped—and all of them were sitting in a circle around Frances, waiting for her to tell the story of her escape.

Axia was feeling very strange. It was as though everything she'd ever known in her life was changing. Her beloved Tode, who had always looked at Axia with adoring eyes, was now looking at Berengaria with love. And helpless Frances had managed to escape from a stone prison and had fried bacon and eggs over a campfire as though it were something she had done a thousand times. But Axia knew that Frances could not even tie her own shoelaces, much less feed herself and certainly not others.

And there was something different in her manner, something . . . Axia thought that maybe it was self-confidence. Frances seemed so much more sure of herself than she ever had before.

"Tell us," Joby urged, stretched on the grass, looking up at Frances and wondering how Jamie could have turned down this woman for Axia. But then she had had some fun with Axia and . . . Well, maybe Axia wasn't so bad after all. "Tell us how you escaped," she said again.

"I painted doors on the walls," Frances answered with a smile, looking about the group expectantly, but there was no enlightenment on the faces of anyone.

But then Tode began to laugh. "Like Axia," he said. When Frances looked at him, Axia saw a look pass between them that she had never seen before. It was as though they shared something private and secret.

Frances motioned for Tode to tell. "It was a trick Axia once played on everyone when she twelve," he said. "She recruited all the workmen on the estate, then stayed up all night painting half-open doorways everywhere. There were mouse holes, tall doors, short doors."

"And a few windows," Frances added.

"The cook drank too much, and Axia almost drove the woman crazy, because for the next several days, she kept walking out open doors, only to find herself running into a wall," Tode said, smiling.

Axia had forgotten the incident entirely, but now she also remembered the time when she painted daisies all over a wall of Frances's bedchamber. Considering what had happened with Jamie and the cloak, she hoped neither Tode nor Frances would mention *that*. "How did *you* get out?" she urged, trying to divert Tode and Frances from a longer rendition of her childhood pranks.

"I asked myself what Axia would do in this situation, then I did it," Frances said proudly, then looking at Jamie, she said, "Axia is very clever, you know."

At that Axia's lower jaw dropped open so far her teeth nearly fell out, and she would have commented if she hadn't been sure the world was in imminent danger of ending.

"I must begin at the beginning," Frances said. "At first everything was fine. Henry was very nice to me because all he wanted was to marry Jamie's sister. He planned to exchange me for her, but then his awful brother came and said, 'Henry, you are holding the

Maidenhall heiress captive, and you want to trade her for some girl who can't afford to fix her own roof?' So he told Henry that he should marry me himself, and I was to be held prisoner in a stone tower until the marriage could be arranged."

Frances took a breath and looked at her audience. Usually, Axia's vivacity overrode any beauty and especially any story that Frances might have to tell. But now everyone was looking and listening to Frances. And she couldn't help reminding herself that it would end as soon as it was found out that she wasn't actually the Maidenhall heiress. For all that she had been kidnapped and held prisoner, Frances liked being the Maidenhall heiress as much as Axia hated it.

She continued her story. "I was trying to make Henry like me, so I told him that I was the one who had painted the dragon wagon. Oh, I was so afraid on the journey south. When I realized he was not the one Axia, uh . . ." She glanced nervously from Axia to Jamie.

"He knows," Axia supplied, nodding toward Jamie.

"Anyway," Frances continued, "Henry thought I was the greatest painter in the world; I just hoped I'd never have to prove it. So later when he locked me away, it seemed natural to him for me to ask for paints, especially since I was so afraid—and so alone. Only Tode was allowed in twice to try to cheer me up. If it hadn't been for him, I . . ." At that she looked away and blushed.

Which made Axia look in consternation from Frances to Tode to Berengaria, whose mouth was now in a prim little line.

Frances continued. "I thought for days of some way

to get out but could think of nothing, as Henry came personally to give me my food. Perhaps I could have persuaded another man, but not Henry. Once he has his mind made up, nothing changes it."

Pausing, she smiled at her audience. "Then I thought, *What would Axia do?* and I remembered all those painted doors. So I begged Henry for pigments, so I could make myself some paints. Just as I've seen you do so often, Axia. When he gave them to me, I stayed up all night and painted three doors on the walls of my room and one window, complete with a bird on the sill."

She looked at Axia, her eyes sparkling. "And out the window was a field full of daisies. I've seen Axia paint a good number of daisies, so I was rather good at painting them," she said with a laugh, looking at Axia's pink face. "Then I painted the back of the real door to look like the stone of the wall."

She looked in apology to Axia. "My painting wasn't very good, but Henry's eyesight was so poor that I thought I might be able to fool him long enough to escape."

"And it did fool him," Jamie said, making everyone turn to look at him. "I did not dare to try to escape from the tunnels myself for fear of what would be done to Frances if they found me gone. But after several days, I heard the guards gossiping that she had escaped, but there seemed to be some great secret attached to her method of escape. However, with some persuasion, I coaxed the guard to tell me all. Henry Oliver opened the door to Frances's room, only to see her lying on the bed, silent and not moving. But when he went to the bed, Frances was hiding behind the door, so she slipped out and shut the door behind her. Oliver then spent hours in that room, wandering around trying to open painted doors and the window. Truthfully, he thought it was the most wondrous thing he'd ever seen, and he wasn't at all upset that Frances had escaped." Looking at Axia, his eyes twinkled. "He swore he could smell the daisies."

Axia was too busy thinking to smile. She did not have to be told that the reason he had been whipped was because Frances had escaped. "But his brother was not amused," Axia said softly, reaching out to touch Jamie's hair.

"True," Jamie said softly, "his brother was very angry." For a moment he looked at Axia with love, letting his eyes talk for him, telling her the things he had not yet had time to say to her. While he had been in that prison, he realized that he had never told her how much he loved her. He had thought of her all the time he was in there, thought of how much she had come to mean to him. Part of him wanted to murder her for endangering herself in attempting to rescue him, but another part of him loved her more for it.

Tonight, he thought. Tonight he would hold her in his arms, they would have privacy, and he'd tell her how he felt.

Now," he said, rising, "it is growing dark, and I think we should all go home."

Frances was the first to rise, and when she started clearing the camp, again Axia watched her in wonder. When they had been traveling north in the wagons, Frances had never once lifted a hand to help. And when they had lived on the Maidenhall estate, she had seemed incapable of doing anything.

"I do not understand," Axia said softly when she and Frances were some distance from the others.

"You do not understand what?"

"How . . . ?" Axia tried to recover herself. "Frances, you are the most helpless person I have ever met, yet you have managed to escape a kidnapping and you have fed us as well as yourself and you have—"

Frances's laugh cut her off. "Axia, I am not helpless."

"But you—You . . ."

Frances looked Axia square in the eyes. "I just pretended to be helpless because that is what you need. You love helpless people."

"I what?" Axia said, half in anger, half in disbelief.

"Axia, you are terrified that no one will ever love you or like you just for yourself. No matter how much someone loves you, you always think it is because of your father's money. When I arrived at your estate, I was just a child, but I had been through more horror than most people endure in a lifetime. And I had decided that I was going to be anything you wanted me to be so I would not be sent back to my father."

"And you think I needed you to be helpless," Axia said with heavy sarcasm.

"Oh yes, Axia. You must feel 'useful' as you call it. You always feel that you have to show people that you are worth more than your father's money, and you do that by working your little fingers to the bone. Please do not get me wrong, you are so very useful that you make everyone around you feel helpless. It is so much easier to sit back and let you do everything."

When Axia managed to quit sputtering, her mouth hardened. "And is it also my fault that you extorted money out of me for all those years? You never gave me the time of day unless I paid you."

"True," Frances said cheerfully, "and I still have every penny of it. Axia, you do have the most amazing ability to earn money. And I am sure you will be the perfect wife for Jamie, what with his blind sister, and that boyish girl, Joby, you will have a lifetime of being useful." She smiled. "I am sure, Axia, that in no time at all you will have them all rolling in money. You'll find ways to turn air into gold—just like your father."

For a moment, Axia was too stunned to speak. She couldn't comprehend what Frances was saying. "Everything is changing," she whispered. "You have changed. Tode has changed."

"Yes," Frances said, her face losing its smile as she glanced quickly at Tode as he helped Berengaria brush her skirt off. Her voice lowered. "Tode humiliated himself in front of Oliver, making the basest jokes about his face and body. It was awful to hear and worse to watch."

She took a breath as though trying to calm something inside her. "He did that for *me*. I always thought he hated me or at least cared nothing about me, but he was—" Quickly, she looked at Tode over her shoulder and closed her mouth.

"He is different," Axia said. "I cannot put my finger on it, but there is something different about him." She looked back at her cousin. "As you are different. What has happened to change the two of you so much?"

"Axia," Frances whispered urgently, grabbing her arm. "I must tell you something. It is very important, and I must tell you before—"

But she never finished her sentence because at that moment Joby came running back toward them. Unbeknownst to Frances and Axia, Jamie had heard horses approaching and had sent Joby to see who they were, all of them hoping the riders were their Montgomery cousins.

"It is Maidenhall himself!" Joby said jubilantly, arms waving, "And he comes now. For his daughter!"

Neither Frances nor Axia had time to think or speak. They merely entwined hands tightly and looked toward where Joby was pointing. Stepping through the trees was a man neither woman had ever seen before but who they knew well. For years Axia had asked every visitor to the estate what her father looked like, and through their descriptions, she had drawn many, many pictures of him, even painted a couple of oils.

Now there was no mistaking the fact that the short, thin man coming toward them, wearing his shabby black wool robe, his lank gray hair hanging to his shoulders, was Perkin Maidenhall—the richest man in England.

Unerringly, he walked straight to Axia. "Well, daughter, what do you have to say for yourself?" His eyes were cold, his voice showing his barely controlled anger.

Chapter 29

When neither Axia nor Frances seemed able to speak, Perkin Maidenhall said, "Come, daughter," then turned his back as though he expected her to follow him and started toward his men, who were rapidly surrounding the little campground.

"I believe you are in error," Jamie said, amusement in his voice, as he slipped his arm around his wife. "This is not your daughter."

Maidenhall turned to look at Jamie as though just now seeing him. He was a small man, with eyes like black glass, and as he turned his hard stare at Jamie, the younger man could see why it was reputed that he had never been bested in a deal.

"Are you saying that I do not know my own daughter?"

Jamie's arm tightened about Axia's shoulders. *This* woman is my wife."

At that Maidenhall threw back his head and gave a laugh, an ugly, rusty sound that showed that laughter was not something he was much practiced at. "And what do you think you have done? Married the Maidenhall heiress? You? Poor James Montgomery? James Lackland should be your name."

Instinctively, Jamie's hand went to the sword at his side, but as he moved, what now looked to be three hundred men, some on horseback, some on foot, all drew their swords and aimed them toward him.

"Please," Axia said, moving out of Jamie's ever-tightening grip. "I must speak to my father."

"Your—?" Jamie said in consternation, then his face changed. "I see," he said. "So this is your great secret. Did you think I was such a mercenary that I would change if I knew of your great wealth? Is this what you thought of me?"

Maidenhall answered before Axia could. "But it is what you wanted, is it not? At first you courted poor cousin Frances, but later your attention turned to my true daughter." He looked at Axia. "Have you never asked yourself why? Why would he stop courting a woman as beautiful as Frances and turn his attention to a plain, drab little thing like you?"

It was as though he were reading her mind, for it is exactly what Axia had wondered.

"I do not know what you are insinuating—" Jamie began, but Maidenhall cut him off.

"I am saying, my lord," he sneered the words, "that you found out the game played by two foolish girls and immediately changed your attentions to the one who was to be my heir."

"I did not . . ." Jamie trailed off, because as he spoke, he looked into Axia's eyes and knew that she believed her father, or at least there was doubt there. He dropped his arm from around her, his pride damaged.

Axia spoke for the first time. "I want to speak to my father alone," she managed to say.

"Yes," Jamie said angrily. "As you *are* the daughter to the great Maidenhall, of course, you must speak to him."

"Jamie," she said, her hand on his arm, but he turned away, so she walked into the trees with her father.

Perkin Maidenhall was short, and his eyes were on a level with his daughter's.

"What do you want?" she said coldly. All her life she had wanted to meet her father. She had worked in every way at pleasing him, but now that he was here, she could see nothing in his eyes. Nothing but money, that is. It was true what Frances had always taunted: her father had never met her because he had never had a way to make money from her—until now.

At his daughter's curt tone, Maidenhall allowed a bit of a smile. "I'd heard that you were like me, and now I can see it."

"Do not insult me," she said quickly. "Talk to me about money. How much is involved?"

He did not hesitate. "I have a contract with Bolingbrooke, and you must honor it."

"I am now defective goods; I am no longer a virgin, so I am not worth the bride price."

"That is all right since Bolingbrooke's son is impotent. If you are with child, I will charge him more for giving him an heir."

At the callousness of that remark, Axia blanched.

"What's the matter, daughter? Did you not believe

what you had heard of me? Did you think I was actually a sweet little man with a fondness for dogs and small children?"

Axia had hoped that perhaps he would have been sweet to her, his only child, but she could see that this man had never loved anyone in his life. Rarely had she seen eyes as hard and unfeeling as his.

Pulling herself up, she stood straighter. If she was to survive this, she must use everything that she had inherited from him. "I am married to him."

Maidenhall gave a snort of laughter. "It was but a moment's work to have that marriage voided. You did not have my permission; you misrepresented yourself when you married him." His eyes glittered. "In truth I think you will find that the parish register recording your marriage has mysteriously disappeared and the clergyman has now moved to France. I think you would be hard-pressed to prove your marriage ever took place."

It took Axia a moment to recover herself. In her daily life and since she had left the estate, she had been able to make any bargain she wanted. She had always found it easy to persuade people to her way of thinking. But now, looking into the heartless eyes of her father, she knew she had more than met her match.

She took a breath. "What will you do to him if I do not go with you?"

Maidenhall again gave his rusty little laugh. "Is it love, daughter? I would have thought I had taught you better than that. I took away everyone you could love except a deformed man and a girl who had a heart as dried up as her face was beautiful."

Standing back, he looked Axia up and down. "I

must say that I am disappointed in you. You believed yourself in love with the first beautiful man you saw. I wondered if you could resist a face such as his. He is—"

"Go on, say what you must but leave his character out of it. I do not want to hear what you have no right to speak of."

Maidenhall smirked at her, letting her know what he thought of her weakness. "I will break him. He will find that he is hounded by burned barns and livestock that dies mysteriously. He and his worthless family think they are poor now, but when I get through with them, they will be fighting swine for food."

Axia's hands clenched at her side. "To do this will cost you much money. What will you do *for* him if I go with you?"

For the first time, Axia saw some human emotion in her father's eyes. She was sure she was wrong, but he seemed to be pleased with her. "I will restore everything to him."

"He is proud, and he will not take charity from you."

"Then I will make it seem that he has incredible good luck in his life. Someone will die and bequeath Montgomery his land. When he takes his grain to be milled, he will find that he receives more than he delivered. His sheep will multiply at an enormous rate."

"Yes, I see," she said softly and looked across the shady woodland to where the others were watching them. Jamie's blind sister. How could Berengaria marry without a dowry? Then there was his sister Joby, who seemed to regret that she had not been born a man. It would take a lot of money to pay a man to marry her. Then what of Tode and Frances? Tode was now talking to Jamie, who had his back to her, and Frances was standing alone, her face showing her terror, for what Axia decided to do would decide her own future.

Axia knew that she had no choice. If she went back to Jamie, her father would ruin him. "I will say goodbye," she whispered.

"And tell him of your noble sacrifice?" Maidenhall smirked. "Will he then draw his sword in order to protect you and give my men the pleasure of running him through?"

"Ah yes," she said, understanding that she could not tell Jamie the truth. Again she was going to have to lie to him. She looked at her father. "Did he know? Did he know that I was the heiress?"

"He found out at Lachlan Teversham's house. Someone there worked at my estate when you were younger; you did not recognize him." He raised an eyebrow at her. "Is that not where Montgomery first started to court you?"

"You seem to know a lot," she said, her mouth a tight line. She needed time to digest this information, that Jamie had discovered that she was the Maidenhall heiress and that was why he had started paying attention to her.

"I find that information helps to make money. Did you know that those two demons you call sisters-in-law planned all of this? They organized the villagers around here to contribute to a grand wardrobe for your lover, so he could return with the Maidenhall gold."

When he saw that she knew of this, his eyes narrowed. *"They* are the ones who paid Oliver to kidnap you."

"Me?" she asked, then smiled smugly. "It seems you have been misinformed. Oliver wanted the heiress."

"No, he was to take you away from their brother and leave him alone with Frances. He had been writing letters home about you, and they were concerned that you were trying to entice him away from the heiress."

When she still did not seem to believe him, he said, "Their welcome of you was not especially warm, was it?"

She did not answer him but stared at Jamie, his back to her, one foot on the ground, the other on a fallen log. She did not have to see his hands to know that he was toying with his little dagger as he always did when he was thinking. Even if he had tricked her and lied to her about knowing who she was, she did not blame him. He loved his family, and they needed him. So, dutifully, he had asked Frances to marry him, but when he had been told that Axia was the heiress . . .

Without bothering to say another word to her father, she straightened her shoulders and walked across the soft pine needles of the forest floor toward Jamie. She knew that all eyes were on her, but she was not about to say anything to them. Had his two sisters really hired Oliver to kidnap her? Were they so naive that they thought an abduction was an innocent prank? Frances could have been hurt, even killed. And Jamie's back had been whipped raw.

All for money, she thought. *And pride.* This poor

Montgomery family had relatives they could go to, but rather than lower their pride, they chose to endanger a woman's life so they could get the Maidenhall gold.

And Jamie had agreed with them in all things.

She knew that he heard her approach, but he did not turn around, and when she was standing in front of him, he wouldn't look at her.

"Did you have a good laugh at me?" he asked, looking off into the distance. "Poor naive Jamie. How you and Frances must have laughed! From that first day when I assumed she was the heiress and later when I said you could not go with us. Now I understand everything. Seize the day. Yes, you would need that when rich little you is going to marry your equally rich fiancé."

When he turned to look at her, his eyes were colder than her father's. "Tode says the man you are to marry is impotent. Did you do what you could to get the child that he could not give you?"

For all that his words hurt, for a moment, Axia wanted to go to him, throw her arms around his neck, and tell him that she loved him and that she understood what he had done and why. But what if he believed her, forgave her? The image of his drawing his sword and attacking all her father's men came to her. Would Jamie, bleeding to death from a hundred wounds, smile up at her and say, "There were only three hundred of them."

"Yes," she said. "I did. I told you our marriage would not hold. My father has destroyed all evidence of it. I am going with him now."

At that, for a fraction of a second, Jamie's eyes looked as though he wanted to beg her to stay, but then they changed. "I hope you do not do this for any misplaced nobility."

He did not say he would do so, but she knew that with one word from her, he'd fight for her. To the death.

With what she hoped was insouciance, she threw back her head and laughed. "Oh, Jamie, how droll you are. Did you really think I was going to give up the Maidenhall inheritance to marry an impoverished earl? Look at you! What do you have that I could want? Just taking care of your eccentric family would be a lifetime responsibility. A crazy mother, a blind sister, and another who cannot make up her mind if she is a boy or a girl. Why would any woman want that? All I wanted was something to pass the time until my father came to get me."

"Yes," he said coldly, "I can see that now. You must have had a good laugh at all the things I said to you in private."

"I shall dine out on them for years. Now, excuse me, I must go. My father awaits me." With that she swept aside her skirt and walked past him. "Come, Tode," she said as she passed him.

But Tode held Berengaria's hand tightly and said, "I am not coming."

Axia knew that if she thought about that statement, she would collapse. It seemed that today she was losing everything. Turning, she looked at Frances and raised her eyebrows in question.

Instantly, Frances held out her hand, and together, without one glance backward, the two women walked toward where Perkin Maidenhall waited with saddled horses.

Chapter 30

$\mathcal{T}$omorrow was Axia's wedding day.

She made no pretense at being happy at the prospect of such a day, for she knew without a doubt that it would be the unhappiest day of her life. No, she corrected herself, that would be the day three months ago that she had last seen Jamie. Yes, that had to be the worst day of her life.

Since then she had many times wanted to write to him, explain what she had done and why, but her fear kept her from contacting him. What if he believed her? she kept asking herself. What if he knew that she loved him and believed that her prank of exchanging places with Frances had been innocent?

With one hand on her belly, she raced for the chamberpot to be sick again for what had to be the thousandth time that day. Maybe some small part of her had known that she was pregnant when she left

Jamie. Maybe she had realized that she had to protect their child as well as her husband.

True to his word, her father had delayed her wedding to Gregory Bolingbrooke until he saw that his daughter was pregnant, and when she was, he upped the bride price. "Selling his own grandchild," Axia had muttered, but nothing that had happened to her since she'd left Jamie seemed to matter to her.

She had been told by the women her father had hired to take care of her that she was going to live like a queen. No more would she "have" to scrimp and save; no more would she spend days in a shed trying to concoct a perfume. From now on she'd have servants who could anticipate her every thought. People would dress her, undress her, cut her food for her. "And shall they chew it?" she'd asked, but no one had understood. It seemed that the goal of all the people on the earth was to do absolutely nothing. It was inconceivable that a woman as rich as she would consider selling cloth from a peddler's wagon as one of her favorite memories in life.

But Axia tried not to have memories, tried not to think or feel anything. She had already been told that her child would be taken from her at birth and given to others to raise. "London is so unhealthy for a child," she was told.

"Then why do I have to live in London?" she'd muttered, but no one understood her sarcasm or her anger.

And anger was what grew inside her daily. Why hadn't Jamie believed in her? Why had he thought only bad of her? And had he actually known who she was? Had he courted her for her money? Her father had said that Jamie did not want her if he could not have the Maidenhall gold with her.

"It is time for bed now," a pretty woman whispered beside Axia. All the women her father had hired were pretty, not as beautiful as Frances, perhaps, but all lovelier than she, Axia, was.

With a sigh, Axia raised her arms and allowed the women to start unbuckling her from the heavy satin dress she wore, a dress that was so stiff it imprisoned her, hampering her movements. Hanging from a hook on the wall was her wedding dress, all of cloth of gold, so heavily encrusted with gold lace that she did not know if she would be able to walk with it on.

And tomorrow she would meet the man she was to marry. In these months neither he nor his father had shown the slightest interest in seeing Axia, for it was her father's money they wanted, not her.

When at last Axia was down to her linen undergarment, the bedcover was pulled back, and she climbed the steps to get into bed. Only at night did she have any privacy, so only then did the tears come.

But tonight she did not cry. Tonight when she was alone in her room, the candles extinguished, her eyes were hot and dry, and the only word that was in her mind was *Jamie. Jamie, where are you? Jamie, do you ever think of me? Do you miss me as I miss you? Jamie, did you ever love me?*

It was very late before she fell asleep, and even then she was restless, tossing about in the bed, thinking she heard odd sounds, waking, then falling asleep again to dream that people were chasing her.

When she did awake, it was to fear, for someone

had his hand over her mouth and a heavy body was on top of hers. Frightened, she could not seem to focus her eyes.

Then she realized it was Jamie on top of her. Immediately, she was afraid, afraid for his life. If her father found him here, he would have Jamie murdered.

"Do not speak," he said softly, and she could see that there was blood on his face and his doublet was torn in several places. What had he been through to get to her?

"I have been to France and found the vicar who married us," he whispered. "And I have found the witnesses, and the parish register has also been found. If it is your wish, I can prove that we are indeed married." He hesitated. "But only if you wish it. If you want to marry Bolingbrooke—"

He was cut off when Axia had managed to get her arms from under the covers to put them around his neck and glue her mouth to his.

"We do not have time for this," Jamie managed to whisper, making no attempt to pull away from her.

It was Axia who finally turned her face away. "I cannot go with you," she whispered. "My father—"

"Hell and damnation to your father!" Jamie said fiercely as Axia put her hand over his mouth and looked anxiously toward the door.

But Jamie pulled it away and began kissing it.

"My father will disinherit me," she said. "He will give me nothing, and he will do awful things to you. You do not know him."

"I know that he is merely rich; he is not a king with

power of life and death. Axia, I want you, not your money."

Axia blinked at him for a moment. "But what of your family's needs?"

"We have moved in with my Montgomery cousins."

"Oh, Jamie, you did not want to do that. You will not like living on someone else's charity."

He kissed her softly. "I will do whatever I have to to be with you. I love you more than I love my pride."

It took Axia a moment to comprehend what he was saying, and she knew how very romantic this was but also how very impractical. "Your sisters hate me. They—"

Jamie kissed her to silence. "If they are angry at anyone, it is at me. Everyone misses you very much."

At this Axia looked skeptical since she remembered that Berengaria and Joby had arranged her kidnapping.

When Jamie saw the look on her face, he smiled. "Much has happened in these months that you have been gone from me. Tode and Berengaria are in love and want to marry. You were right, Berengaria says he is the most beautiful man she has ever seen, and she's been trying to mix perfume, but she says she needs you."

Watching her, Jamie knew he was making some headway when he saw the spark in her eyes at the word *need*.

"Joby does not want me," Axia said.

"Joby feels worse than anyone, except me, of

course. She says that you loved me so much that you were willing to give up the Maidenhall fortune for me. She says she could never love a man that much. Do you? Do you love me that much?"

Axia took a deep breath. "More than that much. I love you—" Shaking her head, she started to push him off of her. "No, no, it will not work. My father will ruin you. He will—"

"Yes, I know, but not even your father is more powerful than all the Montgomery clan. If we must, we will go live in Scotland. My family owns places in Scotland that not even God can find. But it is all your wish, Axia, my love. If you will but follow me."

Looking up at him, she caressed his cheek. "I would follow you to the ends of the earth."

"Even if I have no gold?" he asked softly.

"You have given me all the gold I want," she answered, meaning the child she now carried, but she would not tell him of that now. That would come later.

After a moment she pulled away from kissing him and said, "How do we get out of here? My father's guards—"

"Come," he said, pulling her out of bed, then when she stumbled, he picked her up in his arms and carried her to the window. Four stories below, the rising sun behind them, were what could only be described as an army: thousands of men on horseback.

"Who?" was all she could manage to whisper.

"Montgomerys from England, Scotland, Ireland, and France. I would have brought more, but the ones in America did not arrive in time."

"Jamie," she whispered. "You did this for me?"

"That and more. I love you, Axia. With all my heart and soul. I love you more than gold, more than myself." Pausing, he kissed her lightly. Will you come with me now . . . wife?"

"Yes," she said. "I will follow you, my husband, anywhere."

Epilogue

"What is it?" Axia asked sleepily. Now, in the last month of her pregnancy, all she seemed to want to do was sleep. After much discussion between her and Jamie, she had insisted that the two of them live in the deep, remote mountains of Scotland, away from anyone who could find them. Jamie had protested virulently, but after he'd found out that Axia was pregnant, he'd given into anything that made her feel safe. And safety from her father was what she now needed most. Nothing Jamie could say could alleviate her terror of him. She seemed to think that he was all powerful and all evil and that no one on earth could fight him.

"It is letters," Jamie said, holding up the leather pouch that showed the effects of its journey across sea and over mountains. Since their voluntary exile, they had heard little of the outside world, and Axia liked it that way. She feared hearing that her father was turning the world upside down to find her, then hearing Jamie swearing to kill her father's men upon sight. Or worse, maybe her father was offering great rewards for Jamie's head.

"Axia," Jamie said patiently, "it is not good for the babe to be so fearful."

With difficulty, she sat up. "If those letters can find us, he can."

Jamie did not have to ask who "he" was, so he gave a great sigh as he sat on the bed. "These were sent to my uncle, and he has sent a lone messenger all the way here to give them to us."

"He was sure to be followed."

"Yes," Jamie said sarcastically, "and no doubt I will be dead by nightfall. Do not look at me so, Axia! It was a jest." After some minutes, he was able to loosen the strings that held the pouch shut, then turned it upside down onto the bed. Two letters fell out and with a gasp, Axia saw the familiar writing of her father.

"He has found us," she gasped.

"No, his letter has been forwarded to us. Axia, do not hide under the covers, come and read what the man has to say."

"He will threaten us with death. He will—"

"This is from Frances," he said, holding up the second letter.

For a second, Axia was speechless. She had not heard a word about Frances or from her since her father had separated them after they'd ridden back to London. Many times she had asked, but no one had an answer for her.

"Which shall I read first?" Jamie asked, holding the two letters aloft.

"Frances," Axia answered, wanting to postpone hearing her father's threats as long as possible.

Smiling, Jamie opened Frances's letter, but as he began to read silently, his face changed. "Hell and damnation," he muttered, his eyes wide.

Axia snatched the letter from his grasp.

"My dearest cousin," Axia read aloud, "I know that you always thought that I was helpless and stupid, but I want to know that I learned some things from your clever ways. After Jamie took you away, your father came to tell me what had happened. Yes! that is true: he came to me in person to tell me. He did not seem angry, only very sad, and I was sure it was because he was going to have to go back on his bargain with Bolingbrooke. I know that it is said that no one can best him in a deal, but it is also said that once the bargain is made, Perkin Maidenhall honors his word.

"Oh, Axia, I do not know where I got the strength to do what I did, but I pretended I was you and afraid of nothing, so I made a bargain with your father. We agreed that since Bolingbrooke had never seen you, perhaps he would not be displeased when he saw me standing at the altar beside him."

At that Axia looked up at Jamie, her eyes wide, and in the next second she began to read again.

"So I married Gregory Bolingbrooke, and now I am known as the Maidenhall heiress. I did not think you would mind because I know how much you hate the title. But as much as you hated it, Axia, it is as much as I love it. All the attention! I wear the most splendid clothes!

"But I am sure you are not interested in that. Your father has settled enough on me that I am rich beyond imagining, and if it is not all the money he has, no one but he knows that.

"Axia, I know you will think I am stupid, as you always have, but there is something I must tell you. I am entrusting this letter to Jamie's relatives and no one else because you must burn it. If what I am about to tell you became general knowledge, it could ruin me.

"Axia, I am pregnant with Tode's child."

When she read that last sentence, Axia was so stunned, she dropped the letter, so Jamie picked it up and began to read.

"You must never tell Berengaria, who is Tode's wife now, but only Jamie, for I think he will understand how it was in those days when Tode and I were held captive. He was so good to me, Axia, so very good."

"I should say that he was," Jamie said, making Axia snatch the letter from him and keep reading.

"Axia, do you not think it is ironic that Tode's child is going to be the heir to the Maidenhall fortune? Unfortunately, it is an irony I can share with few people.

"I never thanked you for all that you did for me. And I'm not going to now. You and Jamie will have to come and stay with Gregory and me, and I will thank you then. By the way, I quite like my husband, and even though he never touches me, he is wildly happy about the baby, and he has never asked me a question about who the father is. Nor has his father.

"My love to Jamie and tell him I am so very happy that he didn't marry me. Yours with love, Frances."

When she'd finished reading, Axia fell back against

the pillows. "I have never heard anything like that in my life. Tode! And Frances! And they were doing that while I was so worried about them when she was being held prisoner. They—"

"If you say another word, I will think you are jealous. Now, we shall read this," he said, holding aloft her father's letter.

"No," Axia began, but Jamie paid no attention to her as he broke the seal and began to read.

To my dear daughter,

As you know, I am believed to know more about business than any other man in England. I know how to choose merchandise. I can tell good cloth from bad. I know how to tell quality in furs, in food, in land and ships.

And I know how to judge quality in men.

You think I did not love you because I never saw you. But you are the only thing I ever have loved. I locked you away to protect you, to keep you safe. Had you lived among men as my daughter your spirit would have been tainted, corrupted by the power of money. I gave you what you could not buy: freedom to be a person and not the bags of gold you so often think people see you as.

And yes, I chose a husband for you. As though I were choosing a stallion for the best mare in the world, I searched until I found James Montgomery. His record for honesty, courage, for his care and concern and love for people other than himself, could not be surpassed. No man, rich nor poor, could better him.

But, being a businessman, I did not rely on the

judgment of others. I put him to the ultimate test: love versus money.

For all that you think I do not know you, for years I have been told of your escapades. My "spies" as you call them. Yes, I removed any man or woman who I thought was not worthy of you. When I saw someone getting too close to you for your money, I removed that person. Only Tode and Frances passed the test. Tode loved you, money or no, and even though she did not appear to be, Frances was dedicated to you, as I believe she has proven.

I gave you a good man, your young Jamie, then I did what I could to force him to prove himself to you, to me, and maybe even to himself. Had I proposed marriage between him and the Maidenhall heiress I am sure he would have taken it. Then you, my dear daughter, would have spent your life believing he did not love you. And nothing he could have done would ever have been able to prove to you that he did love you. But I knew that he would. How could he not? It seemed that every other young man who met you asked to marry you. You did not know that, did you? I told them all no. If they returned to me, I told them that if you married against my wishes, I'd disinherit you, and after that, not one of them ever returned.

But your Jamie did. He fought dragons for you. Risked everything, did he not?

And now you know he loves you. Not your wealth, but you.

You are not disinherited. It will all be yours, as I have pledged only a pittance to Frances. A great deal of the money is yours now. You may have as much as you want, as I find the enjoyment in earning, not in owning. I guess I am like my daughter in that way.

I wish you great happiness in your life, and you will have it, as I know you have a good man. As I said, I am an excellent judge of quality, both in men and in daughters.

You have all my love, my dear daughter. All my wealth, and all my love.

> Your loving father,
> Perkin Maidenhall

When Jamie looked up at Axia, there were tears running down her cheeks.

"I would think this would make you happy," he said softly, not knowing how he felt about being part of a bargain made by Maidenhall. But then he pulled Axia toward him, felt her big, hard belly against his body, and he didn't care how he got her, all that mattered was that she was his and that they were free.

"I am the happiest person on earth," she said as she sobbed into his shirt. "The very happiest."

"Second only to me," Jamie whispered as he kissed her hair. "Second only to me."